"All right, you've had your funning. Now take what you want from me and go," Sarah demanded.

"I don't want your jewels. I'm more intrigued by *you*. You seem out of place in this humdrum company. And what of your husband?" Robbie said, grinning.

"My husband was a good deal older than me. He died soon after our wedding—"

"I'm not surprised." Robbie laughed. "Any old fool would expire once he lost himself in such luscious surroundings."

"You're insulting!" she snapped.

"It's no insult to tell a woman she's beautiful, nor to feel her response, no matter what her voice says."

She was outraged. What made it worse was that all he said was true!

"I've never felt challenged by a woman before," he said softly. "It would be my pleasure to tame you, my lovely. I shall leave you your jewels, but I'll take this—for now."

Before she could stop him, his mouth fastened over hers in a long, seductive kiss. She pushed him away, rubbing her hand against her mouth. Black Robbie looked deep into her eyes and then at her heaving breasts. A small smile lifted his lips before he turned away.

"We shall meet again, I promise you," he said, his voice rich with meaning. "I never balk at a challenge. . . ."

Buccaneer's Bride

Jean Innes

ZEBRA BOOKS
KENSINGTON PUBLISHING CORP.

ZEBRA BOOKS

are published by

Kensington Publishing Corp.
475 Park Avenue South
New York, NY 10016

First printing: August, 1989

Printed in the United States of America

Chapter 1

1763

The elegant, sprawling house on Sussex Downs was alive with noise, laughter, and music on that romantic mid-June evening, for the Endor House annual banquet and ball had been arranged this year to coincide with Sarah Huxley's twenty-first birthday. The musicians in the gallery of the Great Hall nearby had played discreetly throughout the evening, their sounds almost drowned out by the exuberance of the house-guests.

Lord Endor rose to his feet with difficulty after the gargantuan meal, his round face even more flushed than usual. The general chatter dwindled away as the toastmaster called for silence.

Lord Endor smiled indulgently at the guests in their jewels and gorgeous attire, some resplendent in lace ruffles and powdered wigs, the décolleté gowns of the ladies putting a gleam even in *his* old eyes. He smiled most particularly at his ward, Sarah, and managed to ignore the feeling of irritation he felt toward his son, Jonas, for not pressing the lovely young widow to be his wife before this important evening. It would have been such a splendid announcement to make.

He brushed aside the uneasy thought that in marrying his ward off to what would surely turn out to be a most unsuitable husband, he was thinking more of his own ends than hers. Sarah's stronger character would be a useful blessing to curb Jonas's fecklessness. A wife might be all the steadying the boy needed.

"Friends, will you all please join me in a toast to our lovely Sarah," he stated instead. "I'm sure there's no gallant gentleman here today who would argue that she's the loveliest gal in the room—"

"Uncle Thomas, please!" Sarah exclaimed from her place of honor at his side, uncomfortable at such public praise.

"Father's right, Sarah!" Jonas spoke up loudly, bold with wine. "The poets have written sonnets about eyes as blue as yours, and lips as ruby red!"

His words were laughed into silence. None of them took Jonas very seriously, to Lord Endor's secret chagrin. The young man acted like a spoiled child, and it infuriated him to know that Endor House would eventually be left in his keeping.

Again, he mused on the prospect of Jonas having a spirited wife like Sarah by his side . . . a wife who had been left widowed at the tender age of seventeen, after a brief marriage to an elderly husband who had left her penniless once his gambling depts had been paid, and grateful to return to the protection of her adoptive family.

"Uncle, please keep this short," Sarah spoke urgently. "You're embarrassing me!"

Lord Endor took pity on her and patted her hand, the costly rings glittering on his pudgy fingers.

"Sarah's asked me to be brief, my friends, so brief it shall be. Will you all please rise and drink the health of my dear ward, who has been all the daughter I could ever want."

Silks and satins rustled and chairs scraped back as the guests rose for the toast. When they were seated once more, Sarah got to her feet. She wasn't enjoying being the center of

6

all this attention, even though she had the composure to carry it off, but she intended to say what she had prepared. At her nod, the toastmaster called for silence again.

"Uncle Thomas, I have a little speech of my own," she announced.

Her voice was soft and lilting. She had planned this moment, but was suddenly nervous. She was a slim, lovely figure, her widowhood giving her a certain piquancy in many eyes. She was still young enough to wear her hair tumbling down her back, caught at the sides with gleaming Spanish combs, her cream satin gown fitting her gentle curves perfectly, the glowing topaz necklace that was Lord Endor's birthday gift to her lying like golden fire against her smooth throat.

"I want to thank Uncle Thomas publicly for all the care he's given me since I was three years old. When Aunt Blanche was alive, she was like a mother to me, and I've been fortunate indeed to have been loved by such devoted people. My cousin Jonas has been more like a dear brother to me, and of course I love and honor Aunt Lily, too. Their support since my husband died has been my mainstay. I ask you to raise your glasses with me to my family, and to the memory of Aunt Blanche."

None could fail to admire the simple dignity and presence of the young woman. When she finished speaking Lord Endor announced that the formalities were over, and they must all leave the banqueting hall for the dancing. He leaned across and kissed Sarah lightly on the cheek, breathing in her subtle perfume.

"Thank you, dear girl. I have only one objection to your charming words."

"I didn't offend you, did I, Uncle? It was not my intention to do so."

"No, no. It was just your reference to Jonas being like a brother to you, when you know very well it has become my dearest wish that the two of you marry. 'Tis time enough for you to have looked elsewhere for a husband, my love, and with his elegance and your beauty, the two of you would take England by storm!"

And with her common sense and maturity, she might yet make a man of Jonas, Lord Endor thought keenly. It was to his credit that he had not considered his own son for marriage to Sarah when she first became so eminently marriageable. But now, time was no longer on his side, and he had a wish to see grandchildren before he died.

Sarah laughed, having heard these words too often lately to take them seriously, but with no intention of leaving him in any doubt as to her feelings.

"Uncle Thomas, you're not dealing with an impressionable seventeen-year-old now. You can no longer manipulate me into marriage!" She spoke teasingly to take the sting out of her words, but there was a gleam in her eyes that told him she meant exactly what she said.

"You're fond of Jonas, aren't you?" Endor demanded.

"Fond, yes—" her voice trailed away as her uncle's attention was diverted by a group of guests who called to him from across the room.

Sarah, thankful for the interruption, mused on her uncle's question. "Fond" was not the feeling she expected to feel for the man of her dreams. Fondness was an eternity away from being so much in love it made the stomach churn as if filled with dancing butterflies. Even though she had been married and widowed, Sarah was fully aware that she had not experienced that feeling yet. At seventeen, she had gone dutifully to the marriage bed with Angus Huxley, but now she was twenty-one and a woman in every sense of the word, and she was still romantic enough and confident enough to know that someday she would find true love.

Aunt Blanche had guessed how much Sarah dreamed . . . but Aunt Blanche had died soon after Angus Huxley, when Sarah still needed her support. Lord Endor's sister, Lily, had come to live with the family and to be his hostess. Aunt Lily

8

was warm-hearted and kind, but none of them ever guessed how often Sarah sat by her bedroom window, listening to the rush of the sea, and wondering what was to become of her.

So many nights she sat watching the beautiful night sky, seeing the glint of silver from the moonlit waves that stretched away into the English Channel, away to distant shores, from the vantage point of the lovely old house high above the cliffs.

Perhaps only Aunt Blanche had had some inkling about Sarah's mixed feelings about the sea. She loved it for itself and its ever-changing mystery, and sometimes felt inexplicably drawn to it. She hated it for drowning her parents, whom she could barely remember now. The generous Endors, her parents' oldest friends, had gladly taken in the small girl, and brought her up as their own.

As a small child, everything about her new surroundings had been magical to Sarah. The quaint old town and fish market at Hastings, and the surrounding countryside with the great hills ablaze with yellow gorse each spring; the ancient castle and network of caves below the cliffs, about which tales of smugglers, true and fanciful, abounded.

All of this added to the young girl's romantic dreams of a lover who would one day come and sweep her off her feet, even if it was to a very different life than the luxurious one in which she now lived. Sarah could never imagine Jonas Endor as her lover. He was her cousin, and would always seem so, despite the fact that they were not related by blood.

Returning his attention to Sarah, Lord Endor momentarily forgot his own dream of uniting his son and his ward in marriage, as he escorted her into the Great Hall. It was late in the evening now, and the room glittered with a thousand candle lights that reflected the sparkling jewelry of the guests. He patted her hand.

"We won't speak of it again tonight, Sarah. Come, let me lead you into the first dance, as an old man's right."

Sarah was drawn onto the dancing space and into the procession of dancers. She was whirled from hand to hand, her skirts rustling in a shimmer of cream silk, her breath quickening as the momentum increased. The room grew hot, and the tall windows at the far end of the room were opened to cool the air. In mid-June, with the heat of the day still lingering, the added exertions of the dance made even the most delicate English skins glow and perspire.

Sarah was glad when the cavorting ended, and even more thankful to see Jonas engaged in conversation with other young ladies. She cooled her warm face with a mother-of-pearl fan, and the elderly matrons seated nearby commented on the beautiful necklace around her throat.

Apart from her wedding ring, which convention decreed she still display, it was the only jewelry she wore tonight, and therefore had even more dramatic impact. Sarah touched the topaz stones with a slender finger, a soft smile curving her lips.

"Uncle Thomas gave it to me. It's the loveliest thing I've ever owned," she said with the disarming honesty people found so enchanting.

"And the costliest, I'll wager," one of the ladies said candidly. "I hope you've a safe place to keep it, my dear. You'll have heard the rumors that the pirate ship has been sighted around these waters this past week, I'm sure!"

"I hardly think pirates will venture inland to the great houses of England, will they, Lady Farlane? Their sport is plundering vessels at sea," Sarah said calmly.

"Not all of them," Lady Farlane replied dryly. "Besides, who could call Black Robbie an ordinary pirate? None can predict what he will do. I've heard that he resorts to cruelty to any crewman who disobeys him, and as for tales of his prowess with the ladies—you'll forgive me for mentioning it, my dear, but you have been married and know what I'm talking about. One wonders if the pirate is superhuman in certain respects!"

"Really, Lady Farlane!" Sarah's clear blue eyes were full of laughter. The dowager lady was renowned for being outspoken, especially when the topic was a little risqué. It was said that the older she became, the less she cared for drawing-room finesse, to the delight of her listeners.

"Anyway, how can anyone with such a ridiculous name be taken seriously?" Sarah retorted.

Lady Farlane pursed her rouged lips.

"Oh, 'tis the newspapers and the excisemen who've dubbed him Black Robbie, on account of his thick black hair and dark skin. There's some that say he's really the son of a gentleman. No one knows his true identity, d'you see?"

"I see that you love a spicy bit of gossip!" Sarah chuckled, and turned reluctantly when Jonas Endor demanded to know when she was going to dance with him.

"What was that old biddy saying to make you look so animated?" he asked as they moved into the line of dancers.

"Is that any way to speak of one of your father's guests?"

"It's true, and you know it!" Jonas was unrelenting.

"We were discussing Black Robbie," Sarah said quickly, not wishing to comment on her uncle's guests while Jonas was in this belligerent mood.

"That scum! His name should be banned from decent society! Especially as—" he stopped abruptly, and Sarah's interest quickened at once. She knew Jonas too well.

"You know something, don't you, Jonas? Tell me! I know you like to play detective—"

"All right, I've been doing some delving, since his name seems to be cropping up so often. It seems he was once a respected privateer, working for the government. Some even hint at noble parentage, but I doubt that." He was scornfully dismissive. "When the need for privateers ended, his greed apparently got the better of him and he turned to piracy. He should be hung, drawn and quartered."

Jonas was still bleating when the dance ended. It was rare for him to become so affected. The pirate's undoubted

11

charisma, as reported in lurid accounts in the newspapers, made many a young man think his own life was deadly dull by comparison. Sarah had never suspected that Jonas might feel the same way. She couldn't really believe it now. Jonas had everything, wealth, possessions, a secure heritage . . . and a sulky and envious nature, especially with regard to gentlemen more dashing than himself.

"I'm sure Black Robbie will get his just deserts, Jonas. When he's captured—"

"*If* he's captured. I'll swear he has a charmed life. If his friends don't protect him, his women do. No one ever betrays him. He's a man without honor, and even the name of his ship, *The Adventuress,* is an insult to all God-fearing folk."

Sarah sighed. Jonas could be unbearably pompous at times. He was barely five years older than she, but sometimes he seemed stodgily middle-aged. He had no need to work, for he would inherit all his father's lands and title, yet Sarah suspected his restless mind could be put to better use than to lord it about the Sussex countryside.

Abruptly, he offered to fetch them both some fruit cup, and Sarah wandered to the far end of the room where the windows were open, and the blissfully cool night air wafted in. The distant chimes from a country church could be heard. It was midnight, the witching hour . . . she gave a small shiver as that thought spun through her mind.

When she had been by herself for some moments, she became aware of a commotion at the other end of the Great Hall, of small screams from the ladies, and sudden shouts of alarm from the gentlemen. And before she could gather her wits, it seemed as though the Great Hall suddenly swarmed with uninvited visitors. It happened in an instant, and the candle-flames nearest the windows blew out in the cold draft. The air was filled with their pungent smell, the end of the Great Hall plunged into sudden gloom.

Lord Endor was elbowing his way through the startled guests, toward Sarah.

"What's happening?" she said in alarm, as the crush of people jostled her.

"Blessed if I know m'dear, but I'm hanged if I'll have folk coming in unnannounced," he said furiously. They both pushed against the tide of people, as utter panic seemed to prevail.

"It's vagabonds, set on a night's free lodging," a lady screeched.

"More likely to be cutthroats, intent on murder. We'll be sliced from ear to ear."

And then someone shrieked a name that stopped Sarah's heart for a second, to send it racing on crazily the next.

"It's Black Robbie and his pirates! They've started plundering ashore!"

Sarah wished desperately that she could see properly. She cursed her inadequate height at that moment, and the melee all around her. Where was Jonas? Gone to fetch a pistol, perhaps, but what use would one pistol be against a band of pirates? Her heart thudded sickeningly at the thought.

"We're all going to be murdered!" Lady Farlane had lost all her aplomb now, and was clutching Sarah's arm, weeping openly, her powder and rouge streaking down her cheeks. "Hide yourself, my love, while there's time!"

"I'll do no such thing!" Sarah said angrily. She burned with rage that this should happen at her birthday ball, to spoil this lovely occasion. "What right does this pirate have to play havoc with our lives? I'm not afraid of him!"

"Well said, my lovely! It looks as though I've met my match at last!"

A strong male voice with a faint Scots burr spoke right beside her. Sarah spun round to stare at the tall, powerfully built man, with a red kerchief tied round his head and another like a cummerbund around his waist. He wore a loose-fitting shirt and leather trousers, and he looked down

13

at her as if he owned the world and everything in it.

Sarah took in his garb in an instant, but it was the man himself who took her breath away. If this was Black Robbie, and undoubtedly it was, then he was nothing like she had imagined. She had assumed he would be old and ugly and thick-set. But this man could be no more than thirty years old, and he was hypnotically handsome, his skin darkly tanned by the hot sun of southern climes.

She took a deep breath, her anger overcoming fear. Her blue eyes blazed into his.

"How dare you intrude on decent folks' lives—"

"That's right," a brave voice echoed nearby. "Especially on Sarah's birthday—"

The pirate looked amused, his gaze sweeping over Sarah in one hot movement in the gloom of the Great Hall.

"Your birthday, is it? And what better night to come calling on a pretty maid?"

There was no logical reason for Sarah to do as she did next, but logic was farthest from her mind in those confused moments when panic seemed to be going on all around her. In some extraordinary way, it seemed to her as if only she and the pirate existed. She thrust her left fist up and shook it at him.

"You're speaking to a married lady, sir, not an innocent." She hoped her frigid tone would have some effect. What it did was make him throw back his head and laugh.

"And do you think such a statement would protect you if I wanted you?" His words were soft and insulting and something more. Sarah was furious to discover the shaft of excitement they sent running through her veins. To be wanted by such a man . . . but she dismissed the thought angrily.

By now, more candles had been lit, and Sarah became seethingly aware of the pirate's interested scrutiny, and knew to her shame that she was still assessing him too. His eyes were an amazing color, like the amber eyes of a cat. His

14

jawline was strong and masculine, his mouth wide and sensual, and in his left ear a golden circlet caught the light.

"What do you want of us, pirate?" Lord Endor pushed himself between Black Robbie and his ward.

The man threw back his head and laughed again. The action had the effect of making him seem head and shoulders taller than anyone else in the room, but his presence alone would have made him dominate everyone around him. Behind him, his unkempt band of pirates sniggered.

"You hear that, laddies? What do we want wi' these fine and dandy folks? Do we show them what we want?"

His companions roared in assent, and Sarah looked on in horror as they ordered the guests to hand over their jewelry and gold. Pistols and daggers held at terrified throats soon had the guests doing exactly as they were bidden.

"I'll have the law on you for this!" Lord Endor roared, his face red as a turkey cock's.

"Save your breath, old man," Black Robbie said sharply. "Do you think we don't know our business? This house has been watched for days. Your servants will be going nowhere!"

"My son will have raised the alarm—"

Even as he spoke, Sarah saw Jonas being led into the Great Hall, goaded forward at the point of a cutlass. Jonas was white with humiliation and badly disguised fear as he watched the pirates trailing necklaces and timepieces from their grimy hands, and stuffing jeweled snuffboxes and valuable rings and bracelets into voluminous pockets.

Sarah pushed past her uncle to confront Black Robbie. Even while she despised herself for it, she admitted that the sexual awareness that had flashed between her and the pirate had a strange way of diminishing her fear of him. If she had been a gauche seventeen, it might have been different. As it was, she recalled his own words: She was a match for him.

"Why don't you get out and leave us alone? You've got what you wanted, so get back to the sea where you belong!"

"And where do you belong, my lovely? Not here with these milksops," he said softly, so that only she could hear.

"How dare you! You insult my family and friends!"

"And your husband? I don't see the brave man coming to your rescue! Is he cowering behind the furniture, perhaps?" He mocked her.

"My husband is dead."

She hadn't meant to say it. The words were out before she could stop them, and she saw the gleam of renewed interest in his amber eyes. As if it mattered. Black Robbie would take what he wanted, no matter who it belonged to, and that went for women as well as possessions.

"So. We have a lovely widow in our midst. And much too lovely to remain without a man. How long has it been, I wonder?"

There was no doubt what he meant. Sarah's face flamed with color, and he laughed carelessly. His slow insolent gaze wandered over her body, and then he turned to the cowering musicians in the gallery.

"Play something lively!" he ordered. "My men would enjoy a dance with these fine ladies before we leave!"

The ladies screamed again, but persuaded by the sharpness of the daggers and the threat of the pistols, they were obliged to swing recklessly about the room, to the frantic accompaniment of the music. The rest of the pirate band kept the angry gentlemen from rushing in to save the dignity of their ladies.

"Now it's our turn," Sarah heard Black Robbie say, and before she could move away, she was caught in those powerful arms and held close to his chest. The other pirates jigged their partners about, but this man held her sensuously, closer than was fitting in the dance, so close that Sarah felt as though she could feel every part of him pressed tight to her. She could feel his heartbeat, and more. It was an insult, and, undeniably, wickedly exciting . . . she pushed back the feeling at once.

16

"Stop this—please—" she said in a low voice. "You humiliate me. Take my necklace if you must, but leave me alone—"

"Do my embraces bother you? 'Tis not only your necklace that charms me, lassie. But mebbe this will please you—"

She half expected him to force a kiss on her then, but to her astonishment he performed an elegant and perfect dance couplet with her, holding her fingers as gently as if they were made of porcelain. Sarah was reminded instantly that some thought he was a nobleman, or certainly the son of a gentleman. Whoever Black Robbie was, he had certainly learned more than the rudiments of the dance at some time in his life. So far he hadn't taken her necklace, but she was quite certain that he would do so eventually. She spoke defiantly.

"All right. You've had your funning. Now take what you want from me and go. My uncle is not well. I fear for him."

"I don't want your jewels. What my men have taken tonight will suffice. I'm more intrigued by *you*. You seem out of place in this humdrum company. And what of your husband? It was an arranged marriage, I suspect."

Was he clairvoyant? Sarah thought in annoyance. But while he held her so close and waited impatiently for her reply, she felt that she may as well give it to him.

"My husband was a good deal older than me. He died soon after our wedding."

"I'm not surprised," Robbie laughed against her body, a rich sound that she felt rather than heard. "Any old fool would expire once he lost himself in such luscious surroundings."

She ignored the provocative remark.

"You're insulting," she snapped.

"It's no insult to tell a woman she's beautiful," Robbie grinned down at her. "Nor to feel her response, no matter what her voice says."

She was outraged. What made it worse was that all he said was true. She did respond to him, in a way that she had never

17

known before. This devil in pirate's clothing aroused some wild free spirit in her, and she couldn't deny it to herself, even if she would die before admitting it to him. She kept her mouth purposefully closed, her eyes distant and stormy, though she knew very well he watched her face as they danced.

"I've never felt challenged by a woman before," he said softly. "It would be my pleasure to tame you, my lovely. I shall leave you your necklace, but I'll take this—for now."

Before she could stop him, he had crushed her to him. He was too strong for her to escape as his mouth fastened over hers in a long, seductive kiss. She *wouldn't* respond . . . but an unbidden thrill ran through her veins at his touch, like a thread of fire. His skin was rough against her own, but this only added to the wanton pleasure of the contact.

She pushed him away, rubbing her hand against her mouth, furious that she felt pleasure at this ruffian's touch, even for a second. Black Robbie looked deep into her eyes and then at the heaving of her breasts against the cream silk of her gown. They betrayed her emotion, and a small smile lifted his lips before he turned away.

"We shall meet again, I promise you," he said, his voice rich with meaning. "I never balk at a challenge."

He snapped his fingers at the musicians in the gallery. They stopped immediately, as if fearful to prolong their playing for a second longer than required. Just as suddenly the pirates relinquished their dancing partners and moved backward toward the open windows.

Sarah could see her uncle and Jonas glance toward one another, and several of the gentlemen begin to look bolder. Once the pirates were out of here, the alarm would be raised, and they would be captured before they reached their ship.

At the last moment, Black Robbie seized a young man who stood near the window, and held the captive tightly in front of his chest, the point of a dagger at the boy's throat.

"At the first sign of pursuit, the boy dies." He spoke

quietly and calmly, and no one doubted that he meant every word.

The terror in the boy's eyes was deterrent enough, and his mother began a noisy wailing.

"All right, you have my word on it," Lord Endor snapped. "'Tis the word of a gentleman, which I doubt you can understand!"

Sarah saw the sudden gleam in Black Robbie's eyes, and sensed instinctively that he understood very well. He had certainly danced like a gentleman well used to being in such company, which was hardly the way one would expect a blackguard to act.

The immediate fear for the household was over, except for the fate of poor Walter Sands, and Sarah knew she was becoming more intrigued by the minute by the mien of the pirate leader.

Walter's mother shrieked at Black Robbie, begging him to show some mercy.

"Don't hurt my boy! He's no more than a babe! Don't harm him!"

As Walter squirmed, Black Robbie spoke with cool arrogance.

"He'll come to no harm. He'll be set free as soon as we're safely away from here. You have *my* word on that."

No one dared to dispute it, with the dagger still held at Walter Sands's throat.

Then Sarah's heart leapt as the pirate leader spoke directly to her.

"Until the next time, my lovely. There is unfinished business between us."

Seconds later he was gone, with the captured boy and the rest of his pirates, as silently and efficiently as they had come. In Endor House there was a sudden hubbub as the tension was released. There was anger and shouting and weeping.

Without thinking, Sarah touched her fingers to the cold topaz stones of her birthday necklace. She remembered how the gaze of the pirate had lingered on it. Somehow she knew with certainty that he had spoken the truth. When—if—they met again, it would be something far more than the necklace he would want.

She shivered, but not from fear or cold. It was as though all her senses were awakening, unbelievably because of Black Robbie's eyes and mouth and the sensuous touch of his hands. She tingled in a way she had never known, certainly in a way that marriage to an elderly husband had never aroused in her.

Angus had never made her feel like a woman the way this outrageous man did. It was as much unnerving as it was exhilarating, and something she had better keep strictly to herself if she didn't want to give everyone here heart failure.

Chapter 2

Between them, Sarah and Jonas, with her aunt and uncle, tried to calm the agitated guests. There was no question of alerting the constables or the excisemen until Walter Sands was safely back with them again.

"I don't have your trust in the pirate to keep his word," Jonas snapped to his father. "Where's the sense in sending for the authorities at that late stage? The scum will be many miles away by then, either at sea or hidden under false colors in some secluded cove. We may as well say goodbye to our valuables."

"I care nothing for that, so long as Walter returns safely! And I don't like your callous tone, Jonas, begging your pardon, Lord Endor!" Mrs. Sands burst out crying once more. "Are none of you here brave enough to follow those evil men?"

"Sarah, please fetch the smelling salts for Mrs. Sands," Lord Endor said crisply. "And Jonas, see what's happening in the servants' quarters. Instruct them to give everyone brandy and hot drinks."

"Very well," Jonas said with a bad grace, clearly furious at Mrs. Sands's remark. He marched out of the hall, while Sarah went to her bedroom for the smelling salts. She was still searching for the elusive bottle when she heard the click of a door-knob behind her. She spun round, her heart in her mouth, to see Jonas glowering at her.

It was almost a relief to see his familiar figure, in rich plum-colored brocade jacket and well-fitting trousers, the silk cravat at his neck as immaculate as ever. Everyone else had looked limp after the evening's ordeal. His mouth tightened as he saw her hand go involuntarily to her throat, until she realized who her visitor was.

"You thought it was *him,* I suppose? I didn't miss the way you looked at each other, Sarah, as if there were no one else in the room!"

"What on earth are you talking about?" she snapped, furious at his perception.

He crossed the room to her in angry strides. Suddenly he frightened her. This was Jonas, her cousin! She reminded herself just as quickly that he was not.

He pulled her into his arms with unusual force. She could smell drink on his breath. He had never acted this way before. But perhaps he'd never seen such a look of desire between Sarah and another man, and realized that he had tarried too long in making her his own. He'd been obliged to stand by while she was married off to that amiable old man, Huxley. His father had thought him far too feckless four years ago to marry anyone, least of all entrust his ward to Jonas, but now . . .

He kissed her, brutally. It was very different from the pirate's kiss. If anything, Jonas shocked her more than the pirate. She could only think of Jonas as a cousin, and that made this the most distasteful embrace of her life. She pushed him away from her.

"That was unforgivable, Jonas!" She rubbed at her mouth furiously. "You're like a brother to me!"

"I am not!" He was hoarse, his voice shaking. "It's time you saw me as a man, with a man's needs. There's no blood relationship between us, Sarah—"

"Nor will there ever be any other kind!" She snapped.

22

"You're mad if you think otherwise, and abuse your father's trust in behaving like an immature pup. Now let me go. I'm needed downstairs."

He breathed harshly. He had felt searingly jealous when Black Robbie had held Sarah so passionately, and he'd guessed immediately that there were depths of sensuality in Sarah that he'd never suspected. Just as suddenly, he knew he wanted her for himself. But he could see now that this was not the best way to go about it. He put a beguiling note into his voice.

"All right. But I've always loved you, Sarah. Perhaps at first it seemed to you like the love of a relative, but we're adults now, and fate sent you to this house a long while ago. There's no reason for either of us to hold back. Father was wrong to marry you off to Angus Huxley. You and I were meant for one another. Remember that."

He left her standing in the middle of the room. She couldn't believe what she had heard. Jonas was being ridiculous. Or was it merely that he couldn't bear to see another man attracted to her? He'd always guarded the things he owned with a possessiveness that had frightened her as a child.

Temperamentally, she was stronger that he, but all the same, he had shaken her. Somewhere in the house a door banged and she jumped. She went downstairs quickly, meaning to lock her door every night from now on, which she had never felt the need to do before. She shivered, knowing that suddenly everything had changed. Not least was the fact that she had been kissed by two men that night, each of them very different, and her senses still reeled from the shock.

Sarah forced her thoughts away from Jonas, only to find them completely taken up by Black Robbie again. She refused to think of him by that ridiculous and colorful name. From now on, he would be Robbie, and immediately she caught her breath as his image swam into her mind.

She admitted that he had a magnetism about him to make a woman forget everything else while she was held in his arms. And despite the fact that he had a price on his head, she would also admit that he came nearer to being her elusive dream lover than anyone else she had met in her lifetime.

Downstairs the guests were beginning to revive, with the liberal glasses of brandy and steaming hot drinks, and only Mrs. Sands continued to wail, convinced that Walter would never survive at the pirates' hands. Sarah guessed that he would probably enjoy his brief fame when he did return. Walter was fifteen years old, and adept at telling a good tale. He would certainly embellish this one.

Lord Endor gave Sarah a glass of brandy.

"Drink this, my love. You look as taut as a violin string. Don't be too distressed. I'm sure the boy will be returned to us very soon."

Sarah forced herself to think of Walter Sands.

"Do you think the pirate will keep his word?" Sarah asked. She realized how much she wanted it to be so, to be able to believe there was something good about the charismatic Robbie.

"I'd say so," Lord Endor said briefly. "All the rogue wants is to get away."

"I hope you're right."

"I wonder what drives such a fellow to piracy. I listened carefully to him, and compared him with his men. It was like seeing the cream above the milk. His voice was educated for all its northern accent, and he turned a pretty shoe in the dancing." He spoke rapidly to Sarah. "Ask the music fellows to play some lively tunes, love. 'Twill take our minds off the troubles, if nothing else."

Sarah was relieved that her uncle didn't pursue the image of Robbie and herself on the dance floor. His comments conjured it up in her own mind, though. The close contact between them, the elegant couplet, the passionate kiss.

Now that she had time to relive the moment, she recalled the freshness of the man. Most men wore scent of some sort, but what Sarah recalled was not the strong perfume of some of the dandies of her acquaintance, nor the rankness of Robbie's own men. Robbie himself had worn a scent that was delicate and manly, and it seemed to fill her nostrils now with the memory.

She must be going mad, but no one had ever made such an impression on her before. The very thought of him brought him instantly to her side, instantly back in her arms.

It was two hours before Walter Sands came limping back to Endor House, his pride wounded, but with no physical harm done to him. His mother wrapped her arms around him, which he suffered for a few minutes, and then managed to extricate himself.

He was given brandy in the hopes that it would revive him. He spluttered this down his cravat in his eagerness to take the unaccustomed spirits.

"Now what can you tell us, boy?" Lord Endor said briskly. "Jonas has sent for the officials, and they'll want to know everything. You're not hurt, I take it?"

"Only my feet!" Walter moaned. "They're cut to ribbons. The devils took my shoes, blindfolded me and tied me up. I could hear the sea crashing against the cliffs, and had no wish to end up as fish bait, so I spent the time sawing the ropes against a rock until I freed myself. The night was pitch-black, and I didn't know where I was—"

"I hope you kept the blindfold or the rope, Walter. They could be useful evidence," Jonas said curtly.

Walter glared at him for interrupting his tale, and shook his head. His mother wrapped her arms around her ewe lamb and snapped at Jonas resentfully.

"Can't you see he gave no thought to such a thing? Nor

would you, I'm thinking!"

Sarah kept her eyes lowered as she listened. It was wrong to feel glad that Robbie and his men would probably escape capture yet again. Robbie was surely not a killer, nor had he harmed the boy. And Walter would have a fine party-piece to tell from now on.

All the same, many of her friends here had lost valuable property. She sympathized with them, although when the constables and excisemen arrived at the house some while later, it astonished her to hear the outrageous tales told in almost hysterical excitement, each guest outdoing the last. Tales were colored vividly, the intruders' appearance made more gruesome, the enforced dancing more terrifying. Sarah could hardly believe what she heard.

"You see, my dear?" Lady Farlane's voice spoke softly to her. "That is how your Black Robbie becomes more demonic than he really is! I'll wager that half of those stripped of their jewels would rather boast that he kissed them the way he kissed you!"

"It's nothing to boast about, Lady Farlane!" Sarah murmured, yet even as she spoke, she was aware of the sweet new sensations racing through her body, remembering his warmth and his caresses. This canny dowager saw nothing so very scandalous in it either, Sarah thought with swift amusement.

"Mistress Huxley, may we have your version of this sea villain?" the constable asked in desperation, after he had heard the garbled stories from most of the other ladies. "Tell us anything you recall. His manner, appearance, his voice and so on."

His manner was the most dashing and flamboyant . . . his appearance made him the most virile of men . . . his voice was richly timbered with that warm Scots burr, and seductive enough to make a lady's toes curl. . . .

Sarah blinked, wondering if she had really said the words aloud, but the constable was still poised, ready to write down her comments.

"I can tell you little more than you've already heard," she said calmly. "It all happened so suddenly—"

The constable sighed and turned away, while Lady Farlane gave a low chuckle at Sarah's side.

"So, Sarah. Even you have succumbed to the pirate's charm!"

She would have denied it, but the mischievous eyes watching her were warm and understanding. Fortunately she was not required to give any reply, since her uncle was beginning to tire of all the fruitless questioning.

"Surely you have enough information by now, Constable? The ladies are fatigued, and we would all like to retire to our beds," he said testily.

"Very well." The man shut his notebook with a bang, throwing one last remark out to the company in general.

"If anyone remembers anything else that may be of use, it's your duty to contact me. The pirate fellow puts people under a kind of spell at first, but perhaps later on your memories will be working more clearly. I bid you good morning."

Morning. Sarah saw with a shock that it was already dawn. She wondered instantly where Robbie was right now. Was his ship already sliding into some secret cove, as someone had suggested? Was he safe? She closed her eyes for a brief moment, praying that it was so. And wondering uneasily about the constable's scathing words. Was she too coming under Robbie's spell? If so, it was something she had never envisaged in her wildest dreams.

The excitement had died down in a week's time, leaving in its wake a restlessness in Sarah, an irritability in Jonas, and a determined avoidance of each for the other. Lord Endor and his sister discussed the situation, since the two young ones seemed to be so much at loggerheads lately. That morning Jonas had gone to visit friends nearby, to Sarah's relief.

"Lily and I have decided that we three must all go up to town for a few weeks," Lord Endor announced. "Jonas has his own pursuits, but we shall stay with the Thorleys in Paddington, visit the theater and get away from the quiet country life for awhile. What d'you say to it, Sarah?"

"Just as you wish, Uncle," she said noncommittally.

Lily and her brother exchanged glances. If anything was needed to prove that the move was a wise one, it was Sarah's reaction. Normally the suggestion would have produced more animation, but ever since the night of her birthday ball, she seemed to be in a world of her own. She excused herself after the meal, saying she needed a breath of air and would take a turn along the cliffs, while the evenings were still long and beautiful.

Sarah felt totally at odds with herself. For the first time in a long while she felt as though she had no purpose in life, and the feeling made her dissatisfied. Even the townsfolk and fisherfolk had their usefulness; the shipwrights; the seamstresses; the lime-burners; the block and mast-makers . . . not that she envied any of them, but they were all occupied, while she seemed to move in a vacuum. By now, she had expected to have children, to be a fulfilled wife and mother. Despite the disparity between her and Angus Huxley in age, she would have been happy to bear his children. They would have provided what was lacking . . . to love and be loved. . . .

She switched her thoughts abruptly, relishing being alone up on the cliffs, where the salt breeze whipped her dark hair into a tangled cloud, and filled her cheeks with color. She paused in her walking, gazing out at the silvery blue sheet of the English Channel, still warmed by the summer sun.

In the distance, there were several tall-masted luggers in full billowing sail on the waterways to France and beyond. She wondered if one of them belonged to the pirate. The thought was in her mind before she could stop it. It was unlikely, of course. By now, he was probably miles away on

28

some distant shore, teasing some other young lady with his swashbuckling charm.

In her heart, Sarah knew very well that Robbie was the reason for her restlessness these past days. In him, it was as though she had glimpsed another life. Not that there was any comparison between life at Endor House and the precarious life of a pirate, but at least his life was never dull, and she was not a woman who enjoyed frittering her time away on idle pursuits.

Robbie was beginning to irritate her, even while she was intrigued by him. It annoyed her that she couldn't seem to rid herself of his image. She lay back on the cliff-top turf and closed her eyes. Her intention was not to dream any longer, but to push the unwanted thoughts of the pirate out of her mind. She would just make her mind a total blank for a few moments, and rid herself of his memory once and for all.

"Sarah, what the devil d'you think you're playing at? I've searched half the county for you, and Father has been thinking all kinds of things!"

She leapt to her feet, her heart pounding as the voice intruded. She couldn't get hold of her senses for a second, and swayed at the dark vision in front of her. She almost stumbled as Jonas scowled, then put out his hands and caught her to him. Feeling her momentarily soft and pliant in his arms, he gave a low oath. He had vowed to leave her strictly alone for a while, while he decided how best to court her, but he forgot all his good intentions and pulled her into a warmer embrace. Sarah resisted at once.

"Get away from me, Jonas!" she snapped, twisting her face from his. "Don't be such an idiot."

"Because I'm like a brother to you?" he mocked. "One day you'll forget all this nonsense, Sarah. There is no bond of blood to keep us from becoming engaged."

She faced him as impatiently as she would an errant pet.

29

Couldn't he see that he was simply not a man in her eyes, but just a boy? He might be five years older than she, but to Sarah he was still a boy.

"Jonas, I won't talk to you while you act so stupidly," she said. "You'll please not speak to me this way again. It's time you looked for a wife, but it will never be me. Why won't you realize that?"

He could overpower her if he wished, he thought angrily, but he had no wish that she go complaining to his father. He told her it was time to get home, marched toward his horse, instructed her curtly to mount, and sat astride the animal behind her.

They had ridden like this many times before, but she was uncomfortably aware of his closeness now, and wished herself miles away from him. Thankfully, she remembered her uncle's decision to take her and Aunt Lily to London.

They rode back in silence, and Sarah made her apologies to her aunt and uncle for any worry she had caused. She had merely dozed off on the cliffs.

"Really, Sarah, anything might have happened to you!" Lily said. "We shall leave for London the day after tomorrow. You need to get some roses back in your cheeks, and although London's not always the most savory of cities, let's hope the bustle of it all will restore your spirits."

Sarah hoped so too. The Thorleys were old friends of the Endors, whose house was always open to them, and there was no need for prior arrangements. When the day arrived, she and her aunt and uncle left Endor House in the carriage. Sarah was glad to get away from home as long as Jonas was there.

En route to London, Lord Endor outlined some of the proposed plans for the few weeks they were to be away. Clearly, he meant to be the complete country visitor, but he spoke with all the arrogance of one who had been to town many times before.

"We shall watch the Foot Guards being drilled and

paraded, and gape at Buckingham House with the rest of the provincials. We shall mingle with the ladies and gentlemen in the Mall. If you feel in need of culture, Sarah, we shall go to the British Museum, or to the Royal Opera House."

"Should we not arrive safely first, and then see what London has to offer, Uncle?" Sarah laughed, clinging on to her seat as the carriage lurched alarmingly on the ill-made roads.

"I heartily agree with Sarah," Lily said feelingly. "At this rate, we shall have no bones left in our bodies."

"At least we shall be far way from pirate ships and the like," Sarah heard herself say dryly. "London society is a mite more civilized."

Why had she introduced *him* into the conversation? She thought angrily. There had been no need. But Lord Endor picked up the thread of it immediately.

"His ship has been sighted several times, still roaming the south coast," he said shortly. "One wonders whether it's best to leave the house in the care of guards, or to stay there and risk another episode like the last one."

"You've done all you could, Thomas." Lily commented. "And surely the rogue would never come back to the same house twice."

"That's my one comfort," her brother agreed. "He's got what he wanted from us, so let's forget the blackguard."

Sarah looked out of the carriage window useeingly. Had Black Robbie got all he wanted from Endor House? Somehow she was sure that he had not. She couldn't forget the way he had danced so close to her, as if they occupied the same skin, in a way that outraged polite society. It had outraged Sarah. She realized that, just thinking about it, her breathing had quickened slightly.

The man had insulted her by his nearness, and yet the recollection of it was enough to make her temperature soar and her heart beat faster. She was not an innocent in the ways of men. Angus Huxley's wooing had been kind and considerate, and she had supposed that was the way all men behaved. It had lulled her into a welcome sense of security in marriage at so young an age and coming from such a sheltered background. But it had never excited her. It had been the role she had accepted for herself.

But ever since the night of her birthday party, she had been aware that there could be more between a man and a woman than she had ever dreamed. She was too much of a lady to wonder if lust coupled with love could be very exciting indeed, but it was a hazy thought that hovered at the back of her mind, all the same.

They finally arrived in London, and it should have been no real surprise to Sarah that the most vivid topic of conversation among the Thorleys and the friends they met in the following weeks was that of Black Robbie and his escapades. To learn that he had actually invaded Endor House suddenly elevated the country visitors to new heights of interest, especially when Lord Endor confided that the devil had the cheek to kiss his pretty ward. All eyes turned on Sarah.

"Is he as handsome as they say, Sarah? The truth now!" One of the ladies said teasingly.

"We were more concerned with poor Walter Sands's fate," Sarah retorted with a smile. "But, well, I suppose the pirate had charm, of a sort. And he didn't harm anyone, so we were thankful for that."

Charm. Was that what it was called when she only had to close her eyes and it was Robbie's amber eyes smiling down into hers, Robbie's arms holding her close, his mouth seeking her own. It was more like some kind of spell, she thought, aghast. The ladies were too engrossed in surmising further about the pirate to notice Sarah's heightened color as she remembered anew the way the pirate had held her in his arms and whispered to her.

The night before they went back to Endor House, they

were to go in a party to the theater in Drury Lane. They arrived early to obtain a box with the best seats and a good view of the stage.

"If we wanted a seat in the pit or galleries we'd be obliged to send a servant to sit there until we arrived," Lady Thorley observed. "There's always a dreadful crush at the door, so be sure we all stay together. There will be music playing before the performance, so you won't find the waiting too tedious."

Sarah found it all enchanting. There was excitement in watching the scuffles over the benches in pit and galleries. Over the stage were gleaming chandeliers alight with several hundred tallow candles. It was so absorbing that Sarah was almost sorry when the play began, but then she became so entranced in the acting of Mr. David Garrick and company, that she was lost to everything around her.

When the play ended, the Thorleys suggested that they wait in their box until the crowd dispersed a little. Sarah was just as happy in watching the fashionable ladies and the dandies, and the less elegant who had paid their pennies to come to the theater.

Suddenly, without any warning, she felt the blood pound in her veins, and her temples throb.

The theater was small, and at times she had felt she could almost touch the opposite box across the width of the hall. It was an illusion, of course. She felt that same illusion now, seeing the tall and dashing gentleman helping a beautiful lady into her evening cloak. But Sarah barely noticed the lady.

The man was the epitome of good taste, from his richly embroidered brocade jacket and fine silk ruffles, to his close-fitting silk breeches. He wore a perfectly coiffured powdered evening wig, and rings gleamed on his fingers. He was flamboyantly handsome. He looked directly across at Sarah for an instant. Their glances met, and held.

His eyes were strange, amber like a cat's. Unusual

enough to be unforgettable, when they had once gazed down into hers in close contact. Amber eyes that widened now, as they recognized her just as surely. Black Robbie . . . Robbie. . . .

The name almost trembled on her lips. If she was public-minded enough, she should shriek it out now, above the babble of the theater-goers, and he would be apprehended at once. One scourge of the high seas would be ended forever, and a gibbet at Tilbury would claim another prize. She gave a shudder.

"Are you coming, Sarah?" she heard Aunt Lily say. And then, "Why, love, you're trembling. Are you ill?"

Sarah moved quickly toward her, away from the edge of the box, before anyone else could see who she had seen. And once outside, she said she had merely felt a little faint, and would like to wait a moment before milling with the crowds. She felt that she would thus give Robbie plenty of time to leave, long before their own party reached the exit.

She couldn't fathom her own reasons for doing this for him. She owed him nothing. He hadn't even tried to contact her again. Not that she wanted or expected him to, and yet, her pride admitted that she was piqued that he hadn't kept his promise, however dangerous such a visit might be.

She let her aunt bundle her out into the waiting carriage, still insisting that she was perfectly well. All the way back to Paddington in the hackney carriage she kept her face averted, glad that there was only the occasional flare from a linkboy to light the dark streets. She was totally bewildered by her own actions.

But late that night, she was unable to sleep as the image of such a different and elegant Robbie danced in and out of her mind. And she remembered vividly something Lady Farlane had said on the night of her twenty-first birthday, when she had seen Black Robbie for the first time.

"Nobody ever betrays him . . ."

Sarah had thought it a preposterous remark at the time,

but that night she had just proved the words true for herself. She remembered the beautiful lady at the theater with Robbie, and the way he had held her cloak for her, caressing the slender shoulders as he did so. At the memory of it, Sarah felt an undoubted stab of envy, and began to wonder with alarm if it was possible for a sane and sensible woman to truly lose her heart to a pirate.

Chapter 3

Sarah's equilibrium was disturbed. So much so that she was glad, after all, to be back in the Sussex countryside. To her intense relief, Jonas was away on one of his frequent visits with friends.

Sarah had dreamed of Black Robbie several times since the night she had seen him at Drury Lane. Strange, seductive dreams, in which he was alternately dressed in finery at the theater, in wait for her as she left it, and in his pirate garb, ready to carry her off to some unknown lair.

What disturbed her even more was the disconcerting sense of disappointment she felt on awakening to find that she was still in her bedroom at Endor House, and the color and excitement of a pirate's life was no more than a fantasy.

Was she discovering another side to her character that she had never even dreamed existed? Sarah thought with alarm about how her parents had loved the sea, how they had died because of its lure. She barely remembered them, but Lady Blanche had told her sorrowfully that Sarah's parents had had a wanderlust that neither she nor Lord Endor could understand.

For some reason she recalled something Aunt Blanche had once told her about her parents.

"Your father always said the best way to conquer fear of

anything was to face it, Sarah. He loved and respected the sea, but he wasn't too big a man to know of its dangers. I think there was something in him made him challenge it, like a big-game hunter worrying a ferocious animal."

"And as always, the stronger beast won," the young Sarah had said bitterly. "In this case, the sea, taking my mother and father with it."

Blanche Endor had been sad. "Don't despise something that your parents loved so much, my dear. Face the fear, as they did, and you'll be all the stronger for it."

She had never wanted to love the sea, nor have anything to do with it. But it was as though the love of it had been inborn in her, no matter how she tried to resist it. She kept her distance, though. She had never set foot on a ship, nor was it her intention to do so. Let others take sea cruises for their health. In this one respect, Sarah was adamant.

But it was undeniable that the sea fascinated her. Sometimes she thought that she felt love and hate for it in equal measure, but she had certainly never expected to share her parent's wanderlust. She had never thought that she, too, would have a strange yearning to break away from normal life. The feeling hadn't been apparent until the night of her birthday, and it was something best kept to herself.

Or had it always been there, unsuspected? Perhaps it had only needed the catalyst that was Black Robbie to stir up all the dormant feelings inside her . . . and already Sarah suspected that there were other longings, deeper and more personal than those of mere wanderlust. She was beginning to learn of her own sensuality, something that her aging husband had never even attempted to awaken in her.

Her daily, brutal appraisal of her own feelings was halted abruptly when Aunt Lily came quickly to her bedroom one morning, soon after their return home, to ask for smelling-salts for Lord Endor.

"Normally he refuses them, saying they're for dolts and old women, but I fear he must succumb today, Sarah. He can hardly breathe, and he has agreed to see the doctor."

Sarah was out of bed at once, throwing on a dressing robe. Her uncle hated to be ill, and would rarely admit to it. She hurried along the corridor and into his bedroom, where Lord Endor coughed and spluttered in a chair near the window. His neckcloth was pushed aside, as if he had dragged it from his throat in his convulsions. Aunt Lily began waving the smelling salts under his nose, and the pungent smell filled the room. He recovered soon, to Sarah's relief, and began blustering loudly as usual.

"Nothing ails me, girl, that a good brandy won't put right, and I'll have it sent up immediately if you please, Lily!"

"I'm sure it's not good for you!" Lily railed.

Thomas roared back at her. "I know what's good for me and what ain't! Fetch it for me, woman, or I'll get it myself!"

"You stay right where you are, then!" his sister said, feathers ruffled. "But don't blame me if Doctor Browning calls you an old fool!"

"He wouldn't dare," Endor growled, as Lily scurried from the room in a huff. "He's well paid for his services."

Sarah knew Aunt Lily's opinion that doctors were paid too well by wealthy men like her uncle. They said what their patients wanted to hear, instead of prescribing proper medication. They had the power to play with peoples' lives. Lord Endor retaliated by vowing that if such services meant a short life but a merry one, then he preferred Doctor Browning's diagnosis to his sister's.

Whatever the remedy, the old man made his usual quick recovery from the attack, long before the doctor's arrival, and spent the day stamping about, complaining about women's interference, and defying anyone to think he was ill.

"I shall slip a sedative into his bed-time drink so that he gets a good night's sleep and doesn't waken half the household with his coughing," Aunt Lily told Sarah with satisfaction. "It'll do no harm, and has the doctor's approval, and we'll see about women's interference then!"

Sarah laughed at the way she intended to score over her irascible brother, and then sobered. "I hate to see him so weakened when he has the attacks, though. He's a tough old gentleman, and it's hateful to see him brought so low."

"It's a pity Jonas doesn't show as much consideration as you, Sarah. I hesitate to put disagreeable thoughts into words, but the boy will gain everything when his father dies, and the least he could do is be here in these difficult times."

Sarah could only nod. Nothing could induce her to wish for more of Jonas Endor's presence, but he was still Lord Endor's son and heir, and a son had a duty to his father, but personally, she felt better knowing that Jonas's irritating person wasn't lurking about Endor House and grounds.

Once her uncle's spirits were restored, Sarah resumed her horse-riding. Her favorite trail took her along the top of the cliffs, descending carefully down one of the narrow tracks leading to the long empty stretches of beach along the coastline.

There was a wonderful sense of abandonment and a glorious freedom in letting the horse have his way in the gallop, in being away from civilized society for a few hours, feeling that strange exhilaration of body and senses at being alone with the elements. She would bend her head over the horse and let the wind stream through her hair, reveling in it all.

On one such excursion, Sarah realized suddenly and with a fright that she was no longer alone. Her horse reared up at the unexpected appearance of a stranger who seemed to walk right out of the cliffs. Sarah clawed at the reins, but the horse whinnied in fright, stumbling even more at her frantic grappling, and the next moment she had slid from his back in an undignified sprawl, and was hurtling to meet the ground with a strangled scream. Sand and sky merged into blackness.

She regained consciousness slowly, a disembodied feeling, as if she were floating somewhere in space. With a great effort, she fought to open her eyes. Her vision was hazy, and she ached all over, but gradually she realized that she was being carried in someone's arms, her head bumping against someone's body, and that they were going inside a dark place . . . she felt utter panic, and her body stiffened with fear.

"Don't be afraid, my lovely."

Sarah knew the voice instantly. She felt its rich resonance against her cheek as she was pressed against the broad male chest. She felt the warmth of his embrace, and she couldn't move out of his arms as he sat down carefully with his burden, still holding her tight. After a moment, he eased himself away so that they sat close together on the sandy floor, his arm still supporting her. Despite the darkness, her vision and her mind were clearing, and she muttered his name through dry lips.

"Aye, 'tis Robbie!" She heard the small smile in his voice then, and knew that he realized she had left off the derogatory adjective that the world had given him. It hardly seemed to matter. He spoke rapidly to reassure her.

"Are you hurt? Try to flex your muscles and to move your head from side to side and up and down—slowly, though! Stretch your limbs carefully—yes, that's right. I think you'll live to ride again, despite the bruises."

"Where—where are we?" Her voice was thick, her feelings a mixture of agitation and pain, but she didn't fail to notice his concern for her as she followed his instructions exactly.

"We're inside a cave in the cliffs. It's best that we hide ourselves for obvious reasons, and for you to recover from your fall. I don't think much harm was done, but you and I have a need to talk."

Through the gloom, Sarah could now see that they were in little more than a fissure in the rocks. Robbie had taken them well inside its twisting turns, but there was still a faint light at a lower level, coming from the entrance. The coastline was riddled with caves and tunnels, and this was evidently one of them. Recovering quickly, despite the dull throbbing in her head and various aches and pains, she was becoming more concerned with Robbie's "need to talk."

"What do we have to discuss?" She spoke defensively, suddenly feeling somewhat ridiculous at having literally fallen at his feet. "And why do I have the feeling this was no chance meeting?"

His laugh was low and throaty. She tried to move away from such close contact, but he kept her imprisoned within his arms. Besides, it hurt to move too quickly. She didn't care for the gloom or the dankness of the cave, either. Who knew what unseen creatures might be here? And guiltily, Sarah admitted to herself that it was not altogether unpleasant to be in this confined space with the intriguing Black Robbie.

It would be an exciting party tale to tell, as intriguing as that of Walter Sands. Yet even as she thought it, Sarah knew that no one would hear of this meeting from *her* lips.

"It was no chance, Mistress Sarah Huxley. Oh yes," he said as her eyes widened, "I've discovered all about you. I know your fondness for this beach, and that you have a wild streak in you that I find enchanting. I told you I found you a challenge, and I suspect that you and I have much in common. Otherwise, why did you not expose me at Drury Lane theater?"

Sarah gasped. He spoke more directly than any other man had ever spoken to her. She wasn't sure whether to be affronted or excited. Her curiosity about the man and his dual activites made her forget much of her pain.

"So it *was* you! Weren't you afraid of being recognized? You know the penalties for piracy—"

"The danger becomes part of it all. There's always the thought that any particular raid might be my last. That the woman in my arms is the last one I'll ever hold."

Sarah bridled at once. She was still being held in the pirate's arms, and she certainly disliked being thought of as the last in a long line of his women.

"So you spend your time terrorizing helpless ladies and young boys, as you did at my uncle's house? What kind of man plunders ships and kills people without compassion?"

He laughed again, as if she merely amused him.

"You shouldn't believe all you hear, sweet Sarah! I'm no murderer, despite all the tales. As for plundering—when a man has had all that he owns taken from him, some might call my actions no more than justifiable retaliation!"

He continually surprised her. His last words were said lightly enough, but with an underlying bitterness, and they were not the words of a common seaman. When something affected him deeply, his rich Scots burr was accentuated too, as it was now.

"Who are you?" she demanded. The imperiousness in her voice might have quelled a lesser man. But not this man.

He bent toward her so suddenly she couldn't have drawn back if she had wished. That faint, pleasant male scent she had smelled before was in her nostrils, seconds before she felt Robbie's mouth on hers. This time it was different. It wasn't in the midst of an outraged company and taken from sheer devilment. That first kiss had been passionate enough, but this one was sensual, seductive, a kiss that told of primitive desire and an animal need. She had never experienced the kind of arousal it could instigate in her, but instinctively she recognized it, and without realizing it, her own arms wound about his neck as he held her captive in his arms. When he broke away from her it was only slightly, his mouth was still touching hers, and he spoke softly against her flesh.

"Someday I'll tell you about myself, when the time is right. For the time being, just ponder on the fact that our destiny is to be together."

The words reminded her of something less pleasant. Jonas too had said it was his fate and Sarah's to be together. For a few moments she had been so captivated by the sheer magnetism of the pirate, she had almost let herself be carried away by the sweetness of seduction. But she had no intention of being fobbed off by fairy tales.

Robbie himself had referred to his "women," and she had no intention of being one of them. If a man wanted her for his own, she must be the *only* one. Her own wanton thoughts appalled her. If she had thought everything in her life was changing before, how much more so was it changing now. To allow these indiscretions with a known pirate was something that would scandalize the entire county!

"I think you assume too much, sir!" she said witheringly. "If you cannot even tell me your name—"

She felt his finger beneath her chin, tipping her face up to his once more.

"You will know it when I choose to give it," he said, an edge to his voice. "We're a match, you and I, Sarah Huxley. You're a woman after my own heart, and I suspect that that husband of yours had no idea of the fire within you. Do you deny it?"

She wouldn't give him the satisfaction of agreeing.

"I don't deny that you can charm any gullible woman!" she taunted him. "Or perhaps you carry them all off in this way, so that no one will hear when your victims cry rape!"

"I have no need to force myself on any woman," he said with careless arrogance. "When you come to me, it will be of your own free will. I want us to share the pleasures of love, not have you begging for mercy!"

She gasped angrily. "You'll never see that day! Besides, I'm as good as engaged to someone else!"

Robbie's eyes narrowed.

"Then he's the loser! I promised myself when I first saw you that no one else should have you. I've dallied with many women, but I've never met one before who touched a chord in me so vibrantly. I've become sick of women who flirt and tease, and think it something of a feather in their hat to have kissed the notorious Black Robbie. It's refreshing to meet one who doesn't primp and preen, and is desirable enough without all that nonsense."

43

Sarah glared at him suspiciously. Was this another of his ruses? She wasn't prepared to take him seriously. She wasn't sure either, whether his assessment of her made her appear quite as desirable as he suggested.

"And what do you suggest we do about this great passion we could share?" She was deliberately flippant. "Do you mean to take me with you as a lady pirate on your exploits? You'd have to tie me down first!"

"That could be arranged," he said calmly. "But you've still not answered my question, which is why you didn't betray me at Drury Lane?"

She looked at him helplessly. Why indeed? She couldn't explain it to herself, so how could she explain it to him?

"I should have done!" she agreed. "It's not too late, of course! I could go to my uncle now and tell him. Who would have expected the infamous Black Robbie to appear in so public a place? Is that what gives it security?"

"Perhaps. And will you also explain to your uncle why you waited so long in telling him?" He seemed quite untroubled.

She pulled away from him in exasperation. It was true. How could she go to Lord Endor now? She had behaved just as every other woman behaved where Black Robbie was concerned. She knew it, and so did he.

"You're quite despicable."

"And you're very lovely." His words stopped her. "I was not born a pirate, Sarah. Which would you prefer to court you? The rake about town, or the dashing sea captain? Either is at your disposal!"

"I prefer that you leave me alone," she said distantly.

She moved, and this time he let her go, and she began to rediscover her aching limbs, and rose awkwardly to her feet. She was stiff and cramped in the small space of the fissure, and its stuffiness was beginning to make her dizzy. "I'm going home, and I'll thank you not to try and stop me. You needn't worry. I won't betray you—this time."

He stood back to let her pass, and she scrambled back the way they had come, mortified to know how undignified she must appear. She was somewhat surprised that he let her go so easily, but as soon as she reached the cave's opening, she understood why.

Sarah caught her breath in horror. While they had been inside the cave, the tide had crept insidiously over the long flat beach, its sound muffled by the twisting passage inside. The outer curve of the bay was filled with water, and it already lapped at her feet. There was nothing to impede its progress. It would fill the cave. It always rose high up the face of the cliffs. They were both going to be drowned! She would share her parents' fate. . . .

She was strong in everything but the thought of drowning. She must have screamed in terror, because the next thing she knew, Robbie was slapping her face hard. She turned to him frantically, clinging to him, face white, the words tumbling out of her.

"Don't let me drown! *Please!* It's been my worst nightmare all my life!"

"I won't let you drown, Sarah!" His voice throbbed against her as he held her fast. "There's another way out if you follow me. It will be as black as pitch, but in ten minutes we'll see the sky again, I promise you. Trust me?"

She was rigid with terror, but she nodded wildly. She would trust him because there was no other choice. She put her cold hand in his, her fingers curling tightly around his as the sea sucked at her skirts.

"Quickly," he commanded.

They entered the fissure again, Robbie leading the way. They went in farther than before, and it was as dark as the grave. The sides were barely an arm's-length apart, and they had to inch their way upwards. The tunnel was rank and cloying. Robbie's hand was her only lifeline, and she clung to it blindly. She realized that the tunnel grew steeper very sharply; it became difficult to breathe because of the

45

claustrophobic atmosphere and her own tension.

"We're nearly there," Robbie's voice came back to her through the blackness. "Hold on to me, my darling."

Sarah couldn't answer. Fear seemed to have fastened her tongue to the roof of her mouth, and then miraculously, at last, there was a glimmer of daylight, and they were pushing through piles of damp bracken and old vegetation to gulp in the clean fresh air and to squint at blue sky and sunlight. Her legs almost buckled beneath her in relief, and Robbie held her close.

"You're safe now." His voice was oddly rough. "We'll rest awhile until you recover."

"I'm safe, but are you?" she stuttered. "You might be seen, Robbie."

She understood in that moment that she had pledged to keep his whereabouts secret for always. He raised her hand to his lips and caressed the poor bruised knuckles.

"We're both safe here," he said quietly. "We're in the old ruins of a lookout tower. The passage ends inside these rumbling walls, which have provided a useful lookout for my men at other times. You may not have known of this place, but if you'll look yonder, there's an animal with true horse sense!"

Sarah looked to where he pointed, and saw that her horse had found his own way up the cliff track and was contentedly munching turf a short distance away. Robbie whistled softly to him, and he cantered toward them.

"It's isolated here, my love, but if anyone approaches, I could easily slip inside the passage again until they had gone. We both have a trust in each other now, I think."

She looked into his amber eyes and her mouth shook.

"You have my word on it."

His fingers touched her soft dark hair, the curve of her cheek and the shape of her mouth, and the trembling spread to every part of her.

"But I want far more of you. A life for a life, Sarah. I saved your life, so now I claim it for my own. You belong to me. Do you admit it?"

How could she answer him? She saw the blaze of desire in his marvelous, expressive eyes. She saw the flamboyance of him, and knew all that was said of him. And still he bewitched her, he filled her with total disregard for all the niceties of her old safe life, and made her yearn for something more.

"I belong to myself," she said. "And yet I hardly know myself anymore."

He gave a low triumphant laugh and pulled her closer. Her eyes closed as she felt his lips move against her cheek and her throat, and her head went back in sweet abandonment to the power of his slightest touch. And yes, yes, yes, he intoxicated her with his nearness. She felt the brush of his palm against her breast, and the sensation was an exquisite one.

"You and I will come to know each other better than two halves of the same heart, my lovely girl," Robbie said softly. "I feel I know you better already than your husband ever knew you. How long were you married to him?"

"Eight months," she said weakly. Eight months of being contented enough, because it was what her uncle had arranged for her, and at seventeen she had been half child, half woman, and unused to the ways of the world. But now she was twenty-one, and discovering more about herself in these past weeks than she had in her whole life before.

"Eight months. And were you happy with an old man?" Robbie persisted.

"Angus was a good man," she prevaricated. "He treated me kindly."

"That's not what I asked. Were you happy?"

"I was not unhappy. And please don't ask me anything more. You refuse to tell me about yourself, so don't expect such confidences from me!" She kept her voice very controlled.

Robbie leaned back against a rock. She admitted that his

extraordinary eyes could be mesmerizing, as could the entire charisma of the man. He was flamboyant and devilish in many ways, but surely not an evil man. Sarah's instincts wouldn't allow her to believe that any longer.

"I think that answers my question for now," he replied just as coolly. "And now I regret that we must part for the time being. May I suggest that you say you had a fall and had to chase after your horse, which will explain the state of your clothes."

Sarah glanced down. Until that instant, she hadn't even noticed how disheveled she looked, her skirts torn from the snagging rocks inside the tunnel, her shoes sodden. She looked the complete opposite from the trimly elegant young widow of Endor House. And yet she had never felt so alive. Despite the traumas of that day, there was a vitality flowing within her that she had never known before, and it had only come about since meeting Robbie.

"Will you be safe?" she heard herself say.

"With you as my talisman, yes," he said. "Now go quickly, before I decide to abduct you after all!"

He was half teasing, but there was a look on his face that said he might just do as he said. He helped her mount her horse, and she dug her heels into its side and rode like the wind away from the old lookout tower. She didn't look back until she was some distance away. By then there was nothing on the horizon but the crumbling stonework.

Once she had stabled the horse, Sarah hoped she would reach her bedroom at Endor House unseen, but luck was against her. Lord Endor was taking his usual afternoon nap, but she encountered Aunt Lily almost at once, who stared at her in horror.

"My dear girl, what's happened to you? Have ruffians set upon you? We must call the constable at once!"

"It's nothing like that, Aunt!" Sarah said. "My horse

threw me, and I had a job to catch up with the beast, that's all. Please don't fuss. I'm not hurt, and a bathe and change of clothes will soon put me to rights."

She repeated the tale Robbie had spun for her, glad of its readiness, seeing the relief in her aunt's eyes.

"I'll send Mabel up to you at once. The girl's useless at many things, but she'll soothe those poor hands of yours. It's a blessing we're not going up to town this week, or you'd look a sorry sight. Pretty yourself up, Sarah, before your uncle comes downstairs and has a seizure at your appearance."

Sarah admitted that her hands hardly resembled a lady's now, all roughened and scratched. Yet there had been a magical moment just a short while ago when Black Robbie had held one of them to his lips, so tenderly that he had made her feel like a queen.

She felt the beginnings of hysterical laughter welling up inside, and wondered just what her prim little aunt would say if she knew the crazy thoughts milling about in Sarah's head. She wondered even more just what Aunt Lily's reaction would be if she knew that Sarah contemplated, even for a second, how enticingly Bohemian life might be on the high seas as the female companion of a dashing pirate sea captain.

All such thoughts vanished from her mind a few days later, when Lord Endor's condition became unexpectedly worse. It was soon obvious that no physician could do anything for him. Within days he was dead, and Sarah wept bitter tears for the generous benefactor who had always done his best for her. As he was laid to rest in the family tomb, she knew she had lost her best friend.

She hardly listened as the will was read out, making small bequests to her and Lily, with the proviso that Endor House be their home for as long as they wished. The entire estate naturally belonged to Jonas now, who took on the inherited title of Lord Endor.

"That's that then, my love. Do you have any plans?" Lily said sadly, when the lawyer had gone, and she and Sarah sat in their somber clothes in the drawing room. Jonas had already departed on business of his own.

Sarah looked at the older woman blankly.

"Plans? What plans should I have? I'll go on living here, I suppose. It's what Uncle Thomas wanted."

She gave a small shiver. It was what Jonas wanted too. He held the purse strings now, and could make her life a misery if he chose. He had become enigmatic and less boisterous since his father's death, and she didn't altogether trust his change of mood.

A few days later he sought out Sarah and handed her a folded piece of paper.

"Read it," he said. "It's a copy of what will be in all the newspapers this weekend. I trust it will please your ladyship."

His grin was sardonic as Sarah unfolded the piece of paper. She gaped at the announcement for a moment, and then went scarlet with fury as the words swam in front of her eyes.

In accordance with the late Lord Thomas Endor's wishes, she read, *the engagement is announced between Jonas, now Lord Endor of Endor House, and Mistress Sarah Huxley. The engagement party will take place at the home of Lord and Lady Thorley in Paddington, London, in deference to the recent demise of Lord Thomas Endor, and the wedding will take place quietly as soon as it can be arranged.*

Chapter 4

"You had no right to do this," Sarah blazed. "I have never agreed to be your wife!"

Jonas didn't attempt to touch her. He lounged insolently against the mantel, a mocking glint in his dark eyes, as if nothing she said made any difference. Sarah felt a cold shiver run through her at the look he gave her. It was that of a large animal with a smaller, helpless one in its claws.

"I hardly think your agreement is necessary, cuz," he drawled. "Without my father's protection, you now come under my care, and he hardly left you enough to live on. I'm damn sure the pittance your aged Angus left you is long gone too. 'Twas my father's wish as well as mine that we wed, and well you know it. It's probably why he didn't leave you the dowry you might have expected."

"I never expected any such thing. I loved your father dearly. He was like my own."

She caught her breath on a sob, missing the man more than she had believed possible. Missing his love and generosity of spirit, and the buffer he provided between her and this oaf. She was sickened by Jonas's assumption, hating him for trying to besmirch his father's image in her eyes. She glowered at him and gathered up her pride as he laughed derisively.

"You seem to have forgotten that I'm no simpleton, Jonas," she snapped. "I have already obeyed your father's wishes once in marrying an old man I didn't love in the way a woman should love her husband. I've no intention of making a second mistake in marrying an uncouth boy who wouldn't recognize the meaning of love if it struck him in the face."

Jonas's eyes sparkled with anger, but he was still too amused by her taut response to his announcement to feel real temper. He had expected this. In fact he enjoyed Sarah Huxley's bursts of temperament. It was part of her character, and made her all the more exciting to him, more than some of the simpering young things who flitted in and out of the London scene. Unwittingly, he echoed the thoughts of the pirate, Black Robbie, who had also seen something more in Sarah Huxley's character.

"Oh, I promise you I know all about love, my dear Sarah," he said softly. "You won't find me completely inexperienced."

She felt her face go hot, knowing exactly what he implied.

"Your kind of love is found between the beasts in the field," she retorted. "It's not the kind I speak of, Jonas, and since I don't love you, nor ever will, you will please do me the courtesy of retracting that ridiculous statement at once, before it reaches the newspapers."

Now she *had* angered him. He strode across the room and caught at her wrist, hurting her. He was physically strong, and a frisson of fear ran through her veins.

"I will retract nothing, Sarah," he said with deceptive mildness. "The announcement will be published, the engagement party will take place, and you and I will be married. I will take great pleasure in taming that wayward spirit of yours. And understand this. If you try to disobey me, I will have you thrown out of Endor House and you will be virtually penniless, thanks to my father's foresight."

Her eyes grew huge and brimmed with the shine of tears she fought to suppress.

"It wouldn't matter to me. There are plenty of people who would take me in. I'm not lacking in friends."

"You would be, because in that event I would have no other course but to deliver a further statement to the press, stating that the marriage will not take place because of Lord Jonas Endor's discovery that his intended bride is a trollop. Naturally any noble house couldn't entertain a liaison with such an ill-bred person. What of your friends *then,* my sweet Sarah? Do you really expect them to rally round a woman with such a reputation?"

She was almost speechless. Her stomach heaved with shock, seeing his eyes so relentless and venomous that she knew he meant it. She protested wildly all the same.

"Not even you could be so wicked! You wouldn't go to such lengths to damage my character. Your father would turn in his grave!"

"Then let my father rest easy," he said calmly, letting go of her wrist as suddenly as he had grasped it. She rubbed at the bruised flesh. "I assure you, Sarah, I will do whatever is necessary to get my way. So what is it to be? I wager that it will not be an unhappy life being the lovely Lady Endor. You and I together will be the toast of the town whenever we go to London. Or you can be tossed into the gutter like so much filth for the rats to gnaw. You see? I'm giving you a choice after all. I'll leave you the announcement to ponder on."

He went out of the room, smiling, knowing he had won. And Sarah sat down heavily on one of the silk-covered sofas, still clutching the piece of paper in her hand, with the sensation that this house she had long thought of as home was fast becoming a prison. And Jonas was the most evil jailer anyone could have devised.

Her Aunt Lily found her still there in the drawing room a while later. She was still numb, but tears had overtaken the shock now, and Sarah's shoulders shook with the prospect opening up before her."

"My dear girl, whatever's wrong?" Lily said in alarm. "I had no idea that my poor brother's death had affected you so badly. Shall I send for the doctor to give you a sedative?"

"No, please." Sarah struggled to sit up, searching for a lace handkerchief in the sleeve of her dress, her voice muffled. "It's nothing to do with Uncle Thomas. Oh, forgive me, Aunt, I don't mean to imply that I'm not still upset over his death, but—"

"But it's something else," Aunt Lily said, stating the obvious. "Do you want to confide in me, or is it too private, my love?"

Sarah shook her head, and the dark curls gleamed in the sunlight through the drawing-room windows. Even in distress, Sarah was still a lovely and dignified figure, Lily noticed.

"It's not private at all, or at least it soon won't be," she said bitterly. "Dear Jonas has begun to sharpen his claws, and shown me what he intends putting in all the newspapers this weekend. He has also told me of the penalty if I disobey him. Perhaps you'd care to see it."

She handed her aunt the piece of paper Jonas had left with her. Lily read it quickly, and then raised shocked eyes to the girl's flushed face. But her voice was somewhat guarded in her reaction to her nephew.

"Yes, I do agree that this is an outrage. To make such an announcement so soon after his father's death will hardly endear the boy to polite society."

She caught sight of Sarah's expression.

"But that is the least of your worries, I can see. My dear, is the thought of marrying Jonas so very distressing to you? It truly is what Thomas wanted."

She gave a crooked smile. "Would Uncle Thomas have wanted me to marry someone I loathed? Someone I could not respect in a thousand years? I think not. If he knew the

54

way I really feel about his son, he would never have wished such a fate for me."

Lily spoke dubiously. "Well, if you really contemplate marriage in such terms, I can see that you have some serious thinking to do. But think about Angus Huxley, my love. I am sure you didn't feel love for him at first, but you were a dutiful girl and did as Thomas wished, and you grew to be fond of Angus, surely?"

"As fond as I might have been of a pet pony or a favorite stuffed animal," Sarah said, more freely than she had ever spoken on the subject before. Lily looked faintly annoyed for a moment, but it only spurred Sarah on.

"Oh Aunt, you've known me a long while. Was I really destined to be the wife of an old man?"

"Well, no," Lily admitted. "But that's why I cannot see why you have such a strong objection to marrying Jonas. He's young and good-looking, and a catch for any girl."

"But I don't love him. And please don't tell me that love would grow between us, because it never would. Jonas is not the kind of man with whom I would wish to spend the rest of my days."

She stopped abruptly, wiping the remnants of tears away from her cheeks. Lily looked at her sharply.

"Is there such a man, Sarah? Have you already met him, perhaps?"

A swift image surged into Sarah's mind. A strangely composite image. Two men in one. A colorful character with jet-black hair, skin tanned by the exotic climate of southern seas, the eyes almost hypnotic, and amber, like a cat's. Tall and handsome and more powerfully built than any other man she had ever known. And then the other side of the man, elegant in a richly embroidered brocade jacket and fine silk ruffles and close-fitting silk breeches. A powdered wig covering his dark hair, and rings gleaming on every finger. Each image of the man as charismatic as the other. Each forming half of an intriguing whole.

"Well, Sarah? You don't answer me, which makes me suspect—"

Sarah gave a short laugh. "And where would I meet such a man? Uncle Thomas kept me strictly chaperoned, and I hardly think the London dandies fit my expectations."

"I suspect that your expectations border too much on the grand romance, my dear. Such things are best left in the imagination, and you'd be doomed to disappointment if you spent your life searching for such a man. You would do better to settle for a harmonious life with Jonas. There's much to be said for security. I shall leave you to consider Jonas's proposal more sensibly."

She swept out, clearly a little ruffled that Sarah was spurning her nephew so vehemently. Despite the way Jonas frequently irritated her, Lily clearly considered it Sarah's duty to comply with Thomas's wishes, to honor them. And so she would, in anything but this!

At that moment, as if he were right beside her, she seemed to hear Black Robbie's voice, echoing through her veins. She heard too much, as if the mere thought of him opened all her senses, expanding her mind, sharpening the memories of that richly timbred voice. . . .

". . . You're much too lovely to remain without a man. How long has it been, I wonder? . . ."

Too long, too long . . .

". . . I've never felt challenged by a woman before. It would be my pleasure to tame you, my lovely . . ."

And mine . . . and mine. . . .

". . . Someday I'll tell you about myself, when the time is right. For the time being, just ponder on the fact that our destiny is to be together . . ."

". . . We're a match, you and I, Sarah Huxley. You're a woman after my own heart . . ."

". . . I was not born a pirate, Sarah . . ."

She gave a sudden shiver, pushing the snippets of conversation out of her mind. Was she mad, to be so un-deniably fascinated by a dashing and plausible rogue? That was all he was, and she would do well to remember it. But in her heart, she strongly suspected that there was far more to him than the world knew.

Hadn't he hinted as much himself? And couldn't that have been merely the way to intrigue a woman, a small cynical voice in her head reminded her.

She was angry for letting her thoughts revolve around the man so much, especially now, when she had other problems to contend with. Jonas. And the thought of how ruthless her cousin could be sent a different kind of shiver down her spine.

For a second she envisaged marriage to him, and shuddered anew. She knew the intimacies of the marriage bed. They were gentle and infrequent in her experience with Angus Huxley, but nevertheless they were intimacies of the most personal kind. She could not contemplate doing such things with Jonas, whom she had always thought of as a brother.

In Sarah's mind, it would be nothing short of incestuous, and besides that, she couldn't imagine that Jonas's approach in the marriage bed would be as considerate as Angus's. The thought of him touching her, seeing her unclothed, feeling his body naked on hers, was utterly repugnant to her.

Sarah felt again like weeping. So much had happened so suddenly, and her world felt as if it was turning upside down. Her Uncle Thomas had been such a stalwart figure in her life, and Jonas had been the brother she never had. Why did he have to go and spoil things! Surely he must have known that their relationship couldn't undergo such a change as this. She had made it plain enough since childhood that she was fond of him, but never more than that. Never could she think of him with the wild sweet love of a woman for a man. . . .

Sarah squared her shoulders, knowing that she must stop this farce at once before it went any farther. She went to seek out her cousin. She had to make it clear to him that it would be hateful for him too, being tied in marriage to a woman who would be so repelled by him. Even Jonas deserved better than that!

"I'm afraid Lord Endor has left the house, Miss Sarah," one of the servants told her, when she had gone through every likely room in the place and become increasingly frustrated at not finding him anywhere.

"What do you mean, he's left the house?" Sarah snapped in unwarranted anger at the girl. "Has he gone to the stables? Did he say he was going riding?"

The girl shook her head. "I was told to pack some clothes for him, and he said he was going to stay in London at his club for a few days."

"Without telling anyone?" Sarah exclaimed.

"I believe he told your aunt just before he left, Miss Sarah. There was a bit of a to-do, if you'll pardon my saying so, with Lord Endor ending up saying he'd do as he damn well liked in his own house."

She repeated the words with a hint of maliciousness, ruffled because Sarah wasn't usually so imperious with the servants. And besides that, only last night the girl had been given sixpence by the young master for special favors, and felt that she had slightly greater status than the other maids.

Sarah stared at her, as if seeing more than was actually said, and the swift color on the girl's pale cheeks told its own story as clearly as if it was written sky-high. And this was the man who wanted to make Sarah his wife! A young oaf who toyed with his own servants. Many men did, but Sarah Huxley didn't intend to marry one of them. She tilted her chin.

"Remember your place, girl. A servant doesn't use strong language in front of her betters. Now leave me."

The girl flounced off, no doubt to rage at the rest of the

kitchen maids at the young Miss's unreasonable behavior. In agitation, Sarah knew she would be partly justified. She wasn't normally so stiff and high-handed with anyone. Jonas was making her that way. Jonas, and the uncertainty of her future, that only a short while ago had seemed so serene.

Two days later, the announcement was in all the newspapers. Since showing it to Sarah, Jonas had added one more refinement to the stark words. He had evidently been in contact with the Thorleys as soon as he reached London, for there was now a date included for the engagement party of the new Lord Endor and Mistress Sarah Huxley. It was to be on the twenty-second of the month, two weeks from now.

The only way Sarah could reconcile herself to the news was to remember that an engagement was not yet a marriage. There must be some way to break it, though she had not the remotest idea how. It was the only way she could remain sane in the nightmare days that followed, when callers left little cards of congratulations, and old acquaintances added a small note that they understood the need for haste, since it was well known that it had been Thomas Endor's dearest wish that his son and his ward should marry. All of this served to ensnare her still more.

Lord and Lady Thorley sent a carefully worded letter to Sarah, assuring her that no one would think badly of her and Jonas for wishing to salvage some happiness in these sad times, and it made her blink with frustration, for nothing could be further from the truth. There was no happiness in such a betrothal for her, only heartache.

Unwillingly, she let her thoughts return to where they so often were these days. This time, she thought how different things might have been had she met Black Robbie in other circumstances, and, more importantly, if he was not the man he was. But another insidious thought followed. Would he have been so charismatic then, so very much a man beyond any young girl's dreams?

She remembered her sight of him at the theater, and knew instantly that a woman could love him anywhere. It was the essence of the man that counted, not the outward trappings. She was aghast and strangely exhilarated by her own assessment, knowing that if she could, she would choose to be the woman to capture Robbie's heart.

Jonas stayed at his club for a week, intending to give Sarah that time to get used to the prospect in front of her, and then he came home to Endor House to make preparations for the few days they would spend with the Thorleys. He didn't seem to be carrying his mourning to any great lengths, Sarah thought irritably, seeing him flirt with Maudie, the young maid she had reprimanded. That kind of thing would be stopped immediately once they were married. . . .

She put her hand to her mouth in horror as the words ran into her head. She was beginning to think of marriage to Jonas as inescapable. Without even knowing how it had begun to happen, she was accepting it, because there was no other choice open to her.

Once at the Thorleys', Jonas had insisted Sarah wear her newest and prettiest gown for the engagement party. This was not a night for somber colors; Thomas Endor would not have wished it. Jonas's favorite was a pale pink satin with bows and frills decorating its hem. The neckline was low and deeply sensual, and in her hair she wore a little coronet of pink pearls.

On the third finger of her left hand was the heavy and unfamiliar opal betrothal ring that Jonas had given her earlier. She had heard somewhere that opals were unlucky, that opals meant tears. In her mind nothing could be more appropriate for this union.

She gave a last look in her bedroom mirror. There had

always been something ethereal about her beauty, enhanced now by the darkness surrounding her eyes. They spoke of some deep unhappiness hidden beneath their lovely exterior. She took a long breath, left the sanctuary of her room and walked down the long curving staircase of Lord Thorley's lovely Paddington home, as if she were going to meet her doom.

Jonas waited at the foot of the stairs with the other guests, who applauded at the sight of her. Some had been present at her twenty-first birthday party, and for a second Sarah experienced a small shiver, remembering the event.

But that party had been so different from this one. It had begun in a sparkling and merry mood, and her dearest uncle had been the host. It had ended somewhat unexpectedly, but as far as Sarah was concerned, not without excitement—she had fallen under the spell of Black Robbie. Her eyes blurred momentarily, because it was suddenly all so real. She struggled against searching for him now, among this fine company. As if such a thing could possibly happen again. As if she would *want* it to.

She was being pressed from hand to hand as one and then another murmured their congratulations and best wishes, some adding their assurances that Thomas would have been so pleased. Jonas was holding her hand in proprietary fashion, and as they moved around the drawing room, her heart suddenly stopped beating for a moment. She wondered desperately if Jonas sensed her sudden rigidity as she looked full in the face of a guest that Lady Thorley was introducing.

"Sarah, dear, this is Mr. David Roberts. He's generously agreed to escort my niece Barbara this evening, as her brother is indisposed. May I introduce Mistress Sarah Huxley, David, our most honored guest, and her betrothed, Lord Jonas Endor."

"How do you do?" Sarah murmured, looking directly into the hypnotic amber eyes of Black Robbie. But such a different Robbie! Gone was the pirate's garb, and he was once more the gentleman Sarah had seen at the theater. His clothes were of the finest make, his hair completely covered by the powdered wig that changed his appearance so dramatically.

"I'm delighted to meet you both, and to be present on this happy occasion," he said smoothly: Sarah noted at once that he had raised his voice to a higher pitch, and there was no trace of a Scottish accent. He spoke with the rounded vowel sounds of a well-educated Englishman. He had achieved the unmistakable air of aristocracy—he was a mild-mannered, harmless gallant. His fussy apparel and manners gave no hint of the daredevil life he secretly led.

Sarah felt a sudden bubbling admiration for his daring. Only Robbie could have risked such a thing. Only Robbie could have gotten away with it.

"It's our pleasure to meet Lord and Lady Thorley's friends," Sarah answered, considering that she was keeping superbly cool under the circumstances, and beginning to enjoy the charade. "Have you known them long?"

"Not very long. You might say we are theater acquaintances. One meets such interesting people at the theater these days, don't you think?"

Sarah was amazed at the way his face never betrayed a thing. No one but she was remotely aware of the double meaning behind his words.

"May I congratulate you, Lord Endor, on your admirable taste in a bride?" He turned to Jonas next, his manners impeccable.

"You may. But tell me, have we not met somewhere before, Sir?" Jonas asked.

"I think not. I have only lately returned to England from the south of France, where I sojourn frequently for my health," Robbie answered, giving a small cough to invite sympathy. Barbara Thorley came to stand beside him, hugging his arm, her tone motherly and protective.

"Do come and have some fruit cup, David. I'm sure it will ease your throat, and I know it's no use asking you to take anything stronger."

They drifted away, and Jonas gave a small snort.

"It's easy to see the kind of man *that* is," he sneered. "Fruit cup indeed. A man who can't take anything stronger is suspect to say the least!"

"Jonas, keep your voice down," Sarah scolded. He had had too much to drink, even before the festivities began. She wished she dared tell him that Robbie's demeanor was all an act, that he was more virile and masculine than Jonas would ever be. She wondered just what the pirate was doing here. Why choose tonight to reappear? Tonight, when she thought that all was lost, that her life would be thrown away on a man she could never love?

It was a long while before she had a chance to speak to him again. Not until after the eating and drinking was done, the toasts made, and the tears held back at the references to dear Uncle Thomas, who couldn't see this happy night. Not until the dancing began, and the elegant David Roberts approached. He spoke directly to Jonas.

"I would deem it a great honor if you would permit me to dance with your lady, Sir."

"Of course," Jonas waved his permission, already feeling hazy, and hardly caring who danced with Sarah as long as *he* didn't have to prance around the spinning room any more. Sarah rose, took the hand held out to her, and glided toward the dance floor with Mr. David Roberts, as the musicians began a new tune.

Chapter 5

The dance was for groups of eight, and there were six sets performing. Sarah was passed from hand to hand several times before she was able to whisper anything at all to Robbie.

"How dare you take such a risk?" she said, under cover of the loud music.

"You should know by now that I would dare much, sweet Sarah, for the touch of your hand," he replied in a tone that was half-mocking, half-serious. "How much more would I dare for all of you!"

A shiver of excitement, sharp and sweet, ran through her veins at his words. He was outrageous! She was both drawn to him and annoyed by him. Yet undoubtedly he colored her life. The grayness that threatened to darken it was momentarily lifted because of him.

"But someone might recognize you, as I did," she whispered frantically.

"No one else seems to have done so, and this is not the first time I've appeared in public as the affable David Roberts," Robbie said, relinquishing her hand as the dance claimed her attention elsewhere. She cavorted with the portly gentlemen, who sweated profusely in their silks and ruffs, until she clasped hands with Robbie once again.

"Do you really intend to marry him?" he demanded. "The announcement in the newspapers took me by surprise. I thought you had more spirit than to be fobbed off on such an oaf."

She bridled at once. It was both a compliment and a censure. She spoke without thinking. "I have no choice. He threatens to discredit me if I do not, and I would have nowhere to go."

Her voice held undisguised bitterness, unwittingly acknowledging that between them there was no need for falseness.

"You would have me," he said calmly.

He let go of her again, and Sarah could have wept with frustration. These snatches of conversation were useless, tantalizing and irritating. The ladies' shimmering skirts whirled around the room in a kaleidoscope of color, and the gentlemen tried to retain their poise as the tempo of the music grew faster. And as if she was in the grip of some madness, all Sarah Huxley wanted was to be alone with Robbie, or David, or whatever he chose to call himself. It was the man that mattered, not the name.

"Will you take the risk, Sarah?" he said the next time they were coupled.

She stared at him, heart pounding. "What risk?"

Robbie gave a short laugh. "My sweet idiot," he said affectionately, "why do you think I'm here? Call it a rescue or an abduction, whichever you prefer. You'll recall the young boy I snatched from your birthday party and know he came to no harm. I'll wager he had a high time in the telling of it."

"And would *I* come to harm?"

"Never with me."

In the midst of this last chance of conversation before the dance ended, she became aware of Jonas. Out of the corner of her eye, she could see him whispering to Lord Thorley, and the two of them were looking hard in her direction.

No, not hers, she realized. It was Robbie at whom they were staring, and a faint look of suspicion was beginning to dawn on Jonas's face.

Could it be that there was something about the man's movements in the dance that reminded Jonas of that other time, that outrageous time when the pirate band had forced its way into Endor House and plundered their guests, an act which Jonas could never forgive? The time when the notorious Black Robbie had danced with Sarah Huxley and kissed her in front of them all . . .

"Robbie, take care. I think Jonas suspects," she said, in sudden fright.

"So I see," he said harshly. "It's clearly time for my departure, so the choice is yours, my lovely. Stay and wed your Lord, or come with me. I have horses waiting, and we'll be at the coast very shortly."

"The coast?" Fear swept through her, reminding her instantly that this was a pirate, however successfully he pretended otherwise, and that if she went with him he would expect her to lead a pirate's life. She would have to live aboard ship, on the sea, which was both her fascination and her enemy. She would be as much an outlaw as he . . .

"Quickly, Sarah." Robbie's voice demanded an answer as the music ended.

The huge throng of dancers was making its way off the floor now, separating herself and Robbie from her betrothed and host. She could just see Jonas and Lord Thorley attempting to move in their direction. They would approach cautiously, not to frighten the guests unduly. Thinking perhaps that Robbie hadn't noticed them, the two men would attempt a triumphant capture of the pirate leader, and all would be over in minutes.

There was still a chance to get away. Either that, or scream and raise the alarm. Sarah glanced at Robbie, saw his amber eyes looking steadily into hers. Jonas or Robbie . . . in an instant she had made her choice.

"Follow me quickly. There's an old servants' passageway I know of that runs to the stables at the back of the house."

She twisted away from the crush of guests, and he followed her with a speed that was surprising in so large a man. But he must be used to fleeing, Sarah thought, as her heart beat crazily, still not sure what she was doing, only knowing that she had to do it. Robbie was her only escape from a life of misery, and it was as if she had always known it.

Seconds later, they had scrambled through the doorway to the dark passageway, and the sounds behind them grew dim. Jonas was not as familiar with this house as Sarah, since she had spent happy times exploring its maze of hidey-holes as a child.

It was dark and musty in the disused passageway, and as she grasped Robbie's hand behind her, it was reminiscent of the old tunnel in the cliffs, when he had led Sarah to safety. Now she was repaying him. She owed her life to him. Now he would owe his to her. They would be equal.

Gasping, they reached an outer door. If it was locked, they would be doomed. Sarah shivered with fright as Robbie pushed past her. He put his shoulder to the door and thrust the weight of his powerful body against it. At first it didn't budge. Then with a great creaking sound it lurched outward, its rusted hinges fracturing against Robbie's powerful frame. For the moment they were free.

The cool night air rushed to meet them. So far, there was no sound of anyone rushing to apprehend them.

"We mustn't tarry. When they realize we're both missing, they'll search the grounds," Robbie said.

He didn't give her time to think. They raced across the ground until they reached the sanctuary of the stables. The stableboys barely looked up from their nightly dice-playing, as they heard what they thought were the sounds of two merrymakers about to take a ride in the moonlight. Robbie helped Sarah, who climbed awkwardly onto a bay horse. She was obliged to pull her layers of skirts most inelegantly above her knees in order to sit comfortably.

Robbie leapt astride his own horse, and the two of them galloped away from the house and across the green fields of Paddington. He must have planned this, Sarah thought. Otherwise, why had two horses stood in wait, completely prepared to carry them to freedom? Sarah's heart pounded sickeningly in her chest. She knew that now there was no turning back. She tried not to think what would become of her if they were caught before they reached the coast. She was an accomplice to a pirate!

They both knew it could only be a matter of time before it was discovered who was missing from the Thorleys' house, and the farcical engagement party would come to an abrupt end.

They crossed the river and began the southward flight. There were other travelers on the road, but very soon they were both aware of the sounds of pursuit. The shrill piercing sound of constables' whistles mingled with shouts and carriage wheels and the rush of hoofbeats some distance behind them. There was no time to tarry. They bent low over the back of their steeds. There was hardly time to breathe, let alone speak, but at last Robbie pointed ahead of them to a fork in the road.

"They'll expect us to take the most direct route, so we'll take the other. We'll ride for a while, then take a short rest if you feel the need."

"I don't need a rest," she said insistently.

He glanced at her. Her hair had come loose from its pins and streamed out behind her. She looked wild and beautiful, and, he realized with a sharp pain, surprisingly dear to him.

"Good girl. Then we'll make for the ship at once. We'll be there in a few hours, and away from the English coast well before daylight."

She wanted to keep riding, because if they stopped she would have time to think. Not about the rightness or wrongness of escaping from a life with Jonas, but about this new and hazardous life she had chosen. She wasn't afraid of Robbie, nor too apprehensive of his men, but her fear of the sea was a personal battle she would have to wage.

It appeared that Robbie was right, that most of the pursuers had taken the more direct route to the coast. But for a short time she had thought that all was lost, as she heard several carriages and a group of riders hurtling closer toward them. Robbie quickly motioned her to a steep bank off the side of the road. The horses slithered down into the sheltering gully, where Sarah and Robbie lay against the beasts, their hearts pounding.

A few minutes later, Sarah was convinced they had been discovered as the followers approached their hiding place off the high road. There was a lot of shouting as the group slowed down a short distance from where she and Robbie lay. To her horror, Sarah heard her cousin's bellow among the melee of snorting horses and loud voices.

"If the blackguard has come this way, you're to show no mercy," he yelled to the group. "Take care with the woman, though she, too, must be taught a lesson. As for the pirate, there'll be a handsome reward for the man who does his patriotic duty."

"Shall we search the land hereabouts, my Lord?" an eager young voice spoke up.

"'Tis time-wasting, you young fool. I say we press on," yelled another. "They'll not be so stupid as to linger about this open country. They'll make for an inn and present themselves as travelers lost on the road."

"They could be hiding anywhere. 'Tis all a fool's errand!"

"Do you want the bloody reward or don't you?" Jonas screamed in fury at this indecision. "We're doing no good standing here like a huddle of washerwomen."

The words goaded the constables and the rest into action, and instead of searching the mounds and hollows near at hand, they took up the chase once more. Sarah hardly dared let out her breath until the sounds disappeared into the night. She was more terrified at the near capture than she had ever been in her life.

"You heard him," she stuttered. "Your life won't be worth a penny if Jonas finds you. He'll never forgive you for taking what is his."

"Then we must make damn sure he doesn't find us," Robbie said grimly. "Are you all right?"

"No. I'll never be all right again," she said, gritting her teeth to stop them trembling. "What do we do now? They're ahead of us. We can't travel the same road, and we can't go back."

She began to know how it felt to be hunted. Was this how Robbie lived every day of his life? And were the risks and the excitement worth it?

"There's another way. It's barely a track and some of it's through dense undergrowth, and your fine dress will be in tatters by the end of it, but I promise they won't find us. They'll begin searching local inns and hostelries pretty soon. It always follows the same pattern," Robbie informed her, confirming her guess that he'd done this kind of thing many times before.

Sarah remounted as best she could, her palms damp and shaking, and they rode carefully along the length of the gully until it dwindled into a track, and the welcome sight of forested wasteland loomed ahead of them. They rode silently to the rhythm of hoofbeats, through the dark night.

"If it follows the same pattern, why don't they know that you wouldn't stay at such places?" Sarah voiced after they had ridden some distance.

He gave a short laugh. "Many innkeepers are my friends. They benefit from a few bottles of fine French brandy, and concoct tales of their own to put the constables off the scent. They'll listen for sounds of any baying pack, standing outside their inns and waving their arms and gabbling excitedly to send the fools elsewhere, knowing they'll be well paid for their trouble. It's a game, Sarah, and so far I've always come out the victor."

A game! But for how long could any man's luck hold out? Especially now that she knew of his audacious trips into the houses of the nobility under the guise of David Roberts. He lived with danger, apparently thrived on it, and she was knowingly about to share that life with him. She must be out of her head.

"Having second thoughts?" he asked eventually.

She felt a mite safer inside the muffled gloom of the forest, and took a deep breath before answering. "I was wondering how long you intend to go on being Black Robbie, when you fit the other role so well."

The adventure was becoming more unnerving by the minute, and she was beginning to feel terribly stiff and sore. The great flanks of the horse rippled beneath her. She suddenly longed for normality, and wondered if she would ever know it again.

Despite the thrill of this flight, she was unused to such a lengthy sojourn, and her horse-riding had been confined to the long stretches of Sussex beaches, terminating in a long soak in a hot fragrant bathtub, attended to by her maid. No such refinements awaited her in the future, she thought uneasily.

Robbie laughed at her words, and she sensed at once that he prevaricated when he answered.

"And neither is the role I truly fit," he retorted. "I promised you I'd tell you the truth someday, and so I shall, when the time is right for the telling."

"And when will that be?" She said haughtily, stung by the male arrogance in his voice. "When you've had your wicked way with me, or whatever it is you intend to do?"

He didn't answer for a minute, then he spoke softly, the rich Scots burr a mere whisper on the wind, the words vibrant with innuendo. Whenever he spoke thus, it had the effect of sending shivers over her skin, as sensuously as the touch of a lover's caress. He was the devil in disguise, she thought weakly, and was maddened by her own weakness.

"I'll do nothing you don't want me to do, Sarah. And whatever you *do* want, I'll be happy to oblige you with."

She felt the heat in her cheeks, because of course she wanted him! She knew it more with every breath she took, every mile they rode. She wanted him with the passion of a woman who had known the marriage-bed, and had gradually come to know what hers lacked. She wanted him with all the anticipation of a woman in love, who knew that this man above any other could give her everything and more.

She loved him, and was both appalled and elated at the thought. She knew too that it would be the most foolish thing in the world to let him know it. He must have had many women, and the last thing Sarah wanted was to be no more than another string in his bow. She set more store by herself than that.

"You don't carry me away merely to seduce me, then?" she said, her voice wavering a little, for truly she didn't know what to expect.

Robbie laughed again. "I don't remember carrying you away at all. I recall that you came of your own free choice."

Her face flushed even more. "So I did," she said defiantly. "In this case, perhaps it was the devil I *don't* know, rather than the one I do, that intrigued me."

She could hear the smile in his voice as they rode through the night. "I take that as a compliment, Sarah, however you intended it.

"Just so long as you didn't do it to hold me for ransom. That would be despicable!"

Even as she said it, the possibility loomed like a specter in front of her. Why had she never considered it before? Whatever Jonas's feelings, he would be obliged to offer a goodly sum for her return. Honor demanded it. And Robbie had to know it. She suddenly felt sick, wondering just how much of a fool she was being after all.

They continued to ride in silence, while she burned up

inside, her feelings totally confused. She had been dancing openly and enjoyably with David Roberts, whose real identity Jonas had clearly guessed. Jonas wasn't a fool. He must have guessed that Sarah, too, suspected the truth. He knew her well enough to know that she had character enough to put up an almighty struggle if it hadn't been her wish to go with the pirate. She could have raised the alarm, but she had done nothing. She had gone willingly to her destiny.

It was natural that Jonas's pride would be mortally hurt by her flight, and after the public announcements he had made in the newspapers, he would never forgive her. If she had thought him her enemy before, how much more would he now consider her his. He would want her back, but he would make her pay dearly for her disloyalty.

And would Robbie be willing to hand her over for a bag of gold? Could she be worth so little to him after all? She wished she dared turn her horse and flee, but she was too afraid of the night and being alone on the road.

When they eventually came out of the forest they went through a series of byways and hidden lanes that Robbie obviously knew well. He must have ridden this trail a hundred times on his daring trips inland. And at last they came alongside a deep river inlet where the tall masts of a sailing ship creaked gently on the ebb tide swirling from the Channel.

All was in darkness, and Robbie slid easily off his horse, and held out his arms to help her dismount. He whacked the horses smartly on their rears to send them packing. There were no more chances for her to get away from him. She swayed slightly, unable for a moment to get her balance after the long hard ride, and he put his arm around her to steady her.

"What happens to the horses? Do you rid yourself of everything you don't need?" She was flustered at the speed with which everything was being taken out of her hands.

"They know their way home," he said shortly. "I have many friends along the coast. But come now. The sooner we put to sea, the better. The tide is on the turn and will aid us. When daylight comes, the coast guard will be on the lookout for us. By the time they're out of their beds, we'll be well on our way down the French coast."

She caught her breath. In her wildest dreams she could have envisaged none of this. She was about to set foot on a pirate ship with this charismatic devil of a man. Her relatives would wash their hands of her. Friends would disown her. She would be branded a pirate's woman and she would be disgraced. Then she felt Robbie's large hand curl around her fingers.

"Why do you wait then?" she asked hoarsely. "Already the dawn sky is starting to appear on the horizon."

He bent his head to kiss her cold cheek. "You're a woman after my own heart, Sarah Huxley. I knew it from the beginning. Remind me to tell you properly sometime."

Sarah had never set foot on a sailing-ship before. As they approached the huge dark shape of it, Robbie gave a series of low whistles that was clearly a coded signal. Several men appeared on deck at once, lowering a flimsy wooden ladder to the bank, and even as Sarah gathered up her stained and bedraggled skirts and climbed gingerly up the rungs with Robbie's help, others were industriously loosening ropes and hauling in the anchor, and they would obviously glide gently out of the inlet the minute their captain was safely on board.

It was all done with such silent efficiency and dexterity that Sarah grudgingly acknowledged their professionalism, if such a word could be applied to pirates of the high seas!

She remembered instead how her own parents had loved the sea, and had tried to instill in her that same love . . . a love that had remained static and dormant all these years, only showing itself in the strange fascination that drew her to the Sussex shores now and then, as if pulled there by an irresistible force. The sea, and Black Robbie. They shared the same magnetism. She pushed that thought out of her mind too.

"Come below, Sarah. I advise you to stay in your cabin until we're safely out of English waters. Follow me, and watch your head. The gangways are narrow."

Far too narrow for voluminous skirts! she thought peevishly as she wrenched at the ruined satin and squeezed through the impossibly small doorway leading down a steep ladder to the deck below. It was stuffy and ill lit, and she experienced a moment of revulsion, knowing she must share these quarters with a company of uncouth men who had been called brigands and cutthroats and every dastardly name the newspapers could invent for them.

"You needn't be afraid." Robbie seemed to read her thoughts as he heard her ragged breathing. "My men won't harm you."

"Can you guarantee that?"

"I can," he said doggedly. "They hurt no one at your birthday party, and they'll respect you on *The Adventuress*. This is your cabin."

He threw open a door, and Sarah gaped when she stepped inside. The cabin was much bigger than she had expected, and far more luxurious. Several lanterns threw soft light across the room, and, far from the basic wood-paneled interior she had expected, the cabin was lined with wall hangings of costly silks. The bed had a cover thrown over it that was soft and supple and made of leopard skin.

Even the air in the cabin was subtly scented, and on the small dressing table, with its lattice-work rail to stop things from falling when the ship lurched in rough seas, were vials of rose and violet and orange water, rouge pots and powders, and other beauty appliances. Silver filigree combs and hair brushes stood beside an elaborate jewel case.

While Sarah stood, stunned into silence by the unexpectedness of it all, Robbie strode to one side of the room and opened a door. Inside were gowns of every hue, and in a box at the foot of the wall cupboard were chemises and undergarments and stockings. Beside them were shoes and slippers, and on the shelf above the gowns was a selection of fashionable hats.

Sarah swallowed, her natural pleasure at seeing such an array stemmed by another thought.

"Whose cabin is this?" she demanded.

He saw the accusation in her lovely eyes and took her hands in his.

"If you think it was ever anyone's but yours, you're wrong. Since the day we met, I've planned for the moment you would set foot on my ship, and now I have you."

She shivered violently at the possessiveness in his voice.

"You planned all this for me?" she asked, in disbelief and anger. "Were you so sure that I'd leave everything I love and come to you?"

"You're here, aren't you? *We're* here, Sarah. And what was left for you to love, but a bastard of a man who'd drain your spirit and turn any spark of affection to hate in a very short while?"

She looked at him dumbly. He knew her so well it was uncanny. Yes, he'd been sure of her. He'd done all this, turning a pirate's cabin into an enchanted place for her. She should be thrilled, yet his very attention to detail, to making everything perfect, alarmed her intensely. Such activity seemed to strip her of her own will, as if from now on she would have to succumb to his. Just as humiliatingly as he intimated she would have succumbed to Jonas's will. And Sarah Huxley was still her own woman, no matter how strong her feelings for a man.

"I thank you, Sir," she said primly. "I appreciate your wish to make me comfortable on this voyage."

76

She heard his rich throaty laugh, and the next minute she was swept into his arms from which there was no escape. She could smell the animal odor of him after the hard ride, knowing that it mingled with her own bodily scent. None of it unpleasant, all of it strangely erotic and sensual in the silken confines of this gently rocking cabin.

"I would give you riches beyond your wildest dreams. You must know that by now! It was no idle whim of mine to bring you here, and this is no mere voyage, to end when we reach English shores again—when and if we ever do."

"What is it then?" she asked in a strangled voice, pressed as she was against that hard masculine chest and feeling the throb of his heartbeat against her own.

"This is our new life, yours and mine. One that will end who knows where? From now on, every voyage will be a new adventure, because you will share it with me."

"You mean to keep me a captive forever then?" She was still unable to breathe properly because he held her so tightly.

"I mean to keep you," he amended. "Your cousin couldn't hold you, but I can. And when you're ready you'll come to me, I promise you, Sarah."

"You presume a lot then! You told me once that I owed you my life, Well, do you not think I've repaid that debt tonight? I could so easily have turned you over to the authorities. We are equal. One shout on the road, one scream, and you would be lying dead in a ditch by now! Were it not for my silence—"

She gave a smothered scream as his mouth came down on hers, stifling the words. She felt the pressure of his fingers against her spine, and the strength of his body made hers unwillingly pliant. She would not respond . . . she would not . . . All the control she could muster made her stand stiffly in his arms, while every nerve in her yearned to melt into him. But he would not make her his slave, she would never submit to such an indignity!

Just when her bones seemed to dissolve from weakness, Sarah couldn't have said. One moment she was standing rigidly in the man's arms while his kiss awoke a primitive passion inside her body as sharp as a flame. His body made small deliberately erotic movements against hers, awakening a thousand pinpricks of desire. Time seemed to merge into sensation, so that it seemed no more than a moment later when she felt a soft little sigh of pleasure deep in her throat, and unconsciously her arms had wound around Robbie's powerful shoulders. Her fingers raked his abundant hair, while her skin felt tinglingly alive at every point where it touched his.

At last he pulled slightly back, his mouth still only slightly away from hers. And immediately when they parted, she despised herself for letting him know how dangerously easy it was for her to respond to his caresses.

"So, Mistress Huxley, you are not as averse to my attentions as you pretend. And as for repaying the debt you owe me by saving my life tonight, I suggest that such an action merely entwines us more deeply than ever. I do not absolve you from your debt to me. I claim you even more surely as my own."

"Your property, do you mean? Or do you mean to sell me off to the highest bidder?" Sarah challenged, her pride coming to the fore once again. She breathed heavily, but no more than he. If she intrigued him by her apparent rebuffs, so much the better. It would do him good to meet a woman of spirit instead of the usual swooning females he probably encountered.

"My property, Sarah. I do not sell what I want for myself."

Her eyes flashed. "How dare you presume so much? You speak as if I'm in bondage to you. You have no right—"

"You gave me the right when you entrusted yourself to me. You're as much mine as any woman who ever belonged to a man. Think on it, my love. And get some rest. In a while I'll send someone with hot water for your bath. You'll find everything you need in the closet with the bamboo door. It will be my pleasure to see you rested and beautifully attired once again. And if you have no more need of this, I suggest you toss it overboard."

He lifted her left hand as he spoke and eyed the opal ring with contempt. "Your cousin gives you a bauble. I will drown you in jewels. Sleep well."

He was gone from the cabin before Sarah could gather her senses. She was suddenly aware of the rocking motion beneath her feet. She rushed to the tiny porthole to peer out. Dimly, she could just make out the dark line of the Sussex coast diminishing as the ship plowed its way on a southerly course into the English Channel. She could hear the creak of oars, and assumed that the crew must be helping *The Adventuress* to speed on her way.

All this time, while Robbie had been keeping her occupied in the cabin, his crew must have been obeying well-rehearsed orders, guiding the ship out of the inlet on the tide, and it was now sliding gently into deeper waters. The great adventure had begun, and there could be no turning back.

Chapter 6

As soon as Robbie had gone, Sarah opened the bamboo door and discovered, to her amazement, a small bathing room, with rails for towels above the basin, and shelves containing perfumes and skin lotions and exotic bath oils. A shielded candle lit the small compartment. She closed the door slowly, and lay on her bed awhile, staring at the ceiling and wondering at this enigma of a man.

What had made a gentleman turn to piracy? she wondered. That he was, or had been, a gentleman, was never in doubt. That he was no ordinary pirate was becoming obvious to her as well. She had already seen him and his men in action at her own birthday party. Where were the bloodcurdling yells, the screams for blood, the threats to the ladies?

Yes, there had been pistols and daggers in evidence, but looking back now, none of it seemed real. It had seemed no more than sport to them, taking just what they wanted and no more. Harming no one, even returning young Walter Sands with a tale to tell that would color his days for many months to come.

She was still puzzling over the strangeness of it all when there was a tap on her cabin door some time later. She opened the door gingerly, her mouth falling open in surprise at seeing the small figure outside, two pails of steaming water in his hands.

"For your bath, Missy," the boy said, his smile wide and gleaming in his black face. He was about twelve years old, his dark unruly hair like a wire mop on top of his head. He wore a once-white loose shirt over dark ragged trousers and his feet were bare. If he had been older, Sarah would have been terrified. As it was, she stood back silently and allowed him into the cabin.

"Cap'n Robbie says Tomby must put water in the tub for the pretty lady," he stated.

"Oh, does he?" Sarah asked, sarcasm dripping from every word. The steam from the pails drifted into her nostrils, and she capitulated.

"All right." She nodded. "But I need some cold water in there first. I don't want to scald myself."

"Please?" he asked, puzzled.

"Can you bring me some cold water as well?" she asked in a loud voice.

The boy grinned. "Cold water pails in closet, Missy. And Tomby daft but not deaf."

She felt her face muscles relax and grinned back. He was a cheeky young devil, but hardly what she expected on a pirate ship. She wondered if Robbie had captured him, too, as he'd captured her. Regardless of the circumstances, she seemed unable to think of her presence here as anything less than a triumph for the pirate captain.

"Carry on then—Tomby," she said. She watched as the boy went to the bamboo closet and lifted two heavy covered pails of cold water out of a small cupboard inside. He emptied them into the tub, then poured the steaming water he'd brought with him.

"Cap'n says you enjoy bath, then he comes have breakfast with you later."

"Does everyone on the ship do exactly what Cap'n— *Captain* Robbie says?" she inquired, irritated at the assumption of a tête-à-tête.

"Sure 'nuf," Tomby said. "Cap'n good man. Cap'n save Tomby from bad men."

"I see. Well, thank you, Tomby. I can manage now."

The boy went out, glancing admiringly at the white skin of the English lady, and ready to tell old Cookie that her eyes were bluer than the bluest ocean and her hair was like long dark silk ribbons.

Left to herself, Sarah selected a bottle of bath oil with the piquant scent of lemons and heady wild violets. She tipped it into the water, quickly shed her layers of clothes with a feeling of relief, and stepped carefully into the tub, shutting the slatted door of the closet behind her. The water was blissfully hot, and in seconds she was enveloped in a fragrant cloud of steam. She closed her eyes and leaned back, allowing the tendrils of her hair to drift into the water.

The rocking motion of the ship and the delight of this luxury almost sent her into ecstasy. There was little room to move, and she had to sit with her knees almost touching her breasts, but it didn't matter. There was a washcloth at hand, and she squeezed it in and out of the water, letting the droplets trickle onto her skin. She felt an extraordinary lethargy. She could happily fall alseep right where she was, with the hot water making her drowsy, and the scent of the oil filling her senses.

A small movement out in the cabin made her look sharply toward the slatted door. Behind it, against the cabin's lamplight, she could make out a dark shape, and her heart seemed to leap into her mouth. She grabbed for a towel and threw it across herself, but even before she heard the rich voice, she knew it was he.

"Don't fret yourself, my lovely. I've no intention of ravishing you just yet, however delightful the thought might be."

"How dare you come in here like this!" She spoke angrily, having no doubt that he'd been able to see something of her through the slats.

"On my ship, I go where I please, Sarah," he said mockingly.

She rose awkwardly, the foaming water still clinging to her skin, when a sudden lurching movement of the ship tugged the flimsy bamboo door open into the cabin. For a moment, as though they were frozen, neither moved a muscle—Sarah, because she didn't know whether to grab at the door and risk losing the towel altogether; Robbie, because of the unexpected vision of her standing there.

The towel was draped across her breasts and shoulders, but below it, soap bubbles glistened on rounded hips and slender legs, and between them the dark pouting triangle that sent his blood surging. Burningly aware of his gaze, Sarah twisted in the tub, scarlet-faced, and, before he pushed the door shut to cover her modesty, Robbie saw the two perfectly shaped buttocks below the curving shape of her spine and tiny waist. Innocently, she had given him far more than she had intended.

"I apologize, Sarah." She heard his voice, thicker than usual. "I have no control over the movement of the sea, and I thought you would have finished bathing by now. I'll return in a while. We have things to discuss."

She heard the cabin door shut firmly as he went out, and realized that she was trembling. She would be a fool to deny the attraction between them. She had felt it from the first. How much more of a fool was she to throw herself into such close contact with him!

She dried herself quickly, and put on petticoats and a dressing-robe, feeling somewhat more respectable, but hardly knowing which gown would be appropriate to wear. Outside the porthole it was almost daylight, and there was no sign of land. She looked away quickly from the gray expanse of water, refusing to let herself panic.

The next time Robbie came to the cabin he knocked at the door and she let him in silently, trying not to think about how he had left her. She pulled the dressing-robe more

83

tightly around her, ignoring the little lift of his eyebrows as she did so.

"Do you feel refreshed?" he asked, as though nothing untoward had happened.

"Yes, thank you."

"Good. Tomby is bringing us some breakfast. He'll remove your bath water while you're on deck later."

"I am to be allowed on deck then?" she couldn't resist saying in a sarcastic tone.

Robbie smiled. "Did you think I intended keeping you a prisoner for the rest of your life?"

"I have no way of knowing what you intend."

"And I have no need to shackle my women, Sarah," he said in that deceptively mild voice he sometimes used that made her shiver. "Yes, of course you will go on deck. You'll need to take regular exercise. But not dressed like that, and this is what we must discuss."

She was about to say scathingly that she had no intention of going on deck in a dressing-robe, when Tomby arrived with a tray of food and a jug of tea, which he put on the little side table. He flashed a look that was almost adoration at Robbie, and went away again.

"Where on earth did you get him?" Sarah was too inquisitive not to ask. "I suppose you bought him at a slave market—or stole him from his mother."

Robbie poured them both a cup of hot, weak tea, spiced with lemon juice and black sugar. It tasted strange and bitter, but not altogether unappetizing.

"You don't think very highly of me, do you?"

"Should I? The notorious Black Robbie, who abducts young boys and women, and robs the nobility—"

His voice was calm and expressionless. "Tomby had been left to die by his family when I found him near to starving. He comes from a tribe steeped in superstition. After a bad harvest, the seventh child is offered to the gods as an appeasement, and to ensure the next year's crops. Tomby

84

was the seventh child. When I found him he was as emaciated as a corpse on a gibbet. Bacon, Sarah?"

She glared at him as he lifted the cover on a dish swimming with bacon fat, on which the rashers were piled high. There was a plate of toast beside it. Normally she had a healthy appetite, but his graphic description of the infant Tomby, allied with the motion of the ship, was doing all sorts of unpleasant things to her stomach. She swallowed convulsively.

"You'll do better to eat," Robbie said. "Dry toast and bacon is a good remedy for seasickness. It'll line your stomach, and the tea will settle it. Eat first, and then we'll talk."

She did as she was told, certain that nothing was going to stop the heaving inside her. Thankfully, it didn't get any worse. She prayed that she wouldn't disgrace herself by throwing it all up again. When they had both finished eating, Robbie looked at her speculatively.

"While they waited for us to come aboard, my men had discussions about what was to be done about you."

"Oh, really?" She bristled at once, not caring to be the subject of talk among a pirate band.

"Simmer down. You're the prickliest female I've ever come across," Robbie said testily. "That's what makes you so interesting to me, of course, but there are times when I wish you'd listen first and jump later."

She sat with her lips clamped shut. Wasn't it just what her uncle had always said of her when she was a child? But she was a woman now, and from the expression in Robbie's eyes, he was only too aware of it.

"The men think it's unlucky to have a woman on board ship," he said bluntly.

Her heart leapt, and she took refuge in sarcasm. "Do they suggest throwing me overboard then?"

"It's one possibility," he said, annoyingly playing to her tune. "There are two others."

"I'm sure I'm not going to like either of them," Sarah said.

He laughed. "I know which one I'd prefer, but I've taken a bet with myself on which one you'll settle for."

She looked at him suspiciously. His eyes lingered on the opening of her dressing-robe. She had loosened it while she ate her breakfast, and the soft swell of her breasts was just visible. She colored at once, and drew the robe together securely.

"I don't see why it should matter so much what the men think. You're the captain, aren't you? Don't they have to obey you in all things?"

He sighed. "You are also the most argumentative woman I've ever met. Yes, they obey me implicitly in matters of seamanship. In matters that might affect the smooth harmony between us, they have the right to be heard."

"Then you'd better tell me what my two choices are to be, hadn't you?" Her voice wasn't quite so steady now.

"A lone woman on a ship is a hazard and many of the crew consider it a bad omen. A ship's captain has the right to have a wife on board, and none will dispute that—"

"No, thank you!"

Robbie smiled slightly. "Then I win my bet," he said mockingly. "And we come to the other alternative, which I will put to the men later."

"Which is?"

"That you look and dress like a boy at all times during the hours of daylight. The crew are well aware of your sex, but providing you disguise yourself moderately well, such a small matter may be overlooked. You will cut your hair and wear boyish clothes to hide your shape, and you'll help Cookie in the galley."

Sarah spluttered in a fury. "I will not! I've never cooked in my life. I refuse to be a skivvy to you and your men. How dare you ask it of me!"

"I don't ask it. I order it," Robbie said coldly. "Either that or marry me."

Her chin tilted. Feelings and desires didn't come into this. She was damned if she'd be held to ransom in this way. Marry *him!* At that moment she'd as soon wed a sea slug.

"I will not marry you!"

"Then you'll do exactly as I say. I will not allow my men to mutiny over a chit of a girl, and I'll have no disobedience from you." He had become steely-voiced now, his dark eyes glinting with anger. If she thought herself a match for him, how much more did he see himself as a match for her, in every way.

She grasped at something he'd said earlier. "During the hours of daylight, you said. Am I to be allowed to don feminine clothes after nightfall then?"

"It will be my pleasure to insist that you do. You and I will stroll the deck every evening, Sarah, and we will take dinner together. When we anchor on the coast of Spain for careening, we'll go ashore and act the dandies together, and perhaps in a few weeks you'll think my alternative not too unwelcome."

She glared at him. "What is this—careening? I don't like the sound of it."

He laughed, teasing her. "You'll find out. I promise you it doesn't hurt. Now then, Tomby will bring you some boy's clothes, and I will send someone to cut your hair."

"No! If it has to be cut, I shall do it myself." She felt her mouth go dry. Her hair was truly her crowning glory. The thought of chopping it short was almost akin to sacrilege. Without warning, Robbie reached forward and twisted a thick tendril of it in his hand and pressed it to his lips.

"Someday, I promise you, it will grow thick and luxurious again, Sarah," he said softly. "You have my word."

Her eyes blurred for a moment. He could speak with such sincerity, but it was still the word of a pirate. She must never forget that. She felt the tug on her hair as he pulled her to her feet and into his arms.

"Do you think I don't regret that I'll not feel this hair

winding around me in my cabin, sweet Sarah?" He was all seduction now. "The scent of it already haunts my dreams, and you have but to say the word and become my wife, and there'll be no need to take the knife to it."

She pulled herself out of his embrace.

"Send the boy to bring me a sharp knife at once," she said imperiously, uncaring if he was master of this ship or not. "No one blackmails me into marriage again."

He turned and left her with a curt promise that he would see her again when she was in a better humor.

An hour later, she looked sickly at the sight reflected in the small mirror in the cabin. She looked like a freak. She had hacked at her hair in a fury and now it was all levels. It had once been so admired, she thought with tears prickling her eyes, as she was both angered and ashamed of her own vanity.

But now the beautiful, richly dark curls lay scattered on the cabin floor. What she was left with was the haircut of an urchin boy. The fact that it suited her piquant features was no consolation. No lady ever wore hair this disheveled or this short.

She might have done better to do as Robbie had suggested, and allowed someone with more experience to shape the unruly tendrils, but that only angered her more. She wanted no pirate's hands holding her head and touching her skin. Only one, the wanton thought simmered in her mind, and she pushed it aside at once.

She sawed briefly at some of the longer strands of hair, and then gave up. Her only appeasement was that at least it curled naturally, without the need for tortuous winding in rags every night. And however short and uneven, it didn't hang in rats' tails.

She heard Tomby's voice outside the cabin door and when she opened it to let him in, he carried a brush and pan and an armful of boyish garb which he handed to her silently. At her changed appearance, his eyes went round and startled in his black face.

"Well? Have you lost your tongue?" Sarah demanded.

The boy studied her and then to her amazement his face relaxed into a wide grin. Two rows of white teeth shone in the darkness of his skin.

"I like," he said. "Missy look good."

"Oh, Missy does, does she?" Despite herself, Sarah felt her mouth twitching. "Well, I think Missy looks like a jack-in-the-box."

And what Black Robbie would think of her, she didn't dare predict. Though if he, too, thought she looked a sight, perhaps he'd leave her alone. She wasn't quite sure that the prospect pleased her.

Tomby proceeded to brush her discarded hair into the pan. For a moment Sarah felt a great sadness at its loss, then resolutely told herself not to be so feeble. What Robbie had said about mollifying the crew made sense. And she wasn't a latter day Samson about to lose all her strength just because she'd lost her hair. Her strength was in her character. She would hang on to *that* at all costs. And there was one thing about hair—it always grew back. She cheered herself up with the thought.

When Tomby scurried away with his brush and pan, she examined the clothes he had brought. Loose-fitting cotton trousers, as full in the legs as those worn by the little Dutch boys in the paintings her Uncle had in his study; a cotton shirt just as baggy, soft flat shoes that were probably well suited to shipboard life, and a battered straw hat that looked as if it had survived a shipwreck. Although clean, to Sarah the whole ensemble was quite hideous.

She rammed the straw hat on her head and pulled a face at herself in the mirror. She threw the hat across the cabin in annoyance. Then she held the shirt up against her figure, and curiosity got the better of her.

Could she pass for a boy? Certainly her feminine features would be hidden beneath the brim of the hat, and the shirt and trousers would hide the most buxom of women. It wasn't as if the crew didn't know who and what she was. Robbie merely wanted to make her presence less evident, for her own safety, as well as his men's peace of mind.

Almost without thinking, she slid her arms out of the dressing-robe and dressed herself in the unfamiliar clothing. Pulling the hat well down over her face once more, the transformation was complete. She gave a slow nod, acknowledging that Robbie knew his crew better than she did, and that she did indeed feel less vulnerable in the strange outfit. Just so long as he didn't laugh at her.

As if in answer to her thought, he arrived at the cabin shortly afterward, no doubt informed by Tomby that "Missy" had been given the clothes. She stared at him defiantly, finally tossing the hat away again, because his gaze made her body feel heated from head to toe. Robbie sprawled on her bed in a proprietary way, studying her from every angle until she felt as if he must know every pore of her skin. His scrutiny made the blood pound in her veins.

"I know it's awful," she said, suddenly aware to her horror that her mouth was trembling. She hated herself, because she knew she didn't want to look awful for him. She didn't want him to jeer at her, or think her a clown. She had been the poised and beautiful Mistress Sarah Huxley until he tore her away from everything she knew, and she wanted to be poised and beautiful for *him*.

"It's not awful," he said at last. "Your long hair, beautiful though it was, detracted from your perfect bone structure. If you had no hair at all you would still be beautiful, and there are few woman who could say the same. I'm awed by you."

He constantly surprised her. His words were so simple and understated they froze the flippant retort on her lips. She felt a dryness in her throat, and knew a sudden overwhelming wish. That they had met and loved in another time and place,

90

in different circumstances than these. . . .

"I'll do for you then?" she said stupidly, unable to take her eyes away from those magnetic amber eyes of his.

In answer he came toward her and took her soft white hand in his. He raised it to his lips in the softest of kisses, yet his touch awoke a searing desire in her, as potent as a flame.

"You'll do very well for me, lassie," he spoke softly, his Scottish brogue becoming more pronounced. She had already deduced that this happened when he was emotionally affected.

So he wasn't entirely immune to her, she thought. Perhaps there *was* something more than mere lust in his response. It was a small sliver of comfort to hold in her heart.

And then, as if he had given away too much of himself, his voice became brusque.

"I want you to come about the ship with me, to let the men see you and accept you. And you'll want to get your bearings on *The Adventuress,* since she's to be your home from now on, Sarah." He became thoughtful. "I wonder if we should change your name."

"No! You've changed everything else, but let me at least keep my name! Besides, what does it matter? The men know who I am, despite the way I look."

Robbie laughed. "I daresay you're right. Anyway, I want you to observe my crew too, to see that they're not altogether the blackguards they're reputed to be."

She was on safer ground now. Instantly, she reverted to the indignant Sarah Huxley who had seen her dearest Uncle's home so rudely intruded.

"Tell that to Lady Farlane and the mother of poor Walter Sands! And what else do you call thieves who creep about the homes of decent folks and scare them out of their wits while taking their most precious possessions?"

Robbie laughed, seeing the sparkle of righteousness in her blue eyes. He leaned forward and kissed the tip of her nose.

"Oh Sarah, Sarah, I love you when you're angry! And I don't remember taking your most precious possessions from you, my lovely!"

She fell into his trap. "Yes, you did leave my topaz necklace!" As her hand moved to touch the jewel beneath her clothes she saw his gaze and her cheeks went fiery red.

"You said you wanted me to meet the crew, I believe?" she said frigidly, and he laughed again, enjoying her discomfiture with a tenderness that took him by surprise. She was beginning to get beneath his skin, this beautiful girl, Robbie thought, and no woman had ever done that before. He chose not to analyze the possible reasons and stood back for her to go out of the cabin before him.

"Does a ship's boy warrant such gallant treatment?" she challenged, and for all that she was his captive, somehow Robbie had the uneasy feeling that Mistress Sarah Huxley was getting the better of him. And far from irritating him, he was beginning to find it a strangely exhilarating experience.

He strode outside the cabin ahead of her, and she had to run to keep up with him in the dark passage until they came to the companionway. At least it was easier to climb the vertical steps in the boyish garb than in her heavy skirts, Sarah thought, and less embarrassing once she had got used to the way she looked.

In fact, she wasn't so different from the men, she realized. From a distance, watched through a spyglass from a customs ship, for instance, no one would think there was a woman on board, just another scruffy pirate urchin.

Her own thoughts shocked her. She was slipping into the role Robbie had mapped out for her far too easily, and she vigorously resisted it. But that spirit of reckless adventure inherited from her parents and, successfully smothered until now, was doing its best to come to the surface, despite all her efforts.

Emerging from the companionway through the small square hatch, Sarah saw that they were up on deck, away from the gloomy bowels of the ship. There was clean fresh air, tangy with the smell of salt. There was blue sky and sunlight and the wheeling of sea birds following the ship on its southerly course. There was great activity among the crew as the sails billowed and the bow of *The Adventuress* plowed through the waves.

There was no sight of land. For a moment Sarah panicked, her turbulent fears subsiding only a little as she felt Robbie's hand on her arm. She felt such a mixture of emotions toward this man, sometimes feeling as if she could trust him completely, and yet never able to forget he was a pirate captain, and she had put her life in his hands.

Whatever he might have said to her at that moment was forgotten as a shadow fell across Sarah's face. She looked up, startled, at the largest man she had ever seen. Swarthy, dressed in similar fashion to herself but with a wide leather belt fastened loosely around his great girth, and a bushy dark beard around heavy jowls, he looked down at her without expression in his cold eyes.

"Well, Quartermaster? Does she pass the test?"

Robbie spoke nonchalantly, yet Sarah sensed that this man's approval was important. He evoked all the old tales of pirates who were mentioned in hushed tones as being wicked and romantic and terrible all at the same time. And of the undoubted hierarchy among every pirate crew, from the captain down. He was the quartermaster, the strong man of the ship, who administered floggings and could order punishment as well as the captain.

"Providing she obeys the rules," the man said sternly. "A woman aboard ship is bad luck, Cap'n, and even now not all the crew have accepted the notion of having her here, nor are we certain on what terms. We've always abided by the majority vote, and 'twould be a bad day for ye, Cap'n, if the vote went against ye and ye didn't pay attention to it."

Sarah felt a frisson of fear at the warning in the quartermaster's voice. This was Robbie's ship, she thought indignantly, and yet right now this bull of a man sounded as if *he* was calling the odds.

"I'll obey the rules," she said in a flash, her chin lifting. "Don't worry, you'll be unaware of my presence as far as possible. And as soon as you see fit to put me ashore, I'll be more than thankful."

"That will not be possible." As several more of the pirate band hovered near, listening intently, Robbie spoke in a different manner, as rough as his crewmen. "For the present you're a hostage on this ship, Mistress Huxley, and you'll leave it when I see fit, which may well be when I've decided what ransom I will ask for you."

The sun dazzled her eyes as she twisted her head to look up at him, and her bones felt like water at the hardness of his eyes and the iron set of his jaw.

So he betrayed her after all! All the tender moments in her cabin, her growing warmth toward him, was all for nothing. He meant to seduce her and leave her ruined, and then to hand her back to Jonas for the highest price he could get. She was no more than bait to feed Black Robbie's greed, sexual and otherwise. She felt a choking sensation in her throat and physically had to force herself not to cry out and shame herself in front of these louts.

"Do you think the dandy will want her back after a sea voyage with ye, Cap'n?" the quartermaster was asking slyly, his meaning clear.

"She'll not be harmed," Robbie said sharply. "Not by me or anyone. That much will be made quite clear at the meeting tonight. We all obey the rules on this ship. Understood?"

"Aye, aye, Cap'n," the man said loudly.

He moved his great bulk away, and the others with him, muttering among themselves. They must all have been aware of Robbie's intentions to bring her here, she thought. They had helped her aboard. Why then, did they all seem so alien to her now?

She could feel the antagonism among them as if it were tangible, and she longed desperately for the safety of home, for Endor House. Even the odious attentions of Jonas might be preferable to the threat of a pirate crewman's cutlass in the silence of the night.

Chapter 7

"Keep that pained look on your face and don't start arguing. I'll explain everything later," Robbie said beneath his breath. Sarah would have preferred to denounce her captor for a rogue there and then, but common sense stopped her. What would be the point, anyway? These men would only laugh and jeer if she began screaming like a harridan, and she had more dignity than that.

At least, she always had, and she prayed she could cling to it now. Dignity and self-respect were about all she had left. She was nervous at being the only woman on board. She would be helpless if any of these men chose to attack her. The pained look on her face was due as much to the rank smell emanating from some of the ruffians as to the outrage she felt.

She vaguely recognized the tall thin man who slouched toward them as one of those who had invaded Endor House on her birthday. Incongruously, he wore a bright sash around his middle, from which a huge knife gleamed. Robbie spoke to him briskly.

"Surgeon, this is the woman. You'll remember her, though I doubt many would take her for the same. Agreed?"

The man looked Sarah over with critical detachment. The surgeon. And probably the carpenter too, since it was rumored that many pirate ships employed one man to do both jobs. For a shuddering second, Sarah had the horrid sensation that the man was measuring her up for a coffin, and then he gave the grimace of a smile.

"Agreed."

"Persuade the rest. 'Twill be to you advantage," Robbie said bluntly, and turned his back on the man.

Sarah felt more and more alarmed as Robbie took her on a tour of the deck, ostensibly to let her get the feel of her surroundings, but she knew at once that it was more to let the crew see her in her new guise. She was relieved to go below once more, away from those hostile faces.

Robbie motioned her toward the galley, where Tomby was busy peeling vegetables. An ancient oriental cook gave her the warmest smile of the day. She had the barest chance to look around at the array of pots and pans and the great stacks of dishes waiting to be scrubbed clean before Robbie led her to the far end.

"You'll be quite safe working here in the daytime," Robbie said quietly.

"Will you please explain to me what's going on?" she asked explosively. "I was terrified on deck. Surely your men knew I was coming on board?"

"Some did."

"And was it true what you said? That I'm no more than a hostage, and that you're holding me for ransom?"

She couldn't say more, because emotion threatened to overcome her. And she would not cry in front of him and the other two, who were grinning at one another like Cheshire cats, obviously not understanding the tension between Sarah and their captain, and getting on with their work as if the others weren't there.

"You mustn't believe all you hear," Robbie said roughly.

"I'm beginning to realize that only too well!" she said bitterly. "But what is tonight's meeting for? Is it to decide what's to be done with me? You've already given me alternatives. Aren't you in command on your own ship?"

"I am. But unless a sea captain wants mutiny on his hands, he's wise enough to allow the crew their say in all matters, and for the quartermaster to act as arbitrator. It's the policy on *The Adventuress* to do things by majority vote." Clearly, he resented her questioning his authority.

"And if they vote to throw me to the sharks?"

"Don't be melodramatic," he said shortly. "It won't come to that. Surgeon knows the way to persuade the crew to do as he says, and as long as we have his vote—"

"How does he persuade them?" She wanted to know.

Robbie gave a slight smile. Since she was so damned inquisitive, he would tell her all.

"He can deprive them of certain privileges. The lack of laudanum to those needing it is so painful as to be almost lethal. Those needing urgent medical attention can find the surgeon is too busy elsewhere to attend to them. A gaping wound can remain untended for so long that it suppurates and becomes gangrenous—"

"Stop it!" Sarah gasped. "How can you condone such horrors?"

"I don't condone them. In fact, they rarely happen, because the crew knows only too well that Surgeon is their lifeline. I only tell you what the threats are."

"In other words, blackmail."

"If you like. Would you rather I hadn't got Surgeon on our side?"

Sarah stared at him. What kind of man was this? The moment she thought she knew him, he showed a different side of himself. And as for blackmail . . . Were all men tarred with the same hateful brush? Her beloved Uncle, her hated cousin, and even Robbie, because of his apparent loyalty to his crew members' wishes.

She glanced toward the cook, chopping at some sort of bony meat as if relishing the experience. To Sarah it seemed symbolic of a barbaric way of life she was only just beginning to know, and she shuddered again. It was really coming home to her what she had done in giving up the comfortable life she knew for one of hazards and danger.

Wallowing briefly in nostalgia, she missed her gentle Aunt Lily with a pang that was almost painful. She missed the brusqueness of her Uncle and her dear Aunt Blanche, both now sadly departed from this life, and the way they had sheltered her after she had been orphaned. She ran her tongue around her dry lips.

"I feel a little faint," she murmured, despising herself for the undoubted truth of it, but thinking she would surely collapse among the cooking utensils if she didn't get away from the galley immediately.

"It's probably the smell of the meat. Cookie, douse it thoroughly in vinegar before Mistress Sarah comes to work with you," Robbie ordered. "She'll report tomorrow morning."

He bundled Sarah out of the galley before she could speak indignantly. But she didn't have the strength to argue at that moment. The meat was definitely off, she thought greenly. How was she going to be able to face hours in the close confines of the galley? It was intolerable of Robbie to force her.

She felt close to weeping again, but he was gripping her arm and leading her through a maze of dark passageways, to the forward end of the ship and upward. She was totally disorientated, even though the ship was small by some standards. It was still frighteningly large and unreal to Sarah.

Robbie opened a door and led her inside, and she gasped. This was no ordinary seaman's cabin. It was obviously Robbie's, and styled in the manner of a gentleman. The room was squarish, though wider at the front and tapering at the door end where they had entered. The other three sides were composed entirely of windows, so that sunlight streamed in, making this the first place Sarah had seen on the ship that resembled real elegance.

The area nearest the great expanse of windows at the forward end seemed purely functional, the rest more personal. There was a table and chairs for dining on the right, and to the left there was a partitioned area, the door partly open. Sarah glimpsed the bunk inside it and facilities that almost turned it into a small bedchamber in a gentleman's house. On the floor near the bunk there was even a fur rug. Her own cabin had been a surprise, but this was magnificent.

And clearly displayed were the spoils of war, in the costly paintings and jeweled mementoes, and the richly embroidered coverlet thrown carelessly across Robbie's bunk. She felt her lips tighten. How could she have been so foolish . . . so *reckless* . . . as to become tangled up with a common thief, however charismatic?

"Is this to be the great seduction scene then?" she burst out, agitation making her speak before she could think. "Now that you've shown me the squalor of the galley, and frightened me half to death by introducing me, if that's what you call it, to your quartermaster and your surgeon, am I expected to succumb to you, as the lesser of two evils?"

"Please sit down, Sarah," he said calmly, pointing to one of the two leather chairs that were placed at each side of the ornate leather-covered desk, on which was the ship's log and a compass, charts, a globe of the world, and other seafaring paraphernalia.

She noted that all the furniture was carefully chained to pegs in the floor, for the occasions when the ship rolled in high seas. She sat down abruptly. She tried to remind herself that she was still a lady, but right now she felt gauche and young and very much at a disadvantage. And, if she truly admitted it, very afraid.

Robbie went to a wall cabinet and took out a bottle of brandy and two glasses. He poured some of the spirits in each glass and handed one to her.

"Drink it," he said. "All of it, and then you and I will talk."

"I thought we'd done enough of that already, and it seems to be getting us nowhere."

"Drink!" he said sternly, and she swallowed the fiery liquid in one gulp, feeling her head spin as it traveled down her gullet.

"What do we have to talk about?" Sarah asked huskily. "It seems that you can do just as you want with me. I'm at your mercy."

He perched on the side of the desk, his back to the sunlight, dazzling through the windows, and she couldn't see the expression on his face as he took both her hands in his.

"My poor little clown," he said softly. She snatched her hands away, mortified, hating the outfit in which she was dressed, and hating him for reminding her of it.

Robbie rose at once and seated himself on the other side of the desk, distancing himself from her, leaning back and looking at her thoughtfully, and now she could see him properly. As handsome and rakish as ever. Into her mind swept the tantalizing memory of the way she had seen him on other occasions, so much the elegant man-about-town, who would personify many a fond Mama's truest hopes as a suitor for a daughter's hand.

Even now, in the midst of her hatred, Sarah couldn't deny those memories, and as always, she was helplessly aware of the powerful hold he had on her emotions. For good or bad, her life was irrevocably intertwined with his.

"Sarah, you must understand that the rules of the sea are not the rules of the land," he said abruptly. "We are a very tight community on board ship and there must be harmony among captain and crew if we are not to court disaster."

He reached into a drawer in his desk and brought out an elaborately scribed document.

"I intended putting a copy of this in your cabin, and you may take it with you to peruse if you wish. These are the articles or rules of *The Adventuress*. You'll see copies like this one posted about the ship, but the original is locked in my strongbox. Every crewman has signed it, swearing to obey the articles over a Bible, or an ax, according to his inclinations."

She glanced at it. It was a set of rules that needed to be studied properly. The incongruity of some of the rules, to one who had been brought up in the house of a gentleman, almost made her smile, even while they sent shivers through her veins.

If any man rob another, he may have his ears or throat slit. If he robs the company he shall be marooned.

Each man shall keep his cutlass and pistol clean and ready for action at all times.

Any man found guilty of cowardice in a skirmish shall be immediately marooned.

Any man found smoking or using naked candlelight below decks at night shall be instantly flogged and later marooned.

Any man found bringing a boy or woman on board for lustful purposes shall be punished by marooning or death.

There were many more such rules, but it was this one that caused Sarah to catch her breath.

"Do you find it amusing?" Robbie asked, noting the smile that was quickly fading.

"I do not," she said. "I find rule seven especially alarming. Who administers the punishment if a man is found guilty?"

"The quartermaster is our magistrate," Robbie said, as calmly as if he spoke of the courts of justice in London. "Every man has a right to his say and we go by the majority vote, but as I've told you, Surgeon is our biggest ally, and the rest will follow, no matter what any dissenters say."

"And these rules apply to you as well as the crew?" Sarah asked in disbelief.

"Why should they not? I cannot be seen to put myself above them. I'm a man, the same as any other."

Oh no . . . He was not the same as any other she had ever

known. She felt a grudging respect for someone who put himself in this situation, dependent on his men for his own safety. And yet canny enough to know which crewman to court when persuasion was needed.

"And what if they decide that you are guilty of bringing a woman on board for lustful purposes?" She forced herself to ask, meeting his eyes and keeping the question as impersonal as it was possible to be while her heart gave that irritating little thrill of awareness.

"I would be marooned or put to death." He shrugged, as if it were of no consequence to him.

Sarah gasped. "What does marooning mean?" she asked quickly, thinking it must surely be better than being put to death by the cutlass or the pistol and thrown overboard to the fishes.

He gave a short laugh. "Did your education about the wicked pirates not teach you of such things? It means stripping a man of everything, his clothes and his weapons, and stranding him on the first available island inhabited by savages. Until that time he is confined in chains in the hold in near-starvation. Death is usually preferable."

"Dear heaven, Robbie, how can you speak so casually of something so horrible!" She leapt to her feet, angered by his nonchalance. Angered too by a ridiculous feeling of guilt that if ever the crew mutinied against him and carried out the punishment, this terrible end would be her fault!

"I told you, it rarely happens, which is exactly why the articles are drawn up," he said edgily. He looked at her through narrowed eyes, so that she saw only slits of amber glittering in the sun's rays.

"You can save me, of course. The captain's wife is above such a fate."

"Oh, spare me that!" Sarah said witheringly. "Why should the captain's wife be any different from any other woman brought on board for lustful purposes! Besides, would you rather not have the ransom money for me, supposing my cousin Jonas would pay it!"

She blushed as she spoke. She had never spoken so boldly to any man before, but somehow they seemed to have cut across all class and social barriers.

"Sarah, please listen. I admit I wanted you here, but because of my own rules I was helpless to do otherwise than bring you here for a definite purpose. The crew must either believe that by the time we return to English shores our intention is immediately to issue a ransom for you, or else that you have agreed to become my wife."

She picked up on one phrase, her whole body shaking.

"When we return to English shores? You make that sound as if it's a long time distant."

Robbie spoke evenly. *"The Adventuress* is not the fastest of vessels, despite the use of oars as well as sails. We're still very dependent on the vagaries of southerly winds."

"How long?" Sarah asked through dry lips. Dear God, the thought of spending days on this ship, with the ground beneath her feet constantly on the move and the contents of her stomach matching it!

He shrugged. "However long it takes. We put in along the coast of Spain for fresh supplies in several weeks' time, and then continue south. Our destination is the Guinea coast."

She stared at him. Her geographical education was adequate as far as the shores of England and Scotland went, but no farther. She had a rudimentary knowledge of the nearest European countries. She knew of the continents of Africa and Asia, but they were alien places, where every white man was at risk. Robbie spun the globe on his desk in front of her eyes and stabbed at a point a very long way down the mass of the African continent. Right down the length of the widest part, and underneath where it curved inland again.

"This is the Guinea coast, where there are priceless pickings for pirates, and even the most notoriously amateurish of the *women* pirates have become rich

103

overnight." He spoke with a light contempt for those of her sex, and Sarah bridled.

"Am I to be included with the likes of them? If so, you may think again!"

He laughed. "You will not. You will remain on board while we go about our business. If you are still a hostage you will receive nothing of our spoils. If you are my wife, I will clothe you in the finest silks and smother you in jewels. You will be a princess, my lovely girl."

His voice dropped seductively as he spoke, but Sarah was too alarmed at the thought of the long voyage ahead to be intimidated or persuaded in any way by his words.

"Why may I not just go home?" She took one last chance of pleading with him, knowing that her mouth trembled and not troubling to hide it. "Put me overboard on a small boat after dark and say that I've escaped."

"But I don't want you to escape. Now that I've captured you, do you think I would so easily let you go?"

She stamped her foot furiously, angry that the soft boys' shoes made little impression on the wooden floor.

"You're impossible. You're just like Jonas—possessive over anything that he thought was his!"

Robbie came round the desk so swiftly she had no time to move back. She was caught in his arms, small and slight in the flat shoes, and held fast against his chest.

"Never compare me to that milksop of a man," he said quietly. "And never think that you were ever his, or likely to be. From the moment we set eyes on each other, we both knew that you were destined to be mine."

He jerked her chin up to meet his gaze. His eyes hypnotized her and she was helpless to look away. Slowly his mouth came down on hers, holding her spellbound, and she could feel the rapid beat of her own heart and his, where her breasts were pressed fast against him. When the kiss ended, he held her close.

"However comical your dress, you still fascinate me as no

other woman has ever done, lassie. But tonight I would see you dressed like a lady once more, and we will take dinner in my cabin, as we will every evening. We'll be civilized and waited on by Tomby, who has learned the ways of service."

"All right," Sarah mumbled inaudibly, because she had no choice, and because she wanted to get out of these silly garments and feel herself once more. And at least this man could hold intelligent conversations. He had all the mien of a gentleman when he chose.

"Tomby will fetch you at sunset, and you will come to this cabin then," Robbie instructed. "I will be at the meeting with the men, which is held directly below here. If you lift the corner of the fur rug you will detect a knothole in the wooden floor. Sit close, and you will hear everything that passes."

"So that's the way you know everything that goes on among your crew and are so well prepared!"

"Of course. Did you think I was clairvoyant?" He gave an amused laugh.

Sarah wasn't sure whether to admire him for it or not. It was somewhat sneaky, and yet it made every kind of sense, especially with an unpredictable body of men who had presumably come from very different backgrounds.

"I think I feel rather unwell," she muttered. "Is it my imagination or is the sea becoming rougher?"

He nodded. "I'm afraid it's likely to be so for a fair amount of time, Sarah. Of necessity we must sail well away from the shelter of land, and this is a particularly difficult part of the journey, as we approach the Bay of Biscay. We have to head westward to avoid being sighted by navy vessels and it means we are often broadside into the wind. The discomfort will pass, I promise you, but in the meantime, I suggest you lie flat in your cabin to ward off the effects of seasickness."

She gave him no argument, not even voicing her doubts that this feeling welling up inside her would ever pass. It had come over her suddenly, ever since she had smelled the meat in the galley. But perhaps that had not been entirely to blame after all, and it was no more than the rolling of the ship on the turbulent sea.

Robbie helped her down the short gangway to her own cabin and she fell thankfully across her bunk.

"I'll send Tomby in from time to time to see to your needs and to bring you fresh water," he said with some sympathy as he left her. "Meanwhile, my presence is needed on deck."

Did he really think she would recover from this, Sarah thought after some hours had passed and she was unable to stop the small moans emitted from her throat as the nausea continued. She wasn't physically sick, for which she was mightily thankful, even though she knew it would probably have been better if she had been.

She was aware of Tomby's tiptoed comings and goings and the native boy's concern. Once, she thought she felt the touch of his palm on her forehead as if to check her fevered skin. No one else came near her, to her relief. She wanted no confident sea captain gazing down on her in this sorry state. She began to wonder if there would ever come a time when she would feel able to sponge herself, and dress, and feel human again.

Miraculously, the time did come. Gradually, she became aware that the heaving of the ship had steadied a little, and that her stomach no longer felt in danger of meeting her throat. Gingerly, she put one foot to the floor and then the other, carefully pulling herself upright in the narrow bunk. She sipped the water Tomby had brought her in a stoppered bottle, glad of its cool caress, and peered through the small porthole in her cabin.

The day had passed without her noticing it. There was a chill in the air and Sarah shivered, reaching for one of the fine shawls at her disposal and wrapping it around herself as she tried to see what was on the horizon. There was nothing, only the swell of the sea and the merging of ocean with sky.

For a moment she felt sick with fear, and then told herself sternly that it would be fatal for her to give in to hysterics. It could be disastrous for herself, and dangerous for Robbie, and if he wasn't here to stand protector between her and these sea villains, who knew what might become of her?

She told herself that that was the only reason she cared what happened to Robbie. Her head acknowledged it, but even though her heart was beginning to tell a different tale, it was one she refused to listen to.

Tomby appeared at the cabin again like a little dark ghost, his face creasing into a smile as he saw that Sarah was on her feet, however precariously.

"Missy feel better now?" he asked.

She gave a weak smile. "Yes, Tomby. I think Missy feels a little better."

"You want tea? Cookie make very fine tea and will make some this instant minute for Missy."

"Yes, please." For some reason the eagerness of this boy and the Chinese cook to please her brought the sting of tears to her eyes.

"And then I bring washing water, and I stand guard outside until Missy ready to be taken to Cap'n's cabin," Tomby repeated, parrot-fashion, and Sarah guessed he had been well instructed by Robbie as to a lady's needs.

He disappeared from the cabin to fetch the tea and the vessel with the washing water, and while he was gone Sarah quickly discarded the boyish garments and slid her arms into the dressing-robe, feeling better by the very act of looking more like her self again. The mirror told her she was very much paler than usual, but there was already a tinge of color returning to her cheeks now that the worst of the ship's motions were over.

"Oh, Uncle Thomas," she murmured sadly to her reflection. "What would you think of me now?"

She turned away quickly, as if to hide from the answer. Her uncle had been a good man who had done his best for her. If his best was to marry her off to an old man, and to bequeath his odious son to her, it was not because he thought ill of her. Lord Endor had loved his ward, and some would say she had thrown his love back in his face by not accepting Jonas's offer of marriage.

Sarah shivered. No, she had not done wrong in refusing him! It went against God's grace for a woman to lie with a man she did not love. She had suffered it for eight months, and even though Angus Huxley had not been an ardent lover, she still burned with humiliation and shame at having been obliged to open herself to him and let him do as he wished with her body.

People spoke of her as a young and beautiful woman, and young and beautiful women should have strong and virile lovers, not the fumblings of old men! Even as the thought came into her head, a strange tingling sensation spread through her limbs and heated her flesh, and the face that flashed through her senses was Robbie's.

The arms she imagined holding her were Robbie's. And knowing as she did the ways of love, the sensation of falling, exquisitely falling into space through a velvet darkness in a lover's embrace, was enough to make the beads of perspiration stand out on her skin. Because everything she dreamed, or imagined, or desired, was encapsulated in one man. Black Robbie, the pirate captain, whose captive slave she undoubtedly was.

"Tea, Missy." Tomby's voice awoke her as if from a nightmare, and the erotic dream vanished. The dampness on her skin made her feel chilled. The very last thing she wanted was to dream of Robbie in that way, she thought, appalled. He might think he owned everything on board this ship, but no man owned her, or ever would.

She took the tea from the boy's hands. Tomby then brought the water vessel and took up his position outside the cabin.

Sarah pushed everything else out of her mind as the hot,

weak tea revived her, and she realized how hungry she was. She had had nothing to eat or drink all day but dry biscuits and water and a glass of brandy. But tonight she was to dine with Robbie in that luxurious cabin and for a little while she could be a lady again.

The thought excited her more than she would have believed possible. She, who had always taken the trappings of a lady for granted, was so glad to be rid of the harsh alien clothing, and once she had attended to her toilet, it was wonderful to slide her arms into silken garments again and to feel their sensuousness against her skin.

She had never removed the topaz necklace, but had let it remain hidden around her throat inside the boyish shirt. Exposed now, it blazed like golden fire against her creamy skin and the shimmering blue silk gown she had chosen to wear that evening, and she felt immense pleasure in its splendor.

There was nothing to be done about her short hair, she thought with a sigh, but at least it framed her face reasonably well and was a novelty. And she remembered instantly what Robbie had said about her face, whether she had a woman's crowning glory atop it or not. She didn't bother to resist the pleasure she felt in that too.

She opened the cabin door cautiously, and the boy scrambled to his feet at once.

"You may take me to the Captain's cabin now, Tomby," she said quietly.

Chapter 8

Robbie's cabin was not far from the narrow gangway leading to her own. Tomby opened his door for her silently, and then withdrew. The cabin was empty, and she remembered Robbie saying he wouldn't see her until much later, after his meeting with the crew. The table with its narrow ridge all the way around the edge was already set with a cloth and cutlery, and Sarah felt a great curiosity at being inside Robbie's domain.

Who or what was he? Not in his pirate's role, but in that other life of which she had already seen glimpses. A Mr. David Roberts, gentleman of leisure? Somehow she doubted that that was his true identity. Despite the charisma of the figure seen in polite society, it was just too mild a persona for someone of his stature.

Her gaze was suddenly caught by the wide spread of windows. No ordinary portholes up here, at the peak of the ship, for the captain! Through the dazzling array of glass was the most glorious sunset Sarah had ever seen.

Of course, they were heading westward and out to sea before they would turn due south along the coast of Spain, and the dying sun's rays were a spectacular flame, red and bronze against the soft blue of sky and sea, with all the colors of the universe merging in between.

It was nature at its most serene and beautiful, and Sarah felt stunned by it, unwilling to move for long moments while she drank in its beauty.

Dimly, she became aware of a rumbling sound, and listened more intently. She identified the sound as the muffled murmur of voices, and after a moment's hesitation she stepped quietly across to open the door to Robbie's partitioned bedchamber, remembering what he had told her.

She lifted the corner of the fur rug with her toe, and the voices became more distinct. She had direct access to all that went on in the meeting that evening, and her heart began to pound as she heard the references being made to herself.

Sarah sat down abruptly on the bunk, with its embroidered coverlet as brilliant as a peacock's feathers. The meeting was clearly in full swing by now, and Robbie was arguing in her defense, backed up by Surgeon.

"I say the woman stays," Robbie said harshly. "Her milksop cousin will want her back right enough, and the longer she remains out of his reach, the higher price he'll be willing to pay. He'll not be willing to lose anything he considers his, especially such a fine piece."

Sarah gasped. How could she ever trust him, when he spoke so degradingly about her, and in so plausible a manner! And then she realized that some of the rougher crewmen wanted her off the ship very quickly.

"Any woman on board is bad luck," she heard a snarling voice say. "She arouses lust in the men and causes brawls, and we want none of it."

"There'll be no lust on this ship," Robbie said sharply. "I promise you that. We all go by the rules."

"And what of you, Cap'n?" another sneered. "All of us saw the way ye fancied the wench the first time ye saw her. We saw the way ye danced with her, as close as if ye shared the same skin, and there's no denying it."

Sarah heard the growls of agreement, and then Robbie spoke up again.

111

"I'll abide by the articles of the ship the same as the rest of you. Unless the woman agrees to be my wife. You'll not deny that as Captain I have the right to wifely comforts."

There were howls of rage at that, and Sarah felt the sickening beat of her heart as they demanded to know how Robbie planned to repay them for the loss of the ransom money if that event should happen.

"We'd decide on a price for her." He had to raise his voice to be heard. "The spoils from the Guinea coast would be divided accordingly, with myself taking a lesser share to compensate. You won't be the losers, whatever happens."

Sarah almost betrayed her presence by screaming out in a fury. How dare he do this to her? Put a price on her indeed! Clearly, he respected nothing but gold. He was a pirate through and through, and she was a fool to ever think otherwise.

She realized that Surgeon was trying to make himself heard among the babble.

"Listen to what makes sense, dunderheads. The wench is prepared to keep her charms as concealed as possible. You saw that today, so there's no cause for any man to get hot in the loins for her. I vote that we follow Cap'n's words. And in case any of you were thinking of disposing of her over the side one dark night, let me tell you you'd be madheads in risking her body being found by navy ships. She'd soon be recognized for the missing wench taken by Black Robbie, and we'd all be branded as murderers of a white woman."

The significance of the distinction wasn't lost on Sarah as she waited agonizingly for the response. It was hard to tell who was getting the better of the argument, until there was a loud hammering of wood on wood, and the melee quietened. She heard the quartermaster's guttural voice.

"Do we put it to the vote then, mates? Those for the woman to stay on as hostage until we return to England and hold her for ransom, unless Cap'n weds her, in which case we'll divide the spoils accordingly."

112

The waiting was almost unbearable for Sarah as she held her breath. Presumably there was a show of hands, counted in silence, and then the quartermaster spoke again.

"And those against, who'd best have some bloody good suggestion to make afore my throat gets too parched to swallow my rum portion. I ain't prepared to spend all night on this piffling matter."

Whether this was an indication that the quartermaster had now sided with the surgeon and his followers, Sarah didn't dare guess, but seconds later he spoke again.

"You have it, Cap'n. Now let's get to the rum keg and some supper, mates."

The meeting was dispersing, and Sarah wilted. She had been crouching on the bunk all this time, so tense that she ached all over. Coupled with the tension in her stomach from the feeling of seasickness all day, and the hunger now, she felt as if there was no substance inside her at all. It was a bit like that other time, she remembered, when someone had gathered her up in his arms after she had fallen from her horse, and she had been taken into a dank, dark cave.

Robbie's arms had been around her then, keeping her safe. She stifled a sob in her throat and the next second she laid her head wearily against the hard pillow on the bunk. It was not the most comfortable bed she had ever lain on, but in her disturbed state it seemed like heaven. She closed her eyes, letting the soft sway of the ship lull her ragged senses.

Dreamlike, almost unaware of where she was, her nerves began to relax. The scent of Robbie was in her nostrils. He was fastidious enough to use soaps and fragrances to keep himself clean, especially on his sojourns on land, as a man of pleasure. The scent of him lingered on his bed linen, and in his closet, captured in the small partitioned room. It brought him close, it soothed and excited her.

Fantasies swept through her mind like quicksilver. Unbidden, erotic fantasies that she didn't seek, didn't want. Robbie was the perfect lover of whom she had always

113

dreamed, strong and virile when passion was at its height, tender and considerate when her needs required it.

She could feel his imagined touch on her skin, and it was so real . . . so real. His hands, not the rough hands of a pirate, but the gentleman's hands that they were, caressing her body, filling her with desire that soared to the skies, sending the swift shafts of response rushing through every pore of her.

Memories of unexceptional love-making during her marriage to Angus Huxley faded to nothing in the vividness of the dream-ecstasy Sarah lived now. Robbie's mouth was touching hers in a light kiss that nevertheless held all the promise of passion, a kiss that he couldn't resist giving, but one that would let her sleep to continue the dream . . . and while senses still struggled to return to normality, she was giddy with the insidious knowledge that she could love this man.

Faint sounds, the chink of china and quiet footsteps, roused Sarah. Her mouth was dry. For a moment of madness she wanted to hold on to the dream, and then she pushed it farthest from her mind with a vigor born of fury at the memory of the meeting she had overheard. She was now in "Cap'n Robbie's" keeping. He would do with her as he wished.

To keep her captive and eventually hold her for ransom, or make her his wife, if she agreed to it, which she certainly did not. But had it ever been anything but that? Hadn't it always been a certainty to Robbie that she was his? And there were more possibilities than the ones the pirate band had outlined!

She sat upright in the small bedchamber, feeling her head swim a little at the sudden movement. The door was ajar, and in the soft lantern-light in the cabin she could see Tomby setting the table properly. Cookie was fussing about with

114

dishes and tureens, and Robbie stood with his back to the cabin, staring out at the dark night through the windows. He looked oddly alone, she thought. Perhaps a man in his position would always be alone.

He heard the rustle of her gown and turned at once, moving quickly across to her.

"Good, you're awake," he said. "I looked in once or twice but you seemed so sound I left you sleeping. Are you ready to eat with me?"

He reached out to assist her and she put her hand in his. A strange feeling flooded through her. The dream was back, vivid in her mind. The touch was the same, the smile was gentle, and his mouth . . . had she really dreamed that light caress on hers, or had it really happened?

"I'm very hungry," she said huskily. "It seems years since I ate anything."

"You'll enjoy Cookie's repast then. He may not look the last word in culinary elegance, but you'll be surprised at his skill."

Sarah went forward warily, wondering what horrors lay beneath the tureens. Cookie lifted the lid of each one triumphantly, and with surprised pleasure Sarah saw the dishes of parsnips and other root vegetaables, the slices of salt beef laid out in a neat pattern to please the eye as well as tempt the palate. The smell of succulent juices made her mouth water. Finally a dish with fresh fruits piled high was set in front of her.

"It looks wonderful," she said, delighted.

"Missy likes." Robbie smiled at the cook, who smiled at Sarah.

"Thank you, Missy. Thank you."

"All right, both of you. We'll serve ourselves tonight," Robbie said.

Cookie and Tomby backed away as if retreating from royalty, leaving the cabin as Robbie held the chair for Sarah to sit.

Sarah began to feel a little intoxicated, as if she had drunk too much champagne, and put it down to the gnawing feelings in her stomach. It really was too ludicrous, to be here in comparative luxury on a pirate ship, where one might have expected to be groveling in filth and privation, or even bound in chains as a hostage. . . .

To be waited on by a Chinese cook and a servant boy, to have this excellent fare placed in front of her, and a handsome sea captain seated opposite her, more virile in the glow of lantern-light than any London dandy . . .

"What are you smiling at?" Robbie said, placing a healthy portion of meat and vegetables on her plate and handing it to her without asking what she wanted.

Sarah spread her hands helplessly. "You. All this. Everything, so different than what I imagined—what anyone would imagine!"

Robbie laughed. "Don't think it's like this below decks, my lovely. The crew sleep and eat in rather more cramped conditions than this! Nor do they get this kind of treatment. Captain's privileges count for something, you see."

She began to eat, and the food tasted as delicious as it looked. She was suddenly ravenous, and didn't say anything until she had cleared her plate and helped herself to more.

"I'm sorry if I appear greedy. I don't usually make a pig of myself like this," she said, half ashamed of her appetite.

"For God's sake, you don't need to apologize to me," Robbie said almost roughly. "I like to see a woman eat. I've no patience with fads of fashion that call for curtailing the appetitie for the sake of being thin."

"You don't need to worry on that score where I'm concerned," she said ruefully, then wished she hadn't, as Robbie's eyes lingered on her throat and beyond.

The neckline of the shimmering blue dress was low, and the rounded curves of her breasts very evident. Beneath the small puffed sleeves, her milk-white arms were shapely and graceful. The waist was nipped in, from where the skirt

116

billowed out to her feet, and the womanliness of her body was never in doubt.

"And you don't need me to tell you I think you are the most beautiful woman I've ever seen, and I wouldn't change one thing about you," Robbie said gravely.

"Not even a hair on my head?" she asked archly, self-consciously putting her hand to her shorn locks.

She amazed herself that she could joke about it. Her lovely hair, her pride and joy, her one vanity. Robbie leaned across the small table, and ran one finger around the nape of her neck, where the dark tendrils curled softly.

"One day, my lovely, your hair will be restored to its full glory again," he said. "But never think that its loss takes away one fraction of your allure. Is that plain enough for you?"

"I wasn't fishing for compliments," she protested, knowing that she was, however artlessly.

"And I wasn't giving them, just telling the truth," he informed her.

For a moment their glances held and locked. Wide blue eyes as deep as the sea, gazing into light amber ones that could be wild as a tiger's or soft as a kitten's.

Sarah dragged her thoughts away from the tantalizing aura of this man, and remembered more important matters. In the ambience of the dream and the much-needed meal, and the return to almost-civilized behavior, she had forgotten. She put down her fork with a clatter.

"I heard what happened at the meeting," she said accusingly.

"And now you're going to spoil our first evening together by reverting to form," he commented.

Her eyes flashed. "What did you expect? You knew I was listening, and you blatantly told your men I was to be a hostage held for ransom, or my price was to be decided on and your next spoils split between them accordingly. How could any lady react to such barbaric words except to be horrified and humiliated?"

"I also offered to marry you."

"Only because you knew you were safe in such an outrageous proposal!" The thought had only just occurred to her, but now that it had, she saw how obvious it was. If she dared, she would call his bluff, but she did not dare, nor did she care to wonder why.

"Is that what you think?" he asked, his voice several tones colder than before.

"Of course! Why should the notorious womanizing Black Robbie ever settle for one woman when he can have the pick of society ladies, and no doubt plenty of serving-girls as well!"

The mere thought that she would be just one more plaything, one of a string of women of all shapes, sizes and colors, deepened her mortification.

Robbie leaned back in his chair, his eyes dark.

"You're probably right. Then marriage between us is not to be considered," he agreed coolly. "You will remain on board at my pleasure until I decide on your ransom price."

Sarah hadn't expected him to agree so readily, and her mouth dropped open.

"Your *pleasure?* You of all people know the rules of the ship, Captain, and no woman is to be brought on board for lustful purposes," she quoted.

"Then it will be my pleasure to ignore you by day and court you by night, and make you so hungry for my caresses that you give yourself to me voluntarily. I told you once this is how it would be. There's nothing in the rules that says a man can't be taken by a woman, rather than the other way round."

She gasped at the arrogance of his words. "No *lady* would ever do such a thing," she said.

"A man is proud to escort a *lady* on all social occasions, but at night he prefers a *woman* in his bed," he retorted. "If he's lucky enough to find one who provides both services, he's fortunate indeed. And why then should he ever look elsewhere?"

She glared at him. "You're insufferable," she said at last. "You're everything bad that they say about you."

Robbie laughed, handing her the bowl of polished fruit. "And you're obstinate and willful and spoiled. So we shall have to learn to tolerate one another, shan't we?"

She took an apple silently and bit into its crunchy skin, feeling the sweet juice ooze out around her lips. She saw Robbie's gaze as she ran her tongue delicately around her mouth, and deliberately slowed down the movement, knowing it was provocative, teasing him, but if he said he intended to court her honorably, then she'd delight in putting him to the test. She'd make him pay for the indignity of her being here, conveniently forgetting that it had been her own choice.

When the meal was over Robbie poured them each a glass of brandy. Sarah wasn't fond of the stuff, but knowing how it had helped to settle her stomach earlier, she did not demur as he handed the glass to her.

"I'm sorry we don't have the comfort of a drawing room in which to sit," he said. "But the leather chairs are rather more comfortable, if you wish."

"I think I shall soon retire," she answered. "I'm feeling very tired."

"The sea air does that to you, but your body will adjust to it in a few days. The brandy will help you sleep."

"And will I be quite safe in my bed?"

Robbie gave a half smile. "I assure you that you will be. None of my men comes near this part of the ship, and Tomby will be posted outside your door all night."

She was appalled. "But he can't. The child needs a bed to sleep in!"

Robbie laughed. "Sweet Sarah, the child was used to

sleeping in the wilds when I found him, and before that in a disgusting hut made from cow dung. The kind that smells abominable after a tropical rainstorm, when the blistering sun heats it up again."

"Please don't be so graphic," she said faintly.

"All right. But I promise you that Tomby finds sleeping outside a cabin door no hardship at all, and besides he requested it."

"Did he?" she asked in surprise.

"You've made a conquest there. Two, in fact, since I suspect that Cookie's also enchanted by you. And several of the men weren't so inclined toward the harsh treatment for you either. By the time we reach the Guinea coast you'll probably have them all eating out of your hands."

"I doubt that very much," she said dryly, but pleased all the same. All her life she had been pampered and cosseted, and she had never really come up against people who resented or hated her. The shock of knowing that these pirates detested her presence so much had shaken her more than she realized. She had assumed that because Robbie wanted her aboard his ship, the rest of them did as well.

"Just why did you bring me here?" she asked directly. "I can't believe it was merely because you were sorry at the thought of my impending marriage!"

He gave her a look that was pure desire. It sent ripples of excitement over her skin, so that the downy hairs on the backs of her arms prickled.

"If you haven't worked out the reason for it yet, then you're less intelligent than I thought," was all he would say.

"But you can't be so desperate for a woman's company," Sarah said, becoming embarrassed at the boldness of her speech. She had never been so bold with any man before.

"But I didn't want just any woman's company, my sweet innocent, I wanted yours," Robbie said, in the seductive voice of the wooer.

She shivered again, remembering that this was just a game

120

to him. He had said as much. He meant to court her until she went to him of her own free will, begging for his favors. And she had every intention of seeing Hades freeze over before that happened!

"Would you care to take a stroll on deck, my lady?" he asked, now altering his tone to that of protector. "No one will approach you after dark, and those men who are not about their duties will be below. Some fresh air will do you good and exercise is to be recommended while we're at sea."

She nodded, saying she must first fetch her shawl, but Robbie merely opened the cabin door and shouted instructions to Tomby, who brought it in a moment from Sarah's own cabin. She was becoming quite attached to the scurrying moppet who was so eager to do her bidding.

She allowed Robbie to lead her back through the dark maze of the ship until they reached the deck. She looked in vain for the distant horizon, but all was black. For a second, the world spun for Sarah; if it hadn't been for her arm held tightly within Robbie's, she was sure she would have fallen.

"What is it? Have you not got your sea-legs yet?" he asked in sympathy.

"It's not that. It's so, so dark everywhere. I had not expected quite such blackness. It frightens me—" she spoke jerkily, not wanting to voice her real fears to him. The fear of drowning, of feeling the cold water closing over her head, of choking as it filled her lungs, leaving her body bloated and weightless, floating down to the bottom of the sea. . . .

She hardly realized she was gasping until he ordered her to take long deep breaths and to close her eyes for a few minutes.

"There's a good deal of low cloud tonight," he said. "It's better for us, but the moon will show itself soon enough and then the ocean will be a different place, with silver lights glittering on the water and strange tricks being played. It can be as enchanting as fairyland, Sarah."

"Not for me," she muttered.

"Come, let's walk. Your eyes will soon get accustomed to the darkness, and it won't seem like total blackness. Is it not getting better already?"

She looked about her uneasily. Yes, she could see the rails of the ship, and the outline of masts and sails. She could see the shadowy figure of a crew member in the crow's-nest, and the bundles of ropes on the deck. She could see the stark masses of the cannons on either side. Dimly, if she strained her eyes, she could faintly make out where the horizon met the sea. But it was all so sinister now, where in the blaze of sunset it had been so beautiful.

"Have you never been to sea before?" Robbie asked, and she shook her head quickly.

"Never. It was the very last place I ever wanted to be, the one place I vowed never to go."

They both heard the tremble in her voice, and he put his arm around her. Her instinct was to resist him, but two things stopped her. One was her need of someone, anyone, to be with her while the sick fear gripped her, and the other was the certainty that this was not part of the great seduction. He seemed genuinely concerned about her.

"Walk, Sarah. First one foot forward, and then the other." He instructed her as if she were a child learning to walk, and that was exactly the way she felt. They walked in silence, once, twice, three times around the deck, and as they finished the third circuit a blustery wind stirred the sails and the clouds began to disperse. Through them the pallor of the full moon lit the sea.

"You see?" Robbie said, as if he had arranged this with the dexterity of a magician's hand. "Isn't it truly beautiful?"

Sarah looked to where he spread his arm expansively. They leaned against the ship's rail and the sea glittered in the moonlight, stretching away to infinity. The greedy little waves sucked at the bow of the ship, and the creaking of the hull reminded Sarah of something the preacher had intoned at her parents' memorial service: *How puny were man's efforts against the fury of the elements. . . .*

She didn't realize that she was shaking violently, sobbing deep in her throat, until Robbie pulled her into his arms and held her fast.

"Devil take me, but are you going to tell me what's wrong, Sarah?" he asked harshly. "I thought you were made of stronger stuff than those who resort to the contrariness of women every time a man tries to please her."

She gasped through her sobs. "If you only knew how I hate the sea you wouldn't taunt me so. How I've always hated it! It took my dearest parents from me. It drowned them, and I've been haunted ever since by the fear that one day it would drown me too. I've tired to keep away from it all my life because of that fear, irrational though it might be. Even so, it's always had a hateful fascination for me that I knew would draw me to it someday. And now I'm here, and I'm very afraid. You wouldn't know what fear is, so how can I expect you to understand!

He held her rigid body tight in his arms, feeling the fear in her and letting her sob it out.

"Do you think I don't know all about fear, my Sarah?" Eventually he spoke gently against her ear. "I live with fear every day of my life. Perhaps it's not your fear, but I too have no desire to end my days in the jaws of a shark. I have other fears. Fears for my men, for young Tomby, for being captured and exposed, aye, for dying too. Such fear is not restricted to women, though men may speak little of it. It's a foolish man who knows no fear, lassie."

Slowly her sobs lessened and she began to breathe more evenly.

"You must think me a fool," she mumbled against his chest.

"Why should I, when you've faced the thing you dread the most? It's always better to face the dragon than to turn your back on it, Sarah."

She gave a small smile at the quaintness of his phrase.

"Well, now you know my secret," she said, unable to still the trembling in her limbs. "And when am I to know yours?"

"Mine?"

He looked down at her, and she could almost sense his withdrawal, even though he didn't move away from her. They were still locked together in what must resemble a lovers' embrace to any onlookers. But there were none on that moonlit night as *The Adventuress* sailed steadily southwest. The only sounds were the sucking of the waves and the surge of sails in the wind, the creaking of timbers, and the thudding of two hearts.

"You once said you would tell me who you really were, when the time was right. Now that you know about me, have I not the right to know about you.?"

"And if I entrust my secret to you, what guarantee do I have that you won't betray me to the authorities when I let you go?"

"Then you do intend to let me go?"

He bent his head and kissed her lips before she could resist. But in those fractured moments, she had no thought of resisting, only of keeping him near until all her fears went away.

"Unless you beg me to let you stay," he answered.

It was on the tip of her tongue to say imperiously that he would never see that day, but at that moment the ship dipped in a current, and they were thrown against the rail. They were in no danger, but once again she was thankful for Robbie's arms around her.

"Perhaps I'll tell you tomorrow night," he said as he led her toward her cabin. "I'll sleep on it, and consider whether I can trust you."

Tomby moved aside from her door to let her enter, and Sarah undressed quickly and crawled into her bunk. The boy's presence outside was comforting, as was the knowledge that Robbie was only a small distance away. And as she drifted into an exhausted sleep, the thought that came to her mind was how incongruous it was that a pirate captain should be wary of whether *he* could trust *her*, when it should surely be the other way around!

Chapter 9

Sarah awoke to the sounds of great activity. There was a rhythmic creaking somewhere below her, accompanied by hoarse shouting. The ship moved through the water less smoothly than before, though with none of the churning that had so upset her. As she rose from her bunk, pulling on her robe in the chill of early morning, the tap on her door reminded her that her small protector was still outside, and she called to him to come inside.

"What's happening, Tomby?" she asked.

"No wind, Missy. Ship becalmed, so men must pull oars." He demonstrated eagerly, and she guessed that his one ambition was to be older, to be like the rest of the pirates and join them as a fully-fledged member of the crew. What an ambition! Yet still preferable to being the outcast of his family and left to starve, the way she had been told.

How little she really knew of the world, Sarah thought suddenly. She had no idea of the cruelty of other places, or the necessity that decreed whether a new child in a family would be welcomed or dreaded. All she knew was the comfortable life of a country squire's home and the occasional sorties into London society. It was only now that she realized what a minuscule part of the wider world it really was.

Not that she rated this pirate ship existence very highly! But there were others outside her experience that she had never even dreamed about until now. How easy it was to become complacent and introverted when one only had to lift a finger and a servant came running to do one's bidding. And how sweet this present little servant, his huge black eyes adoring her as he asked if Missy was ready for breakfast.

"All right, Tomby, and you tell Cookie I'll be along when I've finished," she said with a smile.

When the boy had gone, she asked herself if she had really said those words. Was she really accepting the role Black Robbie had announced for her without a fight? But it would surely be better to keep her hands and mind occupied in doing some useful work than to spend her days aimlessly wandering about the ship.

The days would be so long, and she would have too much time to think and fret over her surroundings. Resolutely, she knew she had made her choice. She dismissed the fact that it was the one Robbie had already made for her.

Breakfast consisted of several hunks of dry bread smeared with some kind of preserves, and weak tea. The alternative was bread dipped in fat, which was the main fare for the crew, lined their stomachs and kept them warm, and which she declined hurriedly. Breakfast had to last her all day. There were only two meals, breakfast and dinner, which the crew called supper, although they could eat fruit if they were very hungry and supplies warranted it.

Though presumably if Sarah worked in the galley, she could help herself to anything. But she was told quite sternly that this was not so, when she presented herself to the cook an hour later, dressed in her somber day outfit.

"Fresh supplies are bought each time we land," Cookie told her. "No one must take more than they need, then we all have enough."

"I see," Sarah murmured, who had never considered such things before. Food was always there in the kitchens of

Endor House. If she was hungry she either called a servant to fetch her some delicacy, or went to the kitchen herself, to perch on a stool while the affable buxom cook made her a succulent snack to last her until the next meal. A wave of nostalgia for times long ago swept over her.

"You want to chop meat?" Cookie said now, pointing to the great leg of mutton waiting to be chopped into small pieces for the stew. Sarah shuddered, seeing how the blood oozed out.

"Can I do something else?" she asked. "Cut up the vegetables or something?"

"You wash dishes then." Cookie pointed to the great pile of greasy dishes. "Tomby do vegetables."

Sarah pushed up her sleeves, feeling the prickle of tears in her eyes. It was nothing short of degrading to be faced with this disgusting pile of dishes, knowing the pirates would have wiped their bread around them with relish, and probably licked the last vestiges of fat from them. It was not the task for a lady.

But she was not a lady here, and she had best remember it. Doggedly, Sarah kept that thought uppermost in her mind, as she scrubbed at the plates in the small amount of water she was allowed, since water too was to be carefully allotted to each task, and then wiped them dry with a piece of cotton rag. She wondered fleetingly how often she was to be permitted the luxury of a bath, and guessed that it would be a rare occasion.

Unused as she was to such domestic tasks, the dish washing and drying seemed to take for ever. Her back ached, and her hands soon began to redden. She dried them as best she could, trying hard not to remember that this day would be repeated endlessly until the voyage was over and she was safely back in England. She had no idea what she would do then, if she were sent back, ignominiously, to Jonas.

She hardly thought Robbie would let things go that far after bringing her here, but then, she didn't really know what to expect from him. She hated the very thought of escaping from this fate only to face a worse one, yet already she yearned to set foot on dry land, with a passion that overcame all else. The great adventure, if such it could be called, was fast losing its charm.

What had she expected, when Robbie had brought her to his ship? Certainly not this. Not to be dressed so poorly by day, in such contrast with the silks and satins he had provided her for evenings! Each revelation had been a mystery to her. And now to be expected to do servants' work!

But what was the alternative? To share his cabin and his life and to be a pirate's woman, for she couldn't possibly take the proposal of marriage seriously. It would surely be a sham of a ceremony, merely to appease his men and abide by the ship's rules. She rejected it out of hand, and refused to let her mind dwell on the thrill of sharing every night with so charismatic a man, in the soft seductive darkness of tropical nights, as they sailed farther south. . . .

She heard the thud of the ax on the meat and jumped as the bones splintered.

"I've finished here," she said abruptly. "Will it do?"

She resented having to look to the Chinese cook for approval. To her own surprise though, she felt a stab of pleasure as his face brightened and he nodded approvingly.

"Missy do well. Plates never so clean before. No more work now until tomorrow."

Sarah stared at him. "No more?" she asked stupidly.

Was this it after all? It didn't seem too much, but perhaps Robbie had only intended to make her do a minimal amount, to prove to the crew that she wasn't a parasite on board, and to make her understand that if she wouldn't agree to his ridiculous suggestion of marriage, then he must find some other way of proving that he was the master here.

For a second, she wondered about the impossible alternative. Marrying Black Robbie. She imagined the outcry if news of such an event ever reached English shores. News of such things had an uncanny way of appearing in the newspapers, and all decent society would be outraged at poor Sarah Huxley's fate.

No, the idea was totally outrageous. And besides, the next time she married, if ever, it would be for love. One mistake had more than proved that, and the way Jonas had tried to blackmail her into making another had more than doubled her resolution.

A shadow fell across the open galley door, and her heart leapt. It was the first time she had seen Robbie that day, and to be seen here, her clothes already soiled from grease and water, her hands no longer those of a lady, made her squirm with embarrassment and anger.

"I presume you've come to check up on me?" She spoke before he had a chance to say anything. "I've obeyed orders and cleaned the filth off the dishes, and I suspect they sparkle more than they ever have before. I'm told there's no more for me to do, unless you think otherwise. Do I pass inspection—Sir?"

Robbie grinned at the aggressive little figure, taunting him with a kind of feminine bravado and doing her best to hide her hands behind her back. He felt a surge of respect for her, knowing how unused she would be to these tasks. He felt a sudden urge to have those small white hands caressing him intimately, and he smothered the feeling with a short laugh.

"I'm not here to check up on you, lassie, merely to say that if you wish to see a fleet of Dutch merchant ships on the horizon, you may come up on deck. They are a fine sight."

She moved out of the galley at once, thankful to be away from its cloying smells. The day was warm and slightly hazy, the sun not yet breaking through, but the wind was beginning to spring up at last. The crewmen scrambled about the rigging, adjusting the sails to catch the first breath of a breeze. With luck, Robbie told her, they would be in full sail once more, and the uneven movement of the ship would regulate itself. Sarah was thankful for that, as she looked to the distant west to try and make out the Dutch merchant ships, but she could see nothing.

"You're looking in the wrong direction," Robbie said in amusement. "There's nothing but ocean to the west this morning. The merchant ships hug the coastline of France and Spain on their way to African ports of call, while we, for obvious reasons, keep well away from it during daylight hours. There's less risk of attack far out at sea."

She understood the reasons very well, and felt the usual little thrill of amazement that she could be taking her new circumstances so comparatively calmly. She looked to the east where he pointed now and could see the graceful lines of three merchant ships in full sail on the horizon, but of the shore there was still no sign. To Sarah it was a lonely and isolated sensation to be so far from land, though for the pirates it clearly meant less risk of attack.

"What happens if another ship sees us?" She asked suddenly. "You fly no flags."

"If we're challenged by a British ship we hoist a Dutch flag. If by a Dutch vessel, we may use a French flag. We have our ways of dispensing with unwelcome attention, and we avoid such encounters in the daylight hours wherever possible. If necessary, there is always the cannon."

"So you spend your life always running, always evading capture," she stated.

"Weren't you doing the same, when you decided to flee from your cousin's attentions?"

"I think that was rather different!" she fumed.

She gazed at the three merchant ships, which were gradually becoming smaller as the distance between them and *The Adventuress* became greater. She felt a sense of loss, as if momentarily the Dutch ships had been a lifeline, a means to take her away from this strange life. And yet, they had never been that. They had never been that close for a start, and Robbie was hardly likely to hand her over, however much she screamed and shouted. Besides, weren't these the very vessels he spoke of as having rich pickings for a pirate ship?

As if he could read her thoughts, his hand was hard on her arm. She could feel the pressure of his fingers through the coarse cotton garment. She already knew how seductive and tender the touch of his fingers could be, but right now it was anything but that.

"Don't ever think of putting my crew in danger, Sarah. Whatever you and the world may think of us, we have a duty to protect one another, and that includes all who sail on my ship. Anyone who disobeys those rules faces the worst punishment of all."

She shivered. "You mean you'd make me walk the plank? That *is* what you call it, isn't it?" she asked.

"That's exactly it," Robbie said, without a hint of humor. "You'd do well to remember it, lassie. The sharks don't fret over what kind of flesh they eat. 'Tis all tasty fodder to them."

He strode away from her as the quartermaster shouted for his attention, and Sarah stared after him in shock. He had meant every word he said. It was the ultimate punishment, and the most hideous. She had seen illustrated sketches in journals, crude and horrific, the unfortunate offender on the brink of falling from the plank into the ocean, a bag tied over his head, hands and feet bound, while greedy sharks waited in the cold waters below.

By the time she looked away to sea gain, the Dutch merchant ships were gone, lost in the haze over the horizon. She missed them as one would miss an old friend. They were a link with all that was real, while none of this bore any semblance to reality. She leaned over the side, watching the scudding waves as if mesmerized by them.

For a second Robbie's words came back to haunt her. *Less risk of attack.* . . . But there was always the risk, she thought. *The Adventuress* wasn't invincible, and one day every pirate's luck ran out. She shivered. It would be the height of ignominy to die in the company of pirate scum at the hands of dutiful fighting men from one of His Majesty's vessels!

"Are you ailing, Miss?" a voice said grudgingly, and she jerked round, realizing she had been gripping the rail tightly. One of the pirates stood nearby, unsure whether this person was to be helped or not, but aware of her distress and wild eyes. He was sandy-haired beneath the bandeau he wore to keep the straggly locks away from his face, and of an indeterminate age, as were most of the men.

"I'm a little faint. I haven't got my sea legs yet, but I shall be all right in a minute. Perhaps if I could just have a little water."

The man looked dubious, glancing around to see if he was being observed, clearly wanting no jeering from the rest of the crew if he helped the woman. But there was no one nearby. Everyone was about their business, and he for one wouldn't have a dog gasping in the road for want of a drink of water. He told Sarah to stay where she was and a few minutes later he appeared with a leather water bottle and handed it to her.

By then her equilibrium had returned, and she gave him a smile all the more stunning because it was the first time any of the pirates apart from Robbie and Cookie and the young Tomby had offered her even a trace of friendship. The man gave a crooked smile back, his lips just baring to show a haphazard set of discolored teeth.

"Thank you," Sarah said gratefully. "You're very kind. What do they call you?"

"Flint, Miss. Flint by name and flint by nature," he said stoically, just in case she mistook kindness for softness.

"Thank you again, Flint. I'm obliged to you."

Someone bellowed his name, and he moved away with an agitated gait, muttering something about concealing the water bottle in her garments, but Sarah hardly registered the words. She felt an undoubted lift to her spirits. It might be demeaning for a lady to socialize with pirates, but there was no escaping the fact that she was here; they had accepted her presence, however grudgingly, and she'd be a fool to be so uppity that it tipped the balance toward the dissenters who had voted against her.

If she had to win their friendship, so be it. She saw Black Robbie striding toward her. By then the cooling water had eased the panic she had momentarily felt, and she knew at once that he was far from pleased.

"Where did you get that?" he snapped, taking the leather bottle that she still held in her hand. She was startled by the anger in his voice.

"I felt faint, and one of the men was kind enough to fetch it for me."

"Who was it? Point him out to me."

Her temper rose. "I don't know what you're making such a fuss about. Is it so wrong to come to a lady's aid when she's in distress?"

"It's wrong to take water without permission. The man risks a flogging."

Sarah gasped. "You can't mean that! A flogging for so simple an act?"

"Mistress Huxley," he said, infuriatingly patient. "How many times must I remind you that we live by a strict code of conduct on this ship, and the rules as set down must be obeyed?"

"I saw nothing in the rules about water?"

"Then please read them again. Any man who takes food or water beyond his portion risks ten lashes. You must realize that if the weather became inclement or we were unable to put into land for any other reason, the lack of water could be disastrous. Men have been driven mad because of it. Now, will you point out the man, or must I question every one of them?"

"That won't be necessary," she said, white-faced. "His

name is Flint, but I implore you not to punish him on my account."

She hated every minute of this. It humiliated her to beg, but she could see by the hardness of Robbie's jaw that the rules were there to be obeyed. If he broke them for her, he would be seen to be giving in to the wiles of a woman, and therefore losing control. And the threat of mutiny was ever-present on any pirate ship, where the majority of the crew was of unsavory character.

As if from nowhere, the quartermaster appeared, his face sardonic; it was obvious that he had heard every word.

"Ye'd best leave this to me, Cap'n," he said slyly, and then turned and roared out a command. "Whoever knows where he is, bring the man Flint to me."

Sarah leaned against the ship's rail, wishing she could melt into its wooden bars, appalled at causing this sudden furor by the simple act of asking for a drink of water. It emphasized the harshness of these men, but also the strict orders of the ship, so alien from the tacit understandings of polite society. To the world Sarah had left behind, pirates were the drunken and bizarre dregs of humanity. Hadn't she herself thought so such a short time ago? And here she was now, angry and upset at being the cause of the punishment of one of them.

Flint was dragged forward by several of the pirates, and a cat-o'-nine-tails was handed to the quartermaster, who brandished it lovingly. He swished it through the air several times, causing it to hiss like an angry snake. As if by magic, other crew members appeared, some standing silently with arms folded, some fingering daggers and grinning lasciviously, anticipating the punishment with relish. Sarah felt physically ill at the way they gathered, like vultures awaiting their prey.

"Is this the man who gave you the water, Miss?" Quartermaster demanded, taking charge.

135

"For pity's sake, it was only a few drops!"

"I ask ye again, Miss," he said belligerently. "Is this the man?"

She swallowed, seeing with sudden dread the determination in Flint's eyes as the cat swished again. Ten lashes from those cruel thongs could lay open a man's back until it was raw and bleeding.

"I refuse to say," she said boldly. Robbie stepped forward and held her arm in a tight grip.

"You must say. Otherwise all the men will be punished. Is that what you want? For every man here to receive ten lashes on account of some female whim of yours to try to save the guilty one?"

She stared at him, her eyes round and disbelieving. Was this the man whom she had found so charismatic, so devastatingly handsome that she had sacrificed everything to be with him? The shame of it flooded through her because it was to be with him, more than to get away from Jonas Endor, that she had fled.

"Then I will say. It was Flint, but—" she spoke clearly, intending to say more, but she had no chance.

Within seconds the two pirates holding Flint had ripped the shirt from his back and twisted him to face the mast, pressing him tightly against it. Quartermaster looked inquiringly at Robbie, who gave a small nod.

"*No!* Stop this, please." She rushed forward as the lash was raised, and stood between it and the victim. The flaying thongs grazed her cheek as Quartermaster drew back quickly—leaving enough of a sting to let her know what it might be like for Flint.

"Sarah, keep out of this!" Robbie pulled angrily at her arm, but she stood her ground.

"Since Flint is obviously not allowed to speak for himself, then hear me," she gasped. "Or are you so barbaric that you'll not listen to a word in a prisoner's defense? Is this how you conduct your so-called justice?"

As Quartermaster hesitated, Robbie took control and spoke grimly. "Let the woman be heard. Speak up, Mistress Huxley. One minute and no more."

She gulped, knowing she had to make a good job of this. If she did not, Flint would likely be ridiculed by the rest of the crew for being defended by a woman.

"This is my fault, not Flint's. I would have fallen overboard if he had not grabbed me," she invented wildly. "I was suddenly very faint and lost my balance. I saw the ocean coming up to meet me and I cried out in alarm. I begged him for water, and he gave it to me, just a few mouthfuls, that's all. But think carefully before you punish this man. If I had gone overboard, where would your ransom money be then? I suspect that his first thought was for the ransom, not for my person. As for the water, you can take half my portion for the rest of the day. Will that not satisfy you instead of flogging this man?"

Quartermaster looked at her through narrowed eyes. Sarah looked back at him unflinchingly, knowing she was probably the first and only woman to challenge the male authority on this ship. It terrified her, but she was damned if she would let them see it.

For once she was glad of the cover the rough shirt provided. She was aware of the rasping of her breath, and the heaving of her breasts. God forbid that any of these men should look at her with lecherous eyes right now, or another rule would be in danger of being broken. She saw Robbie glance toward the back of the crowd where Surgeon stood silently, and a look of agreement flashed between the two men.

"Ye'd do well to heed the woman," came Surgeon's voice, filled with warning. "If she's to be ransomed, we'll not want her tipping over the side. If Flint pulled her back as she says, then such an action must be recognized. I can't think the woman would lie to save any man here."

Robbie reinforced the statement. "Surgeon speaks good

sense. I say Flint's action at the rail outweighs the rest. I vote that we stay the punishment."

The pirates' attention was caught by their captain's strong voice, and the direction from Surgeon. Quartermaster, although officially their magistrate, was known for his hasty punishment, and it was frequently left to these two to cool his hot head.

There were few here who would mutiny against Black Robbie unless swayed by the rest, nor would any put themselves willingly on Surgeon's blacklist. Sarah heard the low mutters of assent all around, then Quartermaster impatiently asked for a shout of aye or nay on the flogging.

"The nays have it," he grunted. "But all of ye take warning. No extra water is to be taken by any person, or we could all suffer. Now get back to your duties."

The men began to disperse, the unfortunate Flint pulling the remnants of his shirt around him.

After a moment's hesitation Sarah said, "If you give me the shirt and a needle and thread, I'll mend it."

He stripped off the garment at once and thrust it into her arms, saying he'd bring her the necessary items, without any word of thanks for what she'd done for him. While he went below, Sarah dared to look at Robbie's dark face.

"I suppose that was wrong, too!" she said defiantly. "Sometimes I wonder if I know you at all!"

"Did you ever really think you did?" he retorted and strode away, ordering the remaining groups of men to get about their work unless they, too, looked for a flogging.

She *would* know him though, Sarah vowed, watching the tall, retreating figure, acknowledging the undoubted power of the man. She had made up her mind to that. Tonight, by candlelight, she would wheedle the truth out of him, if it took every ounce of seduction she knew. Grimly, she ignored the possible consequences.

She wanted to know this man, his background, his life, and most of all, what had turned a gentleman into a pirate

138

captain of the high seas. The more she saw of him, the more he intrigued her. Curiosity had always been one of Sarah's weaknesses.

Were there many others? She thought about this a while later as she sat on a pile of rope on the deck, stitching together Flint's shirt. She was curious and always had been. Lord Thomas Endor had always encouraged an inquiring mind in a boy, but in his opinion a girl shouldn't bother her pretty head with worldly matters. She had a sudden vivid memory of her childhood days, before she really understood the true horror of her parents' death and had begged him for the minutest details with a ghoulish insistence.

What was drowning like? Did the water fill every bit of you so that you blew up like a puffball and floated up to the heavens, or did you go spinning to the bottom of the ocean? How long did it take a shark to rip the skin from your skeleton? If you drowned with your mouth open would the fish swim inside you and tickle you horribly as they went down your gullet? Did fish like the taste of blood? How long did it take before you were no more than a pile of bones, cleaned to shimmering whiteness because of the constant washing of the waves?

All these questions, and more, Sarah remembered asking in the innocence of childhood. Uncle Thomas had been horrified that such thoughts could be conjured up by a small girl. He had been unable and unwilling to answer most, but Jonas had taken a fiendish delight in coloring her mind with his own morbid thoughts on the subject, never dreaming that the memory of them would haunt her long into adulthood.

Jonas . . . Sarah shivered, despite the heat of the sun as the day wore on. In examining her own faults, she could hardly overlook her stubbornness. Otherwise, why would she refuse the soft life Jonas had offered? She was quite sure he would soon have tired of a faithful companion and looked elsewhere for his pleasures. Once she had done her duty and produced an heir or two for Endor House, he would satisfy his lust among the serving-girls, and she would have been free to dote on the children.

She might not know Black Robbie, but she knew Jonas Endor only too well. And she had always thought she knew herself, but these last few days had proved otherwise. That she had spirit had never been in doubt. But she had never thought she had the kind of courage that would allow her to set foot on a ship.

She smiled ruefully. It had been desperation that had led her here of course, and the decision had not altogether been made in the cold light of sanity. Robbie had appeared in the midst of the party like one of King Arthur's knights in shining armor. He had whisked her away into the night before she had time to think.

The stitching was finished, and so were these thoughts that were making her less than comfortable. She could see Flint's bare back, glistening as he attended to the daily cleaning of the ship's cannons. She walked toward him and handed him the shirt without a word.

He merely grunted as a way of thanking her, but the expression in his eyes was warm enough and she sensed that perhaps, after all, she had made one friend.

Chapter 10

Acutely mindful of the need to conserve water now, Sarah decided that, because sponging down the clothes was the only way they were going to be kept fresh throughout the voyage, she would try to get as much wear out of them as possible before they had to be cleaned. She chose to wear the blue dress again that evening. The soft color flattered her. It accentuated the blue of her eyes, and shimmered over her curves and small waist. Without undue vanity, she knew that, in the gown, she was enough to turn any man's head.

Was that really her intention, she wondered uneasily, as she surveyed herself in the small mirror? And if so, was she playing with fire? She already knew the passionate character of Black Robbie, a match for herself, as he had rightly said. A match for Sarah. . . .

For one sweet moment, she tried to imagine the two of them in other circumstances. She pictured Robbie, no longer a pirate, robbing and plundering on the high seas, but assuming his role as a gentleman, calling to court her in the long languid days of an English summer heavy with the drone of bees and the scent of blossom.

And herself, tingling with excitement as she prepared to meet an ardent suitor, a new love. Robbie presenting his visiting card on a silver salver at her uncle's house, and herself being allowed to sit unchaperoned with the gentleman in the rose arbor or the gazebo, because they were affianced and so much in love and so nearly wed. . . .

Sarah halted her wayward thoughts with a little shock. It was madness to dream so! Yet all the same, if things were different, she knew that Robbie, or David Roberts, or whatever he called himself, could be the epitome of all her dreams.

The small tap on her door reminded her that Tomby had taken up his position outside. She called to him to come in, already comfortable with him.

"And how are you this evening?" she asked, eyeing him in the mirror with a smile. He did not look in it, and she put out a hand to him.

"Come and stand by me. Do we not make a fine couple?" She laughed teasingly. To her surprise, he hung back. If it had been possible to detect it in his dark skin, she would have sworn that his face reddened.

"Tomby no like. Bad luck," he said awkwardly.

"Bad luck? To see yourself in a mirror? But how else do you know if your face is clean and your hair tidy!"

But such things didn't matter to him. Whether he cleaned himself or not, Sarah couldn't guess; the tight mop of hair did not seem to need the attention of combs or brushes. But she didn't care to think what might be harbored in those tight black curls.

"Tomby no want bad luck," he said doggedly. "No look-see into devil's images."

"All right," Sarah said gently, seeing his agitation. "I was only funning with you, Tomby. Have you come to take me to the captain's cabin?"

He nodded, cheering up at once. How extraordinary. Sarah had forgotten for a moment that he was totally uneducated due to his unhappy past.

"Tomby, have you ever looked at a book?"

He screwed up his face. "Like Cap'n has? No, Miss."

"Would you like to? I could teach you to read words like the captain. You could read the rules of the ship!"

The boy shook his head vehemently. "Books bad. Not for Tomby to see. No, Miss."

"Don't worry, I'm not going to force you," Sarah said quickly. She felt a moment of disappointment. It would have been something to do, to teach the boy his letters and astound Robbie with her cleverness. She pulled the gossamer shawl around her shoulders and turned to the door.

"Take me to Cap'n's cabin then," she said shortly, not bothering to correct her own slip of the tongue. What did it matter after all? They were all heathens here, in spirit if not in body.

It was a repetition of the previous night. Robbie was not yet there, but the table was partly set, and Tomby waited outside, a miniature guard. A fat lot of use he'd be if any of the pirates set upon her, Sarah mused, feeling more unsettled than minutes ago.

Perhaps it was being in here, she thought, as she watched the sunset begin to spread its spectacular coloring over the sea again, the sheets of fire through Robbie's windows. He wasn't here, yet his presence was everywhere, an enigma that haunted her. And the last time she had seen him that day, his expression had been one almost of dislike. It had disturbed her more than she realized.

Was she so spoiled and petulant that she couldn't accept anyone's dislike? She had always been pampered and admired, protected and loved. Until Jonas had become so despicable, she had thought that he too, loved her in a brotherly way that she missed. He had been her confidant, her friend, and then he had spoiled it all.

"Good evening, my lovely."

Sarah turned with a start. Robbie had entered so quietly she hadn't heard him at all. How long he had been standing there watching her gazing out to sea she didn't know. Yet she

143

had the oddest feeling that it was minutes rather than seconds. She had been completely lost in thought.

He had obviously been back to the cabin earlier. He was clean shaven, he wore clean clothes, and there was a scent of cloves about his person. Gone was the hardness of the morning encounter between them, and she relaxed a little.

"Good evening," she murmured.

He came across the cabin to take her hand in his, and raised it to his lips. His amber eyes looked into hers above the contact, and she felt a sharp thrill of excitement run through her veins.

"Is this any way to greet someone destined to be more than a friend?" he asked softly, and before she could stop him his arms had circled her waist.

One arm held her captive in his embrace, while the other moved up the length of her spine to cup the back of her head. Sarah closed her eyes as his mouth sought hers, and the surge of wanting and needing this man swept over her like a flame. She had never felt like this before. Never in her marriage or her dreams.

For long moments she forgot all about resistance. Why resist, when her own arms were winding around Robbie's neck and she was responding to his kisses as if newly awakened from a long and lonely dream?

Every part of her body was pressed close to his, and she could feel the hard excitement in him as her pulse raced. She knew the effect of a desirable woman on a man's body. She was innocent in the emotions of love, but not in the way it manifested itself. She shivered in the knowledge that a woman could do this to a man.

"So, my lovely," Robbie breathed against her mouth. "You do not find me totally repulsive."

"Have I ever said that I did?" She was unable to deny it, to make the quick repartee of London society belles. This was far, far away from such civilized tête-á-têtes, and honesty seemed the only answer at such a moment. "And how—how do you find me?"

The question was out before she could stop it, and she bit her lip, because it was oh, so foolish, so coquettish and naive.

It was not the question to ask of a sophisticated man of the world, and it must stamp her innocence even more clearly before the man. She had been married and was therefore not a virgin in the true sense, but in matters of the world, she might just as well have been.

She wriggled, trying to get out of his arms and recover from her embarrassment, but Robbie was not yet prepared to let her go. He put one finger beneath her chin, forcing her to look up into his eyes, which were like darkened honey in the last rays of the dying sun.

"How do I find you, my lovely girl?" he echoed. "Like the beat of my own heart."

She caught her breath at the stark simplicity of the words. He voiced no elaborately false sentiments, just a statement of fact, uttered in the husky tones of truth and suppressed passion. For a moment more he held her with his hypnotic gaze and then he let her go.

"We will compose ourselves before Cookie brings our meal, or I swear I will forget myself and lose my own wager," he said lightly, turning to the brandy cabinet and pouring them each a glass, without asking her first if she wanted any.

"And what wager was that?" she asked, trying to calm her rapid pulsebeat and act the lady of composure.

"Have you forgotten so soon?" Robbie asked with mock reproach. "I vowed you would come to me voluntarily, my sweet love, that there would be no need for me to force you into submission."

Yes, she had forgotten. And yes, the tears pricked her eyes at the realization that all this had been part of the big seduction scene after all. He was merely determined to win his own wager, and she had been fool enough to fall for it. But had it not been her intention, too, to seduce him into telling her everything about himself?

Sarah knew she must proceed carefully, for it would be so very easy to imagine she was falling in love with him. And who but a fool fell in love with a colorful rogue such as Black Robbie!

She thought frantically of something sensible to say, to avoid letting him guess at her feelings.

"I offered to teach Tomby to read. Would you object to loaning me a book for the purpose, although he doesn't seem keen on the idea?"

Robbie shook his head, motioning her to sit on one of the leather chairs while he took the other.

"It's a bad idea. He comes from a tribe where there are more taboos than days in a lifetime. The written word is bad medicine."

"And seeing his image in a mirror?"

"That's right. And if you try to make him go against his tribal ways, you'll encourage another taboo. He'll think the Gods are against him and are using you as an instrument to suggest that his time on earth is finished. He could try to kill himself."

"What?" Sarah was incredulous. "But that's the kind of mumbo jumbo witch doctors say to frighten the ignorant, isn't it? I read about it somewhere."

"Of course it is, and it works only too well. Tomby may looked civilized enough now, but he wasn't like that when I found him. He was wild and gibbering and naked, except for the daubs of paint on his body and the gift objects tied to his ankles and wrists."

"What gift objects?" she asked. Robbie drained his brandy glass and poured himself another before she had sipped hers.

"You don't want to know."

"Yes I do! Please don't treat me like a child!"

His slow appraisement told her he thought of her as anything but a child, and then he shrugged. If this beautiful, infuriating, delightful woman wanted to know the facts, she would know all.

"The Gods must be appeased when the seventh child is offered. Unbroken flesh is not considered enough without evidence of some suffering on the part of the dying. The tribal witch doctor invites members of the family to the ritual tying-on of the gift objects before the child is left pegged out in the sun to die. They can range from living things, such as leeches and spiders, to the spines of poisonous plants, or needles, or any sharp object that will cut into the skin as the child begins to writhe."

"Thank you, I don't want to hear any more," Sarah said quickly. It was hideous, and she had only herself to blame for asking Robbie to explain it all.

"It's nearly time for our meal, anyway," he said coolly. "Drink your brandy."

She hadn't wanted it before. Now she hardly knew how she would get through dinner without its stinging support. Why did she always have this compulsion to find things out! She remembered her quest for this evening. Surely finding out about Robbie's past had to be more palatable than hearing of poor Tomby's experience.

"You haven't forgotten your promise to tell me about yourself, have you?" she asked directly, as Cookie appeared with the meal dishes as silently as on the previous night. Again Robbie dismissed him and Tomby and said they would serve themselves.

"Did I promise that?"

"You know you did! I told you of my fears . . . of . . . of facing my dragon, and you said you would tell me about yourself," Sarah said hotly.

Without waiting to be asked, she ladled mutton stew and root vegetables onto a plate and handed it to Robbie, and served herself a similar portion. She broke a crusty piece of bread in two, suspecting that there might not be too many more days when it would still be fresh enough to do so, unless they obtained more land supplies. She hardly thought the Chinese cook would spend his time baking good fresh loaves such as had been on the table every day at Endor House. She brushed the thought aside.

"I approve of a woman who eats heartily," Robbie commented, and Sarah put her fork down in exasperation.

"So you've already told me. Are you going to tell me the truth or not?"

"Is there any reason why I should? Now, if you were going to be my wife, naturally you would want to know of my future prospects, and would have a right to know my family background."

Sarah was both annoyed and amused. "You—a suitor? Spare me the thought! What future prospects can there be for a pirate except a hangman's rope? And if you ever thought Uncle Thomas would invite you to Endor House to ask for my hand—"

She broke off quickly. She forgot that she had been woolgathering such a little while ago about this very thing. She was overcome with remorse that for a dreadful second she had forgotten that Lord Endor was no longer in this world. Her dearest uncle . . . how could she have been so shameful? She swallowed the lump in her throat.

Robbie stretched out a hand to cover hers for a moment. It gave her an odd feeling of comfort while she struggled with her emotions. They ate the meal in silence, and Robbie made no comment on her words until she had pushed her plate away.

"Your uncle may well have preferred Mr. David Roberts to Black Robbie," he agreed. "And even more than that—"

"Yes?" Sarah looked up quickly.

He eyed her thoughtfully, his amber gaze watchful, as if to detect the merest suggestion of betrayal in her face.

"How trustworthy are you, my lassie?"

She felt her face flush. "Do you think I would ever betray you? Have I not given you proof already? I told no one of the rescue in the sea-cave, nor did I tell whom I had seen at the

148

theater in London. I did not raise the alarm when you appeared at my engagement party."

She gave a small twisted smile. "Someone once told me that ladies never betray the dashing Black Robbie. I never believed the tale, and possibly would not believe it now if I hadn't proved it to myself. But for me it's more than some romantic illusion of protecting the flamboyant pirate captain. I don't forget that I owe you my life."

A shiver ran through her. "I might have drowned in the cave but for you. There's nothing greater that one person can do for another, and I shall always be indebted to you for that."

"And I to you," he said gravely. "Already our lives are entwined like the branches of a vine, too much so for us ever to think of parting, my love."

"I was not suggesting that we stay together for ever," she said in confusion.

"Weren't you? Then why did you flee with me? Why not stay in the safety of your cousin's protection? Why not denounce me there and then, or after you had given me a decent amount of time to leave the house? Can you answer those questions in any other way but admitting that you and I were destined to be together, sweet Sarah?"

He hadn't moved from his seat. He didn't touch her, yet across the small creaking table the air was charged with something magical. She could feel his powerful personality sapping her own, drawing her to his will, his needs. And weakly, she began to wonder just what devil in her made her go on resisting, when all she ever wanted was here, in this man. Since the day their eyes met and he had taken her in his arms and danced with her in that outrageously sensual fashion, all she had ever dreamed about, consciously or not, was lying in his arms and being one with him. Being his woman for all time. . . .

"I wish I could offer you the comforts of a silken bedroom, my Sarah," Robbie said softly. "But for the present I cannot.

Will you sit more comfortably on my bunk with me? You have my word that nothing will happen to you that you do not request."

"The word of a gentleman?" She challenged him huskily, her heart beating fast as his gaze lingered on the low neckline of the blue gown.

"The word of a gentleman. And if you would care to hear the rest. . . ."

He rose and held out his hand. Dreamlike, Sarah put her hand in his and allowed him to lead her to the small bedchamber. This room was as she remembered it, luxurious with the furry rug on the floor and the brilliant embroidered coverlet on the bed, fitted snugly against the side. There were two pillows, and Robbie took them both and placed them on the long side wall, so they could recline together, propped up against them.

"I told you you would be in no danger," he said, but to Sarah the words were just words. She might be in no danger from him, if he was to keep to a gentleman's code of honor, but what of herself? How long could she deny the knowledge that her feelings for him were becoming deeper by the hour? How long before those feelings became too strong for her to restrain? A woman's longings were no less than a man's, and if he continued to push her to the limits of her own desires without fulfilling them. . . .

"Please tell me who you are," she said in a half-strangled voice as his arm slid around her shoulders. "I think we should keep this conversation on a sensible level. You have my promise that I will never betray your confidence."

"A promise that must be sealed with a kiss," Robbie stated, and without waiting for a reply he twisted her into his arms. She slid down against the pillow and his body lay half over hers, so that she felt the weight of him, and the throb of his masculinity against her softness. His mouth was hard on hers, sensual and demanding, and her eyelids closed in a kind of ecstasy, her imagination already soaring toward a love that must not happen and yet surely would.

She twisted away and struggled to sit up, and he leaned back, a half-smile on his face.

"All right, my Sarah. But you'll come to me one day soon, and that's a promise I make to *you*," he said.

He leaned his head back against the pillow, and in the splay of moonlight through the open door of the bedchamber she could see the planes and angles of his face, already dear to her. She could detect the pulsebeat at his throat, and guessed that the telling of his own story was as painful to him as facing her own dragon had been to her.

"My real name is not David Roberts. It's Robert Argyll," he said. "You'll not remember the Uprising of '45, lassie. You would have been, how old?"

"Three years old. But of course I know of it, and the tale of Charles Stuart, the Bonnie Prince Charlie."

"Aye, the Bonnie Prince Charlie. We gave him all, and in the end it was all for naught."

Sarah was startled at his tone of voice. There was sadness and bitterness and something else she couldn't identify. One thing she was sure, though. Whatever tale she had thought to hear, this was undoubtedly the true one. Not even Black Robbie could put such raw feeling into words unless they came from the heart.

"I was twelve years old when the English redcoats came burning and ravaging the glens in their search for Charles Stuart. They slaughtered everything and anything that got in their way, including all of my family."

Sarah gasped. "Your parents?"

"Aye," Robbie said, his accent broadening. "My mother and father, my grandparents, my wee sister. I'd been sent to fetch the doctor for my grandfather who was ailing, and 'twas he who kept me from rushing with a boy's madness to try and save them when we saw the house and lands burning. I heard their screams as they were all slaughtered by Butcher Cumberland's bastards while I crouched in the glen, unable to move."

Sarah bemoaned her vivid imagination as she saw the leap

151

of the flames in her own mind, and smelled the acrid stench of burning flesh as if it were real. She shuddered, but Robbie's arm didn't tighten around her, and she knew at once that she had lost him to his own nightmare world. He'd become totally unaware of her except as a receptacle for his tale, his eyes darkened with the pain of remembering. Yet horrific though his story was, she was strangely moved at being permitted to share such tragic memories.

"What happened then?" she whispered, not wanting to break the spell of Robbie's pain by speaking loudly.

"We remained where we were until the redcoats had done their looting. They freed the terrified horses, though I heard my sister's wee pony screaming as it scrambled to get away, its mane on fire. That was also a sight I never wish to see again," he added.

"Please don't say any more if it pains you too much," Sarah said quietly as his words ended.

He turned slowly to look at her, a spark of anger in his eyes. "Should I spare you the rest then, lassie? Has your sensitive woman's heart set you near to swooning to know of the cruelty of your countrymen?"

"*My* countrymen? Do you set yourself apart from the rest of us?" she asked.

Robbie turned his face away from her again, the proud profile rigidly controlled.

"'Tis no matter. How can one expect an Englishwoman ever to understand the passion the Bonnie Prince awoke in the hearts of all true Scots? How can one expect you to share the humiliation when the cause ended with Charles Stuart hounded from glen to glen, and we saw our gallant laddie turned into a fox hunted by a pack of dogs?"

"So as well as everything else between us, we now have political differences, do we?" Sarah said defiantly. And yet she was afraid she might dissolve into tears at the tragedy of it all.

"I do know the story, Robbie," she continued. "It was taught to me in the nursery."

"Aye, and it says much to me that you can call it a mere story. But you can't know the heart and soul of it, lassie. Not unless you lived it. Not unless your own flesh and blood died in the cause and you were left with nothing."

"I do know what it means to be left with nothing."

He looked at her again, running his fingers up and down her bare arm. It could have been a highly sensual movement. It stirred all of Sarah's senses, yet she saw that to Robbie it meant nothing. She doubted that he had ever told this tale to anyone; she was just the catalyst who had forced him to reveal it, perhaps honestly to himself for the first time.

"Aye, so you do. But you had an uncle to take you in, a ready-made family to go to when your parents died. I dare not approach anyone. Everyone lived in fear in those days. There were plenty of folk who would have given me a temporary home, but why should I put them at risk? My family was well-known as ardent Stuart supporters, and it was soon put about that they searched for the young Argyll and wouldn't rest until they had run him through. The doctor was old, and sheltered me in his cottage for a time, but I knew there was no place for me in Scotland any more. I vowed that one day I would get my revenge on all Englishmen for killing my family and burning my home."

"And that's why you turned to piracy?"

"Would you not say it was reason enough?"

Sarah did not know what to think. It was a tale of horror and bloodshed such as she had never known, and put a completely different complexion on the lessons of the nursery schoolroom. She had learned how the foolish Charles Stuart came to Scotland from Europe, having never set foot in the country before, to reclaim what he saw as his rightful inheritance as King of Scotland. King George had had every right in sending his redcoats to disperse the uprising among the barbaric Highlanders in the north of the kingdom, and the Duke of Cumberland had done his noble duty in bringing the treasonable Scots to their knees and sending the Stuart upstart packing.

Now, for the first time in her life, she saw the other side to the story, and questioned the spiteful words of the old tutor who had taught herself and Jonas. Memories came to her out of the past, like hazy watercolor pictures. There was Jonas's gleeful pleasure in hearing how Charles Stuart was relentlessly hunted like an animal, and her own innocent protests, easily quashed, that if his father had been a king, didn't that make him one too?

Her voice was hushed now as the man beside her stared remotely into the distance. Through the open door of the bedchamber and the dimly lit cabin, the blackness of the sea glittered in the moonlight through the expanse of windows. It seemed to emphasize the loneliness of two people who had both lost everything and yet could find no further words of comfort to say to one another.

She could see that Robbie's thoughts were not with her or with his present situation, but far away and long ago, in another time and place where she could not reach him. She touched his arm gently.

"Robbie, I hardly know what to say. I thank you humbly for sharing your sorrow with me." She hesitated. "But do you never want to go back to Scotland? You can't deny your deep love for your country. And your home and lands, were they not of some importance?"

"Aye, they were of importance," he spoke raggedly. "My father was know as the Argyll of Argyll, an influential man in matters of highland justice. My mother was the most beautiful woman who ever lived, my wee sister just beginning to know her letters and to be aware that we were a proud clan, commanding respect from more than just neighbors and friends. We owned a large house and forest land and several beautiful glens and lochs. It's all lost now, but don't ever ask me again if I don't yearn to go back, lassie. Every nerve in my body cries out for Scotland, but I've turned my back on it, and I'd thank you if you'll never refer to this night's conversation again."

He gripped her wrists so fiercely that she had to bite her lips to stop herself from protesting. But this was not the time. Before she could think what she was doing, she had leaned forward and kissed him softly on the lips.

"I will never speak of it again unless it is your wish, Robbie," she said softly. "Your secret is also mine, and I'm privileged to share it. Don't insult me by asking me to swear never to reveal it to anyone, for I think you must know that I would suffer death first."

She drew back from him a little as the grip on her wrists relaxed.

"And you'll forgive me, but I would prefer not to stroll the deck tonight," she mumbled. "I am exhausted, and I suspect that the telling has made you weary too. I would like to return to my cabin now, if you please."

"Or course." He moved away from her at once, holding out his hand to pull her to her feet. Briefly, he held her close, with no vestige of passion. Sarah knew instinctively that this evening had proved too emotional for such feelings, and had drained them both.

He escorted her in silence to her own cabin, where the native boy slumbered outside the door. Robbie raised her hand to his lips, his voice somewhat lighter.

"We've taken one great step forward tonight, my Sarah. You kissed me of your own accord for the first time."

Seconds later he had gone, and Sarah undressed with shaking hands, hardly heeding his last words. All the other words swirled around in her head . . . the little lost boy witnessing such terrible atrocities, and the wilderness years that must have followed before the bitterness made him turn to piracy as a way of revenge. Such a cruel fate for one who was clearly born to a very different life.

Long into the night, Sarah found that she was weeping into her pillow for that small boy who had been Robert Argyll.

Chapter 11

After all his years at sea, Robbie was now an experienced pirate captain. Any British ship that thought to chase *The Adventuress* in pursuit of the missing Sarah Huxley would naturally expect the pirates to sail due south, put into some French or Spanish port and send word to Jonas Endor demanding ransom money.

"So you deliberately sailed out to sea, because you expected the hue and cry to die down?" Sarah queried.

Robbie laughed. "I'm aware that it won't die completely, when there's such a prize as yourself at stake, Sarah. But yes, we simply disappear from the charted routes, and lose ourselves in the swell of the Atlantic for a few weeks."

"Jonas will never give up," Sarah stated, suppressing a shiver at the thought. "He'll want what he thinks is his."

"And I want what I know is mine," Robbie answered.

As the days on board merged into weeks, Sarah became an accepted part of the ship's company, even if some of the crew thought of her as just another piece of baggage *The Adventuress* carried. She was well aware that some still resented her presence, but between them, Robbie and Surgeon had placated most of the doubters, and none dared to abuse her, physically or verbally. There were a very few, Tomby and Flint among them, who would cheerfully have gone over the side and braved sharks for her.

By this time she was forced to grudgingly admire the reckless bravery of the pirates, especially in the face of a sudden vicious storm that had caught them unawares. It was during the storm that Sarah had had to come to terms with her seasickness. It was as Robbie had said. There was no fighting it, and in the end you got your sea legs and would probably find walking on dry land more complicated than accommodating your balance to the rhythm of the ship's motion. She had seen the stoicism of the rest of the crew when one man had gone overboard during the storm. She had accepted with equal stoicism that there was no use risking anyone else's neck in trying to save him.

Her own reactions to people were changing, Sarah thought with some surprise. Along with most people of her class, she had thought that all pirates were the scum of the earth, including the notorious Black Robbie, who plundered the seas and women's hearts alike. She had seen for herself how different things really were as far as Robbie was concerned. She still wouldn't care to meet the rest of them alone in the dark, although some had a few qualities to recommend them . . .

They were getting into more southerly waters now, sailing steadily toward the coast of Spain to drop anchor in a safe, secluded river inlet. Some time before they were due to arrive, Sarah retired to her cabin early one evening, complaining of a sick headache. She was awakened soon after by a loud commotion on deck.

"What's happening, Tomby?" she whispered, venturing her head outside her cabin.

His eyes were round and scared in the thin shaft of moonlight from the hatchway above.

"Some men get very sick, Missy."

Sarah felt her heartbeat quicken. "What do you mean? What's happened?"

The boy shrugged. Death was nothing new to him.

"Men get fever and die, Missy."

Robbie's dark shape suddenly appeared, and he snapped at her to get back inside the cabin.

"Not until you tell me what's going on," she said.

"It could be typhoid. One man's died, and three more are raving," he said briefly. "Now will you get back inside and leave us to get on with our work?"

"What work?" she asked, licking her lips that were suddenly dry.

Robbie cursed beneath his breath.

"We've to tip the dead over the side, find a space on deck for the others until we see which way they'll go. Surgeon can't be certain yet if it's typhoid or not." He spoke brutally, not bothering to tidy up the words, since she wanted to know everything as usual.

Sarah gasped. "But that's barbaric. They should have proper medical care. What's Surgeon doing for them?"

"Sarah, there's no room for beds with clean white linen for those who get sick. You should know that by now. A space on deck is all they can expect. Every man who serves on a pirate ship knows that score. Surgeon will do what's necessary."

"Can I help?" she asked, before she had time to think.

"You cannot. Stay inside and pray that typhoid, if such it is, does not infect you," he said grimly.

He pushed her back inside, and to her rage she heard the sound of a key being turned in the lock. She was no nurse, and her offer had been instinctive, thinking how terrible it must be for three men to be heaped together like so much flotsam, waiting to see which way the fever would turn. If it was typhoid, they would surely die.

"Tomby, go up on deck and come back and tell me what's happening," she said through the door.

"Cap'n said Tomby stays here!" came his agitated voice. "And I say you go!"

She heard a sudden splash as if something heavy had been thrown overboard, and knew that it would be the dead man. There was no finesse in disposing of a body infected with typhoid. She knew the sense of it, but it was against all human dignity to be thrown away like garbage.

She took a deep breath, aware that she was trembling, aware suddenly of beads of perspiration on her face and neck, running in rivulets between her breasts. Her head throbbed at the temples and her legs were beginning to feel rubbery and weak. *Dear God,* she thought in sudden fear, *is this the beginning of the end for me too?* Typhoid took no account of gender or background. When it struck, it could run with lightning swiftness through a house or a town. How much more then were those in the close confines of a ship susceptible to its ravages?

Her thoughts ran on haphazardly as panic overwhelmed her. Hygiene was frequently at a minimum on board, food could go sour and rancid and water become weevil-ridden, since voyages were of uncertain duration due to the nature of the profession. On the plus side, Robbie instructed the decks to be washed daily with vinegar and salt water and this was assiduously done.

To Sarah's knowledge, there had already been some fumigation below decks, with pans of burning pitch that left throats so raw with the acrid stench that she had wondered at the time if the risk of disease was not preferable to the preventive measures. If an epidemic struck, none of it would be enough, she thought. None of it would be the slightest use.

Feeling ill and more light-headed by the minute, a paroxysm of self-pity flooded through her, and she longed desperately for the comfort of her own soft bed at Endor House, and the attentions of the family physician.

"Sarah! Sarah! For God's sake, boy, help me get her onto

the bunk!"

She seemed to be floating somewhere. She had known this feeling before, when she had been in someone's arms in some dark place smelling of the stale debris of the sea. . . .

Robbie's face was a ghostly shape that swam in and out of her senses as she tried to see him clearly. But her vision was blurred and her brain wouldn't function properly. Her skin was burning up. Her only lucid thought was that soon it would shrivel to a crisp and she would die. She heard someone sobbing in a high young voice.

"Stop that noise, Tomby, and fetch some water and a cloth," Robbie's voice ordered.

Sarah was detached from it all. She managed to deduce that the boy had rushed away, and that Robbie had gotten her onto her bunk from where she had fallen on the floor of the cabin. He was pulling off her gown and then her chemise and all her undergarments. She knew she should protest, and that it was unseemly for a gentleman to unclothe a lady, no matter what the circumstances.

But she was incapable of protesting. She could only react like a rag doll, feeling her own arms flop down as Robbie pulled the garments away from her skin. He supported her against him while he fought to get the cambric nightgown over her upper body and to thrust her limp arms through its voluminous sleeves.

Only then did he lay her gently back on the bunk, where she lay as exhausted as if she had ridden hard across the sands below the cliffs near Endor House. Robbie, too, was breathing hard as if from such exertion. Or as if he were deeply affected by something. . . .

Dimly into Sarah's senses came the recollection that he had paused in his ministrations to gaze briefly at her nakedness. If she could have read his mind, she would have known that it had been beyond him to be totally unmoved by the sight of those perfectly rounded milk-white breasts, that sensuous, curving waist. Nor could he fail to be physically

160

aroused as his gaze was drawn down to the dark hair that hid the source of her femininity.

Dear God, but she was even more beautiful than he imagined, Robbie thought raggedly, and if he were to lose her now. . . .

"Tomby!" he bellowed through the open door of the cabin. "Get down here quickly, and tell Surgeon to attend to Mistress Huxley as soon as he's able."

He looked back at the restless figure on the narrow bunk. The cropped hair that lessened her femininity not a bit, as far as he was concerned, curled in night-black tendrils around her face, her lashes lying softly against her flushed cheeks like twin crescents. He felt a strange urge of tenderness mixed with passion.

The sensation surprised him. That the woman had become like a thorn beneath his skin he could accept. That Black Robbie was beginning to feel the beginnings of an emotion he half-recognized as love was more alarming. But when he was alone with her, he no longer thought of himself as Black Robbie. Nor even as the dandy David Roberts.

She called him Robbie . . . and when he was with her, she drew out a tenderness in him that had almost been forgotten in the harsh life he had chosen. With Sarah, he could almost imagine himself reverting to his true role, to Robert Argyll, the young lord of the highland home he would surely have become by now, had circumstances decreed differently.

"By God, but 'tis a foolish man who indulges in dreams," he muttered to himself.

"Robbie," Sarah moaned weakly. "Am I going to die?"

"No, my dearest one," he said savagely. "Not if I have to put you ashore, in a doctor's care, to ensure it."

The tall thin shape of Surgeon entered the cabin, followed by the frightened figure of Tomby with the water and cloth. The boy was dismissed to take up his stance outside, while Surgeon looked at Robbie keenly.

"You'll not risk the ship's company for the sake of the

woman, Cap'n." It was a statement, not a question.

"Then see to her, man. And make her well again."

The pirate captain strode outside while Surgeon made his examination. He leaned his head against the wall and cursed the softness inside him. His men would lose all respect for him if they thought he was weakening for a woman's skirts. It hadn't been his intention. Women were fair game, and he had always had his fill of them. He had never expected to see the day when one of them would work her way into his heart without even trying.

Perhaps that was it, he thought, not ready yet to admit that he could succumb to love like any other mortal. Perhaps when she became his, as she surely would, then the chase would be over, and he would be rid of this madness creeping over him. Once he had had his fill of her. . . .

Surgeon called him into the cabin. He had dampened the cloth and it lay across Sarah's forehead. With her own washcoth he was moistening an exposed area of her flesh at her throat to try and lessen the heat.

"'Tis not the typhoid," Surgeon said shortly. "Just a fever, probably brought on by a drop of tainted water. I daresay 'twill be gone by morning."

"And the others?" For the moment Robbie kept his eyes away from the small figure on the bunk and inquired after his men. Surgeon shrugged.

"I daresay 'twas the same. One unfortunate died and caused a panic, but I suspect that t'others will be recovered by morning. They'll sleep it off, same as the woman."

He left the cabin to keep an eye on his other patients, while Robbie let out a long slow breath, not realizing he had been holding it in check. He looked down at Sarah, who was in a semi-wakened, semi-delirious state, and then knelt by her bunk, turning over the cloth on her forehead to keep it cool. He reached for the damp washcloth and smoothed the white flesh of her throat.

Her breathing was less fraught with anxiety now. Robbie

162

watched the slow rise and fall of her breasts beneath the nightgown, and then, as if compelled beyond reason, his hand stretched out and closed over one soft firm mound. And although not fully aware of what was happening, some primitive response in Sarah caused the rose-bud tip to swell and grow of its own accord, as if it had craved Robbie's touch for a long time.

She gave an involuntary indrawn breath, and without removing his hand, Robbie leaned over her and kissed her mouth, pliant and mobile in sleep, and he could feel her small white teeth and taste her tongue against his own. For a second he allowed the tip of his tongue to circle hers, and then removed it quickly at the surge of pleasure in his loins. For this was not the way he wanted her, insensible and unaware. He wanted the responses of a warm and passionate woman, a match for himself. He stood up.

"Sleep well, my love," he said quietly, stared at her for a moment longer, and left her alone.

And as a pale dawn started to lift the cloak of night, the fever gradually began to leave her. Sarah stirred in her sleep and stretched languidly in the narrow bunk, a strange sense of well-being filling her veins. She had dreamed that a lover had removed her clothes and run his hands over her nakedness, and that instead of being ashamed and afraid, she had felt wanton and pleasured, glorying in the desire in his amber eyes. . . .

She was suddenly wide awake. There was only one man she knew with amber eyes like those of a cat. Eyes that could be cold as ice, or hot as fire . . . Robbie. Quickly she looked down at herself, as if expecting to see her own body exposed and used and abandoned. Instead, she was chastely fastened into her nightgown, with the bedcovers up to her neck, and a damp cloth slipping away from her forehead.

Then she remembered. Robbie had been here, and so had Surgeon, peering down at her, and proclaiming that she merely had a fever, and not the typhoid. Thank God! And the gentle, caring hands had been Robbie's.

It was always easier to be truthful about one's own feelings in the silent hours of the night or early dawn, and Sarah admitted to herself that even if it had all been a dream, it was not the first moment that her soul had craved his touch, and would always crave it.

Whether it was right or wrong, she knew without a doubt that she loved him. She would always love him, and since he only wanted her because he was intrigued by her refusal to be infatuated by him, she knew that the worst thing she could do would be to let him know it.

She turned on her side, the receding fever allowing her to rest peacefully at last, and slept until Tomby came knocking on her door to see if she wanted breakfast.

"Cap'n says you try porridge today," he said importantly.

"I didn't know there was any porridge," Sarah said, a little indignantly, more than tired of her usual dry breakfast fare.

Tomby grinned, pleased to see her looking better

"Cap'n always eats porridge, Missy."

"Does he now? Then I'll have porridge as well, please," she informed him. Of course Cap'n *would*. Porridge was one of Scotland's staple diets, and not so bad with hot milk and honey oozing into it.

When Tomby brought her the dish, she took one mouthful and spat it straight out in a way that would have had her Aunt Lily scandalized at such uncouth behavior.

"*Salt!* There's salt on this porridge!" She rubbed at her mouth to try and rid herself of the bitter taste. "Are there such quantities of vermin in the oats that it needs to be laced with salt, for pity's sake!"

She grimaced at the thought, amazed that she could even bring herself to say the words without vomiting. She marveled again at how differently Mistress Sarah Huxley saw the world these days.

"I can hear that you're better without asking. And do you not like the Scottish way of serving the breakfast dish?" she heard Robbie ask in amusement, and she turned to see him standing at her cabin door.

"You serve it with salt instead of honey?" she asked incredulously, ignoring the rest. "But it's so bitter."

"So *heathen*," he provided dryly. "Perhaps Cookie was over-enthusiastic in the preparation. I suggest you stir it well, and I promise you'll soon get the taste for it. 'Tis much better for the digestion than when tamed by the sweet stuff."

"So you say," she muttered, eyeing the sloppy white gruel with distaste. "I think perhaps I will have bread and drippings, after all."

"As you like. I'm thankful to see the fever has not destroyed your appetite, and in a day or so we shall dine on tastier fare. We put in along the coast of Spain tomorrow night. The next day you may go ashore for a while, under my protection, of course. And in the evening, before we set sail for Guinea, Mr. David Roberts will be pleased to escort his lady to a proper eating-house and then to a small theater. Does that please you?"

Sarah caught her breath. Weeks at sea had deepened the color of her skin to a honeyed hue, and she had at last got her sea legs . . . but the thought of going ashore, of walking on dry land and eating wholesome food prepared in a clean kitchen, of behaving *normally* again, was suddenly, blissfully, wonderfully alluring.

"It pleases me," she said huskily. "And Robbie—thank you, for last night."

"No thanks are necessary. Now eat your breakfast and dress yourself."

He was gone, and Sarah looked down quickly. In the mornings she habitually wore the dressing-robe until she had eaten, and it evoked an intimacy in the small cabin that she hadn't intended. But then she had never invited Robbie in, she thought, and wondered ironically what difference it would make if she tried to bar the door.

Without thinking, she stirred the porridge vigorously, and

put a spoonful in her mouth. The taste wasn't so bad now. In fact, it had a piquancy about it that was certainly missing when laced with the blandness of honey. She concluded that Robbie had been right and that Cookie had probably sprinkled salt rather too lavishly on the top of the dish. She tried another spoonful, and by the time Tomby returned with her bread and drippings, the dish was empty.

Remembering what Robbie had told her, Sarah felt a shiver of excitement. Tomorrow night, under cover of darkness, of course, they would be tying up somewhere in the narrow winding river Robbie had already pointed out on the map. The usual plan, he explained, was to seek out narrow and lonely waterways where larger vessels were unable to follow.

The whole voyage was beginning to take on a slightly different dimension for Sarah. She forgot the ignominy of sailing with pirates and of being captured, however voluntarily. Suddenly this was an adventure of the kind in which her parents had once reveled—not as guests of pirates, naturally, but of seeking out new horizons and new experiences.

Until now, Sarah hadn't realized how cloistered she had been in a world of her own fears, but perhaps at last the dragon was beginning to be slain. She recognized Robbie's own phrase and acknowledged that in some matters he was far wiser than she.

The Adventuress slid along the narrow river inlet. The sails were furled and Sarah heard the small hiss and swish of the oars as the crew strained to move the vessel as quietly as possible. She was allowed on deck with Robbie, peering through the darkness, every nerve straining for possible sounds from the banks.

But luck was theirs, and Robbie was confident that the ship had passed completely undetected. Here, hidden from coastal patrols by the twisting bends of the river, they would tie up for two nights and go out to sea again on an early tide. Tomorrow the crew would attend to the careening in shifts. Their spare hours would be spent in cavorting with certain Spanish señoritas happy to entertain these raucous seamen, asking no questions as long as a few coins changed hands.

Robbie had told her all of this, and Sarah resisted the temptation to ask whether he too was in the habit of visiting these certain señoritas. It was something she didn't care to know, but at least he had promised to tell her about the careening. It still sounded vaguely alarming and he laughed at her curiosity.

"Sometimes, my lassie, you can be as gullible as a bairn," he said softly, at which she bridled at once, then decided to keep quiet if she wished to hear what was to happen.

"There's a flat area of marshland farther up the river where it shallows considerably," he told her. "The ship has to be beached and unloaded, then hauled onto its side to recaulk the seams and burn off any barnacles. It's a necessary procedure and has to be done fairly frequently."

"But isn't that a terrible risk?" Sarah asked, appalled that half her concern was that while this work was going on, there would be no escape if danger threatened.

"It's one we must take, and less risk to us here than on English shores," Robbie said. "If the ship is unseaworthy, then we all risk drowning, and I fancy you'd prefer us to be beached for a day or so than the alternative. But never fear, Sarah. It's unlikely that we shall be discovered. It's a lonely place and one that's given us many a breathing-space before now."

She was remembering that conversation as the dim shape of a wide open area of marshland came into view, and the swish of oars ceased. The night had been chosen carefully. There was no moon and the sky was overcast. The tension of it all, and her unexpected emotion at her first sight of land in weeks, made Sarah very tired. She was thankful to get to her bed, with scarcely a movement of the ship that night to remind her that she was still on board.

In the morning she was roused very early. The ship had to be beached as soon as possible, and there was much work to be done. Even before she dressed in her habitual boy's garb, she was aware of activity on deck and ashore, and peering out of her porthole, she saw that a temporary camp had been set up on the marshland, and barrels and supplies were already being unloaded to lessen the weight of the ship. To her, it seemed an enormous task.

On deck, no one had time to bother with her. The men scurried hither and thither, clearly experienced in their allotted tasks and needing no specific orders. A man was in the crow's nest, scanning the countryside through a spyglass. He came shinning down the ropes minutes later with nothing to report.

Almost before the sun had risen in the sky, the ship was ready to be careened. Everyone was on shore now, and Sarah watched in some awe as men with straining muscles heaved and tugged at a mass of ropes until the ship creaked and groaned safely onto her side. A pungent smell was already filling the air as the protective mixture of tar, tallow and sulphur was prepared for the caulking.

"She's even safer now," Robbie told Sarah. "Her masts are well below any possible line of vision. And now you must amuse yourself, my love, but please don't venture away from camp. My men will only be obliged to bring you back if you do."

There was the hint of a threat in his voice, and she remembered that to the crew at least, she was still no more than a hostage. While to him . . . ? She was still unsure.

She stared at his retreating figure as he strode away to give assistance and encouragement to the men. Like the rest of them, he had stripped to the waist because of the effort involved in the hauling, and his tanned skin glistened with exertion. His back was smooth and powerful, his shoulders broad, and Sarah felt an extraordinary urge to run her hands over his skin.

She turned away quickly as the ground seemed to dip and sway a little under her feet, and she sat down abruptly on a barrel in the shade of the makeshift canvas shelter.

I love him. Once again, the thought filled her head before she could stop it. *Whoever or whatever he is, I love him.*

The ground was still shifting uneasily, and she felt a mild panic. What was happening? Was it an earthquake?

"Does Missy feel green?" Tomby inquired, proud of his new-found expression.

"Missy definitely feels green," she muttered. And the thought of facing a decent meal that evening was suddenly far less attractive than previously.

"Tomby tell Surgeon."

"No, it's nothing," she said weakly, but already the thin man was coming toward her impatiently.

"'Tis naught but the land fever, Mistress Huxley. Your body's got used to adjusting to the motion of the ship and can't adapt readily to ground that stays still beneath it. It tries to compensate for the movement. 'Twill pass soon enough. There's no treatment but close your eyes during the attack, and open them slowly when it's over."

He moved away to more important things, and Sarah glared after him. He may think it nothing to imagine that everything around her was undulating like the waves of the sea, but to her it was extremely unpleasant.

"Do as Surgeon says, Sarah, and the feeling will gradually pass," Robbie said, suddenly close by.

"Will it?" She tried to think sensibly. "Well, just as a matter of interest, can you tell me how you expect me to act like a civilized person this evening if nothing stays still? And just where is this eating-house and theater that you spoke of anyway? I don't believe any of it exists."

Along with her discomfort, Sarah was filled with an acute sense of letdown. Of course none of it was true. There was nothing for miles but marshy wilderness. Robbie had only been taunting her.

"I have a trusted acquaintance here," he said calmly. "A man has already been dispatched to arrange for a small carriage to be sent for us this evening, and there is a small town not too far distant where we will make merry. You really must learn to trust me, Sarah," he said with a mocking smile, and went off to attend to his duties.

She stared after him while the queasy feelings continued to assault her. Trust him? She felt a momentary anger, and then it dwindled to nothing. Once, she might have said she would as soon trust a fox, but that was before she knew him. That was before she fell in love with him.

Chapter 12

Sarah glanced at the gentleman sitting beside her in the ornate little carriage taking them away from the river and marshland. So elegant. So noble a profile, the jaw strong and masculine, a giant among men. So different in appearance from the flamboyant sea captain. Yet in whatever guise, this man had only to look at her with those mesmeric eyes for her to accept that he was now a very dear part of her life.

"Well? Do we look the part, my Sarah?" Robbie asked softly, feeling her gaze on him. He gave all his attention to the reins in his hand, for the carriage had been left at their disposal and he himself drove them to the small town in the hills.

"Can you not answer that question for yourself, Sir?" she asked provocatively, and he laughed, a rich warm sound that she had first heard long ago in her uncle's house, and which had thrilled her even then.

"You look stunning, and you don't need to fish for compliments, lassie, for you must know by now that I'd give you all and more if you give me what I most desire," he said in a shiveringly seductive voice.

Sarah stared straight ahead as the faint lights of civilization appeared ahead of them against a dark backdrop of hills. If only she didn't love him so it would be easy to be flippant and mocking, and indulge in all the light, funning remarks so beloved of sophisticated society. Such drawing-room parryings and flirtations were all nonsense, part of the acceptable charades they all played. She felt the warm touch of Robbie's hand close over her own.

"Enjoy the moment, Sarah. None of us can ask for anything more. Let tomorrow take care of itself."

And tonight? The change in their situation was not lost on her. Until now, on board *The Adventuress*, they had been captor and captive, however ostensibly. Here at last, they were on equal terms, she dressed in one of the exquisite gowns he had bought for her, with a black and gold Spanish mantilla draped attractively over her head to hide the shorn hair. The topaz necklace glowed like fire against her throat, and she felt a sudden fierce gladness at knowing she looked beautiful for him.

And Robbie—Mr. David Roberts for the evening— immaculate in the fairly sober attire of a gentleman, the gleaming white cravat at his neck fastened with a gold pin, the powdered wig a mere gesture toward his own disguise. Together, they were a prize pair. Sarah suppressed a small giggle.

"What have I said that you find so amusing?" Robbie asked, smiling.

"I was just thinking that since we look so fine, it would be ironic if we were apprehended by robbers!"

He laughed, and patted his chest.

"Never fear, Sarah. My pistol is ready for any such emergency, and there's a dirk in my boot."

And that just about summed him up, Sarah thought wryly. Whatever the disguise, he was too steeped now in the ways of piracy ever to change. She doubted that any one woman could ever be the means of persuading him. Until that moment, she had never even considered the possibility of it. But as they rode along the lonely tracks, for a few heady moments she let the dreams take over. . . .

She was no longer Mistress Sarah Huxley, captive of a pirate captain. And he was no longer Black Robbie, notorious plunderer of the seas and women's hearts . . . nor even handsome David Roberts, gallant gentleman of means. They were together in that misty Highland home of which Robbie had spoken so movingly. Together, side by side, sharing their lives, sharing love. . . .

The carriage struck a small rut in the track, and Sarah was thrown against him. His arm went across her to steady her, and the shiver of pleasure such a small attention gave her was enough to dry her mouth. For a long while afterward she could still feel the warm pressure of his hand closing over her thigh.

"The town lies ahead through a small pass," Robbie said, his voice not quite steady, so that for a second she wondered if he too had been affected by her sudden nearness.

But why should he be, when he must have known so many women? Sarah thought, facing the facts honestly. What was one more? Except that so far, this one had refused to surrender to his seduction. But for how much longer? she wondered.

The small Spanish town was little more than a large village, dignified by one theater, visited by strolling players and minor traveling companies, Robbie told her. It was always well-patronized due to its reputation for good productions. They went first to an eating-house where Robbie was known, though in what capacity, Sarah couldn't guess. Certainly they were shown at once to a table in an alcove where their presence would be quite undetected.

The place was comfortable, if undistinguished. The rough stone walls were painted white, different from the English wood paneling she was accustomed to, and were adorned with many Spanish artifacts. It was different from anywhere Sarah had been before, and Robbie promised her that the food would be superb.

She made the dry reply that anything would be superb after the slow deterioration of the food aboard ship. At least when they set sail once more, supplies would have been replenished by the sortie of men sent to fetch them; there would be fresh water, and bread that wasn't rock-hard and suspect with vermin.

"I hope you like fish," Robbie said, as the dark-haired waiter fussed around them with various dishes for their examination. "Naturally, being near to the sea, it's a speciality here."

"Perhaps the señorita would care to try the *sopa de pescado,*" the waiter suggested, openly admiring. "And then *tenemos merluza o calamares muy bien. Despues hay fruta del tiempo—*"

"The señorita *no comprende,* Juan," Robbie said with a smile, and then to Sarah. "He is offering fish soup, then he says they have hake or very good squid, and then there is fresh fruit."

Sarah felt the table begin to sway, and was not altogether sure that it was merely the land fever that was causing it. *Squid?* It sounded disgusting.

"Do they not have meat?" she asked faintly. "I think after all I would prefer anything to fish."

Robbie rattled off something in Spanish to the waiter, who nodded and disappeared again. Sarah was amazed at his command of the language.

"There are many long lonely nights at sea, Sarah," he said, seeing her expression. "I have used them to advantage in studying languages, and the Spanish language in particular. It is useful to know when to be on guard."

It was just something else to surprise her about this complex man, even though he studied the language for purely practical reasons, and reminded her that such an excursion as this must surely be a risk.

"Will you teach me a few words?" she asked.

174

Robbie laughed, leaning across the table toward her, and lowering his voice. "If that is all you wish me to teach you, then for the present I suppose I must be satisfied."

"I'm serious, Robbie!" she said laughingly. "Teach me something now while we wait for the food."

"Very well. Repeat after me," he said, lights dancing in his amber eyes. "*Te quiero, mi cariño.*"

Sarah repeated it carefully.

"Perfect." Robbie grinned.

"What does it mean?"

"I'll tell you at a later date, when I think the time is right," he said, and refused to enlighten her. But as she practised the words, the moments gave her pause to forget the queasy feelings in her stomach for a while, and when the food was brought to the table, rich with gravy and teasing her taste buds, she gave it all her attention.

When they were sated, Robbie said they should leave for the theater. It was only a few short streets away, and it was best if they walked there, leaving the horse and carriage in the quiet courtyard of the eating-house.

The night was still overcast, but the low clouds gave a strange intimacy to the night, and Sarah's arm was tucked firmly in Robbie's as they walked the short distance to the theater. There was a dark sheen on the narrow cobbled streets from the many horses' hooves that had traversed them, and Sarah would have slipped were it not for Robbie's supporting arm.

"We have a small troupe of mime artists tonight," he observed from the poster outside the hall. "Don't expect a London production, Sarah. But at least you will be able to follow the play, since it is without words, and it will be illustrated by a musical accompaniment."

It was the strangest performance Sarah had ever seen. Because of the lack of words, the actors exaggerated their movements and expressions, but the play's message was clear. It was all about unrequited love, and death, and the usual dastardly villain was greeted with hisses and boos that were the same in any language. Finally love conquered all, to the building's musical sounds of triumph. It was amateurish in its way, but to Sarah it was still a breath of normality in her alien new life.

At the end of the performance, the audience seemed suddenly galvanized into speech, as if it had been an ordeal to still their tongues for so long. The Spanish were clearly a voluble race. Sarah was about to say as much to Robbie, when she realized he wasn't listening to her. He was intent on some gentlemen a fair distance away from them, whose eyes were fixed rather too keenly on Sarah, and then reverted with growing interest to himself.

"I think it's time we left, Sarah," he said urgently, and she realized to her horror that the mantilla had slipped from her head, and her cropped hair was very much in evidence. What kind of lady would venture out in public looking such a sketch? What lady would have her hair cut in such a way, expect for suspicious motives?

The two men were peering lower on her person, their hands gesticulating wildly now, and then with a shock she realized they were staring at the topaz pendant. Assuming that their interest could mean they had designs on stealing it, without thinking she pressed one hand across her throat to conceal the jewel, unwittingly giving herself away.

"Dear heaven, Robbie, what do we do?"

"Keep calm, lassie. There's too much of a crush between them and us for them to reach us if we move very quickly. I suspect that your description has been circulated far and wide by now, and I had overlooked that distinctive bauble you're wearing. No doubt your cousin would have given details of it, if only in the hope of recovering what he considers his property."

All the time he was speaking, he was edging her deftly toward a side door which had been opened to accommodate the rush to get out into the fresh air. People were spilling out of the theater from every exit, gathering in groups outside to discuss the performance, clearly in no hurry to move on.

"Fortunately, it's their custom to linger," Robbie said. "Quickly, Sarah, before those men fight their way through the crowds."

Even as he spoke, there was a piercing whistle, and people began to babble excitedly in complete confusion, their voices becoming higher-pitched. News of what was afoot spread like wildfire among the crowd, reaching Robbie's ears. Sarah understood none of it, but he certainly did.

"The authorities have been summoned. It's believed the pirate Black Robbie and a woman companion may be here among the crowd," he translated. "Stay close to me, Sarah. There's a back street leading to the courtyard of the eating-house. With luck we can be away before order is restored."

Her heart pounded as they moved as fast as possible without drawing undue attention to themselves. And then her heart almost stopped as a man seemed to appear from nowhere, his hand on Robbie's arm. She heard Robbie gabble to him in his own language, and the man rushed away.

"What did you say to him?" Sarah asked, almost swooning with fear.

"He wanted to know what was happening, and I said there's been some upset at the theater, and that my wife was ill so we had to get home quickly. I suggested there might be a reward for the pirate's capture, and that was enough to send him running. Men will do much for gold."

She felt sickened to realize how true were his words. But there was no time for such thoughts, nor to ponder on how appealing those other words were to her. His wife . . . To her enormous relief, they reached the courtyard of the eating-house without mishap, and Robbie bundled her into the carriage and jerked on the reins at once.

The vehicle clattered away on the cobbles, and a sharp pain in her side sawed at Sarah as they sped through the darkness toward the sanctuary of the marshy beach.

"Are they following us?" She gasped. "I don't hear anything."

"Then Lady Luck is with us this time." He was concentrating more on getting back to the ship than checking on any pursuers.

This time, Sarah echoed. And if this little diversion had been all for her benefit, how different the outcome might have been. She was still dazed with fear at the suddenness of the discovery and the consequent flight.

Even more so at the realization that there had never been a moment during the entire evening when she had thought to declare who she was, or raise the alarm, or betray Black Robbie. She had once been told that no woman ever betrayed him, but her own reasons went deeper than those of mere fascination for a colorful rogue.

At last the dark shape of *The Adventuress* came into sight, righted now, and riding gently on the incoming tide. It had been Robbie's intention to wait until the early hours before moving smoothly out with the tide with the minimum of effort on the oars. Now, the circumstances had changed.

With a slap on the horse's rump, Robbie sent the nag and carriage away, and hauled Sarah on board, calling out as he did so that they had been spied and must get under way immediately.

"Get below, Sarah," he said tersely. "Stay in your cabin, or mine if you prefer to see ahead, and don't worry unduly. This inlet has always been an undetected retreat. Pray that it continues to be so."

He had half-forgotten her, already busying himself with his men, who were scurrying about like insects to do his bidding, and ready at a minute's notice to be under way. She remembered being told that when necessity made flight imminent, any man not yet returned from an evening's merrymaking would be left behind, but it was rare that any failed to obey the order to be aboard at sundown. They

178

risked death by hanging if they were apprehended on land, probably without even the dignity of a trial.

She went to Robbie's cabin rather than her own, wanting the comfort of his trappings around her, even if he was occupied elsewhere. No lights were allowed on the ship when they were making way, but through the wide windows she could make out the dark shadows of the marshes, and the gradual closing-in of the narrow river inlet and its bordering undergrowth. As the river deepened and narrowed, they were less vulnerable than in the marshy shallows, where the land was flat and easily traversed by horsemen.

But as the minutes passed, and there were no sounds of pursuit or gunshots, it seemed that Robbie had been right, and this time they were safe. Sarah could hear the heavy creak of the oars, and the dip and slide into the water as the crew took *The Adventuress* swiftly out to sea. The crew would be straining against the tide, the power of the tide demanding all their strength.

Sarah wondered uneasily if they would blame her for this hasty departure, thinking that their captain had conceded to a woman's needs in playing the gentleman for a few pleasant hours. She hoped fervently that there would be no repercussions on her account, no revived threat of mutiny.

Slowly she realized that the vista was changing. The undergrowth was diminishing, the river widening slightly at its mouth. The entrance was on a wild and lonely stretch of coast, and ahead of her was the great open expanse of ocean. And she, who had always been so afraid of the sea, had never been so thankful to see it. Once well out among the dipping waves, they would be lost from sight of land, and safe, at least for the time being.

After a time, the creaking of the oars stopped, and Sarah heard muffled orders as the sails were unfurled, and then the more regular motion as the ship plowed through the water under sail, replacing the uneven rhythm of the oars.

Only then did she allow herself to breathe properly and

deeply, and realized that she had been breathing shallowly for a long time. Her ribs felt painful, both from tension and fear, and when she heard the cabin door open and close, she whirled round with a cry, and seconds later she was held fast in Robbie's arms.

"Hush now, my lassie. We're safely away from the coast, and none will seek us out under cover of darkness. Hush now, love, there's nothing more to fear."

He stroked her hair and held her fast for long moments. He spoke soothingly to her as if to a child. His body was warm against her own, and reassuring. But she was not a child, and it was not as a child that she craved his tenderness. She looked up into his face.

Thin wisps of light from the crescent of the new moon between the dispersing clouds revealed the outline of his chiseled features, darkening his eyes so that she could not see them properly. But there was no disguising the rapid beat of his heart, or the way he was aroused because she was so soft and pliant in his arms.

And she loved him so much, and wanted him so much, and it had been so easy all this evening to imagine themselves in another place, another time. She couldn't bear to end this night alone. She didn't want to let the illusion fade.

"Robbie, let me stay," she whispered against his chest. "I want—I want—"

He tipped up her chin so that he could see her face more clearly.

"What do you want, my lovely?" he asked softly, making her say the words, as he had predicted she would. For a second, pride fought with longing, and longing won.

"I want you to love me," she breathed. "Please love me, Robbie—"

He scooped her up in his arms as if she weighed nothing, and carried her gently to his bedroom compartment, laying her on the elaborate bedcover. He pressed feather-light kisses on her mouth and eyes every inch of the way, and when she lay there, trembling, he knelt beside her and his fingers reached for the fastenings of her gown and he began to free them.

Minutes later he had discarded his clothes as well as hers, and he lay beside her, gazing down on her loveliness. He caught his breath, for now that the clouds had dispersed, the clear starry night revealed her perfect body to him, and to his own intense surprise, Robbie felt awed for the first time by a woman.

"You're so beautiful I'm almost afraid to touch you," he said huskily.

She spoke as tremulously, her emotion so great that for a moment she had to be flippant to hide it.

"Can this really be Black Robbie speaking? The one who fears nothing?"

"Perhaps at this moment Black Robbie is furthest from my thoughts," he answered, his palms beginning a sensual trail over her breasts and caressing each tip as they swelled to meet him. "All that matters now is that a man has a lovely woman awaiting his pleasure."

"Then why do you wait so long in pleasuring me, Sir?" Sarah could hardly believe the whispered words had come from her throat. They were the words of a wanton, hungry for a man. But not just any man. Only this man would satisfy her. Only this man, out of all the world.

She heard his deep throaty chuckle. "I am only too happy to oblige you, my lady."

His palms moved downward and outward, curving around her hips, and then meeting over her belly. Sarah drew in her breath as the questing fingers divided the dark hair and sought entrance. She held her breath as the sweet sensations for which she had yearned for so long began to invade her senses. She was already drowning in pleasure when of its own volition, it seemed, her hand strayed and found the source of his life-blood.

A searing excitement ran through her. She was not new to

the consummation of a marriage, but Robbie was new to her, and she was new to the potent desire of a young and virile lover, and it was as though she were awakening after a long lonely sleep to the brilliance of sunlight.

"Are you ready for the loving, my lady?" Robbie whispered against the flesh of her breasts.

"Yes—oh yes—" Every pulse in her body was ready and aching for him. "Please love me now—"

"Y siempre, mi cariño," he murmured almost incoherently, and then the weight of him was covering her nakedness, and her thighs opened in invitation as he entered her. He moved slowly at first, savoring every second, every exquisite sensation, and Sarah gloried in his maleness.

This was no savage piratical Black Robbie, ravaging a woman . . . this was no gentle David Roberts, considerate to a fault . . . this was the lover she had always dreamed of. *This was Robert Argyll*, lord of the glens, master of all his domain, his own man . . . and *hers*, Sarah thought feverishly. Forever hers, for no one else would have him now.

The thrusting movements became more demanding, and Sarah's needs rose to meet Robbie's. They were a writhing tangle of flesh on flesh, heart on heart, and when the climax of desire was imminent, they soared toward it together, and clung for wordless moments afterward.

"Do you remember the Spanish words I taught you?" Robbie murmured against her mouth.

"I don't know," she whispered, still too dazed with love to think properly.

"If you would know what they mean, remember them and say them now, my Sarah."

Sarah struggled to put the unfamiliar words together. "*Te quiero—mi cariño*—is that right? But I think I should know what I'm saying!" She protested weakly, her pupils still enlarged with passion.

"It means, 'I love you, my darling,'" he said.

Sarah caught her breath. "You tricked me."

His mouth covered hers for a lingering kiss. She tasted his tongue as it moved sensuously around her mouth and then teased the tip of her own.

"The words mean I love you, my darling." He repeated the words. Sarah felt a wild tingling sensation run through her veins. *Did he mean it? Had the impossible happened?* She had asked for the moon, and if he truly loved her she would be getting the sun and stars as well.

But she was too afraid to ask, to dare to hope. Robbie pulled her into his arms again, where their glistening bodies made them as near one being as they had been but moments ago.

"Are you listening properly to me, my sweet and lovely lassie? I don't deny that I've fought against the inevitable, but you've captured my heart as surely as I've captured your sweet self."

She leaned against him with a soft sigh of joy, her emotions so intense that they defied words. Soft salty tears ran down her cheeks, and Robbie felt them hot and damp against his chest.

"Does it offend you so much, my lassie, to have a pirate captain lust for you? Does it make you suspect that I might never let you go back to that other life now?"

"Would you ever send me back?" she asked, her voice muffled against him.

She felt him go very still, and knew that he had registered her choice of words.

"Are you suggesting that you do not want to go back?" he asked at last. "You know my life, Sarah. Are you saying that you would choose to share it voluntarily?"

"I thought I had already done that. How many times could I have betrayed you, and did not?"

"Other women have been as charmed by the thought of saving the wicked pirate captain." He spoke with a fine irony against himself.

"But I am not other women." Sarah's voice was no more

than a whisper. She lifted her face to look directly into his. She felt his breath on her skin, and it was as ragged as her own.

"No, you are not other women, my lassie. You are that one in a million every man hopes he will find. And I've wanted you from the first moment."

"Then why are you being hesitant when I offer myself to you?" Sarah suddenly realized that this was not the ardent response she had expected. Robbie smoothed her soft cheek with one finger until it reached the curve of her mouth. He traced its contours, already so known and loved.

"Because, my dearest one, this is not the life for one such as you. Yes, I could make you my pirate woman. There have been others who roamed the seas among men, scavenging and pillaging. But that's not for you, my Sarah. Not for *my* lady."

He moved away from her in sudden anger, sitting up so abruptly that she fell back against the pillows, her eyes wide with surprise.

"The devil of it is, sweet Sarah, that although I desperately wanted you in my bed, I never wanted you in my heart. It was not meant to happen this way. Black Robbie had to be free of all female entanglements, save those he used and discarded." He gave a short laugh. "It does not paint a very pretty picture, does it?"

Sarah stared at him, hardly able to believe what she was hearing. "And yet you offered me marriage, to keep to your own rules—which, I may remind you, we have already broken!"

"I need no reminding! The thought will torment me often enough. And aye, I offered you marriage. Or rather, I taunted you with it!" He was brutally honest now.

"And what if I had agreed to it!"

"But I knew that you wouldn't, so I was quite safe. My plans included marriage even less than yours."

"So why did you even mention it?" Sarah was becoming

184

alternately bewildered and incensed by these changes of mood.

"For your own protection," Robbie said briefly. "I had to give you the choice. But if the crew ever suspected our relationship now, they would mutiny for certain, and God knows what would happen to you then."

She licked her dry lips. "And it could still happen at any time," she whispered.

"So it could, and because of it we must be extra careful," he said grimly. She noted that he didn't mention marriage again, but she brushed the thought aside and reverted to something else he had said, needing to move away from such unpleasant thoughts.

"You said you never wanted me in your heart," she said slowly. She looked at him unblinkingly, her blue eyes wide and luminous. "Is that where I am now, Robbie?"

She caught her breath, knowing that it was where she wanted to be, for now and always. Nothing else mattered. The past was yesterday. All that mattered was now, and beyond. She desperately wanted to erase that grim look from his face and see the tenderness there again.

He spoke softly. "Do I really need to tell you, my lassie? I discover that I'm as vulnerable as any other man when it comes to matters of the heart."

Perversely, Sarah refused to be satisfied with his ambiguous statements.

"Why do you not say the words, then? Say exactly what you mean, for I've suddenly become very thick-headed."

She saw his twisted smile. "Oh, I think not! I think my Sarah is the most clear-headed woman I've ever known. And I always vowed that I would never tell a woman I loved her unless I had a future to offer her."

"So what exactly is stopping you?" she cajoled.

After a moment he bent his head and kissed her swiftly and harshly. He held the back of her head in one hand, and with the other she felt the curl of his fingers around her throat.

"I think you've completely taken leave of your senses. You're my captive, and I could crush you with one blow if I chose, and none of my crew would raise an eyebrow," he said roughly. "Is that not what the world expects of Black Robbie?"

"It's not what I know of Robert Argyll, and he's the one I want." The words were out before she could stop them.

He spoke brutally, still holding her fast. "Now I know you're mad. I told you never to speak of that. Robert Argyll is dead and buried."

"But he's not! He's alive and he's my lover, and he's not remotely like Black Robbie or David Roberts. He has lands waiting to be claimed and a new life to be lived with the right woman by his side."

He let go of her and walked out of the bedchamber in a rage he couldn't explain, pulling on a dressing robe as he went. The fact that he himself had been playing with similar thoughts vanished like a will-o-the-wisp. It was like asking a man to revert to the sweet innocence of childhood.

Sarah lay wide-eyed and afraid, wondering just how foolish she had been in revealing all that she felt about him. Knowing in her heart that she had gone too far by letting herself be carried away by a lovely dream.

Why should Robert Argyll ever want to go back to Scotland? Yet she knew that he did. He had already told her so. She kept the crumb of that in her heart as she struggled with the fastenings of her clothes with shaking fingers and crept out of Robbie's cabin.

She didn't say good night, and he never acknowledged that he was aware of her leaving. At the door she glanced back at the lonely figure standing in front of the windows, gazing out at a vast empty ocean as alien as any foreign shore. With a woman's intuition, she knew she was right. She was his woman now, and one day, God willing, she would be his wife.

Chapter 13

The sound of a loud disturbance on deck seeped into Sarah's mind even before she awoke properly the following morning. For a few brief seconds she was still caught up in the magic of the previous evening, the aesthetic delight of being ashore, visiting the small theater as if everything were perfectly normal again. Even the sudden alarm at the risk of capture had added a certain excitement to the evening, since with it had come the certainty that Robbie would save her, come what may.

And then she was suffused with the memory of that other magic, of lying in his arms and knowing he was everything she had ever wanted . . .

She awoke fully as the sounds above grew louder. Men's voices, shouting angrily, and then the sudden blistering sound of a pistol being fired, as it to restore order. *Or was it worse?* Sarah shivered. There were those among the crew with vicious tempers, and it had not been unheard of in the past for one to shoot out another's brains in a fit of rage.

She sat up quickly, surprised to find her breakfast dishes already in the cabin. Tomby must have crept in while she was sleeping, or perhaps he had been given orders not to waken her. With sudden suspicion, she went to the door and rattled it. It was firmly locked.

187

"Tomby, open this door," she snapped, sure that he'd be at his post outside. For a moment there was no answer, and then she heard his frightened voice.

"Cap'n say no, Missy. Cap'n say you safer inside."

"Why am I safer inside? What's happening? There's no fighting, is there?"

So far, they had encountered no other ships on the journey. Theirs was a small ship and quite speedy when speed was needed, adept at keeping out of sight of vessels that might provoke a battle at sea. Black Robbie's goals on this voyage were the rich merchant ships that unloaded their gold and silver at the coastal trading stations along the Guinea coast. These were his usual haunts. As a diversion there might sometimes be brief sojourns nearer home, a rich landowner's party for his ward, for example, where there would be jewelery and hostages and funning for the crew. . . .

Sarah ignored the thought, waiting impatiently for Tomby to answer. The bedlam on deck had started up again, and she could hardly hear him, even with her ear pressed tight to the cabin door.

"Tomby, are we in danger from another ship?" she demanded to know. Her heart hammered with fear. There could be bloodshed and death. There could be cannon fire from a King's vessel, the pirate ship could be split wide open. And if it was, the sea would pour in . . . she hardly noticed the little moan emitted from her throat for the way her heart was racing now.

"No, Missy. Quartermaster called trial, and Cap'n say to keep you below out of sight."

A trial! So that was what this was all about! And it would be on account of her. Because Robbie had taken her ashore and risked the necks of all the crew. A woman on board was bad luck, unless she were the captain's wife.

The sweet thought of last night was the last thing on her mind now. If he asked her to marry him for the sake of calm among his men, she would refuse. She'd be damned if she'd marry him on those terms.

She forgot about the breakfast and dressed quickly. She ignored boyish garments, and donned the least flamboyant of the gowns, a bronze silk that shimmered and rustled when she moved, but was less revealing at the throat. The last thing she wanted was to incite the men even further, but if trial there was, then she had the right to be present. And as herself, not disguised as a sprat.

"Tomby, open this door," she ordered.

"No, Missy."

After a moment she began to wail as if she was in great pain. "I'm ill, Tomby. Cap'n will beat you within an inch of your life if you let me die. Help me onto the bed, for pity's sake!"

After a few moments, she heard the key turn in the lock, and she was ready for him. As soon as the door opened, she pulled him inside, spluttering and struggling.

"I'm sorry, Tomby, but I'm locking you in. Cap'n will think I overpowered you when you brought my breakfast. I'll see that you're not flogged, provided you agree with everything I say. Do you understand?"

"Yes, Missy," he croaked, his eyes rolling in his black face.

"Good. Eat my breakfast if you want something to do. I'll probably be gone some time," she said hurriedly, and locked the door behind her.

She didn't look forward to her involvement in the so-called trial, but it was impossible for her to sit there twiddling her thumbs, not knowing what her fate was to be. The moment she appeared on deck, the men fell silent, then a dull muttering began among them. Robbie strode forward and gripped her arm cruelly.

"What the devil do you think you're doing? Get back below and leave men's business to men."

"I think it's my business, too, Sir! If I'm the cause of all this fuss, then I've a right to be heard."

189

A few catcalls answered her words in the affirmative. Some of the men were clearly amused at the thought of a woman giving evidence for herself.

"Let the woman have her say!" came the general consensus from the hecklers. "'Twill make no difference to the outcome."

Sarah shivered at these words. She lifted her chin and shook off Robbie's hand as if it were a troublesome insect. She resisted the impulse to rub at the tender, reddened skin, where the marks of his fingers could be clearly seen. She moved to the center of the pirates, afraid of the grinning, lascivious faces, encouraged by the slight sympathy she saw on a few. Flint and Surgeon, in particular, watched her thoughtfully.

"Say your piece then, woman," Quartermaster bellowed above the din. "And make it quick."

Sarah glared at him. He was a bull of a man, and she doubted that he had ever known the pleasures of a woman's love, or softened toward one.

"May I please know the charge, before I start to defend myself?"

"Sarah, for God's sake," Robbie said angrily, knowing that this was a complete waste of time. There was only one way he could redeem this situation, and in her present mood she would never agree.

She stared defiantly at him, and then turned deliberately away, putting every bit of sincerity she could muster into her voice, and appealing directly to the uncouth dregs of men on whose say-so it seemed her life depended.

"Since no one will tell me of what I'm charged, I presume it's the fact that I am a woman. And because your captain is undoubtedly a gentleman, regardless of his reputation as a pirate, and behaved in a gentlemanly way toward me."

She looked around them, fixing her gaze deliberately on one face after another. They had fallen silent, and she felt a glimmer of hope.

"I cannot believe that all of you have quite forgotten what it means to behave like a gentleman toward a lady. Some of you must have known other times, when you dressed in decent clothes and held your head high. You were not always fugitives."

"Get on with it, woman," Quartermaster grunted. Some carped loudly in agreement, while others were just as vehement toward letting her finish. Robbie's face was set and angry, and she knew he resented this intervention.

"I presume most of you chose this life," Sarah went on, trying not to let her voice tremble. "But I did not!"

"Ye put up no fight when Cap'n brought ye to the ship," one man said disagreeably.

She glared at him. "I was escaping from another fate that I did not choose! Am I to pay just for being a woman all my life? I assumed Black Robbie would abandon me somewhere along the coast so that I could be free. I did not expect to be a prisoner for the rest of my life, having to hide myself in urchin's clothes. Nor did I expect to be handed back to my family for the highest price."

"Have ye heard enough, men?" Quartermaster clearly did not like the way some of the crew were shifting uneasily at this impassioned speech, and Sarah decided to resort to more feminine wiles. It wasn't difficult. Her emotions were so heightened, it was easy for the tears to spill over.

"I beg you to think carefully before you decide what to do with me. Remember your own mothers and sisters! What kind of fate would you wish for them at the hands of pirates?"

Surgeon put in his say. "The woman does no harm on board."

"She goes against the rules. There should be no woman on board, unless she be the captain's wife!"

Sarah saw them look toward Robbie. From the uproar at the man's words, some would clearly agree to this way out, others were against it.

"What do ye say to it, Cap'n?" Quartermaster said, a leering smile on his hard face.

Robbie's voice was cold as ice. "I say no. I'll not be blackmailed into marrying any woman. Nor will I put her over the side. She stays on hostage terms until we return to England, and I'll fight every man who says otherwise. Despite Quartermaster's rights to dispense law and order, I'll remind you that this is my ship, and my word overrides all in times of dissent."

The two men stared at each other in a silent clash of wills, and Sarah saw Robbie's hand moved imperceptibly to the dagger at his waist. She had no doubt that he'd use it if provoked, just as the other man would. There was real hatred between them, she thought fearfully, and her presence had probably brought it to a head.

"There's another solution," Surgeon said rapidly, and the crew turned to him with some relief, since the trial appeared to be going nowhere.

"Name it," Quartermaster snapped.

"The woman could be sworn in as a member of the crew. She offered some nursing assistance once, and could be useful to me. The rest of ye are nothing but useless when it comes to holding a man's head when he's racked wi' fever and spilling out his guts."

He watched Sarah steadily as he spoke, and she avoided flinching, sensing that this was some sort of test. The rest would be watching her too, and if she swooned now, she'd lose the small advantage Surgeon was offering her—if advantage it was! But if the alternative was death by drowning, she thought, gritting her teeth to stop them from chattering, then she would take anything.

"We'll take a vote on it," Quartermaster snarled, as the crew yelled their opinions. "'Tis not the first time a woman's been sworn in as crew member on a pirate ship, though never on this one. Do we want her on Surgeon's terms?"

Sarah didn't dare look at Robbie, nor guess what he was

thinking. She knew that he always stood back in matters he considered petty squabbles. They were always settled by the quartermaster. But in this, he was more closely involved.

The voting was not quite unanimous, but the majority of the crew decided there was a certain appeal in being tended by a woman when they ailed. Quartermaster had clearly anticipated this.

"If you bastards think to report sick every morning to get the sniff of a woman's skirts, I'll have your rumps," he roared. He turned to Robbie. "She's to be sworn in, then, Cap'n, if you agree to it."

"If *I* agree to it. You do think to ask my opinion, then?" Robbie asked sarcastically.

"Aye, naturally, but ye've seen that 'tis the general wish," the man said, blustering. In brute force, he could get his way with any man. In intellect and verbal persuasion, his rating was vastly lower than that of the captain, and both knew it.

"What of my wish?" Sarah blazed. "Do I have no say on whether I wish to be made a member of a pirate crew?"

"You do not," Robbie said curtly. "The woman will be sworn in according to the ship's articles at noon this day," he stated to the ship's company, turned on his heel and went below.

Sarah stood in bewilderment as the crew dispersed to go about their business, as if reacting to some silent command. Only Surgeon remained. He towered over her, no compromise in his eyes.

"Don't thank me, Mistress Huxley. There may well come a time when ye wish ye'd been thrown to the sharks in return for your eloquence."

"*Thank* you?" she spluttered. "For giving me the shame of being made a *pirate?*"

"For saving your life," he retorted, and stomped away from her.

Spots of sunlight danced haphazardly in front of Sarah's eyes as the hazy morning blazed into brilliant life. But she felt none of its warmth at that moment, realizing that Surgeon's words were almost certainly true.

She was chilled by the thought. The sentence for endangering the ship's company was death, and not even Robbie could have saved her this time. He had stonily refused to marry her . . . .

Yet the fault had been all his! It had been his idea to take her to the theater, to give her some semblance of normality. And hers was the punishment, merely because she was a woman. The stinging tears were very real now, and she stumbled below to unlock her cabin door and throw herself on her bunk, her shoulders heaving.

"Is Missy still ill?" a frightened voice said.

She sat up, remembering Tomby. He hadn't touched her breakfast, and Sarah realized she was very hungry.

"No, I'm not ill, and I promise that Cap'n won't punish you for opening the door to me," she told him recklessly. "You can go now, Tomby, and tell Cookie he'll have to manage without me from now on."

She'd be damned if she was going to spend hours in the galley doing the menial tasks asked of her now. It would be bad enough to take up nursing duties, which was something she'd never done before. Especially tending to the wounds and the sickness of men who were less than clean, and were more frequently foul. The thought made her blanch, but she would never let any of them know it. It would be just what they expected of a female.

If she had thought Robbie would come to her cabin to try and put things right between them, she was mistaken. The sun rose higher in the sky, and still he did not come. The cabin grew stuffy as the ship sailed steadily southward on a direct course for the African continent, and as the time dragged toward noon, she was still left alone.

Of course, Sarah thought bitterly, Robbie's most pressing need would be to restore his self-esteem among his men. Never mind about her fraught nerves after the farce of a trial that morning. Never mind that in the darkness of the night they had shared the most beautiful and intimate experience possible between a man and a woman.

She drew in a breath that was sharp as a pain. How *could* he treat her so? In a moment of weakness the thought overwhelmed her. When she had believed for one rapturous hour that he was hers, and she was his.

So be it, Sarah thought, hardening her heart with a great effort. If he could show so clearly that he could discard her so easily—that he didn't want her—then she could do the same toward him.

Tomby was sent to fetch her when the sun was directly overhead. Sarah left the cabin with some relief, feeling decidedly uncomfortable in its stickiness. But on deck it was even hotter. Even the deckboards seemed to steam, the underlying smell of stale vinegar causing her to wrinkle her nose. The weight of the heavy petticoats she wore beneath the bronze gown made her think wistfully for a moment of the loose freedom of the boy's garb she had so easily rejected.

Almost the entire crew was on deck, save those whose attention was needed elsewhere. Far above, among the billowing sails, the man in the crow's-nest looked tiny and vulnerable. With a shock, Sarah saw that a black flag was flying from the mast.

"'Tis always so when a new crew member is sworn in," Flint muttered to her, seeing her gape. "'Twill be hauled down as soon as the swearing's done."

"I see," Sarah murmured. For of course, they wouldn't want to risk the flag being spotted by another ship. To Sarah it would have seemed more appropriate to have performed this ceremony at midnight, under cover of darkness. It would be the appropriate time, for shiftless thieves like these. There was no choice left to her but to become one of them, she thought in shock.

Robbie appeared from below, a scroll in his hands, the ship's articles that she had already seen in his cabin. As she had become used to their wording, she had been more amused than horrified at some of the orders they contained.

She felt very differently about them now. She would be obliged to swear to honor them, with as much dignity as if she knelt before her king to swear allegiance. The ceremony was a blasphemy against the Crown of England.

Robbie looked at her coldly. This was obviously to be the captain's duty. Quartermaster stood at his side with a scowl like thunder on his coarse features. Robbie raised his hand, and Quartermaster bellowed out the announcement.

"This here ceremony is to swear in the new crew member, Mistress Sarah Huxley, for good or ill, to abide by the ship's articles and to swear loyalty to the captain and crew at all times. Such failure to do so will result in instant death. Does the new member agree to the terms?"

He fixed his black gaze on Sarah. She shivered, knowing that he, most of all, did not agree to any of this.

"I do," she mumbled, her mouth dry as dust.

Quartermaster glanced toward Robbie and nodded. Robbie looked into Sarah's eyes for the first time, and she saw nothing there but coldness. At this moment they were worlds apart. It was difficult to believe that anything had happened between them.

"You, Mistress Sarah Huxley, will repeat the articles of the ship after me, and swear to abide by them. You will place your hand on my heart, and I on yours, with each article. After each swearing, we break contact, and resume it again for the next. Do you understand?"

"Yes," she said.

At a small rustling of laughter among the crew, Robbie stared frigidly around the company, and they fell silent at once.

"If any man here thinks there's aught funny in the swearing in of a new crew member, let him say so. All here have gone through the same procedure, so let no one put it to ridicule."

But none of them was a woman, Sarah thought faintly. Robbie handed the scroll to Quartermaster, who unrolled it and held it open before the two of them.

Robbie knew his own rules so well that he hardly needed to read them at all. Sarah was unsure how to proceed, and then she felt his hand reach out roughly for hers and put it over his heart. He then placed his own hand over her heart, and began to recite the first article.

The words were a jumble of meaningless phrases to her. Robbie stated each rule first, and she repeated it parrot-fashion, glancing at the scroll from time to time to be sure she was word-perfect.

But for most of the time she stared into the eyes of the man who stared just as intently into hers. She felt the uneven beat of his heart beneath her palm, and knew that he must feel the wild pulsing of her own beneath his fingers.

Each time they broke apart she was still conscious of the pressure of his hand. Each time it returned to her breast she felt a tingling finger-tip pressure that assured her that however much he tried to detach himself from all personal feelings, Black Robbie was not totally unaware of her as a woman.

And even more than from the touch of his hand, she could see the truth in his eyes. They may hide many things from his crew, but Sarah had already known him more intimately than any one of them. She stood close enough to him to be aware of the widening of his pupils, and guessed instantly that her own must be mirroring his. She could read passion in the amber depths that were flecked with little tawny lights she had never noticed before.

What was being revealed in her own, despite her striving to keep her face impassive? He must surely see all the love she couldn't hide, despite the circumstances.

The ceremony went on for as long as it took to read out the

197

lengthy scroll, and afforded an intimacy neither could have foreseen. Or perhaps Robbie had envisaged it, perhaps that was why he had seemed to hold himself so rigidly in check at the beginning, knowing how emotional this swearing-in would be for the two of them.

"No crew member shall bring a boy or woman on board for lustful purposes . . ."

Steadily, Sarah repeated this particular ship's rule, careful to keep all expression out of her voice. Lust? Had it been no more than lust last night? She could not, would not believe it was so. She had seen a small flicker in Robbie's eyes as he had said the words, and knew intuitively that he was remembering too.

At last the scroll had been fully unrolled, and every article had been sworn and accepted.

"There is one final ritual," Robbie informed her, and then spoke loudly for all to hear. "The new crew member will be known as Huxley. And following the faithful practice of swearing-in aboard *The Adventuress*, this embrace is an affirmation that no lust will exist between crew members on board my ship. The ritual will be carried out."

Sarah felt a moment's fright. And then she felt his arms close around her. The final seal of piracy on *The Adventuress* was for the captain to embrace the new crew member with a chaste kiss on both cheeks.

There were subdued cheers from the crew, the black flag was hauled down at once, and the ceremony was over.

"You will take up your new duties with Surgeon as soon as he requires you," Robbie said. "Meanwhile you may come to my cabin for a tot of rum, which is the habitual private sealing of the ceremony."

She followed him numbly. This day was the most bizarre in a life that had become filled with bizarre days. She hardly knew who she was any more. She was *Huxley* now, she reminded herself. Huxley. It sounded cold and impersonal. And despite the gown she wore, Sarah felt that the name imposed on her stripped her of all femininity. She felt more like weeping than at any other time on the whole voyage.

She entered Robbie's cabin behind him and closed the door, leaning against it for a moment because her legs were refusing to hold her up. She would not give in to fainting now, she vowed. She would not.

"Drink this. I fancy you would prefer it to rum, and it is the only concession I will allow," Robbie said.

Sarah took the drink of brandy he thrust at her and drank obediently. The bitter liquid slid down her throat, making her cough.

"Thank you Sir. May I go now—Sir?" she asked woodenly.

He came to her and put his arms around her. They were no longer cruel, but imprisoned her with a sweet and remembered tenderness.

"Oh Sarah, Sarah, do you not think I would have wanted things to happen in some other way than this?"

She remained rigid in his arms, unable yet to yield to him.

"Do you forget my name already, Captain? I am Huxley for the foreseeable future, am I not?"

"Not to me," Robbie said softly.

"Then am I to understand that the captain is suggesting that he and I break one of the very rules to which I have just sworn?" she asked, her mouth half-curling at the edges. She was unconsciously coquettish, and to her surprise, he gave a heavy sigh.

"No, my sweet lassie, I am not."

Sarah stared at him. He released her and led her to one of the leather chairs, seating himself on the far side of the oak desk. But they were separated by more than a piece of furniture, Sarah thought. Whatever his faults, Robbie had a fierce loyalty to his crew, and she knew instantly that he would abide by his rules. *And no boy or woman would be brought on his ship for lustful purposes.* By dubbing her Huxley, pirate crew member, Robbie would be obliged to alienate himself from all repetition of last night's liaison. She knew it even before he told her. She knew too that it was the price he paid for her life.

"Robbie, what's to become of me?" she asked huskily.

"If you've got any sense, you'll get away from the ship and disappear as soon as we return to England," he said brutally. "This is no life for you, though you'll be safe enough now, as long as you abide by the rules and go about your duties sensibly."

His words took her by surprise. "You mean, you wouldn't try to come after me if I wanted to go back to Endor House?" she asked in amazement.

"Is that what you want?"

"Of course it's not!" she said at once. "Although sometimes I miss Aunt Lily dreadfully, and I fret over the heartache I must have caused her."

"And Jonas Endor?"

She shuddered. "No, I do not miss Jonas! And I would never go back to marry him. I would go to the Thorleys, perhaps, and ask them for sanctuary. Anyway, Jonas would probably not want me as his wife now, after—" She felt a blush warming her cheeks.

"You mean because Jonas and the rest of the world will naturally assume that we have been lovers all this while," Robbie said, leaning back in his chair against the windows, so that his hair was lit by a halo of sunlight.

"Yes," she said in a mottled voice. With anyone else, she would have found it impossible to talk so dispassionately in broad daylight about that one perfect act of love that had taken place in the soft intimacy of darkness. With Robbie, she felt able to say anything she chose.

"And I regret with all my heart that it took so long to prove him right, and that our relationship must be so quickly curtailed."

"Must it?" Sarah demanded, uncaring if the question was immodest or not.

"Sarah, you know that it must. I cannot continue to allow one rule for my men and another for myself. The fear of mutiny is always on my mind. I fear for you more than myself, but I don't forget my duty to the men as well."

"Then why did you refuse so adamantly to marry me, so that none of this would have happened?" she cried out, all the hurt spilling out of her.

He didn't speak for a long moment, and Sarah knew she had gone too far. She had humiliated herself by bursting out with such a thought. She burned with embarrassment, and then felt Robbie's finger lift her chin so that her eyes were forced to meet his. He had come around the desk and leaned toward her.

"Because, my lassie, I will choose the time and the place when I ask my woman to marry me. I taunted you with marriage once before, when marriage to you would have meant nothing to me. Another vow to be broken, and too many vows have been broken already," he said with quiet dignity.

Sarah's heart missed a beat and then raced on. The moment was so poignant, she could not bear it, and she answered it with some flippancy. "I hope you'll be sure to let me know when you change your mind, Captain."

He gave a low laugh. "Why would I not? I've found no other woman capable of entwining herself in my heart."

It may have been a promise or a tease. Sarah had no way of knowing. She only knew she was extraordinarily tired, as if she had come a very long way in a very short time.

And since she was not obliged to report to Surgeon immediately, she begged leave to go to her own cabin to rest awhile. She hated the misfortune that had now made her officially Huxley, pirate crew member, but she could never hate the man. For good or ill, he had captured more than her heart. He had captured all her hopes for the future. She accepted unreservedly that he was a most unlikely and unsuitable husband—but he was the only one she would ever want.

Chapter 14

After she had been sworn in as a member of the crew, the voyage took on a different aspect for Sarah. The sexual tension between herself and Robbie simmered like an active volcano, ever ready to erupt. Sometimes it took only a moment when their glances locked, or their fingers touched, and all the vibrant sensations would surge through her again. She guessed that it was the same for him.

But she had seen the sense of his words. While they were on board the ship, there must be no repetition of their passion. She couldn't think beyond the voyage. But she knew only too well that if the crew suspected the captain was breaking his own rules, there would be mutiny. Coupled with her natural fear of what that entailed was guilt that her own sexuality had pushed herself and Robbie into a situation from which there was no turning back. It wasn't entirely Robbie's fault that his own rules had been broken.

By now, Sarah had assumed her role as Surgeon's assistant, and stoically did anything required. She'd begun in defiance and had worn women's clothes, but soon realized the impracticality of it. Skirts were a hindrance on deck, and became too hot as the ship moved into Equatorial waters. She was glad now of the boy's garments, which suited her new status as Huxley. In any case, she felt less conspicuous out of women's clothes, and less likely to invite bawdy comments.

Sometimes there was little to do in her new role. A fairly regular task would be to hold a man's head steady while Surgeon poured distasteful medicine down his throat. But there were more arduous tasks that required her assistance. She had to steel herself while Surgeon picked burrowing weevils out of a man's flesh, and tried not to flinch as a gaping wound was pulled together with rough stitches, with nothing but a flush of brandy over the wound to quell the flow of blood, and a generous swig of the spirit down the throat to dull the pain.

Some days there was more work than others. Before, if a man raved in a fever, he was left to get over it or simply die. Now, providing she had no more pressing work, she was there to wipe his brow with dampened cloths and ease a ration of water through his shaking lips.

Once, a man had staggered about in agony with a pistol wound delivered as a gun went off accidentally, and she watched in fascinated horror as Surgeon deftly hacked out the shot, ignoring the patient's screams as if they were the twitterings of a bird.

"Ye do well, Huxley," Surgeon had said on that occasion, when the man's arm was red and raw, but mercifully free of shot. "Ye stand firm like a man instead of swooning like a woman."

It was meant to be praise, and Sarah took it as such. And gradually, as the time passed, she realized it wasn't only Surgeon who was grudgingly glad of her usefulness. Any crewman she had assisted accepted her unquestioningly now, and if the rest still made snide comments about anticipating the softness of a female hand when they were sick, she froze them with one look from her lustrous blue eyes.

It was the captain's privilege to invite whom he pleased to

eat with him privately, and he had seen no reason to curtail their arrangement of taking supper together each evening.

"There's something that puzzles me about the crew, Robbie," she said on one such occasion.

"You surprise me," he grinned. "With your aptitude for foraging out details, I'd have thought there was nothing about this ship or its crew that escaped you now."

Sarah laughed. They enjoyed an easy camaraderie, but neither dared allow it to develop into intimacy. On Sarah's part there was undying love; in Robbie she knew the lust still burned. Whether it was any more than that, she couldn't be sure. But it wasn't their own feelings about which she was curious at this moment.

She felt the heat in her cheeks, wondering how she could put the question delicately. And then she looked into his amber eyes, and knew it wouldn't matter whether she was forthright or not. All the same, she lowered her gaze quickly, for fear he would see the blaze of love there.

"The crew are all lusty men," she said. "I saw the way they cavorted with the ladies at my birthday ball, and although nothing of a physical nature took place, from the tales some of the ladies told afterward, you would think they had all been ravished there and then!"

A sudden swift image of that lovely time swept into her mind with bittersweet nostalgia. The gorgeously colored apparel of the company that evening; the glittering jewels that collectively would be worth a king's ransom; the gentility of her uncle and aunt; the way Black Robbie had caught her up in his arms and claimed the kiss that unwittingly was to spoil her for any other man. . . .

"Go on, my lovely," he said, in that shiveringly sensual voice that told her he was remembering it too.

Sarah spoke quickly, willing the sweet images to fade, because suddenly they were too heartbreakingly real. "And I recall how you told me that when we went ashore in Spain, some of the crew would visit certain señoritas. I presume it is the same whenever we go ashore?"

"Should it not be so?" Robbie asked, amused. "The men have need of certain comforts after long weeks at sea."

"Yes, so I understand." She did not care to wonder if Robbie, too, had sought these certain comforts on other occasions. Why should he not have? He was the most physical man she had known.

"What is it you want to know, Sarah?" He pressed, seeing her flounder.

She took a deep breath. "Your rules make it clear that no boy or woman is to be brought on board for lustful purposes." She closed her mind to the unpleasant thoughts the word "boy" evoked in her mind.

"True."

"But how is it the men appear to have no inclinations? They appear menacing at first, but I suspect that they are not really aroused by my presence. To my great relief, of course! But are you quite sure that Tomby is in no danger? It embarrasses me even to mention such things, but I've grown fond of the boy and wouldn't wish him to come to harm of any kind."

Her cheeks flamed now at the indelicacy of the reference to Tomby. Until that moment she had not even considered it. She had no real knowledge of such an abomination, except to be aware that it existed, and had, probably since the beginning of time.

She realized that Robbie was tickled by her question, and his reaction annoyed her. "I see you do not take my queries seriously, Sir! Have you no concern for the boy you saved? Nor for me? I've been thrown in close contact with the men since becoming Surgeon's assistant, and am frequently obliged to be alone with one of them. Do you not consider the risk I take?"

Robbie poured some more brandy for himself and looked at her thoughtfully. "You are not at risk, Sarah, and neither is Tomby. Have you not heard of saltpeter?"

"Who is this? Is it some rival pirate I should know about?" she asked suspiciously.

He couldn't contain his laughter any longer, and she got to her feet furiously. Her eyes blazed down into his, her breasts rising and falling in the low-neck gown of chartreuse silk as her breathing quickened. The topaz at her throat caught every vestige of light as though it were liquid gold.

"I won't stay here and be the source of your amusement," she raged. "I shall walk the deck alone, since you consider it to be so safe."

"Calm down, my lassie." Robbie caught at her hands and drew her to him forcefully. "Dear God, but you have the capacity of changing from sun to storm faster than any woman I've ever met. You will not walk the deck alone. I will walk with you."

"I refuse to go anywhere with you until you tell me what I want to know!"

Robbie's eyes sparkled at the thought of this woman defying him. She was the only one who had ever stood up to him, he mused. The only one with spirit enough to match his own. The only one for whom he had ever felt love mingling with desire. The only one for whom he could give up a way of life, if it were ever asked of him. His thoughts raced ahead, startling him.

"Saltpeter is a substance used to dampen men's ardor," he said abruptly, stemming the disturbing thoughts. "Cookie has orders to use it liberally in the men's rations while we're at sea. It's harmless, and renders them temporarily incapable of lustful intent."

"I see," Sarah said, almost wishing she hadn't asked. "Are the men aware of this?"

Robbie shrugged. "It's normal practice. None have ever questioned it, nor have they been told explicitly that it is so."

"But it's not a rule that applies to the captain?"

Robbie laughed softly, in a way that made Sarah catch her breath. One minute she was standing facing him, still annoyed at what she considered his teasing; the next she was pulled into the circle of his arms, and his lips were on her cheek.

"It is not," he agreed. "Though of late I've wondered if perhaps it should be. We have a long way to travel together yet, my lassie, and the wanting grows more persistent, not less."

She was left in no doubt of his meaning as she felt the hardness of his desire against her. It was strange how the masculine power in his body seemed to melt and weaken her, Sarah thought faintly. But one long sweet kiss was all that they shared before Robbie drew away.

"Come, my love. I think a bracing stroll around the deck is best for us tonight, and then we'll be seen to go to our separate beds."

He picked up her shawl and wrapped it lightly around her slender shoulders. The night would be warm, but the sea breezes could be cool, and Sarah didn't want to risk catching a chill. It wasn't that the thought of Surgeon's medical administrations alarmed her, but now she was needed. It was a new way of thinking, and it felt remarkably satisfying. It was good to be needed.

As it happened, there was hardly a breath of wind that night, just enough to allow the ship to glide smoothly through the dark waters on the current. There was hardly any movement in the shrouds. Overhead the moon was high in a cloudless sky filled with a myriad of stars.

"How much longer before we reach our destination?" Sarah asked, as they leaned on the rail staring into what seemed like eternity.

"Soon, barring any intervention," he said guardedly. "In a few days, hopefully."

She twisted to look at him, leaning her back on the rail. She knew that for all his reckless reputation, Robbie was a man who cared about his ship and his crew, and "any intervention" meant an attack from another ship. So far they had been lucky, due mainly to Robbie's skill in keeping *The Adventuress* away from the regular shipping routes. But once they neared the Guinea Coast, they would be vulnerable.

"Is it so exciting, plundering other ships and frightening helpless women and children? Does it serve some primitive instinct in a man to prove himself so dominant?" she asked without thinking.

Robbie gave a short laugh. "Is that what you think, Sarah? You know my reasons for being here. All that was mine was taken from me, so—"

"So you think that makes it right for you to take what belongs to other people. It doesn't, Robbie. Nothing is more stupid than the old saying that two wrongs make a right. They don't."

"And you have no right to question what I do."

She recognized the coldness in his voice. She had displeased him by questioning what he did with his life. The closeness between them was in danger of slipping away once more, but Sarah went on recklessly, taking a deep breath.

"I think I do have the right. I think you and I have committed ourselves to each other, Robbie. You saved me from drowning in the sea-cave and for that I'm forever obligated to you, and I have done the same for you. That gives us both the right to question each other, apart from—"

"Apart from what?" She realized his coldness had lessened slightly.

"Apart from other considerations," she said evenly.

Did he think she was going to blurt out the fact that she loved him? Even worse, that she was about to declare that being as intimate as two people could be gave her some special rights over him? She was not that foolish. Beasts of the field mounted one another, and that did not make them soul mates.

She felt the curl of his fingers around her own lessen. For a moment she thought he was going to retreat into that solitary world of his once more, where a pirate captain undoubtedly belonged. It was a lonely world, Sarah thought, ever on guard, never sure if his crew were friends or foes, ever roaming the seas and dependent on the carelessness of others to obtain riches and rewards. It was a fool's existence, one that was unworthy of Robert Argyll.

"I think you and I had best continue our stroll and speak of other things," he said. "And before we reach the Guinea Coast, there's something you should know."

She was alert at once. "What is it?"

"We shall tie up in a remote river inlet, and most of the crew will go ashore to survey the heavily guarded coastal trading station before we make our move. We know that a rich Dutch merchant vessel will be loading gold and ivory on board from the trading station. While they play back and forth with their cases, we strike. It's a plan that invariably works, and we want nothing to go wrong before we make a quick retreat."

"Naturally."

"But that's only one reason why I must insist that you remain on board, Sarah. There will be no question of any excursion on shore this time."

She felt acute disappointment. They had been at sea for many weeks now, and the journey back to England would be a tedious one. She was weary of the voyage, and longed for a hot bath in proper surroundings, for nourishing food that didn't have to be constantly inspected for grubs, for cool drinks that weren't rancid and bitter. Until that moment she hadn't realized quite how much she had missed the things in life that she had always taken for granted.

"That's not fair," she began.

He gripped her wrist so tightly she almost cried out.

"Sarah, we shall be on African soil, and there are certain tribes in this area unlike ourselves."

"Well, I know that!" she said sarcastically. "I do have some education. They'll be black-skinned, and probably

209

wear few clothes, if any."

"And they're cannibals," he said baldly.

She stared at him, real fear galloping through her. But not just for herself. For the men, all of them, but mostly for Robbie.

"Cannibals?" She echoed the word faintly.

"Perhaps your education didn't go that far. They have a taste for human flesh," he elaborated. "Mostly, they consider it a delicacy when it's cooked, but occasionally they don't wait for that, and consume it raw, sometimes while the victim is still alive."

"Please—don't—don't tell me any more," Sarah said. The sea and sky seemed to swim in front of her for a second at his graphic words. She cursed her vivid imagination which produced a horrific picture in her mind, and swallowed convulsively.

"I'm sorry, but I felt it was necessary," Robbie said. "Now do you see why I must insist on your staying on board while we're ashore?"

"But what about you? It must be terribly dangerous for you, Robbie."

"I live with danger every day, lassie. Our plans are made, and nothing must be allowed to interfere with them. Do you understand? If you force me to, I shall have you locked in your cabin while we go ashore, with instructions that anyone who unbolts the door no matter how much you plead, will be flogged within an inch of his life. Is that clear?"

"Perfectly. And bolting my door will not be necessary," she said stiffly. "I have a great fear of being locked in anywhere."

"How many more fears do you have that I don't know about, I wonder?"

Sarah laughed shortly. "Not many. How could I, after living with pirates? The fear of seeing the disgust and embarrassment in my Aunt's eyes, perhaps, and the turning away of decent people after I return home."

She stopped. Was she ever going to return home? And where was home? Certainly not at Endor House as the wife of Jonas Endor! She shivered at the thought. And in society's eyes, she would surely be as much an outcast as these rogues of the sea were. Perhaps no one would want to take her in, not even the generous-hearted Thorleys, whose opinion she had always valued highly, and who had looked on her almost as a daughter.

But she had changed beyond recognition since those halcyon days, when a visit to London had been a highlight in her life, to attend the best society balls and grace the theater with her renowned beauty, to ride in an elegant carriage through the parks and turn every male head.

What would they think of her now? For a moment she tried to stand outside herself and see the person she had become. To the genteel Thorleys and all her Uncle's old friends, she would appear to have behaved in a totally heathen fashion. Her skin was tanned by the sun and wind, and was far from being the milky-white complexion of a lady. Her beautiful tumbling dark hair was shorn of its former glory. She lived with pirates, dressed like them, attended to their medical needs with as much care as if she tended a dependent child, and did it all without a murmur of protest.

"Old ghosts, Sarah?" She heard Robbie's voice, suddenly gentle.

Her own shook with a vibrant tremor she couldn't contain. "Sometimes I long for home so much, it makes me want to weep for the days that are gone and can never come again. Sometimes I can envisage no future at all, and the pain of it overwhelms me."

"Do you think it is never the same for me?" Robbie queried quietly.

"But you can do something about it!" she said in a burst of anger. "You don't have to continue with this wretched life. You're not a prisoner as I am!"

They stared at one another, suddenly poles apart, and the sighing of a small breeze ruffled Robbie's dark hair. Sarah was filled with a great feeling of self-pity, and he sensed that nothing he said would placate her.

"Shall we go below?" he asked finally. "Perhaps you'd like a drink of brandy before you retire."

"Thank you, no," she said bitterly. "I think I prefer to keep my faculties alert tonight, while I ruminate on what's to happen to me."

One thing was certain in her mind. Robbie never intended to let her go. Any more than he could ever be persuaded to give up the pirate's life for her. Why should he, when he had never done so for any other woman? Why should she think she was so special? But that was what she wanted. If she had ever doubted it before, she knew it now with a sudden rage of longing.

She wanted Robbie to take her away from this life, to be with her and stay with her, and there was about as much hope of that as there was in Africa sinking into the sea. In a fit of dire misery, Sarah let herself be escorted back to her cabin and closed the door without bothering to say good night, more disturbed than she had been for many a day.

The Adventuress slid into the river inlet silently as the first fingers of a pearly dawn lightened the sky. Soon the blaze of the sun would transform the scene into one of vivid color, bursting with tropical life. As the ship inched its way up the river, the oars made hardly a ripple in the deep water. On either bank, dense vegetation reached enormous heights, making a perfect screen for the masts with their sails now tightly furled. Occasionally a screech of an animal or a great rustling of the wings of an exotic bird disturbed their otherwise placid entry.

Together with Robbie and those of the crew who weren't actively pulling on the oars, Sarah leaned on the rail, breathless for the merest whisper of sound that would spell danger or detection. There was nothing, and the jungle noises became a mere lullaby that grew in intensity as the sun rose, the burning heat of the day beginning to beat down. The brief collection of night moisture on the vegetation started to evaporate. Where the fierceness of the sun penetrated the foliage, it hovered in a rosy mist for some minutes and then simply disappeared.

Sarah was aware of the dryness of her mouth, and the fact that already she was sweating profusely. She was thankful that Robbie had told her they wouldn't be here any longer than necessary. It was too easy to lose body liquid and be in serious danger of dehydration. Knowing this, water had been conserved, to give the crew extra rations for the period of time they would be here.

Sarah prayed it wouldn't be long. Within the cloying atmosphere of the dense vegetation, the day promised to be oppressive. Soon it would be hard to breathe and every movement would become an effort.

The ship was tied up safely, and preparations began with precision-like efficiency and the minimum of verbal instruction. Sounds could carry, and an English voice would be suspect at once. During the previous night, they had skirted the Dutch vessel anchored in the bay, enjoying its full right of passage.

Robbie had revised his earlier plan. He intended now to relieve the trading station of the valuable gold and ivory *before* the Dutch seamen were ashore, to be away from the river inlet while most of the Dutch crew were still in small boats reaching the port. This would enable Robbie's crew to evade the chase. By the time the robbery was discovered and the Dutch vessel was fully manned again, *The Adventuress* would be well out to sea.

Some of the crew had considered it an audacious plan, but Robbie was convinced it was the best one. And as Sarah watched them prepare to depart she wondered for the first time what would become of her if anything went wrong and the pirates were caught. With only one or two of the crew left on board, *The Adventuress* would be sought out and found easily. If it was suspected that the ship was deserted, it would be burned as a warning to all other pirate ships.

If not, anyone left on board would be mercilessly killed . . . and that included Sarah Huxley, who resembled a boy, and whose real identity would surely be unknown to Dutch seamen intent on revenge. Fear ran through her as sharp as a knife. She almost begged Robbie to let her go with the crew for the survey, but she knew it would be pointless to ask. Robbie would never agree, and she would only hinder those more experienced than herself.

The men left stealthily to make their way through the jungle. They were well-armed against human attack, but Sarah shuddered, wondering what unknown horrors they may encounter on the way. The waiting would seem endless, knowing they would be gone a considerable time. Tomby was not allowed to go with them, and was sprawled out resentfully on a heap of ropes, his black skin glistening, but not as intolerant of the heat as Sarah. She ran her tongue around her lips, feeling them crack.

"Missy feel bad?" Tomby asked suddenly.

"Missy feel very bad," she muttered, and the boy sat up warily.

"Tomby knows a secret place nearby," he said.

"What do you mean? Have you been here before?" But of course he would have been! This must be a favorite haunt of pirates, to relieve the rich merchant ships of their cargoes, and to raid the trading station.

The boy spoke helpfully. "Tomby take you there and keep watch if you want."

"What kind of secret place?" She was curious, but apprehensive. Robbie had forbidden her to go ashore, and she remembered vividly his warning about the cannibals.

She was in no hurry to become somebody's dinner.

"A small pool under the trees to bathe. Nobody come there. Tomby show you, Missy."

It was unbelievably tempting. Sarah had never longed for anything so much. She could almost feel the coolness of the water lapping around her, as if it were a mirage. It would be much simpler of course, to slip over the side of the ship and swim in the river, but the idea of a small secluded pool was far more inviting. She felt so hot and unclean. She could swim and bathe at the same time, and feel refreshed. And if it wasn't very far, there would be plenty of time . . .

"Where is this place?" she asked quickly.

Tomby waved his arms vaguely in the opposite direction to where she had seen Robbie and the crew disappear, swallowed up by the jungle.

Sarah glanced around. Anyone else still on board was below, well away from the fierce rays of the sun. She made up her mind.

"You'll show me and stand guard," she instructed. "And we must only be gone a very little while, understood?"

"Yes, Missy," Tomby said solemnly.

Sarah's heart beat fast. It might be incredibly foolish and reckless, but the lure of a refreshing pool was suddenly too much to resist.

They crept through the dank foliage, their feet making no sound on the rich carpet of leaves and humus that never saw the sun at all. It surprised Sarah to find the ground beneath her feet relatively cool and damp, when between the restless movement of tree branches, the sun's brilliance stabbed like pinpoints of light and heat.

Tomby assured her that the pool was only a short distance from the ship, but glancing back she realized *The Adventuress* was almost out of sight already. Just the tip of the masts disclosed that anything resembling a craft was there at all. It unnerved her for a moment, and she hesitated, knowing they should go back. Robbie would be incensed if he were to find out, but there was no hint of danger, no sound of being pursued or sense of being watched.

And then the jungle opened up to show the small pool, lit by sunlight. A trickle of water ran into either end, and it was so clear it obviously wasn't stagnant, nor lurking with perils beneath its surface. And it looked so gloriously inviting! Just one quick dip and then back to the ship to don a fresh set of clothes, she promised herself. Not even Robbie could begrudge her that.

"Stand guard, Tomby, and keep your eyes away from me," she said sternly. And without waiting for anything else, she stripped off the outer boyish garments and put one toe into the water to test it, wearing only her shift. The water felt like a tepid bath, and in a moment Sarah had dipped beneath the surface, her eyes closing at the blissful caress of the curling little waves.

Just five minutes, she told herself, she wouldn't dare stay longer than that. She glanced to where Tomby sat on a stump in the shade, his back dutifully presented to her as he guarded her clothes. Sarah ducked her head beneath the crystal clear water, ridding her hair of the dust and grime of the past days. When she surfaced, gasping slightly, the shift clung to her body, almost transparent. She would have to dress quickly when she was ready, making sure that Tomby kept his eyes averted.

A sudden shiver akin to a premonition rippled through her. Nothing touched her, yet it was as though something physical prevented her from turning her head. If she did, she was sure Tomby would still be there, faithfully guarding her. He would never desert her, leaving her with no idea of how to get back to the ship. He *couldn't*. She turned her head sharply.

Sarah stifled a scream, experiencing a moment of pure

panic. There was no sign of the boy, nor of her clothes. It was as if they had vanished in the time it took for her to duck her head beneath the water.

At practically the same instant, she became aware of something else. And she knew to her terror that she was no longer alone.

Chapter 15

Rough hands hauled Sarah, kicking and spluttering, out of the pool. Some voices jabbered excitedly in a foreign tongue she didn't understand. She dashed the water out of her eyes and looked fearfully at her captors. They were black as pitch, and all were naked except for a sheath slung around their waist, in which each carried a crude knife. Their faces were painted garishly, and those waiting on the bank carried spears.

There was not even time to be embarrassed at their nakedness. Any embarrassment was quickly superseded by the realization that the natives peered at her with excited curiosity. Instinctively, she placed her hands across her breasts, only to have them snatched away by the man nearest her. The next instant she felt alien hands grabbing and squeezing her breasts, the nipples made prominent with fear beneath the thin fabric of her shift.

She might as well be naked too, she thought in rising panic. But there was a more urgent fear. If these were the cannibals, then she was in imminent danger of being eaten alive. She opened her mouth to scream, and as the first sounds emerged from her throat she was knocked flying straight back into the pool.

Sobbing and gasping for breath, she struggled to her feet.

What had become of Tomby she didn't dare think. If these savages had killed him, then she was entirely alone. Nobody knew where she was, and the sheer terror of this thought flooded her brain. Then she realized the natives were holding some kind of discussion. They were arguing, their voices raised in anger. She couldn't follow the words, but the implications became suspiciously obvious.

Some certainly saw the white flesh of an Englishwoman as a delicacy, and their assessment sent waves of nausea over her. Others gave her hot lascivious glances that needed no translation. She wondered desperately if there was any chance at all of a quick flight through the inhospitable jungle, and knew it would be hopeless.

And then the dense foliage parted, and a bulbous man, fully head and shoulders above the rest, appeared in their midst. He wore a cloak of feathers, and from the hem hung a selection of bones, bleached white by the sun. Sarah shuddered at the sight, and as the rest of the tribe fell silent, she knew instantly that this must be their chief.

Her heart hammered uncontrollably as the man stepped forward, pinching her arms as if to test the amount of flesh on them. He twisted her head this way and that and poked at her breasts, cupping each one in turn. Then his fat, greedy hands ran down her thighs, the thumbs meeting and making small circling movements through her shift where the shadowy triangle of dark hair was clearly outlined. He grunted approvingly.

The shock of it made her dumb with fear. She wanted to lash out at him, but even if she were not held fast, she dared not. If she provoked any of these natives, she was terrified that a spear would strike straight through her heart.

Finally the chief raised his own spear and struck it into the ground, inches from Sarah's feet.

"Woman—mine," he said.

She heard the smattering of English, disbelieving, and the rest muttered among themselves. The chief turned away to

219

lead the rest, and two of the men grabbed Sarah's arms and began to march her silently through the jungle, the others closely following.

And suddenly she recovered her senses. The numbness was fast disappearing, and she had no intention of allowing this thing to happen without a fight. She struggled furiously, slipping away from the grip of the natives holding her, only to be hauled back savagely. There was to be no escape.

"Let me go, you apes! People will be looking for me, and you'll be punished!" she screamed, knowing even as she did so that it was futile. Hadn't Robbie told her there were no search parties for any crew member who failed to return to the ship by the time they sailed? And wasn't she now Huxley, fully fledged crew member of the pirate ship *The Adventuress*, who could expect no special favors?

The chief paused and turned to her coldly.

"Woman—mine," he repeated. Then as if to pacify her, he gave her a grimacing leer. "Chief—no eat. Chief and woman—" His hand went to his groin and he gave a thrusting gesture that she couldn't fail to understand.

Sarah felt the hot color drain from her face. Hysteria threatened to overwhelm her. She would not, *could not*, contemplate lying with this animal. The thought of it almost made her retch.

"Please," she gasped, trying vainly to appeal to him, since he seemed to know the rudiments of English. "Please take me back. My friends will be waiting for me, and I'm not your sort, please—"

She might as well plead for the moon. There was no response, just the steady silent march through the jungle until Sarah became completely disorientated. All the same, she constantly wrenched her arms against the grip of the natives, and attempted to kick out at one or another. Even though her sense of dignity was outraged, a token fight was better than none at all.

She seemed to have been walking and struggling for

220

hours, and her arms were red and sore, because the natives never relinquished their grip for a second. By the time they reached a clearing where a group of dung huts was clustered, she was utterly exhausted, her spirit defeated. And the one thought uppermost in her mind was that nobody would come for her. Nobody knew where she was, and her fate was sealed.

Robbie and his men crept stealthily through the undergrowth toward the trading station. All was quiet, the guards still slumbering in the first light of dawn, not expecting any business dealings until the Dutchmen came ashore in a day or so.

The pirate raiders circled the low wooden building, knowing from past visits that there would be only a handful of men inside, and that an arm around a throat with a cutlass held fast against the skin was usually enough to persuade any one of them to open safes and strongboxes.

Even the most loyal guards could be lily-livered when it was a case of risking their necks or losing riches that were not their own property, Robbie thought cynically, and privately thanked God that they were. He had no wish to add unnecessary killings to his record of misdemeanors, despite the wishes of men such as the quartermaster, who would kill for the sake of killing.

When it was clear that there was no other presence in the vicinity, Robbie raised one arm. Instead of rushing in with bloodcurdling screams and curses, firing indiscriminately and bursting open the doors before the terrified guards had a chance to gather their wits, they moved silently. The plan was to surprise the guards without the sound of gunfire, which would have alerted the waiting Dutch ship in the bay that something was amiss. A few heavy shoulders on the doors, and the pirates were inside, brandishing weapons and cutlasses.

Robbie strode inside the building where the men cowered at the back of the main room. One of them let his hand stray toward his waist to grab his pistol, and had several fingers sliced off by the expert throw of a knife by a keen-eyed crewman. The guard fell to his knees with agonizing screams, blood pouring from the wound.

"Let that be a lesson to you," Robbie said coldly. "The next one who attempts being a hero may well lose his head. Now, gentlemen, we'll relieve you of the gold and ivory awaiting dispatch to the Dutch. The crates, if you please."

There were no further arguments. The guards scurried about, faces terrified as they brought out the crates of riches for the pirates to gloat over. Two men to a crate were needed to transport them all back to the ship, and meanwhile Robbie and several of the crew stood watch over the guards, finally leaving them gagged and bound so they were unable to raise the alarm.

The entire expedition was done speedily and efficiently, and Robbie was confident that they could be back on board and ready to glide out of the river under cover of nightfall. The Dutch ship was still far out in the bay, and Robbie calculated it was unlikely they would send in their small boats for at least another day. By then *The Adventuress* would be well on her way out to sea.

There was no sound of their being followed, and as they neared their own ship, Robbie began congratulating himself on the success of the venture. There was gold and ivory in plenty to share among the crew after their long journey. As captain, his was the largest portion, the rest shared out according to rank.

There was jewelry among the crates too, and his plan was to give some special piece to Sarah. The thought of it gave him an unexpected pleasure. And then, as the masts of *The Adventuress* came into view among the trees, something like a small hurricane came bursting out of the undergrowth.

*　　*　　*

"What the devil are you doing on shore, Tomby?" Robbie lashed out savagely. "You could have got your head blown off. Get back on the ship."

The boy's eyes rolled in terror as he was bundled aboard behind the perspiring crew with their crates of booty. He'd been crouching in the nearby bushes for so long he could hardly move. He'd been too afraid to board, and too afraid to take his chances on this alien soil. Now he was almost incoherent as he spilled out the words. Robbie snatched at his shoulders, swearing beneath his breath.

"Is this the truth?"

"Yes, Cap'n," he sobbed. "Missy want to see pool, and Tomby take her. Tomby know it wrong. Tomby sorry—"

"Never mind that now. What happened?" Robbie snapped, half-guessing, half-dreading the rest.

"Men come with spears. Tomby hear them, and Tomby hide with Missy's clothes. Tomby watch from bushes. Men take Missy away!"

"Which direction did they take?"

The quartermaster spoke up warningly at once, his face as dark as thunder, his supporters gathering around him.

"You'll not go after the woman, Cap'n. 'Tis against the ship's rules, and you've no right to put the rest of the crew in danger to satisfy—"

Robbie quelled him with a glance.

"I'm still the captain here, and I'll have the last word," he snapped. "Where did they take the woman, Tomby?"

The boy waved a shaking hand. Robbie nodded briefly.

"It will probably be Chief N'Oga's men. We may be in time if we move quickly, and no doubt he'll be willing to bargain."

"I say no!" Quartermaster said loudly. "No wench is worth risking all our necks."

Howls of agreement passed around the men, then Surgeon added his words to the argument.

"Ye're forgetting that this is no ordinary wench. Huxley's proved herself as good as any male crew member."

"And there's a rule that says we wait for no crew member

223

who delays sailing," Quartermaster shouted. "Do we have one rule for the men and another for the wench?"

He spat noisily, while the crew muttered among themselves, clearly divided now. Robbie took command.

"I say we bargain with the chief for the woman's return. We offer tobacco and a cask of rum. 'Tis little enough from our supplies. And to show my good faith, I'll relinquish all my share of today's spoils in return for the woman. She'll belong to me, and once back in England I'll be rid of her. Since you consider her so much trouble, I suspect that would be the majority wish. Is it agreed?"

Quartermaster's eyes narrowed. "Seems to me you're getting the best of the bargain. What of the ransom that was intended?"

"The ransom would be worthless, man, and ye know it," Surgeon snapped, adding his authority. "After all this time with Black Robbie, her people won't offer a fig for the woman. Take what's offered, and remember that Huxley has her uses on board. Let's get her back and be away from here as quickly as possible."

"Then who's with me for rescuing Huxley?" Robbie said at once. A chorus of ayes assured him of a significant group to track down Chief N'Oga's settlement through the jungle. Normally the savages' path wouldn't be easy to follow, but he counted on Sarah's kicking and struggling to have made their trail as evident as possible.

Sarah huddled up in a corner, trying not to notice the appalling smells inside the dung hut. Opposite her, a naked black woman with pendulous breasts sat unmoving and unblinking hour after hour, while outside the tribe indulged in some kind of ritual by fire before the public initiation of the white woman by their chief.

Sarah peered through the gap in the hut that served for a window. The chief squatted before the twig fire while his men paid court to him as if he were a god. He terrified her. The cloak of feathers had been removed, and layers of flesh hung over his engorged stomach, which did not hide the thing below. She shuddered, not daring to think of it entering her body, invading her flesh, taking that which belonged to Robbie.

She stifled a sob. Robbie ... she knew how foolish she had been in not heeding his warning. She had never wanted anything so desperately as she wanted him now, nor been so despairing that he would never find her. Out of all the world she had grown to love the man who had abducted her, she thought sorrowfully, and she would never have the chance to tell him.

There was a sudden commotion outside, and the woman in the hut sprang to her feet and held Sarah's arms as she stared disbelievingly through the window gap.

"Robbie!" Sarah croaked. "Robbie! I'm here!"

Her mouth was so dry that hardly a sound came out. She had begged for water, but either the woman didn't understand or was under orders to give the prisoner nothing.

And then Sarah's eyes widened. She saw Robbie stride toward the chief and hold out an arm as if in friendship. There was a group of pirates behind him, already encircled by natives, their spears forming a formidable screen. She recognized Surgeon and Fling among them, and as they all fell silent, she heard Robbie's voice rap out something in a language she didn't understand.

The chief got clumsily to his feet, and the cloak was wound around him at once to give him status. Sarah shook off the woman's hands and strained to listen. The chief answered in pidgin English, as if to air his knowledge.

"Woman—mine!" he stated.

"No. Woman is *mine,"* Robbie said just as harshly.

At his words the natives closed in still farther, bunching the pirates together, and Sarah's heart raced with fear. But Robbie stood unmoving and spoke rapidly in the

225

strange language.

"Where, this offering?" the chief challenged, the arrogance in his voice telling Sarah he was just as determined to use his stilted command of English.

"Bring the woman to my ship and we exchange her there," Robbie said shortly.

Sarah gasped. They were *bartering* for her. The shame of it made her sick. But if it was the only way . . . there was gold and ivory from the trading station, so presumably Robbie was prepared to pay a good price.

"What you offer?" Chief N'Oga said, greed shining out of his black face.

"One cask of rum and a box of tobacco."

Sarah could hardly believe her ears. The fear was replaced by outrage. Was this all she was worth to him? One measly cask of rum and a box of tobacco! It was an insult.

She saw the chief shake his head vigorously, and fear raced through her again.

"Woman worth more," he stated. "Chief and woman—" again he made the disgusting gesture she had seen before, and now Sarah saw Robbie's jaw tighten.

She felt tears of rage and despair slide down her cheeks. Surely he'd give in. He must offer more! There was no longer any thought of self-respect in her mind, just the need to get away from here, to be saved from what was truly a fate worse than death. It was true, she thought hysterically. She would rather die than be forced to fornicate with that hideous savage.

"Two boxes of tobacco then," Robbie said loudly. "No more, Chief. One cask of rum and two boxes of tobacco. No woman is worth more."

Sarah held her breath, and then saw the chief's face pull a grimace of a smile as he nodded and slapped his thigh until the flesh rolled. He gave a great roar of laughter and gripped Robbie's arm in agreement.

"You right, pirate. And white woman got no meat." He

226

spat on the ground, and Sarah felt faint. Presumably once the chief had satisfied his lusts, she'd have been for the cooking pot.

She heard the chief give orders in his own tongue, and the next second the hut door was opened and a stream of daylight entered, hurting her eyes. Two of the natives pulled her outside, and she was instantly aware of her own lack of clothing.

Robbie looked at her coldly, as if no tender feelings had ever existed between them. She was aware of a few sniggers from the pirate crew, and desperately tried to pull her shift down around her thighs. The next minute Robbie had ripped off his own shirt and told her to cover herself.

She dragged it around her shoulders. She felt dirty and degraded and ashamed. Robbie barely acknowledged her, and within minutes they were moving back through the jungle. She was still held captive between two of N'Oga's men, and there were natives at the front and the rear of the silent column as they tracked back toward the ship.

Ahead of her, Robbie marched stolidly. His bare back was broad and tanned a deep hue by wind and sun. She could see the muscles working, taut and pronounced, and remembered how she had clung to that responsive flesh in what already seemed like another time, another world. Her nostrils were filled with the male scent of him as she hugged his shirt to her body, and her spirit ached for something that might never come again. He would only despise her after this.

Once they reached the ship, the natives refused to let go of her arms until the cask of rum and boxes of tobacco were placed on the ground and examined thoroughly. Only then did they relinquish their hold on her. She stumbled and half-fell into Robbie's arms.

"Get on board quickly," he said. "We've tarried far longer than we ought to have. You will go to your cabin, Sarah, and wait there until I come to you."

The only small comfort she took from his words was that

227

he still called her Sarah.

The Adventuress moved out of the river with no heed of the usual caution. All speed was necessary now. The trading station guards were unlikely to release themselves from their heavy bindings, but the Dutch would be ashore at any time, and once it was discovered that Black Robbie and his pirates had been at work, alarms would be raised, and they would be hunted mercilessly.

There were many creeks and inlets along the Guinea Coast, but their best hope was to get out to sea as quickly as possible. Besides, they had got what they came for, and the spoils of this raid alone would see them rich for many months.

Sarah sat huddled on her bed as the motion of the ship told her they were already under way. She was totally exhausted, and furious at her own foolhardiness. She had put everyone at risk. And the savage face of the quartermaster when she was bundled back on board told her that he at least didn't welcome her back. For the moment, the knowledge that he was her enemy allayed the indignation of knowing her worth. A cask of rum and two boxes of tobacco.

Some time later there was a tap on her door and Tomby came inside, his eyes still wild with fright.

"Tomby, are you all right? Cap'n didn't punish you, did he?" she said in a strangled voice, remembering that she had persuaded the boy to show her the pool.

"No, Missy. Cap'n no punish," he mumbled. "Cap'n say you stay here till we out to sea. Cap'n say—"

Whatever Cap'n might have said was lost in a sudden burst of cannon fire that rocked the ship and nearly deafened Sarah. She screamed in terror, and flung her arms around the boy without thinking.

"What's happening?" she whispered, as fear laced her voice again.

228

"Cap'n say we under attack," Tomby croaked. "The Dutch ship want gold. Cap'n take gold from trading station while Missy in pool. He say Dutchmen kill for it."

"Kill for it?" Sarah gasped, clinging to Tomby for dear life as another burst of firing rattled the timbers and shook several pots of toiletries from a shelf.

She ignored them and rushed to peer through the porthole. Another ship was frighteningly close. Its cannons spat furiously and she could see the billowing smoke on its deck wafting through the sails. Her mouth was dry with shock. All around both vessels was a thick pall of smoke, and she realized that the stench of it was already permeating *The Adventuress*. It was acrid and choking, and she wondered wildly if the noise of gunfire from both ships threatened to burst her eardrums.

She would end up either stifled or deafened, and in neither care was she going to remain here and just let it happen! She was Surgeon's assistant, and if ever there was a time when she was needed, it was now. She didn't pause to think of anything else. She suddenly realized that the boy had gone. She rattled her door, but to her relief it wasn't bolted from the outside.

Quickly, Sarah changed out of her filthy clothes into her usual garb of baggy trousers and coarse shirt, and went swiftly up on deck. The stink caught at her throat and made her cough uncontrollably, and her eyes began to stream at once. She had difficulty in making out where anyone was, until she stumbled over something limp and inert.

"Flint!" She felt bile rise into her mouth, and gagged for a moment. His stomach was ripped open, and blood poured from the wound. She tried to move him, and then felt Surgeon's hands pull her back.

"Leave the bugger be until we can tip him over the side," he said savagely. "There's more important things to attend to than a dead 'un. If ye want to help, then help."

She followed him numbly. She'd seen instantly that Flint

was in a bad way, but she hadn't thought he was dead. His eyes had been open, and there had been a kind of smile on his lips . . . oh God, she couldn't stand it! Another great shudder of gunfire seemed to lift the ship out of the water and then hurl it down again, sending water pouring over the deck and washing it clean.

"'Twill help clear the blood," Surgeon said, with no thought for her feelings. Sarah realized for the first time that there were others moaning and hurt all around her. She was paralyzed with a new fear, worse than the fear of Chief N'Oga's ravishing. Was she about to drown after all, as her parents had drowned, as her worst nightmares had prophesied she would?

"What's the woman doing here?" Quartermaster's voice suddenly roared through the din. "Get her below."

"*Sarah!*" Robbie's voice was just as incensed. "I told you—"

His voice was cut short by a hideous cracking sound, and the mainmast, already weakened by repeated shot, toppled across the ship, taking Quartermaster with it. He let out a scream of agony as his legs were pinned beneath the heavy timber, and then fell silent.

"Help me get him out!" Robbie yelled. Several crewmen rushed to the man's aid, and lifted the heavy mainmast out of the way. The quartermaster's legs were crushed and bleeding, and his face had already gone a waxy gray color.

"Cap'n, we've seen 'em off!" somebody yelled gleefully. "They're taking in water fast."

Sarah raised her eyes from the wounded man for a moment. The Dutch vessel was indeed limping toward the coast. She prayed that it would get there safely. She was degraded enough by consorting with pirates. She had no wish to be an accomplice to murder. A deep sob left her throat. It was exactly what she was, for the Lord knew how many men had been killed or maimed this day in so short a space of time.

How long could she go on living this way, even for the love of Robert Argyll? But he no longer existed, she thought bitterly. The Robert Argyll she dreamed about lived only in her imagination, and Black Robbie the pirate had taken over his life.

She was utterly confused. From what Tomby had said, the raid for the gold had already taken place, and presumably the Dutchmen were out for revenge and the capture of Black Robbie. But they hadn't won. It had been their necks or Robbie's, and Robbie had won. She heard a ragged groan, and looked down quickly to where Surgeon was examining Quartermaster's legs, pulling the ripped clothing away from the wounds.

"Will he live?" she asked sickly.

Surgeon laughed shortly. "He'll live, once we stitch him up. How do ye fare with a needle and thread, Huxley?"

She looked at him in dumb horror as he held up his right hand, peppered with shot and looking painfully raw. Sarah gulped.

"You can't expect me to sew a wound!"

"I can't manage it with this arm, and the scabs will all faint away like painted doxies if I so much as mention it."

"And you think I won't?" she asked.

There was no sign of Robbie. Why didn't he come and tell this impossible man that it was no job for a lady? But Robbie was far too busy ensuring that the vessel got quickly away to safer waters to bother with Mistress Sarah Huxley's problems.

"Boy, fetch my tool bag and a good supply of brandy," Surgeon yelled to Tomby, hovering near. His left hand snatched at Sarah's.

"Ye'll do it, Huxley. I'll instruct ye, and 'twill go well for ye. Quartermaster will thank ye for it."

She didn't want his thanks. She only wanted to run and hide and never set foot on a ship again. She was sick to her stomach at the thought of dragging two pieces of flesh

231

together with a crude sewing needle. But there was no one else. The thought hammered into her brain. And she was humane enough not to let any creature die without trying to save him, even the wretched quartermaster.

He was regaining a semblance of consciousness by the time Sarah stabbed the needle into the flesh under Surgeon's instruction. She tried not to think what she was doing, as liberal doses of brandy were trickled down Quartermaster's throat. She tried to imagine she sewed a fine seam for her governess's inspection. She tried to think herself anywhere but on the open sea, performing an operation while the recipient of her labors gagged and spluttered and finally became drunk and filled her ears with the most foul abuse she had ever heard.

"He'll do, Huxley," Surgeon said keenly at last. "Go and wash off the muck and leave the tending to me. You'll be glad of a rest."

She looked down at herself mutely, knowing it was all the praise she would get from this stern man. Once again she was covered in filth, and she staggered to her feet and blundered down the companionway to her cabin. She stripped off her clothes, sponged every part of herself and scrubbed at the stubborn bloodstains on her skin between sobs of sheer exhaustion. Finally she crawled into bed, aching all over, wishing she need never face another day.

Chapter 16

Dusk came, swift and spectacular. One minute a blood-red sunset turned the sea to a sheet of flame, and the next, the soft blue-black of night provided a blessed shield to vessels of dubious allegiance roaming the high seas.

Sarah was only dimly aware that, despite the loss of the mainmast, the ship was moving fairly steadily out to sea. The rhythm of its motion soothed her ragged nerves, and instilled in her a sort of peace, a peace disrupted by restless nightmares.

It was pitch-dark when a small noise awakened her. She had been in the middle of a horrendous dream, and for a second she was completely disorientated. In her mind she was somewhere in the jungle, and the terror of Chief N'Oga's lecherous plans for her was vivid and real.

As she felt someone move next to her, she let out a scream, which was instantly muffled by a hand clamping over her mouth.

"Sarah, be still," Robbie's voice said quietly. "It's all over, all of it. We're going home."

He held her fast in his arms, while she took in the shock of his words. Robbie cursed his own vulnerability where she was concerned. He'd come here to censure her, but now that he saw her, cowed and defenseless, he didn't have the stomach for it.

"*Home?*" she asked in a cracked voice.

"To England. And then you'll be free to go where you wish. My men won't try to hold you."

He spoke brusquely, not wanting to betray how his own words struck a chill in his heart.

She stared into the darkness, unable to comprehend what he was saying. Did he mean he wouldn't try to hold her here? That he no longer wanted her? But after what had happened today, how could she blame him? She had nearly ruined his entire mission to the Guinea Coast.

"And you?" she whispered.

He was bitter now. "I doubt there's any place left for me in the world but this ship. I'm bound to it as fast as any wife to a husband."

"You don't have to be."

"Don't patronize me, Sarah. I've a loyalty to my crew, even if theirs to me is sometimes questionable."

"I had no thought of patronizing you," she said hotly. "I merely meant that you have another identity, one less scurrilous than Black Robbie, and less of a nambypamby than David Roberts."

She felt, rather than saw, his smile.

"So you find David Roberts a nambypamby, do you?"

Sarah's face flamed. Hadn't she been overwhelmed by the elegance of the gentleman when first she'd seen him in a theater box? Hadn't she resisted renouncing him, just like every other woman who had ever been mesmerized by those amber eyes?

"I didn't mean that exactly," she muttered.

She felt her chin tipped up by his hand. There was very little room on the narrow bed for them both, and Sarah was pressed against the cabin wall as Robbie eased his large frame fully onto it beside her. With an oath, he flung back the bedclothes. She felt the tips of her breasts respond as his free hand circled them sensuously.

"Then what did you mean? That you'd be willing to take a chance on returning to my homeland with me, and attempt to claim what's rightfully mine?"

Sarah's thoughts whirled. She wasn't sure if he was mocking or serious. Whether he teased her or tested her. She waited too long before answering. The caressing hand left her body and the voice was edged.

"Or perhaps you're just like every other woman who became a pirate's mistress, dazzled by the thrill of having men lust after you, when the idea of settling into a normal life with just one man seems extraordinarily dull."

Sarah's temper rose. She was desperately tired after today's ordeal, and to have him come here to torment her was more than she could stand.

"If that's what you think, then you don't know me at all!" she snapped. "Do you think I was thrilled at the thought of those disgusting natives pawing me?"

She gave a great shudder at the memory of black hands tweaking her nipples, seeing the blatant effect in their male organs as a result of it. But her words reminded him of his purpose.

"There's to be no repeat of such flagrant disobeying of my rules." Robbie stood arrogantly now, his arms folded. In the thin light of the porthole, Sarah could make out the hardness of his features, as if carved in marble. Perhaps he, too, was imagining the outrage. Perhaps he even cared. But right now, she would never have guessed it.

"No, sir," she said sarcastically. "Am I to be put in chains and kept in the hold?"

"It may have come to that if I had not bargained for you. And not only with Chief N'Oga."

She gasped, sitting up straight in the bed, forgetting that she was naked until Robbie reached forward to cover her. His hands were gentle, and it brought a sting of tears to her eyes. But his words made her overlook everything else.

"Are you telling me that you *bargained* for me with the

crew as well?"

"I did. You now belong to me. There will be no ransom demand, since it's been agreed that probably not even your despicable cousin will want soiled baggage." He ignored her furious gasp and went on relentlessly. "You're bought and paid for with my share of today's spoils, Mistress Huxley. And since it's not my wish to have you roam the high seas with me indefinitely, you will be returned safely to English shores to go your own way."

She wanted to shriek abuse at him in a way no lady ever had. She wanted to hit out and pummel him with her fists and take that cold, distant look from his eyes. She wanted . . . *dear God*, Sarah thought desperately, ashamed at her own feelings, she wanted *him* so much. The very last thing that she wanted was to be abandoned when they returned to England.

"Where will I go? I'll be as much adrift after all this time as if you had abandoned me on a desert island," she said huskily.

"I have friends. I know a reliable couple in Cornwall who will take care of you. And I shall see that you're provided for, never fear."

It wasn't enough. It wasn't how she envisaged her future life. If he wasn't part of it, then she simply didn't want to live. Even while the thought stunned her mind, she felt the touch of Robbie's lips on her mouth, a brief hard kiss. He stared down at her for a moment as if wondering whether to say more, but the words never came. She couldn't see the color of his eyes in the dim light, but she could imagine them. Oh, she could *imagine* them . . . one last long look . . . and then he was gone.

During the next weeks, Sarah became aware that the crew was treating her somewhat differently. Officially she was still Huxley, but she defiantly disregarded the boyish garb and wore the pretty gowns Robbie had provided her with. Her hair was growing to a more feminine length, curling into her nape, and she absolutely refused to cut it again.

There were still men recovering from their wounds after the skirmish with the Dutch ship, and although Surgeon said curtly that it was no longer necessary for her to assist him, she preferred to do so than be totally idle for the journey home.

The idleness of old seemed to belong to another life now, and Sarah realized anew how she had changed. Perhaps she no longer had the pale complexion beloved of society ladies; perhaps her hands were not quite milky-white, and her fingernails not manicured. But she felt herself to have grown in maturity and strength. And she had found true love, whether or not it had been returned.

She had also commanded a unique respect among the crew since stitching Quartermaster's legs, even though the memory of that occasion still sent waves of disbelief and nausea flowing through her. The man himself had growled his thanks, tempered with complaints that the skin felt taut, and that his legs would probably be stiffened permanently from such clumsy attentions. But at least his legs still functioned. They both knew he owed that much to Sarah.

In the evenings, the old routine was resumed. She dined with Robbie in his cabin, and walked the deck with him. Outwardly, they looked like two lovers enjoying a moonlit stroll on an ocean voyage. Two lovers in a world of their own, with only the moon and stars and the glittering sea to hear their whispered words of love.

In reality it was very different. Robbie was careful to keep their conversations light and impersonal. He stuck rigidly to his own rules. No person to be brought on board for the purposes of lust . . . no crew member to indulge in lustful pursuits with another.

If she had never known how it felt to lie with him, to be part of him, to know that this man above all others was the one she loved and desired, then Sarah might have accepted his terms gladly. Such a little while ago she had ached for England and home, but now . . . .

Now it meant that their days together were numbered, that Robbie would simply discharge her to some well-meaning folk and provide for her in the way one would provide for a pet animal. Much as she longed for news of home, and to see her dear Aunt Lily once more, the thought of losing Robbie was traumatic to her.

They were drinking brandy in his cabin one night, after a dinner in which Cookie had outdone himself, considering the dwindling rations. Robbie was talking blandly about the theater, when Sarah decided she simply couldn't stand his pretense any longer.

"Why do you torment me so?" she asked in a low voice. "Do you not think women have the same feelings as men?"

He looked at her gravely. At least he didn't do her the indignity of pretending to misunderstand.

"It's better this way, Sarah."

"No, it is not," she said passionately, her pique making her bold. "I can't bear it when you behave like a dandy toward me. No, not even that! A dandy would make flirtatious remarks, and you don't do even that! I might as well be a piece of furniture for all the interest you pay me."

"Would you wish me to treat you like a whore, the way some pirate captains treat their captives?"

"If that's meant to shock me, then you fail miserably! No, I do not wish you to treat me like a whore, nor like a slave, nor a sister! I want—I want—" Her voice cracked a little.

She realized he was very still, watching her with expressionless amber eyes. It was as if he willed her to say the truth, to reveal all her innermost feelings. He tried to extract more from her than he was willing to give back, Sarah thought bitterly.

"What do you want, my Sarah?" he asked in a soft voice that oozed with sensuality, and which she was totally unable to resist.

She stared at him blindly for a moment, and then said huskily, "I want you to love me."

He didn't answer immediately, and in those shivering seconds she was conscious of so many things: the ornate clock on his desk, ticking away their time together; the movement of the ship through the ocean, diminishing the space between them and England; the moment when Robbie simply held out his hands to her, and the way she seemed to watch everything in slow motion, savoring each sensation, glorying in the knowledge that the blankness had finally left his eyes and that what she saw there made her hold her breath.

"Then if that is what my lady wants, that is what my lady must have," he said gently.

He pulled her into his arms, and the distance between them became nothing. She felt instantly safe and warm, with a growing excitement and need that was physically matched in Robbie.

"You see what you do to me, my lovely." His mouth moved against hers as he said the words, and at the hardness of his body against her softness, she was in no doubt as to his meaning. It didn't shock her as the natives' crude gestures had. It exalted and thrilled her to know she could produce such evidence of life's perpetuity in this man.

"You see what you do to *me,* my love," she whispered back, knowing the fundamental truth that between true lovers there could be no false modesty. She took one of his hands and placed it tremulously over her breast, where the nipple strained for his touch.

The next minute she was swept up in his arms and enclosed within the small compartment containing his bed. He undressed her tenderly but with great speed, because his need for her was stretched to the limit, and the only thing that would assuage it was to sink himself into her softness, to be surrounded by that sweet receptive flesh that cradled him and welcomed him.

Sarah breathed in his scent as his arms crushed her to his body. Robbie made no pretense at preliminaries; neither did she want them. All they needed was to be part of each other, one flesh, one love. She felt him slide inside her, filling her, and her spirit rejoiced.

The movements began, slow and sensual at first, sending exquisite shafts of desire through every nerve-end, until the final glorious moments when the thrusts were hard and furious, and her passion rose to meet his, culminating in an explosion of sensation so spectacular it caused silent tears to run down her cheeks. Robbie kissed them away, still not leaving her, still part of her, until the pulsing inside her became a sweet spreading lethargy in her limbs and her mind.

"God, but I love you." As they still clung, he spoke raggedly against her breast, and Sarah realized he went very still once more. Her heart beat so fast she could hardly breathe. His weight fully covered her, but she dared not ask him to move. Not when the words she had so longed to hear had been practically torn from him. Robbie was not a man to say them lightly. Once said, they were irrevocable.

It seemed a long while before he lifted his head to look into her face.

"It seems that you've managed to do the impossible, my Sarah."

"Why should it be so impossible for you to love?" she whispered.

"Because I vowed it must never happen." He sounded almost angry, but her fingers curling around the dark hairs on his chest made him groan softly. "I knew if it ever happened, my life would change."

Sarah felt her heart leap. But she dared not press him now. It was too fragile a moment to tempt fate by trying to extract promises. Even though she held him in her arms and he was hers, she dared not risk asking Robbie to give up this life and return to Scotland. And just as instantly she knew it was what she wanted, needed, above all else. But the decision had to be his. It was enough for her now to know it could become more than a fleeting idea in his mind.

"But do you love me?" She was woman enough to persist, wanting him to say it again and again and again.

"Yes, you beautiful witch, I do love you," Robbie said. "But what we're going to do about it is something else. Nor can I think sensibly while you're in my arms like this. You know what I'm talking about, don't you?"

Sarah moved restlessly, knowing the idyll was over for the moment. He would never allow her to remain in his cabin all night, nor was the bed accommodating enough for the two of them. But she was woman enough to feel piqued at his words.

"Your old mutiny," she muttered. "Sometimes I think you exaggerate the danger."

She gasped as his hands gripped her wrists tightly.

"Sarah, don't ever underestimate the ambition of a man such as Quartermaster. I warn you, if he ever suspected that we were lovers, he'd do his damnedest to turn the others against me and take command of the ship, and you and I would be fish bait."

She shivered, hearing the certainty in his voice. He knew these men better than she, and she knew she would do well to listen to him.

"I'm sorry," she said in a small voice. "I know you're right, but it all seems so improbable to me. It's a different world—"

"Sarah, you're part of this world now, and you must face up to it. We live with danger all the time, on board ship as well as off. Don't ever forget that."

She moved away from him carefully, donning her clothes with shaking hands. She would rely on him anywhere. He had strength and integrity, and if the thought was an incongruous one applied to a pirate, it no longer seemed strange to her. It was true. She was now part of his world,

241

and must accept it for what it was.

If she wouldn't have him beside her all night, she had the sweet knowledge that he loved her. He *loved* her. It was a thought wondrous enough to sustain her through all the days of her life.

Now, however nobly they resisted the temptation to abide by Robbie's rules, it was just too difficult. Now that they had been lovers again, they couldn't bear to stay apart, and most evenings ended up the same way. But for them both, the joy of being in each other's arms was constantly laced with apprehension. They dreaded a moment of discovery, when the ship's crew would mutiny because their captain had done the unforgiveable, by breaking his most stringent rule.

As the ship sailed into northern waters, tempers became short and voices agitated, because there was always danger until they were securely moored in a safe harbor, and the tension touched both Sarah and Robbie.

"We make for a remote Cornish creek under cover of darkness," he told her, when the English coastline became a hazy black shape in the distance. "We shall stay there for several weeks while the repairs to the ship are carried out. And I shall see you safely to the home of my friends."

"Robbie, I want to see my aunt," she said tremulously. The idea had been simmering in her mind for days, and the nearer home they got, the more urgent it became. "I want her to know I'm alive and well. I wouldn't stay at Endor House. Contrary to what you and your men think, I still believe Jonas will want to marry me. He doesn't let go easily of something he considers his."

She shivered. Jonas wouldn't be deterred by anything that had happened to her. She knew him too well. He would try to prise everything out of her, and find a vicarious pleasure in hearing about the native capture. She knew he would glory in the fact that Sarah belonged to him after lying with the notorious Black Robbie. She also knew that a visit to Aunt Lily was fraught with risk, but love and family loyalty demanded it of her.

"I can't allow it," Robbie said at once.

"Please, my love," she said in frustration. "At least let me send a message to Endor House, to let Aunt Lily know I'm well. Don't forget, I could easily go there when you return to sea."

Her hand was soft on his arm. She could plead with those large, expressive eyes in a way that threatened to wear down his resistance, Robbie thought with annoyance. His feelings for this woman constantly took him by surprise. He tightened his mouth at the sparkle in her eyes, knowing that he went against his own wishes.

"You would be very foolish to attempt to take up the old life in any way, and I think you have sense enough to know that, Sarah," he said coldly. "I'm very much against messages being sent. But if you feel that you must see your Aunt, then I'll take you to Endor House myself, and see you safely back to Cornwall."

She looked at him with a mixture of gratitude and resentment. "You don't seem to appreciate that I have family feelings. Don't you ever miss your own, or wish that things could have been different?"

Robbie's face gave nothing away. "There's no use in wishing. We can't change what fate decrees for us, and besides, nothing stays the same for ever."

"But sometimes we make our own destiny," Sarah said defiantly. "You could change yours even now. We both could."

He looked at her, and she knew he wasn't yet ready to change his chosen way of life, not even for her. If she had a loyalty to her family, then his was to his crew, the only family that he had.

She would have to be content with his offer to take her to Endor House. And when *The Adventuress* finally nudged her way gently into the darkened Cornish waters, into the remote creek overhung with trees and grasses, Sarah's sense of joy at finally being home was almost overwhelming. With or without Robbie in her life, she was home.

The crew, too, seemed more buoyant than in past weeks. They had gold to exchange; the money would be burning holes in their pockets while they indulged themselves in taverns and bawdy houses. In a county in which seafaring men constantly came and went, the pickings of the notorious Cornish wreckers regularly found its way into such establishments, and nothing was ever questioned. A pirate crew looked much the same as any other ship's crew after a long voyage, and raised few eyebrows.

Robbie organized the repair of the ship under the scrutiny of Quartermaster, who would be in charge of the work.

Before they were to leave, Sarah hugged the small native boy she had become so attached to.

"You behave yourself now, Tomby," she said sternly. "Don't let those others lead you into bad habits."

"No, Missy," he said, innocent-eyed, and she gave him a rueful smile, knowing that even if it hadn't happened already, the boy would soon be initiated into everything these men stood for.

She wondered briefly if she would ever see him again, or if Robbie himself would visit her at the house where he intended to place her. She refused to dwell on the thought, and as she resolutely said goodbye to Tomby, she saw the shine of tears in his eyes.

She felt a lump in her throat. Taking her leave of the crew was more emotional than she could ever have supposed. She had shared their lives for too long now to be unaffected by the parting. She begged Robbie to make it brief as they left for Sussex.

* * *

She glanced at him in the small swaying carriage he had hired. He was dressed as soberly as Sarah herself, in the garb of a genteel person making a journey across the country to visit relatives. Neither of them looked overly rich or ostentatious, not wanting to draw undue attention to themselves or succumb to the irony of being accosted by highwaymen.

"It will be a tedious journey," Robbie told her. "We will have to cross from one side of the country to the other, and we'll need to put up at a wayside inn tonight and tomorrow night, before reaching Endor House."

"I prefer to go to the house alone," Sarah said at once. "It will be too great a risk for you, Robbie. Jonas is sure to recognize you, and would show no mercy. The reward for your capture would be very alluring to him, but I suspect he would run you through first, for the insult you did him in taking me away."

"I can't agree to your going alone."

"You must," Sarah insisted. "Please, Robbie. I couldn't bear it if anything were to happen to you. I'll take no chances. Jonas may not even be at home, but I'll slip inside the house by a side door, go to my Aunt's rooms and send a message, through the old housekeeper, that she's needed. Both of them will be loyal to me, and I'll rejoin you later, you have my word on it. Do you not trust me?"

"I don't doubt your word," he said roughly. "Only the wisdom of your going there unprotected."

She leaned over as the carriage lurched on the uneven ground, and kissed his cheek. He felt the softness of her skin against his, and the fragrant scent of her filled his nostrils.

"Please, my love," she said softly, and he heard himself agreeing without really knowing why. He hadn't planned for this, but Sarah Huxley had a way of twisting herself around him in a way that was both delightful and infuriating.

"Very well. But first I shall go to Endor House and see how the land lies. There's a hotel just outside Hastings where we shall stay for a night. Once I've decided that all is well, I'll agree to your visiting your Aunt alone and await you at the gates. This visit must not be prolonged, Sarah. I've much to do in Cornwell before we set sail again, and it's unwise for *The Adventuress* to remain in home waters for too long. And I'll want to see you safely settled with the Trewithans."

She had had to agree to that, though the mention of him setting sail again sent a pang of dismay running through her. The end of their association was very near, and there seemed nothing at all she could do to stop it. In the future there would be only Robbie's infrequent visits to the home of this Cornish family, until he forgot her—or she decided to make a life for herself elsewhere.

But there was no point in worrying her head with that for the moment. The pain of it would come later; she needn't anticipate it. There were still these days and nights together, without the rocking motion of the ship beneath their feet. It took a while for the strangeness of being on dry land to wear off, though the swimming sensation of land fever occasionally overtook her.

And there were the two nights spent in wayside inns, whose landlords understood them to be man and wife. Sarah secretly thought of their shared rooms as a private heaven. Cocooned in Robbie's arms, it was easy to say all the things her heart dictated, which in the cold light of day seemed to be a mockery of reality.

"How I wish these precious hours together could last forever," she murmured sleepily against his bare shoulder, wrapped in his arms in the aftermath of love.

"No more than I do, my sweet lassie," Robbie said, but further than that he would not go. "We've struck our bargain. You know the risks I run in even bringing you here, and I trust you not to ask more of me than I can give."

"I do not ask," Sarah said in a low voice. "But that does not mean that I do not want."

How could she not want all of him, for always and beyond, when every nerve in her cried out to him for love, for

246

the spiritual and physical belonging that came only through marriage? She craved above all things to be married to him, to belong to him in every sense, and with God's blessing . . .

She felt him move slightly away from her, and the loss of contact sent a little chill through her skin, which moments before had been so heated by his passion.

"Accept what cannot be changed, Sarah," he said gently, and wearily she knew she waged a hopeless battle in trying to change Robbie's will. She was strong, but he was stronger. It was the nature of things that, even in her acute disappointment she would not have him any other way.

The hotel outside Hastings was within several miles of Endor House. Near enough for Robbie to go out in the carriage on the afternoon of their arrival, while Sarah ostensibly rested in their room. In reality, she paced the floor in a fever of anxiety. Until now, she hadn't fully realized what danger she put him in—even from herself. He was miles from his ship, and if she were to turn traitor . . . but of course, he knew that would never happen. He trusted her, as she had always trusted him.

At long last the door handle turned and he was back from his sojourn. She clung to him, feeling the coldness of the night air on his face and clothes. She was flooded with warmth that he had made this journey with her, for her.

"It's all right," he said reassuringly. "I watched your cousin leave the house, so it might be wise for you to go now, Sarah. I still think I should be with you—"

"No! You made a promise, and I refuse to go at all if you insist, and then we'll have made this long journey for nothing!" She was adamant. Robbie's sighting of Jonas brought her spurned fiancé distressingly clear to her mind. Jonas would show no mercy to Sarah either, but she gave no thought to that. Robbie's safety concerned her more.

"Then as planned, I'll take you to the gates, and wait there for you. I'll expect you to take every care, my brave and foolish lassie," he said, and she knew that she had won. She leaned upward and kissed him full on the mouth, winding her arms about his neck as she did so, feeling his instant response as his arms closed around her.

"Every care," she said huskily. "Nothing but the devil in disguise would keep me from my love tonight, however late the hour."

Their kisses were a sweet promise of that late hour. The thought that her words could be construed as a warning never entered either of their minds.

Chapter 17

Robbie wouldn't waver from his resolve to accompany her part of the way to Endor House, fearing that a woman alone would be fair prey to rogues and vagabonds. Sarah laughed softly at his words, her heart swelling with love for him.

"Oh, my love, you sound just like a fussy old husband," she teased, her breath catching at the very thought. How wonderful it would be, if only . . . if only . . . she closed her mind to something that was unlikely to ever happen, and instead concentrated on the sense of his words.

When night had cloaked the countryside in darkness and a fine mist spread out over the land, they rode in the carriage for the first part of their short journey. Robbie helped her alight within yards of the impressive gates of Endor House.

Sarah's throat was thick as the dim outline of the house stood out against the sky. So much of her life had been spent here, and yet this was no longer her home. But how could she forget the many happy years of childhood under her uncle's loving protection? Even her marriage to an old man of her uncle's choice had been arranged with care and consideration.

She might have fared far worse than sharing a marriage-bed with Angus Huxley. She might have been forced to suffer the lust of her cousin Jonas! She gave a sudden shiver at the thought, and felt Robbie's hands grip hers tightly as he prepared to move the horse and carriage into the shadows and wait for her.

"It's not to late to change your mind, Sarah. You don't have to do this."

"Yes, I do," she said simply. "Both for my own peace of mind, and Aunt Lily's. Now that we've come this far, it would be madness not to finish what we've begun."

"One hour then," he said, raising her hand to his lips. "If you're away for longer than that, I shall come looking for you."

"I'll remember," she promised. "But give me a little longer. Aunt Lily and I will have a few tears to shed, and I'll have so much to tell her."

"A little longer then. But be careful how much you tell, Sarah. I can only request that you say merely that you are safe and well, and have chosen to move far away from here because of your cousin's intentions. Walls have ears, however solid they may seem."

His voice reminded her that she must be careful. Many lives would be at stake if she revealed the whereabouts of the pirate ship, not only that of her beloved. She hugged him swiftly, promising to do as he asked, and then sped silently away across the wide lawn, feeling the dampness of the evening dew through her thin soles.

It was easy to skirt the side of the house by way of the thick hedges around the rose arbors. Sarah knew it all so well. So many times she and Jonas had played among these shrubberies in the innocence of childhood. So many times she had dreamed of a lover spiriting her away in the night to a fantasy land that was forever filled with warmth and sunshine and love . . . .

She pushed away the dreams. This was no time for allowing her thoughts to wander. She must be alert, and careful. She slipped inside the servants' door, from which a staircase led to the corridor where her Aunt Lily's room was situated. She would go there and ring the bell-pull and await the housekeeper.

She went inside the room without being hindered in any way, and breathed a sigh of relief. The room was very tidy, as if no one ever used it. Aunt Lily had always been very particular. Sarah pulled the long tapestry rope impatiently, filled with a great longing to see someone from her past once more.

A few minutes later she heard footsteps outside the door, and then it was opened as if in anger. When she saw Sarah sitting on the bed, the old housekeeper's face registered varying emotions. Anger was quickly replaced by disbelief and then shock. She finally became suffused with color as she stumbled across the room, her hands outstretched.

"Miss Sarah, can it really be you?" she cried out. "Or is it a ghost I'm seeing? You look so changed, and yet I'm sure it must be my Miss Sarah!"

"Oh, Binny, of course it's me!" One minute Sarah was wondering if her trembling legs would hold her up when she stood, and the next she was being held close to an ample bosom, hugged and wept over, and her own tears mingled with the old woman's.

"Oh, it's so good to see you again," Sarah wept. "For a time I thought I never would!"

"Neither did we when that terrible pirate took you off in the night," Binny said feelingly.

Sarah hesitated. It would have been so good to say that Black Robbie wasn't a terrible pirate at all, and that after all, she had gone willingly, and would stay with him forever if he asked her . . . but it was wisest to keep the truth for her Aunt's ears, and even then, she could reveal very little.

"Will you let Aunt Lily know I'm here, Binny? But tell her discreetly, and don't let any of the other servants know. I can't stay very long, so please be quick!"

She felt the old woman stiffen, and felt a horrible presentiment as Binny made no attempt to move away. Her tongue seemed to stick to the roof of her mouth, and she swallowed thickly.

"Miss Sarah—your Aunt—she passed on soon after you left us," Binny stammered. "Master Jonas reckoned it was the shame of it all that did it, begging your pardon if I'm speaking out of turn. But she took it all real bad, and he made her pay for not keeping a proper eye on you. If you ask me 'twas his wicked tongue and the thought of living with it forever that made her give up trying to fight off the influenza!"

Sarah felt sick as the voice went on indignantly. All this time she had counted on Aunt Lily being just the same, wanting her back. And all this time she had been dead, and Sarah had never known. Her breath caught on a sob. And Jonas—that bastard Jonas—had probably made Aunt Lily's life a misery. And all because of Sarah. She felt a swift shame pass through her.

For a few moments all sense of purpose seemed to leave her. She was drained. After all her determination to reach here, it had been all for nothing. Bitterness washed over her. She had so wanted to vindicate Black Robbie in Aunt Lily's eyes! And now her Aunt would never know that the reputedly notorious pirate was her niece's one true love.

"There now, you mustn't blame yourself, dearie," Binny went on sympathetically. "She'd be glad to know you're back safe and sound, and she's probably somewhere up there a'knowing it."

"But I can't stay. I'm—I'm married now, Binny, and I'm in the neighborhood for just a few hours," she invented quickly. "Of course I couldn't leave without coming here, but I'm sure you'll understand if I don't stay long enough to see my cousin."

"Ah, love, I understand. Then you don't want a bed for the night?"

"No, thank you." Sarah managed to avoid a shudder. "I'm

252

staying at The Bell Hotel just outside Hastings with my husband. I must get back there very soon."

Sarah knew Binny would understand her reasons for not wanting to remain at Endor House. The old housekeeper had always had a pretty shrewd idea of what went on. She was a loyal servant and Sarah knew she could trust her. Some of the younger maids would go running to Jonas with the tale at once, hoping to get a few favors from him, monetary or otherwise.

While she and Binny consoled one another, Sarah gave only the briefest of details as to what her life had been like all these months. But neither saw the shadow hovering outside the half-open door. Neither saw one of the new maids, well aware of the tale of Sarah's abduction, listening at the door, agog with the sudden realization of who this stranger must be.

Neither saw her speed down the stairs and out of the house, to the tavern where she knew Lord Jonas Endor was in the habit of going, to take an ale with his cronies instead of going up to town as he used to. She was quite sure that her information would produce a few pennies to spend on herself, and more than a few cuddles in the gentleman's bed to spice up the long nights.

"You're back sooner than I expected," Robbie said with relief as the slight figure reached the carriage waiting in the darkness of the trees. "Is everything all right? Why, my dearest girl, I see that it is not."

She fell into his arms, weeping with sorrow and disappointment and the sheer frustration of it all. It was a few minutes before she could tell him of it, and when she had sobbed out the words, he smoothed her dark hair back from her hot forehead.

"My poor wee lassie, to have lost the one person in the

world who you love," Robbie said softly.

She drew a deep breath, leaning against him. Her voice was exhausted and tinged with bitterness.

"She was not the one person, Robbie, and you know it. I love you so much, and now that I've lost Aunt Lily it makes me all the more devastated, knowing I'm so soon to lose you. I would give anything and do anything to keep you from going away again."

He folded her in his arms and let her cry until she felt there were no more tears left inside her. He hardly registered her words. He only realized that she seemed unable to move or to gather her senses, and he became alarmed at the length of time they were standing there, locked together in her grief.

"Sarah, we must get back to the hotel, where it's safe. Come, my love, let me help you into the carriage."

She moved numbly, like a sleepwalker. She sat beside him, not touching him, huddled up in the corner of the carriage while he urged the horse on. She felt totally alone and bereft, as if her aunt's death had only just happened.

When they had returned to the hotel, she refused to go downstairs for supper.

"Perhaps you could arrange to have something sent up for me a little later, Robbie. Just a morsel, for I'm sure I couldn't stomach more. And, forgive me, love, but I think I need to be alone awhile."

His heart went out to her. "I understand, lassie. I'll away downstairs and see about some food, and I'll return when you've composed yourself. We must leave here at first light tomorrow, and you need a good night's sleep. Get undressed, my love, and slip into bed."

She followed his instructions without knowing it. She crawled beneath the bedclothes, her teeth chattering with cold and nerves. She felt a great need to curl up inside the bed, to burrow into a cocoon the way a hurt animal did, as if to barricade itself against all the world's ills. She couldn't think of anything but the awfulness of knowing her aunt was dead, and she was quite unable to shake off her own guilt at not being there.

Jonas Endor looked up irritably as one of his maids peered round the smoke-filled tavern. He enjoyed these evenings with the lower orders, when he could act the lord that he was and know that they hung on his every word like the bumpkins they were.

"Is this one of your wenches, me Lord?" one of them muttered slyly, with a lascivious grin.

Jonas looked at him coldly. There were barriers these companions were not permitted to cross, and this was one of them. "One of my servants, yes," he said frigidly, putting the man in his place at once.

"Oh, yes, sir, I was forgetting the props—prosps—yer Lordship," the other sniggered, giving up the attempt to find the word.

Jonas was unable to stop himself from grinning back. Truth to tell, his head was near to bursting with the drink he had imbibed. If this bold-eyed wench wanted servicing from him tonight, she'd have to wait a long time for his body to oblige. Even the brief flicker in his loins at the thought of bedding her dwindled to nothing as she worked her way through the benches toward him.

"Can I have private words with you, me Lord?" she asked quickly.

His companions guffawed, mouthing obscenities among themselves. *Private words* . . . that would be a new name for it! Jonas leaned back against the wall, feeling the room spin somewhat as he growled at her to say what she wanted.

"I can't—not here," she said. "It's *very* private, and—it's about someone you used to know."

Jonas was not so befuddled that he didn't guess by the meaningful tone of her voice who the somebody he used to know might be. He stood up too fast and staggered against the wall before he was able to walk across the room and hustle the girl outside. He gripped her arm so tightly that she cried out, but he needed to hold her fast to help keep himself steady.

"Now then," he rasped. "If you've got information, let's hear it. If you've got me out here on a fool's errand, I'll make you sorry you were born."

"'Tis no fool's errand," she gasped, twisting her head from the abomination of his breath, "'Tis your cousin come to the house seeking your aunt, and swearing the housekeeper to secrecy about her visit."

Jonas stared through red-rimmed eyes. This was hardly what he'd expected to hear. He'd assumed the girl had got hold of some garbled tale about a young woman resembling the missing Sarah Huxley being seen in the neighborhood. There had been other such tales from a fortune-hunter out to gain some reward from Lord Endor. Jonas had relentlessly followed up every lead to no avail.

"Sarah's *here,* you say? She's come back to Endor House? Are you certain of it, or is it mere kitchen gossip?"

"I seen her with me own eyes," the girl said indignantly. "I've seen enough portraits of her to recognize her, though she looks a mite different now."

"You'll come back to the house with me until I've proved your tale," Jonas said rapidly. "If you're funning with me, you'll be sorry for it."

"She won't be there. She was going back to some hotel near Hastings, to be with her husband."

She squealed as the cruel fingers pinched her arm even tighter.

"*Husband,* you say? Are you sure about this, you baggage?"

"'Course I'm sure. That's what she said. She's staying at The Bell Hotel with 'im."

There was a small triumph in her voice. It was well known that Jonas Endor had wanted the luscious Sarah Huxley for himself, and this girl, like many others, had cause to wish him to hell. He had his attributes, but he could also be a cold devil, casting off an old female-fancy for a newer one as easily as if he threw out an old glove.

"Get on back to your duties," Jonas growled, letting her go so quickly she nearly fell. He didn't watch her go. She was nothing to him, and her only use this night was to alert him that Sarah—*his Sarah* was no more than a few miles away, in the company of someone she called her husband . . .

Jonas wasn't stupid. He'd seen the way the pirate could charm women, and he hadn't missed the way Sarah was bemused by the catlike eyes of the man. If she'd been in his seductive company all these months, she might well consider herself to be married, but Jonas was willing to wager it was no marriage sanctioned by the church.

She'd be no more than bed sport to Black Robbie, and he felt a savage jealousy envelop him at the thought of her sharing another man's bed. He'd had to put up with it when his father had arranged her marriage to the senile Angus Huxley, but he'd been prepared then to bide his time until the old man died and Sarah inevitably turned to him.

And all this time, thwarted by the abduction by the pirate captain, he had seethed and burned, imagining himself outwitted and betrayed by a woman he considered rightfully his. His obsession had not lessened with her disappearance.

And now that she was in the vicinity, he had only to alert the constables that Black Robbie was close at hand, and he could snatch her back, the way the pirate had snatched her from him. The thought of it was very sweet.

But he had to go carefully. To alarm the pirate would be to put the two of them to flight, and first of all, Jonas had to be sure of all the facts. With the peculiar canniness of the roaring drunk, he clarified certain things in his mind. He must go to the hotel as an ordinary traveler and make discreet inquiries about friends he was supposed to be meeting there before he took this further. It would be

257

humiliating for Lord Endor to make a fool of himself over false information.

But there was an undoubted thrill of excitement racing through him. With luck, he was about to get Sarah back. This time, he'd make damned sure she wouldn't get away again. And as a bonus, the reward and glory for the capture of the notorious Black Robbie would be his.

Having made his plan, he went blindly to where his horse was tied up at the back of the tavern, threw himself over the nag's back and headed in the direction of Hastings.

Robbie glanced up idly from the tankard of ale he had allowed himself. All this traveling was thirsty work, and it was a novelty to get so much ale on tap; aboard ship, there was just so much room in the hold for storage of ale barrels. He had organized a light meal for Sarah to be sent up to their room in half an hour, and thinking she would probably fall asleep from sheer grief, he had decided to let her be. Mourning a loved one took time, and she would be sorely grieving the sorry news of her aunt.

As the door of the hotel opened, bringing with it a bluster of cold wind, Robbie felt a moment's revulsion at the fellow who swayed inside. Yet this was not some country yokel, but a man of quality, judging by the cut of his clothes.

The fellow looked about him keenly, and then made for the desk and spoke rapidly. As he did so Robbie felt his heart stop for a moment and then thunder on. He couldn't hear all the conversation, but he could get the gist of it.

The newcomer was asking about two friends recently arrived, and just as instantly Robbie realized that this man was no stranger to him. He had seen him several times before. This was Sarah's hated cousin, Jonas Endor. It had to be more than coincidence that brought him here.

Robbie sat in a secluded alcove of the hotel, as was his habit in any public place, and thought back quickly. If Jonas had seen Sarah at Endor House, he would surely have prevented her from leaving. If he'd followed her and seen her get into the carriage hidden beneath the trees, he would surely have brought supporters with him and apprehended them at once. Robbie felt a sharp and searing suspicion as he thought of the only explanation for Jonas's presence.

Sarah had betrayed him.

Robbie felt as if he had suffered a mortal blow to his stomach as the thought stormed through him. Brief snippets of memory whirled through his senses, all seeming to point to that one end.

The way Sarah had wanted to send a message to Endor House in the first place, until Robbie had insisted that written messages of any kind were dangerous and could be used as evidence of his presence . . . .

The way she had wanted to go to the house alone; and before they left the hotel, the way she had told him so passionately that she would give anything and do anything to keep him from going away again . . . .

And on their return . . . the tiredness . . . the insistence that she couldn't eat and needed time alone . . . was all that no more than a ploy to get him out of the room so that she needn't be witness to what was imminent?

Robbie had been too long in the business of keeping his eyes peeled for danger. Too long to take chances, and too long to allow sentiment for a woman to threaten the lives and livelihood of himself and his crew.

Bitterness toward what he saw as Sarah's betrayal was paramount, but above and beyond that was the need for survival, ingrained in him from the day he saw his parents die and his home burned.

He saw the landlord of the hotel and Jonas Endor in a deep conversation now as they leaned toward one another. He saw money pass from Jonas's hand to the other's, and Robbie wasted no more time.

He was seated near the rear door of the hotel, a position he

259

had taken up out of long habit, and he slipped through it inconspicuously. He wore no outer garment, but he gave no heed to that. He was fired with such a burning anger he didn't feel the chill of the night as he made quickly for the horse and carriage that had brought him and Sarah from Cornwall.

His one aim was to get back there as fast as possible. Sarah would have no idea of the exact location of *The Adventuress*, only that it was moored somewhere in a remote Cornish creek. But if he had to be hunted at all, Robbie chose to be hunted and slain at sea where pirates were considered fair game, rather than be trapped in a river inlet and taken into custody. A one-sided trial and an ignominious public hanging held little charm for him.

The rage he felt burned too fiercely for him to give too much thought to what Sarah had done. She had clearly made her choice, despite all she had said about Jonas Endor. She preferred the soft life . . . and how could he honestly blame her? Robbie thought bitterly. But he had never expected this. He had trusted her. . . .

The carriage clattered out of the courtyard and he prayed that Endor didn't have constables hiding in the shadows watching for a speedy escape. But the hotel was well frequented, and as other vehicles sauntered in and out, no one made a move to stop him.

Before he could even begin to mourn the loss of what he'd begun to believe was his true destiny after all, Robbie was well on the road west, and still there were no sounds of pistol shots following him.

Sarah was unbelievably exhausted. The past months had taken their toll, and the sorrow of today's discovery had drained her totally. She lay huddled up in bed in the unfamiliar hotel room, hardly aware of where she was. She hoped Robbie wouldn't come back too soon. For the first

ime in a long while she wanted no one. She wanted to mourn
n complete privacy.

Besides that, she didn't want to think about the future.
Whether she would ever have contacted Aunt Lily after
oday, she hadn't really thought. There had been some vague
dea in her head that letters might be exchanged, and some
ontact with her relatives could continue.

She knew now it would have been a futile idea. Robbie
vould never have approved. It had been a dream, and even
hat dream had been taken away from her. Very soon,
Robbie would return to sea, and she would be left with
trangers in a place she didn't know. A sob escaped her
hroat. It would almost have been better to have taken
onas's hand in marriage than to feel so abandoned.

As she lay dulled in a half-sleep, she heard the click of the
loor handle as it opened. She didn't really want anything to
at. How could she think of food when her heart was
reaking?

The next minute she gave a smothered scream as a rough
and was clamped over her mouth, and she breathed the
trong odor of drink on someone's rancid breath. She knew
astantly that this wasn't Robbie, and at the guttural sound
f the voice she knew exactly who it was.

"So, at last we meet again, my fine Sarah," Jonas Endor
louthed softly. "And in the pirate's bed, where no doubt
ou've been for many a month."

He pressed against her mouth more cruelly, and although
er instincts were to scream and shout, when Sarah opened
er lips, she tasted the sweat on him and felt an urge to
omit.

"It's no good protesting, my beauty," Jonas went on. "By
ow the landlord will have sent for the constables and they'll
ave apprehended your precious Black Robbie. He'll be duly
ung as befits such scum. And that leaves you and me, dear
ousin. Now, if you promise not to struggle, I'll remove my
and. If you try to escape, I'll have no alternative but to

punish you. The landlord understands that we're closely related, and sees nothing strange in my staying here to protect you. You can expect no help from your lover, for like you, he's beyond anyone's help now."

He ended mockingly, and Sarah felt the weak tears gather in her eyes, She had no reason to doubt Jonas's words. Somehow he had discovered their presence. He must have followed them after her reckless visit to Endor House. And now, after all they had been through, Robbie had been taken into custody, and it was all her fault. She loved him more than life, and she had been the unwitting cause of his capture.

She nodded wildly, and the odious hand was taken cautiously from her lips. She brushed it away and scrubbed furiously at her mouth to remove the taste of Jonas's flesh. She heard him give a soft laugh.

"Are you telling me the truth?" she sobbed. "Have the constables taken Robbie?"

He stared at her, fury darkening his fleshy face.

"It seems you care more for the pirate than for your own fate, my dear," he sneered.

"I care for him because he knows how to behave like a gentleman," she flashed back in a moment of spirit.

Jonas gave a raucous laugh. "A gentleman?" he spluttered "Your opinions clearly need sharpening, Sarah. I fear that your months at sea with scurvy companions hasn't diminished your volatile nature. What else has it done for you, I wonder?"

Sarah realized that his voice had dropped to deceptive softness, and felt a new fear. Jonas had always lusted after her, even though she had been unaware of it until quite recently. Now, his thoughts were quite evident in his eyes. It would give him a twisted delight to take what she had so freely given to Robbie, whether he knew the facts or not. Like an animal stalking its prey, he would want to put his mark on her.

"If you touch me, I'll shout for the landlord," she said desperately.

He laughed coarsely. "No one will come, Sarah. I've taken care of that. The landlord has been told that my poor cousin is somewhat deranged after her ordeal and is in need of my comfort. I've instructed that we should be left alone. The walls are thick and we shall be undisturbed. And we have the whole night ahead of us."

Her hysteria rising, Sarah saw tht he was unbuckling the belt of his breeches. He meant to rape her, to force her into submission. Knowing his brute strength, she shuddered violently. She would be helpless to stop it.

Chapter 18

Jonas Endor cursed his luck with blasphemies no lady should ever hear, and Sarah welcomed them as if she listened to a soothing lullaby.

His lecherous intentions were clear, but the means to carry them out was miserably denied him. He had been drinking too freely for too long, and try as he might, there was no possible way his flaccid member would do as he wanted it to. He could expect no help from Sarah in the way of assistance. She was as frigid toward him as if she were made of ice, which only added to the dampening of his would-be ardor. She fought off his pawing advances with more confidence as the realization came to her.

"Why don't you leave me alone, pig?" she hissed at him finally. "You must know how you disgust me!"

She gave a cry as the back of his hand lashed out and caught her cheek.

"I will have you, Sarah, make no mistake on it," he said venomously. "You belong to me, and you've made me wait too long for you already. But by God, I'll see that you know it soon!"

Whatever else he might have said or done was lost as there came a loud hammering on the door. Sarah gasped in relief, twisting to free herself from where Jonas had pinned her beneath him. He struggled impotently with drink-sodden nerves to fasten his breeches as the landlord's voice penetrated the door.

"All right, damn you," he bawled out uncouthly. "Give a man a chance to get to the door, can't you?"

He lurched across the room, his temper still violent at his lack of success with Sarah, and threw open the door.

Sarah saw the large figure of the landlord standing there, and behind him, several constables discreetly averting their gaze from the lady in the rumpled bed.

Used to assessing situations that threatened to become unpleasant, the landlord took in the scene at a glance. He'd heard tales of the new owner of Endor House, and even without such tales, had quickly formed his own opinion of him.

He was new to the area, but when he had requested the presence of constables on Jonas Endor's say-so, they had surmised who the lady might be, and her circumstances. If it was assumed that the erstwhile visitor had been Black Robbie, it was too late now to do anything about his capture, and he was not in the business of witch-hunting a man, pirate or not.

Also, the landlord decided it was nothing to him whether the couple were married or not. All his sympathies were with the young lady. Especially now, with the news he had to impart. He spoke briskly to Jonas.

"Sir, I'm afraid your bird has flown," he said enigmatically. "By the time the constables arrived, there was no sign of either the stranger or the carriage in which he and the lady arrived. I'm sorry, but there's nothing more I can do."

Sarah was unable to resist a cry of relief. She never gave a thought to herself. All she could think of was that Robbie had gotten away. Thank God. *Thank God* . . . .

The look Jonas flashed at her was pure hatred. So, the bastard had run, and the reward for his capture was lost. The brief fury disappeared, because he still had the bigger prize.

265

All the same, claiming the pirate's capture would have sent his status rocketing among his contemporaries, and the reward would have eased the growing concern over his heavy gambling debts.

"Sir—is everything all right here?" the landlord said pointedly. "I trust you will be leaving the hotel shortly."

"I think not," Jonas growled. "I shall remain here with my cousin and escort her back to her rightful home in the morning. We need no chaperones."

"And I need no guardian!" Sarah said spiritedly. "I refuse to have you remaining in my room, Jonas!"

"It's my right to look after you in case the ruffian returns," Jonas snapped.

"But it's *my* right to suggest that for decency's sake, the lady remains in this room while you use another one, sir," the landlord said quietly but with a hint of menace in his voice. He was burly enough to use force to eject Jonas if need be, and they all knew it. "The lady is clearly upset, and I cannot allow any further distress to a patron of my hotel. If it is her wish to remain alone, then I must insist on it."

"It *is* my wish," Sarah said fervently, and at the sight of the constables still hovering, clearly wondering if there was going to be any further disturbance from this objectionable man, Jonas gave in.

"Very well. I'll take a room for the night, and my cousin and I will leave this miserable establishment first thing tomorrow morning."

Sarah went weak with relief. Somehow she seemed to have gained the sympathies of the landlord, who must be wondering just what kind of people had arrived at his hotel. But faced with Jonas Endor and his vile moods, anyone's sympathies could be roused toward his victim.

The constables retired reluctantly, and the landlord called for a servant to show the gentleman to his own room. Clearly, Jonas didn't intend to go far from Sarah, and loudly insisted that it should be a room adjoining hers.

She felt a kind of desperation listening to his bombastic voice as he went along the corridor. She felt trapped, knowing he would still be there in the morning. Unless she too did as Robbie had done, and fled during the night. The thought came to her immediately, and she swallowed hard, knowing what a risk a young woman took traveling alone at night. But to be with Robbie, she would take any risk, go anywhere.

"Have you recovered, my dear?" The landlord came into the room and spoke more kindly. "This has been an ordeal for you."

"Yes, thank you," she mumbled, and became aware of the rumblings in her stomach. It would be foolish not to eat. "But perhaps I could have the food sent up that was ordered for me? I have not eaten for some hours and I do feel a little faint. And please—do you know what became of my—my husband? Did he really get away safely?"

"Apparently so," the man said. "I was not aware of him leaving, but there's no sign of him or the carriage in which you arrived."

He hesitated, and then said what his own feelings dictated him to say. "I suspect that your cousin will soon be in a stupor and will sleep soundly all night. And if it was your wish to slip away, his own horse is tethered at the back of the hotel in the stables. Your bill was paid on arrival, and paid generously, so no one would be pursuing you on that account. Food and drink will be sent up to you directly, enough to sustain you in case you think fit to take a journey." He smiled slightly. "I'm only passing on idle thoughts, you understand."

She couldn't speak for a few seconds, choked by his rough plan and the sudden hope flaring inside her at such idle thoughts.

"I do understand, and thank you, so much."

She understood fully that he was giving her a chance to get away, to find Robbie, to be free of the shackles with which

267

Jonas threatened her. Even in the short time the three of them had become known to the hotel landlord, he couldn't fail to see which of the two men was the true gentleman, no matter what the guise.

An hour later Sarah was replete with food and drink, and thankful that the sober clothes she wore would make her less noticeable at night. The clothes were dark, and since she would be obliged to put up at several lodging houses during the long journey, she would say she was a poor widow going to her husband's family, and hope she would be given a night's accommodation without charge as was common enough in such circumstances.

She had been touched to find a small bag of provisions for the road accompanying the tray of food sent up to her, and knew this was the landlord's way of giving her his blessing. There would be no irate cousin or any constables tracking her down.

She waited a while longer until it seemed likely that the entire hotel slumbered peacefully. Cautiously, she crept out of her room and into the darkened passageway of the hotel. She paused outside Jonas's door, and heard the weighted snoring of the inebriated coming from inside. She went silently down the stairs and through the hotel lobby, where the night porter dozed peacefully in his corner.

And then she was out into the cool night, making toward the stables, where horses and carriages belonging to hotel patrons were housed. She knew Jonas's horse at once.

"There, Jewel, old boy," she whispered to the animal, gently fondling its nose. "You remember me, don't you? You and I are going to take a long hard ride."

Jonas's horse responded with a soft nuzzling against her hand, recognizing her scent. She led him quietly across the cobbles of the courtyard, hardly breathing in case anyone should wonder who was about at such an hour, but no one stirred, and no lights appeared.

Once out onto the road, Sarah quickly climbed astride the horse's back, leaning low to make herself as inconspicuous as she could. She could ride faster astride than sidesaddle, and besides, she wanted no rogues of the night to suspect she was a woman. Her skirts hampered her, but she pushed them down over her legs as far as she could, uncaring that it was totally unladylike.

For a moment she had a strange feeling of déjà vu, remembering how she had once felt so affronted at being forced to wear the clothes of a boy, on board *The Adventuress*. What would she not give now, for such a disguise!

But there was no time for reminiscing. She must travel as fast as the horse would allow. She would not dare to ride in this fashion in daylight, of course. If she rode at all then, it must be with decorum, but it would be far more frustrating than a gallop across open country, knowing her destination was Cornwall and Robbie.

A surge of exhilaration gripped her as the horse trotted away from the vicinity of the hotel and she was at last able to give him his head. There was much open country on the road to Cornwall, and with luck, she might even be there as soon as Robbie, since the horse and carriage would be obliged to travel slower than her own mount.

Sarah could imagine his joy when he realized how clever she had been in following him so swiftly. She hardly dared think he would be willing to come back for her. Sorrowfully, she knew his first loyalty must be to his crew, and it had taken enough persuasion on her part to get him to agree to this journey to Sussex in the first place.

She couldn't expect him to linger and seek her out again, no matter what his own feelings were. She respected him for his loyalty, even while it was her loss.

Never once did she stop to think why he had vanished without a word or without trying to save her skin. It was

269

obvious in her mind. The risks were too great, and he dare not think only of her when more lives were at stake. If Black Robbie was on land, then so were his crew, and his ship must be moored up somewhere. Jonas and the constables were now aware of it, and the witch-hunt would be on.

Sarah knew that her life was not in danger as his was. Had Jonas forced her to stay in Sussex, she would have been welcomed back as the prodigal daughter from whatever hell society imagined her to have been in. She understood and accepted Robbie's decision to do as he had. Never once did she imagine that his flight was for very different reasons.

Some hours later, Sarah slipped wearily from Jewel's back. Darkness still shrouded the countryside, but it was a slightly less dense darkness than previously. Morning could not be far away. How far she had traveled she could not guess.

She had encountered no vagabonds ready to pounce on her, even though she'd heard some revelers in the distance, and had hid breathless in a thicket of trees for some while until she was sure the only noises came from small insects and animals and the rustlings of leaves in the branches.

She was stiff and sore, and very hungry. She tried not to admit that she was frightened too. In her imagination, every shadow held a beast, every softening of the ground a marsh ready to suck her down. Before daybreak, she found a flat rock at the side of the road to sit on, and reached feverishly for the provisions the landlord had sent her.

There was bread and cheese and several apples. She bit into a piece of fruit hungrily, the juice helping to assuage her thirst. She rationed the bread and cheese carefully, in case it must last her for some time. There were even a few hard biscuits for Jewel, which touched her anew, and she fed them to him, feeling his soft mouth gratefully nudging her fingers.

And then she encountered something hard and round at the bottom of the provisions bag, and a few coins glinted in the pale light from the stars.

Tears rushed to her eyes. How very kind of the landlord to do this! She remembered how Robbie had overpaid the bill, and presumably this was the landlord's way of reimbursing him, when there had been no need. And in her headlong flight, Sarah had given no thought of how she would pay for anything, failing completely to remember that she had no money, nor had she ever had to deal with any. How narrow her life had been until now.

She had believed her old life to be the epitome of social convention, but she realized she knew nothing of the way others lived. She had always been cared for by family and elderly husband, cosseted and loved, and yet she was almost useless when it came to the everyday things of life that others took for granted. After last night, she would never take anything for granted again, Sarah thought shakily.

There was very little movement on the road during the early hours of the morning; the occasional farm cart going about its business, or traveling men with all kinds of cooking utensils and quack potions to cure all ills going to the next town to set up temporary camp to sell their wares. She could hear them approaching a long way off, pots and pans clanking against their carts, their owners usually bawling at a tired nag to get a move on.

She remounted carefully, ignoring the aches and pains, and rode until she came to a small town, as sunrise came over the horizon. It was easy enough to find a respectable-looking house with a sign advertising rooms, and at least this time she wouldn't need to rely on charity.

The buxom owner took one look at Sarah's drawn face and somber clothes and hardly needed to listen to her tale of being a poor widow. She was welcomed inside the house, offered a breakfast of eggs and bread dipped in tasty hot drippings, and then shown to her room, where she slept for most of the day. She was assured that Jewel would be attended to by the woman's husband.

She awoke with a start to hear a church clock chiming. Two . . . three . . . four . . . five . . . she tried to leap from the bed, only to find the stiffness hadn't subsided. She ached in every muscle, and for a few seconds she closed her eyes again and wished she could be lulled back to sleep by the everyday sounds going on outside the house. She knew it would be madness to tarry, but she did ache so. And this bed, though not the softest she had ever slept in, was manna to her senses right now.

But other thoughts crowded her mind. Once Robbie returned to the ship and the repairs were done, he would go back to sea, and Sarah intended going with him, even if she had to stow away to do it. She would not be fobbed off in some stranger's house, allowed only occasional visits from her man, being almost a kept woman!

She was still not fully awake, and thoughts were fleeting and insubstantial. But during her exhausted sleep, she had dreamed restless dreams, and in them the unthinkable had gradually edged into her mind, and now it began to overtake her wanderings.

If Robbie had seen Jonas arrive at the hotel so soon after they had returned from Endor House, he didn't think . . . he surely *couldn't* think that Sarah had led him there?

She was fully awake in an instant, the dreams becoming vivid and believable. Why had she never thought of it before? The sick thoughts made her faint. *Robbie must have thought she had betrayed him.* And if she had needed to reach him urgently before, the need was increased a hundredfold now, to tell him the truth. She couldn't bear it if he sailed away believing the worst of her.

"Why don't 'ee rest awhile longer, Ma'am?" the lodging-house woman said in her rich country voice when Sarah descended the stairs ready to leave. "You look fair wore out, and a few more days won't make no difference to your man's folks, I daresay. Sudden, was it, dearie?"

Sarah looked at her blankly, and then remembered she would be referring to the supposed death of Sarah's "husband." She almost wished she hadn't started on this tale. She was sure it was bad luck to invent a death, but she couldn't retract it now.

"Very sudden," she murmured. "And if you don't mind, it pains me to speak of it."

"Oh, I understand," the woman said at once. "Well, you know your business best, dearie, and if you must go, then at least let me give 'ee directions. Where is it you're making for?"

Instinct made Sarah avoid mentioning Cornwall. She had never been to the south of Wales, but it was the first name that sprang to her mind.

"You've a distance to go yet then," the woman said, staring. "I can't think who told 'ee to keep to the coast. You should have headed northwards, not west. Can I pack 'ee up some victuals for the road?"

"Oh, I would appreciate that," Sarah said gratefully, knowing how keen her appetite would be once she was traveling. And the bread and cheese had long since gone, shared finally with Jewel. Though the horse fared all right. There was always a nose bag and drinking trough even at these humble establishments for a hungry animal, and the woman assured Sarah he hadn't starved.

But she waited impatiently until daylight faded before traveling again. She felt a great urgency to get to Cornwall, and there were many miles to cover. All went well during the second night until the horse reared up at a small animal scuttling across the road in front of him, and unable to save herself, Sarah was thrown heavily with a cry of pain, landing on the dirt road and wrenching her shoulder in the process.

She tried to get up after a second or two, and fell back

gasping. As well as the knock to her shoulder, she realized her ankle was throbbing and swelling badly. Sobs of frustration mingled with the pain, and then she lost her senses as she seemed to fall into a black velvet space.

How long she lay unconscious she had no idea, but her first awareness was that of a large hand holding her steady, and moving experimentally down her leg. Her instinct was to scream, but her throat was so dry with terror that no sound came out as she tried to gather her wits. But she struggled to be free of the nameless horror.

"Hold still, Missy, or you'll only be making things a sight worse for yerself," a thickly accented male voice said. "'Tis a fine and dandy sprain you've got there, sure it is, or me name's not Dublin Dan."

Sarah groaned. She couldn't have a sprain. She didn't have *time* to have a sprain!

"How do you know? Are you a doctor?" she muttered. She instantly refuted the idea. What would a respectable doctor be doing on the road in the middle of the night, and smelling of whisky!

The man laughed. "Sure and am I not Ireland's finest!" He said cheerfully. "Known to man and beast as the curer of all ills, with me patent medicines gracing the homes of rich and poor alike for a pittance of payment, and your honest Dublin Dan asking only that patients recommend me to friends if they be cured, and to foes if they be not."

He chuckled, as if congratulating himself on his own verbosity, and Sarah guessed this was the usual spiel he used in front of crowds of gawking locals at fairs and revels, and felt a mite easier that at least she was not about to be ravished. Dimly she saw the flamboyant features of the showman, a thick shock of white hair and waxed mustache, the rather garish outfit that matched the cart standing nearby, its horse nuzzling contentedly at the sweet, dew-fresh grass of early morning.

There was painted lettering on the cart, and if Sarah

strained her eyes in the dawn light, she could make out the legend: DUBLIN DAN, YOUR MEDICINE MAN. HONEST AS THE DAY IS LONG, WITH POTIONS TO CURE ALL KNOWN ILLS AND THOSE YOU HAVEN'T EVEN THOUGHT OF.

The man saw her glance, and chuckled again. "Get's 'em every time, Missy. If summat ails 'em that hasn't got a name, then Dan's your man for inventing the ailment and providing the cure."

"But does the cure work?"

Sarah grimaced as she flexed her foot cautiously and felt the pain race through her ankle. For a few moments the company of this curious man had made her forget her purpose, but now it rushed back to her.

Dublin Dan cocked his head on one side quizzically.

"Depends how much the patient wants to be cured. Some enjoy being ill, see? But take yourself now, Missy. I'd say you were going somewhere in an almighty hurry to be on the road alone at such an hour, and you'd want a cure that was fast and lasting."

Sarah overlooked the fact that Dublin Dan was also an amateur philosopher, and what was popularly known as an observer of human nature. Her interest quickened.

"And do you have such a cure for a sprained ankle and a sore shoulder?" she demanded. "I must tell you I have no money. I'm a poor widow joining my husband's family."

"And I'm Joan of Arc," the man said dryly. "No matter. We all have secrets, and there's no obligation to share 'em. But to prove my words, I'll guarantee to have that ankle fixed in a shake of a lamb's tail. You may not be dancing on it for a night or two, if that's one of your requirements."

"I don't need it for dancing," Sarah said. "I told you, I'm a poor—"

She caught his shrewd glance, and amended her words. "I have a great distance still to travel, and I can't afford to waste the time in being sick."

Dublin Dan grunted. "There's many a patient who's said

the same thing, and had cause to be grateful to Dan. As for payment—did I ask for any?"

"No, but surely it's your livelihood."

He laughed. "Sure and if a drop of kindness along life's road is mine to give and yours to take, then we've both been paid our dues," he said extravagantly.

She wasn't quite sure how she had paid anything, but she lay back with a bit less apprehension as Dan strode across to his cart to fetch the appropriate potion that was supposedly going to cure her sprain.

He was a very large man, which presumably gave authority to his pronouncements regarding his wares, and Sarah suddenly saw the absurdity of the situation. Here she was, the Lord knew where, in the early hours of the morning, dependent on a stranger who professed to do something even the best doctors couldn't do.

The Endor family physician had always insisted on at least a week's bed-rest as a matter of course for any ailment, from a whitlow on a finger to an attack of the rheumatics, a fact that her Uncle Thomas had dourly remarked was to extract the highest possible fee for his visits.

Now, she watched a little apprehensively, as Dublin Dan returned with a bottle of colorless liquid and a great roll of wadding.

"'Tis a spirit mixture of my own concocting that I call enimum, Missy, and 'twill feel icy cold. Your ankle must stay bound for several hours to let the enimum do its work. After that, I guarantee you'll be walking with barely a limp and hardly a twinge."

Several hours . . . it wasn't so long, and by then she would be looking for a place to spend the day anyway. She felt the tenderness in the ankle as the man poured the mixture onto a piece of wadding and wrapped it around her ankle with surprisingly gentle hands. It numbed her almost at once, and then the wadding was bound tightly with a length of coarse cotton material.

"Thank you," Sarah mumbled.

"Now, the shoulder. How badly does it hurt?"

She moved it gingerly. It wasn't too bad, and clearly nothing was broken. She certainly didn't feel like removing her clothing for any further attentions, and he read her unspoken words accurately.

"Perhaps you'd care to place a pad of wadding wrung out in enimum inside your clothing. 'Tis an awkward part of the body to treat, but the spirit will still work its magic, if slightly slower than on the ankle."

She did as she was told, almost mesmerized by the man's confidence. This was obviously how such men worked their magic, if magic it was, by instilling the belief of a cure in their "patients." Sarah suddenly saw this episode as a new adventure. Nothing like it had ever happened to her before, and if Aunt Lily might have been horrified at her consorting with such a traveler on the road, Aunt Lily no longer had to be considered.

"Do you have other pains?" Dublin Dan enquired at the sudden shadow across her face.

"Only the pain of bereavement. As you suspected, I have not just become widowed, but I have recently learned that my aunt is dead."

"Ah. Then you do right to go on a journey. Nature is a great comforter. Where do you make for now?"

How far could she trust him? Sarah wondered. With that uncanny way of reading her mind, Dan went on speaking.

"Travelers such as meself are all free spirits, and have an unspoken respect for one another's reasons for traveling. Now what's to be done with you?"

When she didn't answer, he went on thoughtfully. "You can stay where you are and rest awhile until the ankle recovers, in which case I shan't see the result of my handiwork, and you may be at the mercy of any rogues abroad. Or you can ride with me for a spell. I've enough food and drink for two, and I'd be glad of the company. I'm

277

headed west where the mood takes me, through Devon and perhaps into Cornwall."

Sarah hesitated no longer.

"Then I'd be more than glad to ride with you if you'll have me—Mr. Dan."

"Good. and the name's Dan. So what do I call you? Or perhaps I should invent my own name for you. What about Primrose since I found you at the side of the road? Does that suit?"

"Why not?" Sarah heard herself laugh, the pain in her ankle and shoulder already pleasantly numbed as Dan helped her to her feet, and she felt suddenly buoyant.

With luck, she would soon be well on her way to Cornwall in the company of this eccentric and delightful Irishman, and far more safely than if she were traveling on her own.

Chapter 19

At the end of two days, Sarah and Dublin Dan had reached deep into the county of Cornwall without mishap. By then, Sarah had become used to country folk stopping the cart with inquiries for potions, or thanks for past services, sometimes with the gift of a pot of honey or homemade preserves, or a few coins for a new supply of a successful linament or rub. Sarah had been introduced as Dan's niece Primrose, and hearing the praises heaped on her unlikely benefactor, she had discovered a way of life about which she had never dreamed.

Sarah was amazed at how quickly she became fond of the outrageous character. It would be quite a wrench to part company with him, but she never forgot her purpose in reaching Cornwall for a single instant. And as promised, his magic cure had worked, her ankle was as good as new and the stiffness in her shoulder nonexistent.

Dan had cared for her as if she truly were his niece, she thought, and decided that there was good as well as bad in the world, however bizarre the outward trappings. Robbie himself had shown her that, as had the small kindnesses of the less raucous pirates, Surgeon and Flint, and then there was the undisguised and freely given adoration of young Tomby.

Her eyes misted for a moment, thinking how appalled she had been in what seemed like another life. *Was* another life, she corrected. When the word "pirate" was only to be uttered in polite company in hushed and disdainful tones. If the world only knew what she knew of the fierce camaraderie and loyalty!

Her reverie was interrupted by Dan pointing out a distant town, and telling her that they were fast approaching Helston. There was to be one of the regular country fairs in Helston over the next few days, and Dan would be taking up temporary residence to sell his wares.

By studying his map of the area, Sarah realized that this town was within a few miles of the coast where *The Adventuress* was hidden for repairs in a lonely creek. She studied the large map carefully, ostensibly to acquaint herself with their journey, but in reality to ascertain just how far she would have to go on alone. Not even to Dan did she reveal her true identity, or that of the man she sought.

She recognized the name of the fishing village nearby where Robbie's friends lived, and knew it had to be her destination. It would be easy enough to cut across the moorland and reach it. Even on foot it wouldn't be too difficult. But she still needed to repay this good Irishman for all his trouble, and she came to a decision.

"Dan, will you take my horse as payment for all your kindness?"

"Don't be insulting me, Primrose," he said almost angrily. "Sure and the company of your sweet self has been payment enough for a lonely traveler."

"But you'd be doing me a kindness," she insisted. "I shall have no more need of Jewel, but I can't just turn him loose. If you don't want him, then at least I know you'll sell him to a good home, and I'd be happy for you to take what you can for him—in the cause of furthering your research, of course."

She invented the last bit quickly, and knew that his pride

was restored as he accepted the gift graciously. If he was doubly curious as to why this young and beautiful colleen was prepared to go the rest of her journey on foot, he kept his curiosity to himself. Travelers on the road asked no questions of each other. It was an unwritten rule.

Truth to tell, Sarah was glad to be rid of Jewel, reminding her as he did of Jonas, and she gave the horse one last hug before parting from him, and then did the same to Dublin Dan.

"Sure and there are days when I wish I was forty years younger," he said gallantly. "Whatever it is you're seeking, Primrose, I wish you hearty luck in finding it."

"The luck of the Irish?" She teased, her eyes soft, but feeling a jaunty lift to her heart all the same at his words.

Blarney it might be, but to Sarah it was a sweet omen, just like the new and rugged landscape surrounding her, with its mingled salt tang and earthy scents of heath and moorland. She had read somewhere that Cornwall was a place of magic and mystery, and in the early dawn of a beautiful day, she could believe every word of it. There was sea on either side of the long finger of England's extremity, isolating Cornwall from the rest of the country, and adding to the legend that it was a land within itself.

The risks and fears of traveling alone quickly vanished. Now, she could be any young woman going on foot to a neighboring village to inquire after friends. But after the exhilaration of actually reaching her goal, Sarah began to feel dispirited.

She had no way of knowing the exact location of the creek hiding the ship. Its virtue for the pirates was that it was remote and secluded. But it had to be somewhere in the vicinity, and in a fever of anxiety, she decided to try and locate it first. She needed to find it before Robbie set sail, which must surely be soon, and she meant to sneak aboard as soon as it grew dark.

Once at sea, she knew there was no way that Robbie would turn back to abandon her. She stolidly refused to contemplate the event of a trial, with Quartermaster's thunderous voice condemning her for bringing bad luck to the ship.

But she soon realized how alone she was in her quest. She could hardly ask for information about a pirate ship undergoing repairs! But could she ask if anyone had seen a giant of a man with charismatic amber eyes, a traveling man dressed as a gentleman? It sounded a bit hazardous, but gradually she realized that surely no one would recognize such a description as belonging to the pirate Black Robbie.

Sarah began to admit that searching out one creek among so many in the maze of Cornish inland waterways was hopeless. She was very tired, her ankle reminding her, despite Dan's magic cure, that she had so recently sprained it, and she knew she was being extremely foolish. She would never find the creek. Robbie was too professional to allow a casual observer to locate its hiding place.

Suddenly the name of the couple she was meant to stay with came to her mind, and her spirits lifted again. Trewithan! That was the name. She would ask where a couple called Trewithan lived, and hope that they could direct her straight to Robbie.

But first she must find a tea room and quench her thirst. The sun had risen high in the sky by now and she had been walking aimlessly for hours since leaving Helston. There had been times when she had almost thought someone was stalking her, but every time she turned swiftly, there was no one there. It was like a shadow that disappeared every time she tried to see its elusive form.

It began to unnerve her, and ascribing the feeling to the fey quality of the moors had unnerved her even more. It was broad daylight, yet there was an uncanniness about this place, and she was thankful to return to the tiny fishing village she had already traversed several times.

The village boasted several respectable-looking establishments offering refreshment, and Sarah entered one of them and sat down with a sigh of relief as a woman came forward to take her order.

"Tea, and a bun, if you please," she said. She was ravenously hungry. Breakfast with Dublin Dan seemed like hours ago.

"With preserves and cream, me dear?" the distinctive soft Cornish voice asked.

"Yes, why not?" Sarah said recklessly. She could afford a bit of extra flesh. During the intense heat of the sea voyage and the restricted diet, she had lost weight. And Dan had been lyrical about the thick Cornish clotted cream in these parts, making her mouth water with his praises.

"You must try the Cornish pasties too, me love," he'd gone on, positively drooling at the thought. "Fresh baked with pastry as light as moondust, filled with a savory mixture of tatties and meat at one end, and jam at t'other. A meal fit for a king, and one that the Cornish miners take underground with 'em. When they're working in the dark they don't have to scramble about for different portions of the meal, see? 'Tis all in the one luscious pastry package."

Sarah smiled, remembering. Dublin Dan's gift of the gab was enough to persuade anybody that the moon was made of cheese, she thought.

But he hadn't exaggerated about the cream, she decided a short while later. Cornish cream and wild strawberry preserves on a bun still warm from the oven was like nectar. She delicately wiped a corner of her mouth, and saw that the serving woman was hovering nearby.

"Would you want anything more, Miss?"

"No, thank you. Unless—can you tell me if there are some people called Trewithan around here, please?"

The woman didn't hesitate.

"Oh, ah, me dear. There's the Trewithans at the cottage on the slope, and old Abel Trewithan who keeps the chandlery. Then there's the young 'uns come recently to live here from Falmouth, and I b'lieve the new exciseman living over to Lizard Town be called Trewithan. Or mebbe it were Trewinth—"

"Thank you very much," Sarah said faintly, aghast at this last piece of information. Excisemen spelled certain trouble for pirates. She had no idea where Lizard Town was, but it obviously couldn't be far for this woman to know someone there. And to Sarah it seemed annoyingly true that every other person in Cornwall had the same or similar names.

"Which one of 'em were you wanting?" the woman asked.

"Well, now that I come to think of it, I'm not sure if it was Trewithan at all," Sarah said quickly, the mention of a new exciseman still sending small shocks through her. "It's no matter anyway. I'm only passing through and had the name mentioned to me by a friend."

The woman went away and Sarah shivered, despite the warmth of the day. How easy it would be to say the wrong thing to the wrong person! The tea room was evidently a popular one, with frequent changes of customers, and any one of them might be listening, and wondering about this stranger inquiring after some people called Trewithan. A word in the wrong ear and she could put Robbie in danger without even knowing it. Her anxiety exaggerated the slightest risk.

She glanced around, thankful to find that other people were busy with their own affairs. Several matrons were gossiping over tea and buns, a group of fishermen bringing a whiff of the sea with them were huddled together in a corner, and a man on his own sat back in the shadows, watching her. *Watching her. . . .*

Sarah realized with a sudden stab of fear that the man had been there most of the time she had been in the tea room. With the memory of hindsight, she recalled him entering as she was giving her order, and without giving thought to how or why, she wondered fearfully if it could be some henchman of Jonas's who had been following her all this time, hoping that she would lead him straight to Black Robbie. Her mouth was dry as she turned her head swiftly away from the man's surreptitious gaze.

Then, quite unbidden, she remembered Robbie's words about facing the dragon. And if this unknown man was her new dragon, she would be better equipped to deal with it by knowing the man's business.

She had to pass him on her way out of the tea room. He sat in an alcove nearby, and as she rose to leave, she paused at his table, her heart thudding.

"Do you think you know me, Sir?" she asked in a low voice, taking in briefly his shabby garb without looking into his face. A fisherman, perhaps, or someone who worked on the boats in the harbor for a pittance.

"I think perhaps I do."

Her heart lurched crazily before it settled down again. The voice that answered was one that she knew. One that she had dreamed about and longed for, and had heard, deep and seductive, in the most intimate moments she had ever known. Sarah's head jerked up to look at his face. The eyes looking back at her were amber, though darkened with an expression she couldn't read. Not desire, not love. Sarah felt faint.

"Robbie—" she whispered. She sat down abruptly at the chair alongside him, not knowing if it was wise to do so. They were enclosed in a small private world of their own in the alcove, yet she was numbed by the hardness in his face.

"Aye, 'tis Robbie. I've been tracking you for some time, lassie. I've followed you over the moors all this day, and I'm still not sure for what purpose you're here."

"So it was you," she said involuntarily, thankful for a second to know she hadn't been followed by goblins or the reputed underground creatures of the tin mines that were

285

worked in these areas. Thankful to her soul it hadn't been Jonas. . . .

He sat unmoving, waiting for her to speak, and she ran her tongue around her cracked lips. It was hardly credible that this was her beloved, watchful and alert, as if he suspected that at any minute the door would burst open and the military would march him away to the gallows.

"Robbie, I was desperate after you left the hotel. I understood your reasons, but I thought, I expected that you'd be waiting for me, that you must have known I'd come after you, that you wouldn't want me to make this long journey by myself—"

Her voice dwindled away. It was as if she had never consciously given thought to these things before, but now that she did, she knew precisely why he hadn't waited. She could see it in those eyes that she loved, so accusing and unrelenting. He thought she had betrayed him! And the words he had just spoken—he had been tracking her all day—he thought she had come to Cornwall with Jonas, to give him up to his enemies! The swift pain of it gave way just as instantly to rage.

"You couldn't honestly believe that I'd betray you to Jonas," she was forced to speak in a low, bitter voice, for this was not the place to rant and rave, even though her instincts made her want to beat against his chest in a fury.

"What else was I to believe?" He leaned forward, his voice as harsh as she had ever heard it. "First of all, you insist on going to Endor House alone, then you're in a fever of anxiety and want me to leave you alone in the room."

"You know why! I was bereaved on account of Aunt Lily!"

"So you said. But I know how accomplished an actress you've become, lassie. That too may have been a ruse for all I knew, and when I saw your cousin at the hotel there was no time for speculation."

"So you ran and left me," Sarah said bitterly.

286

"You know my life, Mistress Huxley, and this was not the time for sentiment."

They stared at one another, two who had once shared love so glorious that each would have given the world for the other. As remote as two enemies now, each fearful of the other in different ways, Robbie unconvinced of her loyalty, Sarah bitterly hurt at his mistrust.

"So what do you see now?" she asked sarcastically. "Do you see my cousin with me? Since you've been tracking me all day, you'll know he is not in Cornwall! Do you see the military, or the excisemen? And do you think I enjoyed being a woman alone on the long road to find you? Does that not in itself speak of something more than betrayal?"

To her fury her voice broke a little, and several matrons at another table glanced their way. Sarah swallowed. Dear heaven, she thought hysterically, didn't he know that her emotions were near to the breaking-point! She had traveled the width of England to find him, risking danger at every turn in the road, risking everything.

And from the look on his face, he no longer wanted her. A sob caught in her throat and tears shimmered angrily in her eyes as she brushed her hand across them.

Robbie saw the gesture. Saw the trembling in the soft hand that had caressed him so intimately, remembered the way he had wanted to love and cherish this woman for always. Savagely, he reminded himself of his own rule. Neither sentiment nor lust could play any part in the need for survival.

"Are you saying I was mistaken? That you didn't give your cousin the information that I was at the Bell Hotel?" he demanded. "The truth now, Sarah."

She found a crumb of comfort in the fact that he had used her name for the first time since their reunion—if that was what this unreal confrontation could be called.

"Of course you were mistaken," she said, her voice vibrant with passion. "Dear God, do you think I would betray the

287

other half of myself—which is what you were to me?"

And still are . . . the words danced inside her head, pride making her ashamed of her own womanly weakness at loving this man so much that she would willingly die for him. Her eyes closed, hating herself for the weakness, and then she felt the pressure of Robbie's hand on hers.

"My love, I think perhaps we should leave this place and go somewhere where there are fewer interested eyes on a fisherman deep in conversation with a lady," he said gently.

She searched his face for meaning. Had he really called her his love? Her heart stopped for a moment and then raced on, because it seemed that the impossible had happened, that the mistrust had gone from his eyes.

"Then you believe me?" she asked in a strangled voice.

He gave her a rueful smile. "It seems that the ties between us are stronger than any outside influence, my Sarah. Yes, I believe you. No woman could lie so convincingly. But now I shall leave here quietly, and I suggest that you go out in a few minutes' time. I'll be leaning over the harbor wall until I see you emerge, and then you will follow me up the hill they call the slope. When I go into a cottage, follow me there."

"Is that where your friends live?" she murmured, remembering that this was one of the places the serving woman had mentioned.

"That's right. Don't rush, Sarah."

He got up and moved away from the table as if they had never spoken, and Sarah tried to recover her breath.

It was all right. She had found Robbie. Yet for some reason an inexplicable air of impending disaster seemed to gather her up and leave her weightless, as if she floated somewhere in an alien atmosphere in which she couldn't breathe properly, and unconsciously she fought for air. The feeling was one of total mindless panic as it gathered her up and then plunged her down into an abyss. As if she were drowning. . . .

"Are you all right, Miss? That roughneck wasn't accosting

you, was he? You need to be careful o' strangers, me dear."

Sarah realized the serving woman was watching her curiously, wondering about this customer who seemed to have the hallmarks of a lady, and yet had sat down of her own accord with the uncouth-looking stranger.

For a moment, Agnes Killen had wondered if the lady was such a lady after all, but the poor mite looked quite ashen now, as if she'd just seen something not of this world. And Agnes, who believed implicitly in such things, looked at Sarah with more interest.

"I'm quite well," Sarah said in a small voice. "I felt very strange a few moments ago and had to sit down here to recover myself. I'm sorry."

"Don't be sorry, me dear," Agnes said stoutly, and then her voice dropped to a mysterious softness. "There's times when we none of us keep full control of our senses and see things we're not meant to see."

She might have expanded on this, anticipating some snippet of delicious spine-tingling revelation from this young lady with the beautiful face and the unfashionable hairstyle, had not Sarah got to her feet unsteadily, and moved quickly out of the tea room, with a mumbled apology about needing fresh air. The last thing she wanted was for the woman to start attributing Sarah's pallor to some supernatural experience.

Especially since she half-suspected it herself, and she didn't want it, choosing to put it as far from her mind as she could. To her wild relief she saw Robbie, standing solid and dear against the railings of the harbor wall. There was nothing fey about him, and she was probably being an impressionable woman, caught by the enchantment of Cornwall and the emotion of finding Robbie again.

She saw him glance her way and then look away again, before he moved casually away from the harbor, with its jumble of fishing boats and lobster pots, where men in thick woolen garments sat on the sandy beach mending nets and

289

talking in a language as strange to Sarah's ears as any she had heard on her travels.

Robbie walked steadily toward the hodgepodge of fishermen's cottages up a narrow cobblestone hill. This then was the slope. Above it the ever-present gulls wheeled and dipped, giving out their peculiarly unattractive mourning cries. In Sarah's nostrils the luring smell of the sea was suddenly very strong, making her shiver.

She followed Robbie at a distance, thankful that very soon she would be welcomed inside the Trewithans' homely cottage, assured now that Robbie believed her story. It was strange to realize that she had felt more at home on *The Adventuress* than here, the sight and sound and scent of it, its dangerous attractions glittering in dazzling diamond points, gradually fading and merging with the faraway horizon.

You could believe in anything here, Sarah thought, wishing such sensations didn't keep washing over her. Sirens luring men to their deaths with their sweet unearthly voices, mermaids whose charms could make mortal men forget wives and sweethearts and long for a life below the waves, an obsession that could only end in death. . . .

She stilled such thoughts with a huge effort. What was wrong with her, for pity's sake! She was not clairvoyant, and never wanted to be, and the day was as it had always been, blue and fresh and scented with sweet aromas. She must be so intoxicated with it all that it was allowing her mind to expand and become so unwillingly receptive.

Robbie opened a small gate and went inside one of the cottages, and when Sarah was sure no one was watching her, she did the same. As soon as she reached the front door it was opened, and she was inside, where an extraordinary air of safety and friendliness dispelled the more unnatural sensations, to her intense relief.

For a moment her gaze encapsulated the scene; the homely fireside and the rag rugs on the stone floor; the knickknacks on the mantel and the evidence of a life spent near the sea—a collection of shells and flotsam shaped into bizarre ornaments, clearly whittled by a man's loving hands. The old man sucking on a clay pipe in the corner of the room, rising stiffly to greet this newcomer; the wife, round and small and smiling.

And Robbie, who opened his arms to her and folded her inside them.

Sarah blinked away the tears of joy at knowing in her heart that nothing was going to part them again. And if this certain knowledge was a small inheritance of Cornwall's magic, then it was one facet that she didn't push away.

"Meet my good friends, Sarah," he said quietly. "Jude and Freda Trewithan."

"Welcome to our home, and yours for as long as you want it, me dear," Freda Trewithan said in the creamy-rich accent Sarah was coming to know.

"Thank you, Mrs. Trewithan," Sarah said, startled by such instant hospitality.

"Lord love us, dearie, but the name's Freda, same as 'tis to this lovely man here," the woman said at once, smiling at Robbie. "And this 'ere's Jude. Don't you go standing on ceremony with us, or we'll have to behave like we've got company."

Sarah smiled, liking her at once, even though to her, etiquette had always counted; a person had to know another very well before becoming so familiar. It was the done thing, even though it sometimes stifled a promising relationship before it had even begun. Yet here, between these four walls, there was a warmth that she had never known before. It seemed to be borne in the very stone, as if this was a cottage that received and gave out love in equal measure. How fanciful she was being now! she thought with a little shock.

"You've chosen well, Robbie." Jude Trewithan spoke up for the first time, his hand, gnarled as an ancient oak, taking hold of Sarah's and giving it a fatherly squeeze. "She'll do nicely for 'ee."

She just managed not to laugh out loud, touched by the simplicity of his words. It was a recommendation the pompous Jonas Endor would have thought outrageous. But here, and now, with Robbie looking ridiculously pleased at this voice of approval, it was exactly right.

"You'll be wanting to see your room, lovey," Freda said suddenly. "'Twill be here any time you're needing it, whether for a short time or more permanent."

She saw more than Robbie did, Sarah thought, as the two women exchanged a look of understanding. A woman needed to be with her man, not parted from him while he roamed the high seas, and awaited his pleasure with impatience.

His pleasure . . . her throat caught again. For a while she had wondered if that unique and exquisite pleasure they had known would ever come again. But now she knew that it would. He had always belonged to her, and she to him, and in her heart, Sarah had always known it.

She followed Freda's heavy footsteps up the creaking staircase to a small bedroom at the front of the cottage. There was barely room for anything more than a large bed covered in a patchwork quilt that Sarah suspected had been worked by Freda's own hands, and a chest of drawers with a mirror above it. Through the small window was a view of the harbor and beyond it the sea.

"We've only two bedrooms, and me and Jude prefer the back one. We can allus see the sea, but Robbie likes to be in sight of it."

Sarah felt her heart leap. So this was clearly Robbie's room and Freda saw nothing wrong in assuming Sarah would want to share it. The frankness of these people astonished her, yet she was not offended by it. She guessed instinctively that Jude and Freda would take such things to be normal. If two people loved, then they would want to be together. It was as natural as birth and death and everything that went between

As if in a dream, she saw the woman retreat and heard the door close behind her. And then there were only the two of them, together as they were always intended to be. Robbie opened his arms to her again, and she went toward her destiny willingly and passionately, and that little room became a warm and beautiful place, a haven of ecstasy Sarah had begun to think would never be hers again.

"Don't leave me here, my darling," she whispered in his ear when they lay close and fulfilled in the afterglow of love. "Much as I love your friends, don't ever leave me again—"

"How could I leave you now?" he whispered back, kissing the softness of her breasts where the shine of love still glistened in a rosy fullness. "How could I ever leave my heart?"

Chapter 20

They remained in each other's arms until the evening sky deepened into darkness. No one disturbed them, and neither felt any inclination to stir, even though they knew they must do so very soon. But to move from this haven meant returning to the real world, to be sociable with others and eventually to go silently through the night to rejoin Robbie's ship. By now, Sarah knew that the repairs had been done, and that the crew would be uneasy at remaining too long in one place.

They had already stayed longer than usual because of Robbie's journey across the country with her, and when he left them getting the ship ready that morning there had been strong signs of unrest and more than a hint of mutiny among Quartermaster's followers. Robbie had been in two minds whether to sail the previous night, or to keep a last glimmer of hope alive that Sarah might yet come to him, and prove his suspicions groundless. To their mutual joy, they now knew that it was worth the wait.

But they both knew also that tonight the ship must glide smoothly out on the tide into safer waters. It was the last night of no moon and *The Adventuress* would be as well concealed by a thick Cornish mist as she was ever likely to be. The crew wouldn't wait any longer, and they had still to see their reaction when Sarah returned with their Captain.

She stirred regretfully in Robbie's arms as his hands smoothed back her dark hair, grown longer now and curling around her cheeks.

"Do you come with me then, my lassie?" he asked softly.

"Anywhere, my love. To the ends of the earth if need be," Sarah answered, and he held her close to his heart for a last close embrace. And then she became aware that he had grown very still and was no longer listening to her.

She lifted her head from the pillow and then she heard it too. The sounds had grown insidiously and yet now they seemed to fill her head. The sounds of running feet on the cobbled streets, as if the whole village had suddenly come alive.

Robbie was out of bed in an instant and moving toward the casement window and throwing it wide. Sarah followed, a strange dread already worming its way into her gut. As if she already knew.

In the late evening light, she could see people running down to the harbor, some already in nightclothes and shawls, women with curling-rags in their hair, and men pointing excitedly out to sea. Just as instantly both Sarah and Robbie became aware of the distant heavy rumbling sound that was like thunder, and yet she was certain was not thunder.

The noise could have been going on for some time, Sarah realized, in the way that something dully insistent only reached the consciousness when the mind was freed from other occupations. And theirs had been too occupied with rediscovering each other. . . .

"Dear God," Robbie mouthed. "Surely it canna be—"

"What is it?" Sarah asked fearfully, but he was paying no heed to her. And she found her gaze irresistibly drawn to where he pointed far out to sea.

By now there should have been only inky blackness in the moonless night. Instead there was a red glow in which was etched the black skeletal shape of a sailing ship. Even as Sarah scrambled to see behind Robbie, she heard a renewed burst of gunfire as the ship's own cannon spat fire on its pursuers.

"Robbie, it doesn't have to be—"

"What other ship could it be but mine?" he said harshly. "'Tis *The Adventuress,* lassie. 'Tis clear those fools have been persuaded by Quartermaster to mutiny and he's taken charge of the ship. They must have sailed in daylight, and probably been watched every bit of the way while a fleet was assembled to make light work of her."

"But you don't know that, love!"

"What other vessel besides a pirate ship gets such treatment? Don't humor me, Sarah. I know my own business, and I know my ship, and right now I'm watching her death throes."

He was struggling into his clothes as he spoke, and Sarah hurriedly did the same, not knowing what he was about to do. If it was *The Adventuress,* as it surely must be, then he could do nothing to save her nor Surgeon and the rest . . . young Tomby must be scared out of his wits by now . . . Sarah felt a prickling in her eyes at the thought, and then the blood pounded in her ears. She knew that, but for fate, it would have been herself and Robbie who perished, as those other were surely perishing right now.

Her attention was caught by the onlookers on the beach, circling the harbor like black vultures, lit only by the lantern lights that had appeared in their hands. Even little children were clapping and cheering, and Sarah realized sickly that they were actually celebrating the death of the pirate ship and all those on board.

She gasped, beginning to shake all over as the enormity of what was happening and the vicious glee of those watching swept through her. Robbie pulled her back from the open window and slammed it shut. It made no difference. She could still hear the cheering and merrymaking.

In her head she could hear the screams of Tomby and the others, she could almost taste the smell of burning as their flesh caught fire and shriveled like parchment dissolving into ashes; she could feel the world closing in for those who tried to escape by leaping into those enticing dark waves. . . .

She felt the slap of Robbie's hand against her cheek, shocking her back to reality, and gulped at the pain of it. He held her fast as she seemed near to swooning.

"I can't bear it," she wept, managing to gather her breath. "Poor Tomby—and all of them—"

"It's too late to think of them. They're all doomed. One way or another, they'll all end this night the same way. God help those who are captured and face the gallows. Far better to end it out there where they belong."

He spoke savagely, not daring to let sentiment enter his voice for a single second. Not daring to let her see how he, too, ached inside for his companions of many years. If he did, Sarah would surely go completely to pieces.

"How can you be so hard?" she raged against him, not understanding. "They're your friends!"

"They wiped out our friendship when they took command of my ship. You know the rule that says if any crew member fails to return in time for sailing, the ship sails without him. But one thing they do not do is take her out to sea, leaving their captain defenseless. They've disobeyed that rule, and therefore it was mutiny. I know them, Sarah, better than you think."

They heard voices outside the door, and then a rapid hammering on it. Sarah felt a frisson of fear that somehow the excisemen had tracked down Black Robbie after all, and then she heard Jude Trewithan's voice, followed by his wife's. Robbie put Sarah away from him and strode to the door to let the couple inside. Freda's face was white.

"You'll have heard the firing, Robbie? Jude's been down the harbor to find out what's afoot, and they say 'tis the excisemen who got wind of the pirate ship moving out to sea from Widow's Creek."

"We heard it, Freda. We see it," he said briefly. And then his voice was drowned as an almighty burst of gunfire shook the cottage. Robbie rushed to the window, the others crowding behind him.

The Adventuress was brilliantly silhouetted now, flames leaping from bow to stern and crawling up her masts like giant glowing serpents. All around her were the ghostly shapes of other vessels, moving in for the kill.

Robbie's ship was too far out for anyone to see whether any of the crew jumped overboard or were burned alive, but Sarah's vivid imagination supplied the horrific images all the same.

"I can't bear it," she sobbed. "Nor can I believe those ghouls at the harbor are rejoicing because men are being killed. It's barbaric!"

"Thank whatever God you have that 'tis not your man among them, me dear," Jude's voice reminded her. "And don't think too badly of fisherfolk. We're simple souls down here, and all pirates be tarred with the same brush to most minds. There's many a household that's lost its man to the sea, and plenty of ships that have fallen foul to brigands. Remember, 'tis a pirate ship out there. They see only the ship and not the men inside it."

"I thought Robbie was your friend!" she said, not liking these words at all. "How can you condemn him so?"

"Aye, so he is, and I'd defend him to the death, but I don't like pirate ways and never have."

"Leave it, Sarah. These are good people, and I'll not have them criticized," Robbie snapped as tension in the bedroom seemed to mount. "Besides, I think that no one need worry any longer about my pirate ways," he added, his voice suddenly as hard and unyielding as stone.

They followed his gaze, and even as they crowded in front of the window, the ship seemed to turn turtle and throw her stern into the air. It hovered there for a moment like some agonizing beast, before plunging into the sea with a great cracking noise as if its back had broken, echoed by a roar of approval from the wildly dancing onlookers at the harbor and the beach.

"May God have mercy on all their souls," Sarah heard Robbie say quietly.

She felt a tightening in her throat at the dignified words, undoubtedly the only benediction the pirates would ever have allowed be said for them. And in such stark contrast to the crazy prancings of the village folk. Sarah felt such disgust at their rejoicings, and yet despite it all, she could understand it. Pirate ships were the scourge of the seas, and the notorious Black Robbie one of the most sought-after.

She caught her breath. What of Black Robbie now? She suddenly noticed Freda Trewithan hugging Robbie as though he were a bereaved child, and saw Freda's old eyes filling with tears. Sarah heard the woman give her own form of consolation. A full belly was Freda's panacea for all ills.

"'Tis a sad day for 'ee, and I doubt that you'll be wanting the meat pie I've baked specially for 'ee. But come downstairs when you're ready, and try to eat a morsel."

"How can I think of eating, Freda?" Robbie's voice was strained. "There's no heart in it for me."

Sarah realized how hungry she was, and felt almost shamed by the fact as she felt the gnawing in her stomach at the mention of a meat pie. The smell of the baking was permeating the upper rooms by now, and it was a long time since she had eaten.

"Robbie, I think we should eat," she said in a low voice. "It won't help any of those in the sea if we starve ourselves, and Freda's gone to all this trouble."

His eyes seemed to burn as he looked at her. Amber eyes that were suddenly molten fire. *Dear God,* she thought fearfully, *he's not turning against me because of this, is he? He doesn't blame me for the loss of his ship and his men . . .?*

But she realized he wasn't really looking at her at all, but beyond her to some place of memory to which she had no access. And then she knew. She remembered the home that had been burned to the ground, and the family with it. And she knew the bereft young boy that had been Robert Argyll was reliving every moment in seeing his ship and his surrogate family burn. She was numbed by his look. It shut her out, and enslaved him in a private hell of his own.

"Can I have some supper, Freda?" She turned roughly to the woman, unable to bear Robbie's expression any longer. "I fear I shall faint if I don't get something hot inside me, and that will be no help to anybody."

"'Course you can, lovey, and I think perhaps Robbie will do better to be by himself for a while," Freda said with more perception than Sarah might have expected. "Come you downstairs, Jude, and find a bottle of brandy to bring up for the boy, and the rest of us will have some with our supper. We're all in need of a bit of extra strength."

Robbie hardly saw them go. All his thoughts were wrapped up inside himself as past mingled with present, so painful he could hardly bear it. He needed neither food nor drink for sustenance, but he took the bottle of brandy Jude brought him, and deliberately proceeded to pour the contents down his throat, the effect of the spirit managing to dull the worst of the pain, at least temporarily.

"I'm thinking 'twill take more'n a few days to put the boy to rights after this," Freda said to Sarah, who realized she could only pick at the food after all. Ravenous as she was, much of her appetite seemed to desert her as soon as she put a fork to her mouth. Her brief amusement at hearing Freda refer to Robbie as "the boy" quickly vanished from Sarah's mind at the seriousness of the other's voice.

"I'm thinking the same," she murmured.

"Aye, 'tis a bad blow to have two tragedies in one lifetime," Jude said heavily, and Sarah concluded they must know more than they let on about their visitor.

"Do the people around here never wonder about Robbie when he stays here?" she asked carefully. "A stranger appearing at about the same time as any reported pirate activity must surely arouse suspicion."

Even now, she thought fearfully, if someone thought there was still such a prize to be captured, Robbie could be in dire danger.

"Folk in these parts know Robbie as our nephew," Freda told her. "'Tis a long while since he first came, and nobody ever questions it. He always dresses the same way as we, and fits in with the rest of us. We make no bones about our humble surroundings, lovey, and Robbie always said 'twere as fine as a prince's palace as far as he was concerned."

"He's right," Sarah said honestly. Of what use were the fine trappings of the grand life without peace of mind? These two old folk here had that in abundance. While Robbie . . . when had he last felt that state? Sarah wondered. He had had his fill of excitement in his life, but never real peace of mind.

And never the exorcism of his parents' deaths. Perhaps until now, when the burning of his ship must have brought that time searingly back to him. The effects of this day could go either way with him.

It was the same for her . . . Sarah shivered. She had been forcing herself to keep at bay the hated images of people drowning, conjuring up as they did the images of her own dear parents. She and Robbie both had to come to terms with the past and the present. If they didn't, then there was no peace in the future for either of them. They each had to face their dragons.

"Laying ghosts, lovey?" she heard Freda ask gently.

She smiled crookedly. "A little," she said, thinking how kind these people were. They knew nothing about her, yet they took her in and made her welcome. How generous were these simple souls, who had nothing to give but their loving hearts, and gave them freely. She felt her eyelids prick with emotion coupled with sheer exhaustion. But she dare not go back to that front bedroom yet, where Robbie needed to be alone. And she too needed to be alone with her thoughts.

"Do you think I dare go down to the harbor?" she asked suddenly. "I wouldn't be in any danger, would I?"

"That you wouldn't, me dear," Jude said. "You may get some curious looks, being a stranger, but pay no heed and if you're asked, just say you're visiting the area. City folks sometimes come among we rustics for a bit of countrifying. Mother and me never go out at night, but your limbs be younger than ours, so the cobbles won't worry you. And I reckon you'd like to find out what you can."

"Yes, I'm sure Robbie would want to know exactly what happened," Sarah said, escaping thankfully from those too-knowing old eyes as she reached for her shawl. Had she sounded too superior for a second? God knows she hadn't meant to!

She went out of the cottage into the cool night air, and was instantly aware of the stench of burning. Even from this distance, where the red glow of the doomed pirate ship had long since disappeared beneath the waves, the strong smell of burning hung in the air, and wafted toward the village and the harbor.

She shuddered, glancing back toward the bedroom window, thankful to see that Robbie had fastened it shut. He would need no reminders such as the stench of burning. Behind the drawn curtains the bedroom was all in darkness. She could imagine him lying on his bed, eyes wide and unseeing, reliving too much.

"'Ere, mind where you're going, me dear, or you'll end up in the drink same as that scurvy bunch!"

She was startled by the voice right beside her, and realized she had already walked down the slope and straight into a crowd of revelers swinging jugs of ale about.

"I'm sorry. But what's been happening? I'm a stranger here."

"A stranger, be 'ee? And a mighty handsome one at that!" one of the fishermen said gloatingly at the sight of her, and was quickly shouted down by his companions.

"Please, can you tell me what happened?" She turned to one of the others, less in his cups than the first.

"Why, 'tis the death of the pirate, me dear. The one they call Black Robbie. Surely you've heard of 'im?"

"Well, everybody's heard of him," Sarah said faintly. The fisherman laughed more heartily, and pointed out to sea.

"'Is ship were spotted earlier today coming out o' Widow's Creek, and the excisemen 'ave had their eyes on it ever since. They waited till dark and then circled her. The tale is they was going to try to get aboard the pirate ship, and bring 'em back to be strung up as was right and proper, but the blackguards started firing, and the excisemen had to do the same. There were too many of 'em for the pirates to stand a chance, and the only sorrowful thing is that nobody gets the reward for Black Robbie's capture. Swallowed up by the fishes by now, I daresay, and good riddance to 'im."

A roar of approval followed his colorful tale, and Sarah slid away from them as one and another brandished a jug of ale for her to sample. She moved swiftly in and out of the various groups and chattering fisherfolk, none of whom seemed eager to leave the scene of such excitement. It gradually dawned on her that it was totally accepted that Robbie had been on his ship and perished with it.

Black Robbie was dead. Time and again she heard the words. And the rest? No one could claim the reward for Robbie, unless his body washed up somewhere along the coast in due course, and by then it would probably be so bloated and distorted from being crushed against the rocks as to be unrecognizable. Sarah began to realize the implications behind the words.

Black Robbie was dead. But David Roberts was not. And neither—if his own sensibilities would allow it—was Robert Argyll. A fevered possibility began to take hold of her. A small shiver of hope amid the turmoil of this terrible night. A hope to cling to, for now. . . .

By the time she went back to the Trewithans' cottage up the slope, she had been pushed and jostled, and the excitement of the village folk had filled her with a strange resentment. And yet she couldn't entirely condemn them. These were simple folk, the way Freda and Jude were simple. They saw things in black and white, and since a pirate ship contained the worst scum of the earth, it had come to its rightful end.

It puzzled Sarah therefore, just why the Trewithans should be so loyal to Robbie, since they obviously knew exactly who he was, and what he was.

They welcomed her back to the cottage with a hot drink and a plate of biscuits still warm from the oven.

"What news then, lovey?" Freda asked sympathetically. "Was it an ordeal to be among 'em?"

"A little," Sarah admitted. "The general opinion is that Black Robbie's dead, and good riddance to him."

She waited for a response to this, and saw Freda shake her head sadly.

"Aye, 'tis time for the boy to stop his wanderings, and I feared this was the only way he'd ever do it. There's not a pretty maid yet who's managed to persuade him, though I fancy present company's come very near to it. But 'twas always obvious to we that a man such as Robbie had to control his own destiny."

"I'd say destiny was controlling him now," Sarah said. She found that she needed to talk with these people who knew Robbie, to restore this night to something less traumatic. She needed to keep the conversation alive.

Jude shook his head decisively. "He's seen his ship burn and die, and when a thing's finished, it's over and done with, and to go against it is to play against whatever fate puts in

304

your way. No, he'll make a new life now. He's done it before, and he'll do it again."

"Then you know all about him," Sarah stated quietly.

"Oh, ah, my love, we know all there is to know," Freda said softly. "We've known him from the time he brought Jude home half-drowned, his boat smashed to matchwood, and near to putting an end to his life when he got the fears for going back to sea. 'Twas Robbie who talked him out o' the fears and put new life back into him—aye, and bought a new boat for the remainder o' Jude's fishing days. We owe 'im more than we can repay."

It revealed much about Robbie the man, but it still didn't tell Sarah if they knew of his early life.

"Who do you say is visiting you, when folk ask? Your nephew?" she asked cautiously. "Forgive me if I'm prying, but you must know that I'm to be trusted."

"If we didn't, you'd have been out of here afore you crossed the threshold," Jude said in a mild but surprisingly menacing voice. "We say 'tis our nephew David, o' course."

He left them then, saying it was time for him to go to his bed, and wishing the women good night. Sarah looked at Freda, sitting on the other side of the fireplace.

"David Roberts?" she asked. "I must say, he doesn't look like the David Roberts I saw in London!"

"Nor yet like Robert Argyll."

Freda said the name so softly Sarah wondered if she had really heard it. She looked across the hearth where the wood fire sparked with sudden brilliance, and through the heat haze old Freda's face looked oddly young and old at the same time. It was a wise-woman's face. Sarah caught her breath. A woman with the sight, as they say of certain people. Without stopping to think, she plunged right in.

"Do you think he'll ever be Robert Argyll again, Freda? Is there a chance of it?"

Cast a spell . . . burn incense . . . deal the cards . . . spin the dice . . . just do whatever a wise-woman with the sight did on these occasions to illuminate the future, Sarah thought wildly.

"Who can tell, lovey?" Freda said gently. "But as long as there's life there's always a chance. Sometimes even chance can do with a little help, o' course."

"What kind of help? What must I do?" Sarah almost begged, hardly knowing that she did so.

"Why, just be your sweet self, Sarah. Love is the best help any woman can give to a man, and 'tis certain sure that Robbie loves you. Be everything to him, and put your hope and trust in the rest."

It told her everything and nothing. If she felt disappointed, Sarah instinctively knew she wouldn't get any more out of Freda. After its brief flaring, the fire was quickly dying down, the heat haze diminishing, and the old woman looked very tired. The strange look of youth and age in her features was fading quickly and leaving her as wizened as before, so that Sarah wondered if she had imagined the whole thing.

Perhaps it was just Cornwall, she thought tremulously, and the undoubted empathy she felt toward it, as if earth and sea and sky and things beyond explanation existed here in some supreme and powerful concentration of nature. And she needed to bring her thoughts down from the ethereal plane to which they had gone.

"I think I'll go to bed too," she said. "I'm tired, and who knows what tomorrow will bring?"

Impulsively she leaned forward and kissed Freda's old cheek. It felt cold and not the way a cheek should feel after being heated by a fire. Sarah shivered again. She went quickly up the rickety stairs and into the front bedroom, thankfully closing the door behind her. She might be over-receptive to a feeling of enchantment all around her, but she was not quite ready to relinquish her preference for things that were natural and normal.

In the bedroom, she could hear Robbie's labored breathing, and stumbled against the empty brandy bottle.

306

The room was filled with the fumes of the spirit, but she couldn't blame him for sinking every drop and passing into oblivion. The forgetting lasted such a little while, and tomorrow the pain of remembering would be all the sharper.

She undressed quickly, and slid into the bed beside him, careful not to disturb him. She didn't think it likely, because he was in a deep sleep that was almost a stupor. She was heavy with sleep herself, and yet it was difficult to rid her senses of all that had passed, and it was a long while before she finally closed her eyes.

It must have been some time later when she awoke very suddenly. The room was still dark but beyond the window the sky was beginning to lighten imperceptibly, a thin yellow dawn beginning to streak the sky. There was a terrible sound in the room that she didn't immediately identify. When she did, she lay tense and unmoving for long minutes, wondering what to do.

Beside her, Robbie's whole body shook. He was sweating profusely, and Sarah could feel the heat emanating from him. He moaned in his sleep as if in pain, and she tried to understand the meaning of the tortured words he muttered.

"Robbie, don't—please don't—" she whispered at last, unable to bear witness to the physical effects of the nightmare which held him in its grip.

He flung out an arm, not even aware that she was there, and it caught her on the side of the head, causing her to cry out. He was immediately alert, twisting his head toward her with the shock of awakening.

"How long have you been here?" he asked in a ragged voice, the drink having lost its drugging effect long ago, and reality swamping him.

"Long enough," she said quietly, and knew she must speak out. "My dearest love, don't blame yourself. For pity's sake, none of it was your fault, not your parents' fate or that of the ship—"

"So I came out with it all, did I? It seems there are no

307

secrets from a woman who shares a man's bed. Eventually even the strongest become dependent on her to keep silent about his private weaknesses."

Sarah was stunned and hurt by the bitterness in him.

"I thought I was more than just a woman who shares your bed. I thought I was someone very special to you, as you are to me. Why do you begrudge me an insight into your private moments, which I do not call weakness!"

"What else do you call it when a man weeps in his sleep?"

"I don't think him less of a man because of it," Sarah said tremulously. "I think him a bigger person for caring so much. Why don't you let me share your grief instead of turning me away from it? We both lost companions today, and I know how you feel for your parents, Robbie."

She swallowed painfully as he said nothing, and went on slowly. "Don't you think I hurt for my parents at this time, when everything brings it back to me? Don't you think I wish that things could be different? But nothing stays the same, and we just have to go on as best we can. Be grateful that we have each other, and that we have love. We do have love, don't we?"

He continued to stare at the ceiling for a time, and Sarah felt a deep ache inside, wondering if the events of the day had made him revert to that wilderness time, when his childhood had been snatched away from him. And then he turned to her, and held her tightly in his arms until his breathing calmed and he gradually relaxed, and she gave up a small prayer of thankfulness.

The thought of physical love was never in either of their minds, because now was not the time. But each of them knew and acknowledged silently that Sarah's words were all that mattered. They had each other, and they had love.

Chapter 21

The next day, posters were fastened to every tree and secured inside the window of anyone willing to display them. The triumphant news of the burning of *The Adventuress* off the treacherous Lizard Coast quickly spread throughout the county of Cornwall. The excisemen and their runners had been up and about early to distribute them, and county folk commented jocularly that they must have been up all night preparing them. Unless they had already been partly prepared for just such a day of rejoicing as this, the sages said, which wasn't at all unlikely.

Sarah awoke slowly the following morning, still mentally and physically exhausted after all that had occurred. The memories of the night rushed back at her, and although she felt the urge to weep, weeping was a luxury she wouldn't allow herself until she knew what the future held.

She stretched out a hand for Robbie's comforting presence, but she was alone in the bed, and she sat up at once, fearful to know where he had gone. And then she heard the church bells ringing and wondered in a fever of disorientation if it was already Sunday, and if she had somehow lost several days.

She dressed quickly and went downstairs to the scullery where Freda Trewithan was stirring a great pan of porridge. For Robbie it would have to have salt sprinkled on it instead of sugar, in the Scottish fashion, Sarah disjointedly remembered.

"Do 'ee hear them?" Freda tossed her head at once, obviously referring to the church bells.

"I couldn't help hearing them," Sarah said. "I began to think I was imagining things. It's not Sunday, is it?"

"Lord love us, no, 'tain't Sunday. They're ringing the bells to announce special news. 'Tis the usual custom in these remote parts, me dear, whether 'tis for a royal birthin' or somebody of certain fame dyin'."

Just for a second, Sarah looked blank, and just as instantly knew she should have guessed already. It wouldn't be just the burning of a pirate ship that was causing celebration. The bells were ringing to announce Black Robbie's death. The thought was quite sickening, and yet in its way she knew it was just as much a celebration for her, and she should remember that.

As far as the world was concerned, Black Robbie was dead. But David Roberts was not, and Robert Argyll. . . .

"Where is he, Freda?" she asked at once, not needing to say his name.

"Don't you fret yourself now, he's gone wi' Jude to see what's to do in the village. 'Twould be odd if the visiting nephew didn't show himself now and then and show a bit o' curiosity about the celebrating, and plenty of folk have taken a liking to the young 'un who keeps Jude company in his fishing boat from time to time."

Sarah breathed more easily. For a while she had been afraid, but of what she didn't know. The feeling of being afraid was all too familiar, she thought uneasily, and it occurred to her that it was a luxurious feeling to feel totally safe, and one that she hadn't known for a very long time. It was even worse to feel constantly afraid on someone else's behalf.

When Robbie returned, she went to him gladly, and he gave her a brief hug. She didn't expect him to be too demonstrative in public, but there was a remoteness in his eyes that alarmed her. She felt as if she could read his mind, and guessed that he couldn't break the bonds with his recent past with the speed with which his ship had gone down. How could she expect him to, she thought, when piracy had been so much a part of his life for so long?

She had been thoughtless to imagine that it was all over for him. Without comment, he handed her one of the posters fastened everywhere, and her eyes blurred as she scanned the words.

"Wicked pirate meets his maker," she read aloud. "The notorious Black Robbie was drowned last night along with his vicious band of men when *The Adventuress* was fired on and sunk by our heroic excisemen. Let us give grateful thanks to excisemen Trewithan, Polgenna and Brelade for successfully leading the attack. It is unlikely that any reward will be paid for the recovery of the body unless it can be positively identified, and with the spring season's high tides, it's to be expected that the rogues will be smashed to pulp against the cliffs. Such is the fate of pirates. God Save The King and his upholders of law and order against the scum of the seas."

Sarah felt nausea rise up inside her at the blatant dismissal of men's lives, concentrating instead on the irony that the leader of the excisemen should be named Trewithan, when these good people who shielded Robbie so generously shared the same name.

"Amen," she murmured. "The King is dead. God save the King. Isn't that what they say?"

"I believe so," Robbie said, but she couldn't miss the unconscious bitterness in his voice. "What you really mean is that Black Robbie is dead—God save David Roberts—or would that be blasphemy?"

"I don't think so," Sarah tried to smile, though her heart was heavy. What she really meant was that Robert Argyll could also be alive and well, if Robbie wanted him to be. But perhaps it was a thought that hadn't occurred to him yet. Or if it had, it was one that was swallowed up in his mourning for his ship and his men.

And it was such a private mourning. There could be no public show of grief, no black funeral garb or decent burials. Without a proper wake, it was all so unfinished, the way her own parents' death had been unfinished. And Robbie's too, she remembered. They shared so much, yet she had the instinctive feeling that he felt totally alone, and wanted to be.

Sarah tried not to think what effect all this would have on herself. She grieved for the crew too. Any drowning at sea would always be a reminder of a time of agony for her, but guiltily she knew that the loss of the pirate ship also offered a new hope for the future for herself and Robbie. But seeing his controlled, frozen face now, she knew that the time for such a discussion was not here.

She concentrated on her breakfast, and heard Freda scold Robbie for not making a hearty meal. She guessed he was finding it difficult to do such a mundane thing as eat breakfast, but he persevered at Freda's insistence. They ate the porridge, and then a dip of bread and bacon fat, washed down with a thick milky drink.

Sarah found it nourishing enough fare, but she doubted that Robbie knew or cared what he ate. She began to wonder how much longer they would be staying here. It was probably unwise to disappear too suddenly, but Robbie's thoughts for the immediate future were a closed book to her. He had withdrawn inside himself, to a place she couldn't reach.

She began to think with some anxiety about her own predicament. There was no question of her going back to London or the southeast of the country. It wouldn't be too long before someone recognized her as the missing Sarah

Huxley, and if Robbie accompanied her, suspicions would soon be aroused as to his identity. And besides, there was something else to consider.

The news about Black Robbie's presumed death would be circulated around the whole country very quickly. It would reach London and its environs and the newspapers would be full of it. The usual ribald and derogatory cartoons would appear, and polite society would be gleeful that the pirate had met his deserved end.

And news would certainly be revived of the lovely young widow the wicked pirate had abducted all those months ago. If Jonas Endor added his own vicious account to it, it would be to state that his cousin had recently appeared at Endor House and then fled in pursuit of the pirate once more, with whom she seemed to have formed a romantic attachment.

Unable to resist the little bit of sensationalism and sympathy toward himself, Jonas would confirm what the country would come to believe, that Sarah Huxley and Black Robbie had rejoined the pirate ship and had been drowned together.

The realization came sharply. As far as the world was concerned, neither she nor Robbie had any identity any more. They didn't exist, and could simply disappear. Just as long as Robbie wasn't still too wrapped up in the past to face the future.

"You know that you and I have a great deal to talk about, Robbie," she said ambiguously, because it was too important to discuss with other people listening.

"Yes, we do, lassie," he said. "But it must wait until another time. I'm not in the mood for talking just yet, and Jude and I are going out in his fishing boat this morning. Things must appear to go on as normal between a man and his nephew, and this afternoon I have to go to Helston. I may remain there for several days, and you will stay here and be looked after by Freda."

It was said mildly, but it was an order all the same. Despite

313

her first reaction to bristle at his short words, they both knew she would obey. Where else would she go, and what else would she do?

She had a chance to be alone with him in the bedroom for only a short time before he left for the day.

"Why do you have to go to Helston, Robbie? And why must you stay away? I don't understand."

If it was a bad time to question him, she didn't heed the thought. They had come too far together for her to be the reticent female now.

"I have private business there, Sarah," he said. "As for staying away, you surely realize that I need time to be alone with my thoughts."

"But we have to talk, you said so yourself."

"Aye, so we do, but talking comes second to thinking, and I'll not be swayed from my decision by a—"

"A woman?" she asked bitterly. "Not even by a woman who loves you?"

"Not even by the woman I love," he answered, and the tears stung her throat, because this was a strong man whom she would not diminish by her weeping. And if he had his own personal battle to fight now, it was clearly one that he must face alone. His own dragon . . . she moved into his arms and clung to him for a moment.

"Come back to me," she whispered against his chest.

"Always," he said.

She spent the days listlessly. In the mornings she helped Freda bake bread. It was the season when nature sprang into new life and they picked strawberries and nettles in the hedgerows and little wild apples from wind-stunted trees, and stirred pans of preserves that had the whole cottage scented with their piquant aroma.

Each midday they ate a meal of bread and cheese, and afterward Sarah found she was so tired from the morning's activities that she needed to rest on her bed, amazed to realize she slept for the biggest part of every afternoon. The Cornish air was soft and sultry, dulling her senses to a degree, and when Freda explained that it was always so for a time with upcountry folk who visited, Sarah gave in to its seductiveness.

As the days passed, Sarah became apprehensive about Robbie's absence, and waited for him with an impatience that had the two old folk smiling sympathetically at the ache of young love. They had no living children of their own, though they had once had a daughter who died in early womanhood and whom they never spoke of. They accepted whatever fate decreed for them. Their lives were humdrum compared with the danger of a pirate existence, but Sarah felt a definite calming influence in their natures.

Most evenings, Jude came back to the cottage with a fine catch of fish that they would have for supper, along with potatoes he grew in the little patch of earth at the back of the cottage, which were boiled in their skins for goodness.

They were all thankful that the first flush of excitement over the pirate ship had died down in the village. Several bodies had been washed up farther down the coast, and because of their bloated and battered condition, dressed in tattered but flamboyant garb, it was simply assumed that one of them was Black Robbie's.

Locally, interest in the pirates' end was virtually dismissed as the spring tides came in, with their usual crop of promised shipwreckings on the granite cliffs, and rich pickings to be had by folk eager to salvage what they could from the broken vessels.

Sarah was preparing to face another night without Robbie, having had no news of him for eight days. She was standing forlornly in her chemise, attending to her toilet at the washstand in their room, when the door opened and suddenly he was there. She hadn't heard him arrive, and his appearance caused her heart to jolt.

315

But by now she knew better than to rush straight into his arms. Robbie had been gone from her more than physically, and she didn't yet know if he had recovered from his loss. For a moment they stood apart, and then he held out his arms and she was enclosed within them.

"I missed you so," she mumbled.

"Good. A woman should miss her man while he's away on business." His voice was husky, and she thought she could detect a smile in it, but she couldn't be sure.

But then she was caught by his words. What business was this? He wouldn't, he *couldn't* contemplate buying another ship for any reason whatsoever, could he? She simply couldn't bear it if it were so. He lifted her chin to look into her face, as if he could read every thought in her head.

"Don't take on, lassie," he said softly.

"Should I not?" She spoke with some heat, and then bit her lip. "But of course, your business is no concern of mine."

"Everything I do is of concern to you, and I'd not have it any other way."

She looked at him, and couldn't resist saying the words, "But you had to stay away."

"Aye, I had to stay away. Sometimes a man canna bear it for anyone to see his hurt, not even the one closest to him. And sometimes 'tis the one closest to him he hides his hurt from the most. But it's past, lassie. Life goes on."

She swallowed, sharing the sadness in his voice. "And are you going to tell me what you did in Helston?"

He gave a forced laugh. "I'll tell you what I didn't do! I didn't play the gambling dens or take up with loose women!"

"I never thought you did!"

"Then you disappoint me! Wasn't my lassie just a wee bit jealous that I'd solace myself?"

"Robbie, *please,*" she begged. She didn't want his teasing. There was too much of importance at stake.

"Aye, all right, 'tis not fair to keep you guessing. Well then. For many years now, there's been money deposited in a

316

Helston bank in Jude's name. The banking folk believe he inherited some wealth that brings in irregular amounts and that his money is there for safekeeping. But because he's old and doesn't travel far, his visiting nephew collects whatever he needs. It's an arrangement that's continued easily for some years."

"I see," Sarah said, her heart beginning to beat faster. "But the money really belongs to you, and you need it now."

"Just enough to get to Bristol," Robbie said.

She gasped. "Bristol? Why would you want to go there? I don't even know where it is!"

"But you'll have heard of it. It's a sea-faring port at the head of a great river."

Sarah felt stricken. It must be true then. He meant to put his money back into some kind of ship, perhaps to renew the old ties of piracy with a new crew. She could imagine his brazenness at proving that Black Robbie was still alive when everyone thought he was dead. So he couldn't let go of the hold that the sea had on him.

Sarah felt her whole body begin to shake and knew that tears weren't far away. She opened her mouth to speak but nothing came out, and she moved away from him and sat down heavily on the bed, already feeling his loss as if it were tangible. She knew she was losing him, and she was as certain of something else. If he begged her on his knees to go with him now, she couldn't ever face the sea again. Not now. Not ever . . . not even for love of him.

"For God's sake, my lovely girl, what damnable thoughts are going round in that head of yours now?" Robbie asked, sitting beside her and taking her hands tightly between his. In the thin cotton chemise, she shivered visibly, and his hands were warm on her bare shoulders.

"You say Bristol's a sea-faring port, so I presume that you intend to buy another ship, to go back to sea?" The words were whispered, and she couldn't say more.

He gave her a look that was half-teasing, half-impatient.

"Does the fact that Cornwall is noted for its cream mean that everyone owns a cow?"

She didn't understand him for a moment and stared dumbly. He pulled her close, his mouth moving softly against hers as he spoke slowly, deliberating over every word.

"I do not intend buying another ship, my dearest, nor do I intend going to sea again. That part of my life, and yours, is over for ever."

The touch on her mouth deepened, and his kiss was long and sweet. When they broke apart, she felt lightheaded, wondering what was still to come, a wild feeling of buoyancy sweeping through her.

"Tell me why you intend to go to Bristol," she pleaded. " I think I shall go mad if I don't know what plans you have."

"I have yet to ask my woman if she agrees with them," he said gravely.

"Then I am included in them?" Sarah asked, waves of thankfulness surging through her veins, as if she were suddenly coming to life again after a long sleep.

And Robbie's amber eyes were already darkening with passion as he saw the release of tension in her, in this woman who had captured his heart more surely than he had ever captured any treasure. His fingers touched the peaks of her breasts and she gave a small sigh of pleasure and swayed toward him.

Downstairs in the cozy parlor of the Trewithan cottage, Freda glanced up the rickety staircase and mentally put the cooking of the supper back an hour or so. There would be time enough for eating. Right now, what was happening in that small front bedroom was probably far more important. She smiled across the hearth at her man as she said as much, and received his usual grunt of agreement. It was good to be so much in accord with a man, whether he was great or humble, Freda thought contentedly, and felt no more than a moment's envy for those two above, whose lives together were only just beginning.

When their passion was spent and the aftermath of love still held them in its glow, Sarah lay on the bed in Robbie's arms, atop the patchwork quilt that Freda had stitched so lovingly. It was a good place for telling secrets and making plans, the best place of all, she thought, her eyes still filled with dreams. And there were such plans to be made.

"We go to Bristol because most of my assets are there," Robbie told her. "Mr. David Roberts, gentleman, has his account deposited in a respectable merchant bank in the city. The money in Helston is a lesser amount, enough to tide things over whenever I'm in Cornwall, and to see that the Trewithans are provided for all their lives."

"I see," Sarah said. She'd never had anything to do with money or banks. Uncle Thomas had always seen to that, and then Jonas, and she had no idea of the value of it or the handling of it. It wasn't her fault, it was the way a lady was brought up, but her own lack of knowledge made her impatient with herself.

"Are you very rich, Robbie?" she asked bluntly.

He laughed. "You could say so," he agreed.

"And what are your plans, for us both? Do we set up residence as people of quality in this city of Bristol?"

She tried not to sound too disappointed. A seafaring port, even at the head of a river, with its constant reminders of the sea, held no charms for her. But she would hear him out before she voiced her opinion.

"That is not my intention," he said carefully. "But what I want most dearly depends very largely on you, Sarah."

Her heart began to pound. If all the gods were with them, then what Robbie wanted most dearly must surely coincide with what she wanted too.

"You've never been to Scotland, have you?"

"No," she said, hardly daring to break the spell of these moments by saying more.

"The highlands are very beautiful," Robbie went on, almost as if he were talking to himself. "The mountains are covered with snow in winter, turning it into a fairyland, and even in summer the peaks are always snow-covered, the slopes a mass of purple heather. In the glens the little burns gurgle over the rocks, as clear as spring water, and the lochs are deep and silent, reflecting the mountains. 'Tis a place nearer to heaven than any I ever knew."

Sarah swallowed, hearing the longing in his voice he found impossible to hide now.

"And these highlands—are they near to the sea?" she asked, feeling that she had to contribute something.

"Oh aye, they stretch from coast to coast, rugged and remote. But the Argyll land belonging to my family was central, in a wild and beautiful glen."

"And you hunger for it," Sarah stated.

His eyes focused on her slowly, as if reluctant to come out of a lovely dream.

"Aye, lassie, I hunger for it," he said huskily. "More than I ever realized. All these years the bitterness inside me had refused to let me dream of home. I accepted what fate had in store for me, but now I want more. I want what's rightfully mine."

"Do you intend going back to the highlands and rebuilding your house? Didn't you once tell me it was burned to the ground?"

"So it was, and even though the land is irrevocably mine, I wish it were as simple as that." His mood changed and he moved away from her, to stare up at the ceiling.

"Why should it not be as simple as that?" Sarah asked quietly. "You're still Robert Argyll, no matter what you've been in the meantime. No one can take away your birthright."

"But who would believe me? My home is remote, and such places are scattered in the highlands. There were no near neighbors, and the doctor who befriended me is probably dead. He was ailing then. I was a mere laddie of twelve years old and I'm now a man of thirty. Who's to say I'm not an imposter? And if my story is not believed, the land will be left to go wild and the foundations of the house continue to rot."

Sarah was aghast. "But they must believe you! There must be someone who would vouch for you, someone who knows you and remembers you!"

"There may not be, and it's something I shall have to face."

Sarah felt a shiver run through her. To be so near to achieving her heart's desire and not know if it were possible after all!

"Will you face it with me, Sarah?" Robbie asked quietly. "Will you come with me and share a life of obscurity? For that is what it must be, with no unnatural attention drawn to us."

Her eyes filled with tears of joy at his asking.

"I can think of no better life," she said honestly. "But any that I shared with you would be heaven on earth."

Robbie held her close and his kiss confirmed his love for her.

"Oh, lassie, lassie, I ask so much of you," he murmured against her hair. "And never once do you press me with promises the way most women would."

"But I'm not most women," she said unsteadily.

"That you're not. You're the only one I've ever wanted to be my wife."

She caught her breath.

"Will you marry me, Sarah? I canna ask you to travel the length and breadth of England and Scotland without making an honest woman of you!" He tried to make a joke of it, but it didn't hide the real emotion in his voice.

"No, my love, I won't marry you," she heard herself say softly. "Not yet, anyway. I won't marry Black Robbie, nor

321

will I marry Mr. David Roberts, gentleman. But I will marry Robert Argyll if he asks me, and be happy and proud to do so."

Robbie leaned up on one elbow looking down at her. The evening was deepening, the shadows lengthening in the small bedroom, and she couldn't quite see the expression in his eyes.

"Even if Robert Argyll has nothing but the shell of a house to offer, and mebbe not even that if my claim is not proven?"

"Especially if all that happens," she said shakily. "For I have nothing to offer either, and we shall begin on equal terms."

"Then I ask you, Sarah—will you marry Robert Argyll?"

"I will," she breathed, and their close embrace was as meaningful as a vow.

A moment later Robbie held her slightly away from him.

"Does this mean you're content to continue as we are now? A man and woman traveling together and living together out of wedlock?"

She nodded slowly. "I can't believe that a caring God will think us any less married because we have not had words spouted at us from a preacher! Society might be scandalized, but truly I could never feel more wed than I already do, Robbie."

By the time they descended downstairs, the couple in the cottage could see that a momentous decision had been reached. Jude had already guessed at some of it, because Robbie had instructed him to appoint a trusted friend in the village to collect money for him from the Helston bank in the future. Jude and Freda knew that the visits from this particular guest were almost at an end.

"We'll be leaving tomorrow after nightfall," Robbie said as they sat at the table laden with the evening meal.

"And God speed to the pair of you," Freda said, the shine

of tears in her eyes. "I'll not bother telling you how you'll be missed, for you know that already. You'll tell us where you'll go?"

Robbie shook his head. "It's best that we don't. I have much business to settle before we go to our final destination, Freda. I wish I could say what I feel for all that you've done for me over the years."

"There's no need for thanks," Jude said roughly. "Besides, who's to say who owes the bigger debt? You've been more'n a son to we simple folk."

Sarah realized the truth of it, and guessed that in a way it was reciprocated. And this night was in danger of becoming maudlin if they didn't make it otherwise.

"Shouldn't we be glad for all the good times you've shared?" she said quickly. "I'm sure there must be many. Freda, you always have a story to tell. Has Robbie ever disgraced himself in the village and caused you to chastise your 'nephew'?"

The woman laughed, her old eyes brightening. "That he has, some nights when the drink flowed too freely and Jude had to help him to bed, lovey!"

"Never over a pretty maid, though, Mother," Jude added. "Robbie were always careful not to let one reputation spill over into another."

"Oh yes! The notorious Black Robbie had quite a reputation with the ladies, didn't he! I could be quite jealous!" Sarah said teasingly, and was thankful to find an answering laugh in Robbie's eyes. For a moment she wondered if she should have reminded him, and if the bleakness would be back. But it seemed clear that the bad moments were fast receding with the new propects ahead.

"So he did, and you never had any cause to be jealous, Mistress Huxley!" Robbie said, his hand closing over Sarah's. "But I think these good folk deserve to know our news, don't you? They're all the family we've got, at least for the present."

Sarah felt the heat in her face as she caught his meaning, and heard Freda laugh softly.

"Go on with you, but there's no need to tell us this sweet girl's captured your heart, me dear! I saw that the minute she arrived, and not before time either. 'Tis well time for 'ee to be putting down roots on the land, and to leave the sea to the fishes."

"Aye, we both think the same," Robbie agreed.

"So let's drink to it," Jude said, bringing a jug of mead to the table. "You'll enjoy this, Sarah. 'Tis the sweet-drink, a potent brew fit for a couple of lovebirds to celebrate the start of their new life together."

Sarah knew that the most potent brew between them was the love that burned bright and strong, but she drank deeply of the heady sweet-drink and felt her senses swim. And later, in the privacy of their own little haven, Robbie took her in his arms once more, and she felt the hardness of him melt into her welcoming softness. They moved together in the exquisite rhythm of love, and the one thought that shivered through every pulsebeat was a simple prayer of thanks to all the powers above and beyond the earth for bringing them together out of all the world.

Chapter 22

Sarah had wondered about how they would travel to Bristol, but she learned that Robbie had organized everything while he'd been in Helston. They were to be a genteel couple traveling together, and he had hired a carriage and horses, which the driver would bring to the Trewithan cottage in the evening, to load their baggage onto it at their convenience.

"Baggage? But we have no baggage, Robbie," Sarah said in consternation. "How shall we act our parts in these simple rags?" She blushed as she spoke. Their "rags" were little different from the humble clothes the fishing folk of the district wore, and she was glad that only Robbie could hear her words, lest they be misconstrued.

"We have all we need for the present, my love," he said. "Come, and I will show you."

Mystified, she followed him to a tiny attic room above a rickety staircase that looked as if it was seldom used. Sarah had assumed it was a mere storage room, filled with the usual flotsam collected over the years, and so it was. The only thing that looked of any worth was a large leather trunk. Apart from that the narrow room was filled with dusty boxes and bric-a-brac. There was also a broken rocking chair, a child's cot and several faded rag dolls that she guessed had once belonged to the Trewithans' daughter, and which Freda hadn't been able to throw away.

Sarah felt her throat tighten, feeling that she shouldn't be here, that she was somehow witnessing something very private. The very mustiness spoke of times past, of things held dear that once were and could never be again.

But Robbie was seemingly unaware of such thoughts. He pointed to the tiny window that was the only source of light in the room. Through it, a majestic lugger could be seen far out to sea, riding the waves with apparent ease. Sarah drew her eyes away and glanced downward, nearer to home. From here, the harbor and cove were clearly visible, the fishermen attending to their nets and jawing noisily over last night's catch and prospects for the next.

"Most of these harbor cottages have such a window," Robbie observed. "It's ideal for keeping a watch."

"You've used it before now, I presume?"

"Many times," Robbie said dryly. "But it's not the view I brought you up here to see. The trunk contains my belongings, and Freda wishes you to take whatever you need from these boxes."

She felt a fatalistic premonition. She knew instinctively what would be in the boxes, and she didn't want to wear a dead woman's clothes.

"It's Freda's gift to you, Sarah," Robbie said, seeing her face. "It's all she had to give, and she would never part with Wenna's precious things to anyone she didn't think very special."

Wenna. Wenna Trewithan. The daughter had a name and now that she knew it, in Sarah's mind she immediately assumed a personality, however unreal. She saw Robbie open one of the boxes, and fearfully, she half-expected the specter of the dead girl to rise up and face her. Instead, there was only the scent of rose petals and dried herbs emanating from the neatly folded gowns inside.

Sarah shook off the momentary horror. She was being

ridiculous! This was Freda's gift to her. She must hold that thought in her mind and accept what Robbie was saying rapidly and sensibly now.

"We must appear as normal a couple as possible, Sarah. There's no time to visit dressmakers and deck ourselves up to our own taste. We'll take time for that in Bristol, since my business there cannot be done in five minutes. We'll probably need to stay for several weeks, and do the town a little. In the meantime, don't deny Freda her pride in this last gesture to her nephew and his lady, whom she'll never see again."

Sarah nodded, her throat full. It was full. She, at least, would pass this way but once.

She picked up the first dress gingerly. It was a pretty enough creation in russet brown, simple and discreet as befitted a countrywoman, with fewer trimmings than someone of quality would wear, but nonetheless perfectly suitable attire for traveling. She held it against her. Wenna Trewithan may have been a little plumper than herself, but she guessed they would have been about the same height.

Beneath the dress was a pair of matching slippers, so Wenna hadn't been entirely without vanity, Sarah thought with a slight smile. As she held up one garment after another, finding surprising clues to a personality in everything, she began to warm to the unknown girl, thankful that the weird sense of stepping into Wenna Trewithan's aura was leaving her. The clothes were slightly old-fashioned as if from another era, but with the uncanny way that fashions came full circle, they were not so outdated as to draw attention to the woman who would be wearing them.

"Will it suit?" Robbie asked quietly.

She smiled shakily, holding up a gown of midnight blue in heavy linen fabric. "It will suit," she answered. "I think I might have liked Wenna Trewithan." A thought struck her. Did you know her, Robbie?"

He shook his head. "She died some years ago, and our

327

paths never crossed. She fell madly in love with and then married an impoverished landowner who lavished what little he owned on her, hence the reasonable quality of the clothes. but when he died she came back for a brief spell."

"And then she died," Sarah said, guessing the rest.

"She walked into the sea one warm September morning and was found some days later down the coast. Everyone said it was an accident, of course."

Sarah felt her skin prickle. Was she to be dogged by tales of drownings for the rest of her life?

"But it wasn't. She chose to die because her heart was broken without her love," she said, as if she could see right into Wenna Trewithan's soul as the scent of the old garments filled her nostrils.

Robbie gave a crooked smile. "Are you sure you're not a true daughter of Cornwall after all, my lassie? You seem to sense things the way they do."

"I'm just a woman in love, who knows how another would have felt, and grateful that my lot is not the same as hers," she said softly. "I never forget that but for good fortune, I might be mourning you now, Robbie."

"And but for waiting for you, I might have been on my ship and gone to the fishes with the rest of them." He spoke lightly to minimize the truth of it, but they clung together for a moment, knowing the strange debt of life each owed to the other.

By the time the soft purple shadows had fallen over sea and sky that evening, the goodbyes were emotional and quick, for both Robbie and Sarah could see that to prolong them would be too much for the old couple. The trunk had been loaded onto the carriage, the driver already seated silent and obliging as he waited for his charges.

"I'll never forget you, Freda." Sarah clasped the old woman tightly, her own eyes brimming. Such a read friendship had been forged in the short time she had known the couple that it was like parting with dearly loved relatives.

"Nor I you, my lamb. 'Tis truly like seeing a vision o' my sweet Wenna one last time to see you decked out so fine. Me and Jude both thank 'ee for that."

Sarah swallowed, forcing the shivery feeling to subside at the gratitude she saw in Freda's face. Then she was held fast in old Jude's embrace as he nearly hugged the life out of her.

"You mind what you're doing wi' they furbelows," Freda's voice admonished him severely. "Sarah don't want to arrive all crushed and weary-looking."

Sarah laughed, and the fey moment was gone. The serviceable midnight-blue gown was perfect for traveling, with a warm shawl around her shoulders, and as Robbie handed her into the carriage she knew that another episode in her life was over.

Where to now? she wondered, as the vehicle began its dipping movements over the rough road. She and Robbie waved frantically until they could see the Trewithans no more, and knew they had gone out of their lives.

She glanced at the man beside her, tall and strong, and handsomely made. A man above men, Sarah thought, with a great rush of love for him. And of course she knew where they were going. First to Bristol, and then home . . . it was already as if the scent of the highlands was filling her senses. Yet suddenly it no longer mattered where they went, for as long as Robbie was by her side, anywhere with him would be home to her.

"Sad thoughts?" he asked, turning toward her with a sympathetic smile.

Sarah shook her head. "Not any more," she said steadily. "Only good ones from now on. I was just thinking how much I love you."

His hand closed over hers in the rocking carriage, and its warmth sustained her through the chill of the night. She vowed to remember those words. Only good thoughts from now on. And as if to approve her words, the scent of Wenna Trewithan's rose petals and herbs drifted into her nostrils as she shifted more comfortably against her man. As her eyelids dropped in sleep, all the loving ghosts of the past let her be.

They stayed at an inn that night, still in the county of Cornwall, and after two more wearisome days and nights of traveling, they arrived in the bustling city of Bristol in the late evening. Robbie retained the carriage and driver for the time being and Sarah was never more thankful to see the end of a journey as they were shown their room in the elegant wide-fronted hotel.

Sea travel was by far the most comfortable mode of travel after all, she thought, much to her own surprise. At least you didn't have the constant discomfort of being jolted about on rutted roads and the constant risk of being apprehended by highwaymen or vagabonds.

Not that they had seen any such rogues, she admitted with relief. The journey had been particularly uneventful, except for the bumping and bruising and the indignity of climbing down from the carriage. She was as stiff as if her bones were as creaky as old Freda's.

The hotel was in a smart part of town, high above the river Avon and the deep gorge that forged its way between towering cliffs, Robbie told her, and tomorrow he would take her on a guided tour of the city. She cared little for it at the present time, and related her discomfort and observations to him in a whimsical way when they were at last ensconced in their comfortable room for their stay in the city.

"Aye, the English roads are hardly to be recommended," he said feelingly. "But be warned that this is only a small part of our traveling, lassie. We still have a great distance to go before we reach the highlands."

He heard her groan, and spoke cagily.

"There's always an alternative to traveling by road, Sarah."

She felt her heart lurch.

"You mean go by sea? But you said that Argyll land was in the middle of the country!"

"So it is. But we could get a passage on a ship from Bristol to the Kyle of Lochalsh. It would mean only one day's ride inland from the coast, instead of several weeks overland from here to the north of Scotland."

Several weeks . . . the very thought of it appalled her. But so did Robbie's alternative. She wanted to be done with the sea.

"We don't have to decide right away, do we?" she asked quickly, putting off the moment. "Perhaps when we've recovered from this last journey I'll be able to think more sensibly about it all."

"Not having regrets, are you?"

Her look was reproachful. "I don't know how you can even think such a thing!"

Robbie's amber gaze became more intense. He took her in his arms in the hotel room, relishing in the luxury they hadn't known for some time. Knowing he would give her the earth, moon and stars if they were his to give.

"How sufficiently have you recovered from the journey, my lovely girl? Do your shoulders need a gentle massage, perhaps? Or your neck need the touch of loving fingers?"

She felt the tiredness being replaced by something more vibrant. Desire was etched in every pore of Robbie's face, and in the hardness of his body closing in on hers. She was tired, yes, but the hunger of her need for him superseded all the weariness. His fingers were already gently kneading her neck, and she arched her body backward, flexing her muscles, and glorying in the sudden quickening of his breath.

There was something strangely humbling in knowing how

331

sheer womanliness could bring a powerful man to such need. There was glory in knowing their needs matched so perfectly.

"I think perhaps a bath after the journey would relax my muscles even more, dearest," she murmured, her blue gaze never leaving his face.

"I'll arrange for the water to be brought at once," he agreed. "Enough for us both, I think."

His intention was obvious, and Sarah felt a shiver of excitement run through her veins. The hotel was very modern, and their accommodations were really a small suite of rooms. There was a door at either side of the main bedroom and there were long French windows leading onto a small balcony where private meals could be served when the weather was accommodating. At other times they could have meals in their room if required, and Robbie had requested as much for this first evening, because they were tired, and for their morning breakfasts.

Sarah had already explored every corner of the suite, and walked out onto the balcony, but she could see nothing beyond it since the night was already so dark. Behind one of the side doors was a small dressing room. Behind the other was a bathing room, with a large bath, big enough for two people if so desired. She and Robbie had taken one look at it and smiled at each other, knowing it was going to be put to good use.

He left her to unpack the trunk and hang the clothes in a wall closet while he ordered hot water and bath salts to be sent up, and for dinner to be sent up in one hour. Would one hour be enough? he mused. And then decided with a grin that it would.

They had been apart too long too often, and these days on the road had been too exhausting to indulge in delightful bedroom activities. He knew full well that his desire would permit no lengthy exchanges of loveplay this night. He wanted Sarah, and he wanted her now. It was only the tantalizing thought of the delightful bathtub that allowed him to restrain himself this long.

A short while later, he closed the door of the suite on the frankly admiring maids, who had delivered the pitchers of hot water and sprinkled the fragrant bath salts into the bath until it foamed. The whole ambience was seductive and so was Sarah, Robbie thought with a catch in his breath, as she divested herself of her clothes without false modesty.

She was stunningly beautiful, he thought, her skin still tinged with the lingering honeyed tones from their journey to the Guinea Coast. Her shape was womanly and proud, curving and dipping as a woman's body should, the breasts full and invitingly rosy-tipped. So much so that Robbie paused in his own undressing to take each one in his hands, caressing their delightful fullness, as he pressed his lips to each one and felt the instant arousal of each rosebud tip.

"I canna wait for ye, Sarah," he said, suddenly hoarse, and at his urgency her hands as well as his were wrenching at his breeches, his shirt, sending them flying as the flaring desire fired her soul, matching his every need.

"Nor I you," she whispered in answer, and her eyes took in every part of him, from the magnificent strength of his shoulders to the manly crest of dark hair on his chest that trailed downward to the engorged, proud evidence of his desire for her.

Driven by a wild and wanton compulsion, her hand reached down and fondled him swiftly, only to be stayed by Robbie's murmur of warning and the gentle pressure of his hand on her hair in a silent plea. Her head dipped to continue what her fingers had begun, her tongue flicking, teasing and arousing and pleasuring him to a state of ecstasy.

And then she allowed it to forge deeper, and time and again she heard him gasp as she drew him into her mouth as if she would take the very life-source from him.

"Dear God, Sarah, but I must have you *now*," he gasped, jerking her away from him, pushing her against the wall and straddling her where she stood, her legs wide.

No time for finesse now, nor did she want it, not now, when the feeling was so dazzlingly sensual and unlike anything she had ever experienced before.

He thrust inward and upward, until her back felt raw from the fierce ramming against the hard wall paneling. None of it mattered as his seed exploded inside her, and the exquisite mind-freeing sensations radiated out from the very core of her being, spreading through every part of her as if heaven and earth merged into one.

He held her tight as they rocked together, while the climax of love enveloped them both, and she was still part of him, feeling almost weightless, floating somewhere in space as shimmering, incandescent lights filled her mind in a meeting of body and spirit. And slowly, slowly, slowly, it seemed, she came down to earth as Robbie's voice murmured raggedly in her ear.

"My lovely, lovely girl. My own lassie, I never meant it to be like this. If I've shamed you—"

She stilled his words by moving her mouth tremulously across his own.

"Nothing you do could ever shame me, my dearest. I thank you for showing me another facet of love."

His mouth pressed hard against hers, and she could feel the dwindling of his passion against her. It didn't matter. Passion might be momentary, but love was forever.

"I think perhaps we should have our bath now, before our dinner is brought to us," she whispered. "It would be rather embarrassing for anyone to find us in this state!"

Robbie laughed, the brief moments of doubt in his mind gone with the sure knowledge that his woman loved him, as passionately as he loved her. She was everything he needed in life.

They romped in the bathtub, as naturally as two children.

334

Released from the urgency of desire, their instincts were to play and tease, facing each other in the foaming fragrant water that had lost some of its heat but was nonetheless warming and refreshing. A little like their own feelings now, Sarah thought. The fierce heat had diminished for the moment, but the more valuable warmth remained.

By the time their dinner was brought to the room, there were never two more decorously attired gentlefolk. Sarah's russet brown dress was buttoned to the neck, and she sat demurely while the waiter placed the dishes in front of them. He was so stiff and starched that she could hardly contain her mirth as she sat opposite Robbie, composing all kinds of imaginary outrageous remarks to say aloud to her lover as though the manservant were quite invisible, just to see if the steady hand would waver over the serving of spiced potatoes and succulent pork slices.

"By the way, dearest." Her imaginary remark went casually. "Please don't be quite so amorous the next time we make love, or I fear you will bite my nipples clean off!"

She was hard-pressed to hold back her giggles until the man went away, and Robbie asked her smilingly what was so funny. Admittedly, he'd been a funny little man with an unfortunate tic at the side of his mouth, but surely it wasn't just that.

"I couldn't tell you!" she said, blushing now. "My thoughts were too vulgar for a lady to even allow into her head, and, well, I suppose I can hint—I was imagining what that man would say if he knew what we had just been doing!"

"He probably does," Robbie said casually, his hypnotic eyes betraying his pleasure that his beloved could speak so freely of love. "Even in large hotels like this one, there are intimate tête-à-têtes and lovers' meetings, and not all couples who take a bed for a night are legally wed, my love."

"Neither are we yet, remember!" she said. "So do you suppose these maids and waiters take a vicarious delight in surmising all that goes on?"

335

"Of course. And the next time I make love to you, what do you say if we pretend that little man with the tic has his eye pressed to some knothole in the wall? Do you think it may make our performance even more exciting?"

He spoke extravagantly, not knowing what way Sarah might take this. The idea had come to him in an instant, and although he had always disliked the idea of voyeurism, there was a certain frisson of excitement in the thought he had outlined. To his pleasure, Sarah laughed aloud, her blue eyes sparkling like sapphires.

"Why not? There's surely no harm in it! Just as long as the beastly little man doesn't *actually* watch! If he did, he would surely expire at the exertions of my man." And this time she blushed more fiercely at her own daring words.

"Aye, that he would." Robbie grinned. "Always remember this, Sarah. Nothing that occurs between a man and woman who truly love one another is wrong. Nothing, whether it be fantasy or lust, or however bizarre it may seem, because none but the two of them will ever know of it."

At her quick nod, he felt a renewed stirring in his loins at the thought of all the love-pleasures they would experience in the years ahead. To have such a companion, who shared his every whim, was a God-given blessing, and he sent up a silent prayer to whatever deity was listening.

Sarah awoke slowly, unwilling to remember for a moment where she was. The aches of the tedious journey from Cornwall had gone, and only the briefest remnants of back pains from Robbie's delightful ravishing remained. She smiled, still half-asleep, because the reasons for the pain were far from unpleasant to recall. Gradually into her half-consciousness there came a strange high-pitched screeching sound that was not unduly alarming, but not unfamiliar either. . . .

She was instantly awake, and stretched out an arm to find

Robbie's shoulder. He wasn't there, and she sensed the breeze coming in through the French windows as the curtains rustled slightly. As well as the screeching, which she identified at once as the sound of sea-birds, there was a strong pungent odor in the air, a mixture of salt and tar and fish and everything she associated with something she would rather forget.

She saw Robbie's shadow on the balcony, and when she called to him, her voice was tinged with disappointment. She had hoped to be far from the sea, and it seemed he had brought her back to it again. Another coastline, another jogging of her memory.

He came inside the room at once. He was already dressed for going out, elegant in close-fitting breeches and shining black boots, his favorite mulberry-colored waistcoat with the gilt threads running through it over a crisp white shirt and cravat. Despite her feelings for their location, Sarah's heart filled with love for him.

"Good morning, my lassie." She still smelled of sleep, musky and womanly in his arms now, and but for the business appointment he had to set up, he would keep her in sweet imprisonment and make love to her, wantonly and passionately. Even as the temptation almost overcame him, he realized she had tensed in his arms and he looked at her quizzically, her dark hair tumbling into her eyes now and giving her the look of a gamin child in a woman's body.

"What is it?"

"Are we by the sea?" she asked, trying not to sound accusatorial. "Oh Robbie, you know it would not be my wish!"

"It's not the sea. Come and look for yourself," he said at once. She slid out of bed, wrapping the quilt around her in the chill of the morning, and stepped out onto the balcony. What she saw caused her to reel back for a moment, gasping, glad that Robbie's arms were supporting her.

The hotel was perched atop a cliff, and stretching out

dizzyingly below them was the Avon gorge, the winding river a silver ribbon in the thin morning sunlight. The river was tidal and already on the turn, and several craft were already busily plying their way toward the sea on the ebb. The gorge was steep-sided and seemingly narrow from this height, and the opposite side of it was thickly wooded in an impenetrable dark forest. Throughout the gorge the sea-birds swooped and hovered, escorting every boat within sight.

"Is it not a magnificent sight?" Robbie exclaimed, as if he had personally engineered the spectacle.

"Magnificent," Sarah muttered, feeling slightly green as she witnessed the depths below them.

"I predict that one of these days someone will construct a bridge across this gorge and open up the whole of that rugged little unknown corner of the country," he said cannily.

"Do you know it?" she asked in surprise.

"Only from the sea." He shrugged. "No, I'm just day-dreaming, Sarah. Though sometimes I wish it could be possible to return to this earth a century from now, and see what man has made of his heritage."

She turned to go back inside, shivering. Such thoughts always made her a bit depressed. The past had already happened, and some said the future was already ordained; it was surely best then, to live in the present.

"I'm sorry. Did the unexpectedness of the gorge alarm you, love? I should have warned you," he said now, seeing her pallor.

"No, I'm all right," she murmured. "Perhaps I need my breakfast."

But when it came, she couldn't eat it. She felt upset for reasons she couldn't fathom. Last night she had been so blissfully happy, and today . . . today it seemed as if some sixth sense was impressing on her that they shouldn't remain in Bristol any longer than necessary.

For a moment she remembered the woman in the tea room

338

in Cornwall who had been so interested in Sarah and thought she may have had the sight. If ever she had felt the power of such a possession, she felt it now. She was sure there was danger here. Danger for Robbie, who even yet might be recognized as Black Robbie, the scourge of the seas, whose days would end with the twist of a hangman's rope if ever he were discovered.

"Please don't go out, Robbie," she said in a panic as he prepared to put on his coat.

"Why, lassie, of course I must go out. I have to get things settled before we make our final move. I'll be back in a couple of hours, or less, and this afternoon I'll take you on that promised tour of the city. There's nothing to fear. You can spend the morning on the balcony if you wish. The air is a little strong, I'll admit, but you'll be well used to that. I'll ask that some newspapers and journals be sent up to the room."

She could hardly beg and plead. It wasn't her way. But she kissed him goodbye with dire apprehension in her heart, and a little later, when a maid brought her a bundle of newspapers and journals, she spent most of her time scouring them for the remotest reference to the pirate. Although there was none, she read and re-read until the words danced in front of her aching eyes and her head throbbed unmercifully. She realized how very alone she felt in a hotel she didn't know, in a seafaring port she instinctively feared.

Chapter 23

He returned to the hotel before the sun was high in the sky, and Sarah called herself every kind of a fool for allowing her imagination to run away with her. Nothing was wrong here. Robbie told her that everything was going ahead as planned.

"Am I to know what these plans are?" she asked, slightly piqued at all her foolish fancies. "What can it be that takes so long to do here?"

He smiled, seeing her usual impatience.

"I have to settle Mr. David Roberts's affairs. The gentleman is going abroad, emigrating to the colonies to an unknown destination, so everything he owns must be calculated and collated and put at his disposal, either in cash or bonds. I have given broad hints that it may be necessary for me to change my identity for government purposes, so the bonds will be unnamed, and for the use of the holder, but of the type that may be cashed at any legal merchant bank. Once we establish my claim in Scotland, they will be transferred at intervals into various banks in the name of Robert Argyll. Everything is taken into account, Sarah, so you may get that worried little frown off your forehead."

"I'm sorry," she said. "It all sounds so—so hazardous, that's all."

He laughed out loud this time.

"My darling girl, are you not talking to the erstwhile Black Robbie, who lived with danger every day of his life? I'm sure the distribution of a few bonds is going to be no problem."

"A few bonds?" she asked, raising her eyebrows.

"Well, perhaps a considerable number of bonds," he agreed. "More than enough to see us handsomely settled in Scotland." He hesitated. "Even if my claim is dismissed out of hand, there will still be sufficient funds for us to start building our own destiny, Sarah."

"But it won't be the same."

"No," he said briefly, his amber eyes clouded for a moment. "It won't be the same. And if I have to move mountains to prove that I'm the legal heir to the Argyll estate, then so be it."

"There's no one likely to contest it, is there?" she asked in sudden alarm, the thought just occurring to her.

"There was an older cousin," Robbie said thoughtfully. "But before the burning he'd gone to India to settle. I have no idea whether he stayed there, of course, nor if he had any family. He could pose a small problem."

Sarah was aghast at this. "But why have you never spoken of this before? Robbie, by now the cousin could have claimed your land and rebuilt the house. Word would surely have reached him that you had disappeared. Perhaps even then it was presumed that you were dead, and everything you ever dreamed about could already belong to someone else!"

In her mind's eye, she could already see the house, built of greystone and solid as a rock, forever out of Robbie's reach. He put his hands firmly on her quivering shoulders, a smile in his voice.

"Hold fast, my love. I think you're more besotted by the idea of rebuilding my home than I am!"

"I want it for you, Robbie. And I want it for us," she said, a shine of tears starting in her eyes. "I feel very strongly that it's our destiny, and I can't bear the thought of some cousin snatching it away from us. You've been away so long.

341

For all you know, he might have been living there for eighteen years."

It seemed to her that he wasn't taking this as seriously as he should. She felt him give her a small shake.

"Will you please listen to me, lassie! For pity's sake, am I going to have to go through life trying to curb your impetuous tongue!"

She glared at him. And then she listened properly to what he was saying.

"No man can rebuild on my land for twenty-one years, nor put in a rival claim to the heir before then. I've known this all my life. It was one of the things my father drummed into me. If anything were to happen, he insisted that I get away from the glen as quickly as possible and stay away. But I was to be sure and return within the time limit, or all would be lost. When you're a child, you don't take such things seriously, and twenty-one years seems like a lifetime to a lad of twelve."

Sarah repeated her rapid calculations.

"And you've been away for eighteen years?"

"That's right," Robbie said. "So the land is still mine to claim."

"Does this mean that you would have given up your seagoing life within three years whether or not you had met me?" She felt somewhat dashed at the thought, and his smile was crooked and tender as he noted it.

"No, love. You've been the catalyst to revive all the old longings, and I'm ever in your debt for it. I doubt that Robert Argyll would ever have surfaced again without the incentive for a man to put down roots and raise bairns of his own."

Sarah drew in her breath. "And that's what you want now?"

"Aye, it's what I want. A man needs perpetuity."

He stopped, looking at her oddly. There was a faint pink flush on her cheeks and a look in her eyes he had not seen before. Her eyes were a clear and beautiful blue, and right now they looked bluer than ever. There was something in them that momentarily shut him out, as if she looked beyond the present to somewhere distant he couldn't see. As if she hugged some great secret of her own that was not yet ready for the telling.

Surely she could not be changing her mind at this late stage, he thought in alarm.

"What is it, Sarah?" he asked anxiously.

She shook her head vigorously. Just as she thought it an omen of good fortune to refuse to marry him until he was truly recognized as Robert Argyll, so she kept this new and precious secret as an omen too. She was not even sure there was a secret to be kept, or to share, as yet. It was only a flicker of hope in her mind that came from a feeling of unease in the early morning, a distaste for breakfast and a slight heaviness in her breasts. It could be nothing, or it could be the beginning of something wonderful, the miracle that was to bind them together for all time, and ensure the dynasty that must surely pass into Robbie's hands.

"It's nothing. A goose walked over my grave, that's all," she said, and drew her thoughts back to the issue they had been discussing.

"But you say your cousin might pose a small problem," she persisted.

Robbie's eyes hardened, recalling the past.

"Callum never liked me," he said shortly. "I can see now that he resented the fact that the land was my heritage and not his. His father owned a far smaller estate, which would eventually be Callum's, and which meant little enough to him because of this grand idea he had of going to India and making something of his life. He frequently taunted me with it because I was too young to think about such things. He said I'd have to be content to be a paltry lord. Even then I could see the jealousy behind his barbs."

"And instead you rose to heights in a more spectacular way than Callum," she surmised.

"Aye, as a pirate captain." Robbie's mouth twisted. "But

'tis hardly the recommendation a man takes to a lawyer with a claim to his inheritance, is it, lassie? And believe me, if Callum's back in Scotland now, he'll contest every claim I make. We may not find it as easy as we had hoped."

Sarah felt alarm rippling through her with every word he spoke. What if this cousin was so determined to gain the Argyll land that he began to probe deeper into Robbie's whereabouts for the last eighteen years?"

"Robbie, I'm afraid," she said tremulously.

"There's no need, I promise you."

But she couldn't be sure that his words carried conviction. Nor that his hearty promise of taking her on a tour of the town that afternoon, and on a visit to a dressmaker this morning, was anything more than a placebo. For Sarah, it was one that simply wouldn't work.

They had dispatched the carriage and driver to Cornwall, and would hire various ones while they stayed in Bristol. Robbie decided it was better this way, since new drivers asked no questions and showed no curiosity. And that sparkling late-spring morning, they rode down from the heights of Clifton and their hotel overlooking the gorge, to the teeming streets of the city. Sarah still didn't like it. She found the language coarse, without the softness of the Cornish or the quick, cultured tones of her family's acquaintances in Sussex. It wasn't that she was snobbish about their speech, it was simply that she didn't understand it easily. Robbie showed her the splendid buildings and then the river where tall ships jostled for position. The all-pervading smells almost made her gag.

"I don't like it here, Robbie," she gasped, putting a small handkerchief to her nose. "I think I've seen enough."

He looked at her face, whiter than usual, and decided that it must be the sight of the ships that was distressing her. A pity, because he had almost decided that a sea voyage would be their best route to Scotland. The journey by land would be wearisome.

"I'm sorry, Sarah," he said. "Listen, love, I've discovered that the Holtby Theater Company is performing at the Alhambra in Halfpenny Lane in three days' time. By then you'll have some new finery and we shall do the town. Perhaps then I shall prove to you that this fair city of Bristol is not filled only with ruffians and sea-scabs!"

"Yes, that would be lovely," she said faintly. "Though any finery I may obtain here will hardly be up to *proper* city standards, I'm sure." She tried to tease him, to cover the fact that her stomach felt as if it were turning somersaults.

She thought swiftly of the gowns of Wenna Trewithan she had brought with her. They were not a pauper's clothes by any means, but neither were they elegant, and for a moment she thought wistfully of all the beautiful silks and satins she had taken so much for granted as her uncle's ward. The sensual memory of silk next to her skin made her sigh with a small regret that she tried to hide. Robbie guessed her feelings and nodded.

"I know a place that sells Spanish shawls of the finest lace, and we shall go there next. Then to a reputed dressmaker who will be instructed to work at top speed to make all the gowns my lady needs to take with her to Scotland. And for the theater—well, these establishments often have sample gowns made up to show their best clients, and I'm sure we can persuade Madame Dupont to part with one that's suitable for the Alhambra, and to make any alterations necessary in three days' time."

Sarah hugged his arm.

"Have I told you today that I love you?" she said huskily as they seated themselves in the carriage for the ride through the busy streets, up to the fresh air of Clifton Heights, where the dressmaking establishment was situated.

He laughed, squeezing her arm against his side, adoring this lovely woman more with every day that passed.

"If you have, I shall never tire of hearing it again," he said quietly, and Sarah knew a moment of pure happiness, because their hearts were one.

She leaned her head against him, and once up on the vast green area known as the Downs, she looked around her and saw it all with different eyes. It was beautiful, she conceded, and the deep gorge was truly breathtaking, cutting through the towering steep-sided cliffs as it did, dividing the city in half. Though the other side was not Bristol, she remembered Robbie telling her. Beyond was a wilder countryside that ran the entire length of the Bristol Channel Coast, which bordered Somerset and Devon until it narrowed into the long finger of England that was Cornwall.

To traverse it all by sea would be to reach the north coast of Cornwall, while the Lizard Peninsula and the tiny cove where the Trewithans lived was in the far southwest. She had already discovered as much from one of the articles in a magazine she had been reading that morning, where a sketch map of this unfamiliar southwest of England had been of great interest to her.

Robbie gave the name of Madame Dupont's dressmaking establishmend to the driver and smiled at Sarah, thankful to see her taking more interest in everything around her. This morning she had looked quite frail for a time. It would be fatal for either of them to be ill now, to be forced to remain here any longer than was necessary.

He felt a renewed eagerness to be home, back in the north of these islands, to feel the ruggedness and grandeur of scenery still vivid in his memory, where a man could walk for hours and see no one, and feel at one with the earth and sky. It struck him that the sea never once came into these thoughts, and he knew at last that he was done with it.

"Have you been to this Madame Dupont's before?" Sarah asked him, so casually he knew there was a reason behind the words.

"Hardly," he laughed. "I'm not in the habit of dressing in

346

women's clothes!" And then he saw her face and his hand covered hers. "No, my lassie, I have never brought another lady to Madame Dupont's, nor ever bought fine gowns for another. Does that reassure your jealous little heart?"

She gave a sheepish smile. "It does. And I didn't mean to offend you, but I can't quite forget your reputation with the ladies, Robbie."

The fingers holding hers were suddenly tight, and as she looked at him, she saw his sharp warning glance. At once, she realized how careless she was being in talking so freely when the carriage driver might be listening. Her face whitened as she accepted anew how careful she must be from now on. She gave Robbie a quick, embarrassed nod.

The carriage slowed down, and she was glad to alight and look about her. The shop looked like an ordinary house from the outside, white-porticoed, clearly the abode of a well-to-do person.

Her spirits lifted. She'd had enough of roughing it, and she remembered with nostalgia the Endors' favored dressmaking establishment in London. There, Mistress Sarah Huxley had been waited on with samples of silks and satins, and offered cups of tea in bone china cups, with petit fours and chocolate dainties, pampered as an honored client should be. Here, everything was much the same, she saw with astonished delight.

Madame Dupont was a charming, middle-aged French-woman of renowned elegance. She sized Sarah up surreptitiously, quickly and expertly. When the measurements had been noted down by an assistant, Sarah was taken to the fabric room, where great shimmering bolts of silk rippled across long narrow tables to show the effect of light and shade, and then various fabrics were draped against Sarah's body for her to admire in the floor-length mirrors.

"It's all so beautiful," she said, bemused at the choice, which must surely rival anything London had to offer. "I hardly know which to choose."

Robbie turned to Madame Dupont.

"Mrs. Roberts will require half a dozen gowns of after-noon or evening quality," he said. "And we wondered if you have a sample suitable for the theater that would fit her, or could be altered by this weekend?"

"Of course," Madame gushed, clearly stunned by the elegance of this handsome man, as were the young assistants rushing around like bees to do her bidding.

Sarah noticed that he never addressed her by name, always referring to her as Mrs. Roberts. He did the same in the company of anyone at the hotel. She must therefore speak to him as David, if anything at all. There was so much to remember!

After a considerable time, they emerged from the shop, an assistant carrying a large box which was placed reverently in the waiting carriage. One of the sample gowns had fitted Sarah perfectly; a beautiful creation in shot gold water silk, with a matching cape. To complete the display ensemble, a parasol had been supplied. Sarah's persuasive plea had made Madame agree to part with it that very day.

Though perhaps it wasn't solely for the young lady's smile of thanks that she did so, Sarah thought with a glimmer of amusement. Robbie had clearly charmed everyone in the place, and their order of six gowns was to be completed within the week, an accomplishment which would surely require the most diligent fingers to work to the limit.

On Saturday night they were going to the theater, and Sarah would wear the golden gown that made her look like a princess. She felt a burst of excitement run through her. It was so long since she had behaved in her true role, that of a society lady. Robbie, too, was not born to a life of scheming and roguery, and adapted more readily to his rightful heritage than one might suspect of a pirate captain.

Just for a moment, Sarah let the memories fill her head. Had she loved him less when he was the dashing and flamboyant Black Robbie? Could she ever love him more, in whatever guise? The memories faded. The past had made them what they were, perhaps, but today was theirs, and they would enjoy it to the utmost. And on Saturday . . . the thought of attending the small theater he had pointed out to her, the Alhambra on Halfpenny Lane, drew her like a moth to a flame.

They went out riding several times more before then, to the northern confines of the city, which gave way to rolling countryside and distant hills. To the left, the narrowing funnel of the Bristol Channel before it merged into a long winding river that Robbie told her meandered through part of England and Wales.

A river sounded so harmless, Sarah thought, while the sea could be so treacherous! She shivered, glad to her soul that they were rid of it, reliving for a moment her horror when she had realized that the alternative to marrying her hated cousin was to flee to sea with the notorious Black Robbie.

Would she do it again? One look at her love on that Saturday evening, when they were both dressed in their finery for the theater, and she knew she would risk everything she had to be with him.

A small frown puckered her brow. Did they take a risk in appearing in public? Sarah wondered for a second. The Holtby Theater Company was well-traveled and popular in London as well as the provincial towns, and drew a faithful following. But surely there was no risk to Robbie here. The news about the pirate's death had quickly died down. Since Black Robbie was no longer a threat, his legendary exploits no longer attracted interest.

So much for the fickle public, Sarah thought cynically, who by now were exaggerating claims of having seen or been apprehended by the newest rogue of the highways and byways, the scandalous Jed Porter. She thanked him silently for taking the attention away from themselves.

*   *   *

The exterior of the Alhambra Theater in Halfpenny Lane was small and elegant, the lane itself narrow and cobbled, and congested with carriages by the time they arrived. Ladies and gentlemen clearly attired for an evening's entertainment, obviously trying to outdo each other in silks and satins and brocades, smiled and nodded and pretended passing acquaintance with strangers who looked of any importance.

"Let's play a guessing game," Robbie whispered in her ear as they walked into the plush interior, with its dark red carpet and paneled walls proudly displaying portraits of its most eminent players. "Let's look around and see if we can spot the wicked pirate."

She looked up into his face, and knew at once that he had guessed how her heart was thudding. It was at the theater that she had first caught sight of the handsome David Roberts, seated in a box with a beautiful lady beside him. The theater where her startled blue eyes had locked with his amber ones, and she had known him instantly. Was there not a chance, even now, that others might do the same?

"Please don't jest," she muttered, feeling it was bad luck to play with the past. They had been so lucky so far. Even in Spain, there had been bad moments. In another theater, there had been another risk of discovery. A portent of doom washed over her, as if she were suddenly sure that this was to be the place where their end was destined to be enacted. She clutched at his arm.

Suddenly panicked, she said, "Robbie, I think we've made a mistake. We shouldn't have come—"

His hand was firm beneath her elbow.

"Calm yourself, lassie, and forget my foolish suggestion. Look around instead, and see how everyone is intent on minding their own business. We're all out for an evening's pleasure, nothing more. Come, we will take our seats."

Not in a box this time, where she knew all eyes would be on them, Sarah thought thankfully, but anonymous in the middle of a row. She took up the tiny magnifying eyeglasses

put at clients' disposal, as if to hide herself behind them, and
began to gaze about her at the rest of the populace.
Gradually she relaxed. It was as Robbie had said. All here
were intent on enjoying themselves. She doubted if Black
Robbie's name ever crossed their minds now.

Without more ado, the performance began with a swish of
curtains and thunderous applause from the audience as the
whole company lined up on the stage to acknowledge
themselves as true professionals. Already in their stage
costumes, it was easy to identify who was to play the various
parts by the program they had purchased in the foyer. It
was to be a tragicomedy, and Sarah hoped faintly that the
comedy would outweigh the tragedy. A little laughter was
far preferable to her just now.

But the players themselves showed such expertise that it
was easy to lose oneself in whatever role they played. With
the rest of the audience, Sarah was totally captivated by the
performance, whether she was laughing to the antics of the
fool, or wiping a discreet tear when tragedy struck the
heroine. She joined in the rapturous applause when it all
finally came to an end. The cast took half a dozen encores
before they were finally allowed to leave the stage.

There was an instant melee as ladies and gentlemen rose,
searching for shawls or wraps that had slipped beneath seats,
foraging for programs to take home as mementos. It had
been a wonderful evening, and Sarah and Robbie had been
able to lose themselves completely in the welcome return to
something like normalcy.

Sarah replaced the eyeglasses in their holder with a small
smile as Robbie moved away, making a path for her to
follow. How foolish she had been to think that anyone
would even remotely connect her dashing and attentive
escort with anyone as dastardly as a pirate!

"Sarah! Sarah Endor! It *is* you, isn't it? I've been puzzling
and puzzling all evening where I'd seen you before, and
you're not going to tell me you weren't at one of Lord

Gressingham's summer balls a few years back, are you? I believe it was just before your uncle married you off to that what-was-his-name—Huxley, wasn't it? That's it, Huxley. And wasn't there something else I should remember about it all? I'm afraid my memory's not what it used to be, but I never forget a face. Now do come and join my husband and me for supper and tell me all that's been happening to you, and assure me I've got the right person."

Horror swept through Sarah as she heard the trilling voice, and felt the restraining hand on her arm. She turned very slowly to face the elderly woman with the powdered cheeks dabbed with rouge, and the viciously sculptured gray curls. She was wearing an outfit totally unsuitable for her age and size, the garish purple silk straining tight over a bolstered bosom and vast hips. Sarah knew her at once.

"You are mistaken, Ma'am," she said, striving to sound haughty and firm, while wishing with rising hysteria that the hand on her arm didn't have such a clawing grip. "I know no one by the name of Huxley."

"No, *no,* gel," the Honorable Aileen Montague said, assuming the vexed look Sarah well remembered. It belonged to a lady of esteem in high London circles, and Sarah prayed she would soon be well rid of the woman.

Where was Robbie? she thought desperately. She saw him at the end of the row of people, enveloped for a moment in a swirl of colorful gowns as the ladies all pressed to get out of the theater and into their waiting carriages, and at his sudden look of alarm, she gave him a small imperceptible shake of her head.

The Honorable Aileen Montague tapped her fan against her teeth, frowning slightly at Sarah.

"When we were at the same gathering, your name wasn't Huxley, but Endor, I'm sure of it. Even my tired old eyes registered the prettiest gel at the ball, along with most of the young bucks there, I recall. Now don't tell me I'm wrong, pray, for I already have the devil's own job in persuading my family that I'm not going quite senile."

She smiled encouragingly, but with a hint of desperation, and for a moment Sarah felt quite sorry for her. But only for a moment. She seized on the woman's words, praying that her husband wouldn't return from wherever he'd gone, and express a similar certainty that he had seen her before.

"I'm sure they only tease you, ma'am," she said with more gentleness. "But truly you are quite wrong. I have never been to London, nor do I know anyone as grand as Lord Gressingham. Indeed, I've never heard of him. 'Tis said everyone has a double, and I presume I must slightly resemble the lady you mention. I thank you for the compliment, but if you will excuse me, I have someone waiting."

She wrenched her arm away from the clawing hand and rushed along the row of seats blindly. If the woman screeched after her, accusing her of deceit, or perhaps recalling the "something else" that she should know about Sarah Huxley, she would die of shame.

But there was no shout of discovery behind her, and still gasping with the shock of it all, she found herself in Robbie's arms. She would have wilted like a flower, but there was no time for that.

"Quickly, outside and into the carriage," he said swiftly. "You can tell me everything when we reach the hotel. Not a word out of place on the way there, love."

She shivered as if with the ague, and was unable to stop the shaking as he held her fast on the carriage ride back to the hotel.

All this time, all her fears had been for Robbie's discovery, for someone to point the finger and denounce him as Black Robbie. All this time, she had never given a single thought that *she* might be the one to be recognized.

The shock of it was still too great to let her relax, even when Robbie sat beside her on the bed, rubbing her chafed hands that were as chilled as if it were midwinter. He tried to

353

make her drink some brandy.

"Robbie, I'm so sorry," she finally choked out.

"Why should you be sorry? It wasn't your fault!"

"But I should have more sense! The Holtby Theater Company attracts a wide audience, and people like that woman—the Honorable Aileen Montague—follow them around the country avidly. I never thought—and I *should* have done so—"

"No more than I should have," Robbie acknowledged. "But no harm's done, my love. You handled things admirably. I was proud of you. Black Robbie couldn't have done it better."

She couldn't smile at his gentle teasing. All she could think of was that they had come so far, and there was still a risk. They still weren't safe. There was only one place they could be safe, and one safe way of reaching it.

"Robbie, please get us a sea passage to Scotland as soon as possible," she whispered. "I can't bear any more of this. I want to be home—I want to feel truly safe."

He took her roughly in his arms, touched at her use of the word "home," and promised that he would do so first thing in the morning. His business was almost complete, her gowns would be ready in two days' time, and they would be on the first available passenger ship to Scotland.

Chapter 24

Three days later, two late-booking passengers arrived at the docks in the early morning to embark on the *Sea Sprite*, a small but sturdy vessel that regularly made the journey from the port of Bristol through the ever-widening Bristol Channel, then north along the Welsh Coast through the Irish Sea. There would be one stop at the port of Liverpool, and then the *Sea Sprite* would continue sailing until it reached the Scottish Islands and eventually its destination—the Kyle of Lochalsh.

It would take them a week's sailing, providing the weather was good. Robbie was still marveling that Sarah had opted for the sea voyage after all; he had explained to her that at times the Irish Sea could be almost as rough as the Bay of Biscay.

"I hardly care," Sarah said feelingly, "just as long as the ship gets us home. I want no more frights such as I received the other night. You may have thrived on such dangers in the past, Robbie, but I confess that it does not suit me!"

He looked at her with some concern. She had been badly shaken the night they had been to the theater. The sight of someone from her past, of however slight an acquaintance, had taken away all the pleasure of the evening. Like her, Robbie had always assumed that his was the greater danger.

After all, his was the head with the price on it. But Sarah would be in dire disgrace if she were apprehended now. And her cousin Jonas would doubtless make her pay cruelly for his humiliation.

Robbie grew concerned about her. Her eyes seemed to be more brilliant than usual in her white face, though not a healthy blue. They looked as if they burned with an intense blue heat.

The *Sea Sprite* was not a luxurious ship, and their cabin was small and cramped. They had paid for one of the best, but even so, their trunk and all the other baggage, some containing Robbie's precious bonds, took up most of the available space. They remained there for a while upon boarding to settle themselves, and once the ship was under way, he took her gently in his arms.

"Sarah, are you quite well? We didn't have to leave Bristol quite so ignominiously, my dearest. We could have remained quietly in the hotel until you felt recovered enough to travel. You look decidedly peaked."

She didn't answer at once, not wanting to alarm him, but she did feel decidedly queasy as the familiar undulating motion of the ship began beneath her. Through the small round porthole she saw that they were already sliding out of the river toward the Channel.

The gaunt high cliffs of the Avon Gorge on either side of them took on a new majesty from here, yet she felt oddly as if they were protective of the frail man-made craft below. She pushed aside her anxieties. They were leaving England for the last time, and she felt the sliver of a new and reckless freedom, and knew that the time for telling secrets had come.

She ran her fingers down Robbie's anxious face, the face she loved so well with a love as deep as the ocean itself, and her voice was husky-soft when she spoke. She looked steadfastly into his eyes, wanting to be sure to gauge the first nuance of his awareness.

"I'm quite well, my darling—as well as a lady in a certain

condition can be—"

She drew in her breath as she saw the startled light of realization change those hypnotic amber eyes into glowing golden orbs. A delighted smile widened his sensual mouth and then it was claiming hers with a kiss that said more than words could ever convey. A kiss that said here was their destiny, their future, an omen for life to take on a new meaning, which was everything Sarah herself saw it to be.

After breathtaking moments, he put her slightly away from him. His voice was deepened by emotion.

"Are you sure of this? You've given no hint, lassie—"

"I'm sure in my heart," she said unsteadily. "And by certain signs, of course. But I know it's true, Robbie. There's a baby growing out of our love, and I want—oh, how I want it to be born in Scotland, where it will be free of everything bad that's touched our lives."

"Aye. It will be born an Argyll." He couldn't hide the swelling pride in his voice.

Defiantly, he had registered them on the ship as Robert Argyll and wife. Now, more than ever, he wanted to uphold the truth of that.

"You'll promise me that as soon as we reach the mainland, we'll be wed," he said fiercely. "There'll be no more holding back, Sarah. I'll not have my son born a bastard."

My son . . . he repeated the words inside his head, and the sound and the taste of them was more heady than the most potent wine.

"No, sir, and nor would I want it either! But I had a thought, that perhaps before then?"

She spoke meekly, and then laughed, because meekness did not become her fiery nature. She caught both his hands in hers and pressed them to her face at his inquiring look.

"Oh Robbie, do you not think we could be wed by the ship's captain? I know we're already supposed to be married, but surely you can say it's the whim of a pregnant wife to want the romantic words repeated to her on board ship by

357

moonlight! No captain with half a heart could refuse such a request."

His hands cupped her face, knowing that he for one could refuse her nothing. Let the other passengers surmise what they would, he thought grimly, but his Sarah would have her romantic shipboard wedding beneath the stars. And he did not deny to himself that it appealed to him too. What more fitting marriage-setting for a pirate?

"I'll arrange it at once," he told her. "How clever you are to have thought of it, and the sooner I know you're truly my wife, the better pleased I shall be."

Sarah said shyly, "And I have one last request, my love, which you may dismiss as superstitious nonsense if you like. But I'd like us to be wed as we're passing the coast of Cornwall. I'd like to think that somehow Freda and Jude will be thinking of us and giving us their blessing."

He held her close. He had often thought very strongly that she had some of the Cornish in her, some of that Celtic awareness that went too with his own Celtic ancestry. Sarah would have her offshore Cornish wedding. If he had to hold a cutlass to the Captain's throat, he would see to it . . . He smiled ruefully at the flippant thought. It was hardly a thought for the wealthy Robert Argyll to be taking to his homeland!

He wanted to let Sarah rest in the cabin for a while, but with a new vigor she insisted on going up on deck to see the city of Bristol diminishing behind them, to know just when they sailed out into the Channel with England on one side and Wales on the other.

The sea, that had once been her enemy, now seemed like a haven. Perhaps never again would she feel such a dreadful antipathy toward it. At last, the fate of her parents seemed no longer to color her life quite so appallingly.

Robbie left her leaning over the ship's rail while he went to have words with the Captain. She breathed in the strong salt air, which was undeniably tainted with the thick mud that fringed the river's passage, and the heavy smell of fish from the cellars along the water's edge, but part of its extravaganza.

Out of the corner of her eye, Sarah noticed another young couple strolling along the deck and whispering together. The brief moment of apprehension faded as they paused beside her, the young woman smiling at Sarah in a friendly way, and glancing at her husband. There was nothing remotely familiar about them, and Sarah gave a small sigh of relief and looked inquiringly at them both.

The young man was thin and earnest, with sandy-colored hair and a fine mustache, and a habit of clearing his throat a good deal as if not quite sure of himself. His wife was young and dainty, dark and vivacious and about Sarah's own age. The husband spoke in an apologetic way as if egged on by his companion.

"Forgive me for intruding on you, Ma'am, but we saw you and your husband boarding earlier, and my wife and I couldn't help noticing that we four seem to be the only passengers under a hundred years old on the ship."

His eyes twinkled as he spoke, and Sarah guessed that once his diffidence was put aside he could be good company. "We wondered if you and your husband would care to join us for meals during the journey? Our names are Emily and John Morgan, and we don't travel all the way to Scotland, but leave the ship at Liverpool."

"Do say that you'll join us," Emily Morgan put in eagerly. "Sea voyages can be so dull, can't they? And it would be so nice to have company."

Sarah hid a smile. Sea voyages in her experience were anything but dull! She wondered briefly what this nice young couple would say if she were to comment casually that for much of the past year she had been at sea with the notorious pirate captain, Black Robbie. That she had been ravished and loved by him, and carried his child. The thoughts were so powerful in her head she wondered for a

359

moment if she had said them aloud! But clearly not! And the Morgans were still waiting for an answer.

John Morgan was holding out his hand in a gesture of friendship and as Sarah took it, she felt her spirits lift. They did look an agreeable couple, and obviously took herself and Robbie at face value. She saw him returning, tall and handsome, head and shoulders above everyone else in every way, and she spoke for him.

"I'm sure we would be delighted," she said rather breathlessly. "We're the Argylls—Robert and Sarah."

The unexpected glow of pride she felt at saying the words for the first time made the blood rush to her cheeks, and she turned to hug Robbie's arm as he reached them. She explained quickly what John Morgan had suggested. Robbie smiled broadly.

"Then perhaps our new friends will act as witnesses at our little ceremony this evening," he said enigmatically, to Sarah's delight, knowing at once that her dream was to come true.

He spoke evenly to these new friends, his voice carrying such conviction that none could doubt that every word was true. "You'll think it a strange whim, but I gather that ladies in a certain condition do have these strange fancies—" He paused as Emily Morgan gave an exclamation of pleasure at this news.

"Sarah wishes our marriage vows to be reaffirmed on board ship in sight of the Cornish Coast, since she has strong connections with the county. The Captain has agreed to perform the ceremony, so I hereby invite you both to join us and celebrate with champagne afterward."

"How lovely!" Emily Morgan's pretty face showed that she was clearly enchanted with the idea. "And our best congratulations—on both counts!"

Sarah and Robbie smiled at one another, and just for a moment the look shut out everything else. They heard nothing, saw nothing, except the love that burned bright

360

between them, until the dimly heard excitement from the other pair penetrated their minds. And then the joy of making this journey to Scotland was doubled because they were to share it with new friends who accepted them for what they were.

They would be truly ships that passed in the night, Sarah thought, the old phrase slipping into her mind. They had met, their lives would briefly touch and be all the richer for it, and they would part. It was the way of things. It was good, and portended well for the future.

By that evening, the Argylls and the Morgans felt as if they had known each other always. The Morgans were to take up residence in Lancashire, where John would take on the management of his ailing father's cotton mill. The Argylls were ostensibly traveling back to Scotland from a long spell away from home in the southern hemisphere and preferred to forget all about the heat and dust and resume a quieter life.

Without being rude, Robbie managed to convey that this background was to be a closed book from now on, and respecting it, the Morgans didn't probe any deeper. It was the most refreshing kind of friendship, instant and superficial but nontheless real.

And on that moonlit evening, with the stars forming a canopy of brilliants in the night sky, Sarah Huxley formally became the wife of Robert Argyll. She wore a gown of cream silk, embroidered with little lovers' knots in forget-me-not blue, with the Spanish lace shawl about her shoulders. From somewhere on the ship, Emily had produced a small posy of roses for Sarah to carry, and Sarah had breathed in their scent, thinking of Wenna Trewithan, and all the loving ghosts of the past.

Robbie had asked the captain to dispense with too much formality, since it was assumed that there had already been a church ceremony and they were merely to be joined in wedlock as Robert and Sarah. It simplified everything, and gave it a more poignant dignity than could have been dreamed of. Sarah stood very still with her hand clasped in Robbie's, seeing across the captain's shoulder the distant darkened shape of the Cornish coastline. And then she thought of nothing but the words that were to bind her to Robbie for the rest of time.

"Do you, Robert, take this woman Sarah, to wife?"

"I do," Robbie said gravely, his eyes never leaving Sarah's face.

"Do you, Sarah, take this man Robert, to husband?"

"I do," she said softly, repeating the haunting and beautifully simple words.

The captain put his hand over both of theirs and put a gentle pressure on them. "By the power invested in me, I bid you both go in wedlock and happiness together as man and wife," he said.

As the vows were exchanged, the coast of Cornwall seemed to be lightened for a moment as a lingering cloud drifted away and the panorama was flooded with a more intense moonlight. Almost as if she ran barefoot and free over the wild and beautiful moors of that mystical place, Sarah was vividly aware of the scent of wild heather and yarrow, and the musk of Wenna Trewithan's roses as well as her own filling her senses.

Her throat was full as her husband took her in his arms for their first kiss as man and wife.

And then the spell was broken as she heard Emily Morgan say gaily that there was to be a special wedding feast for the four of them. The captain had offered his cabin for the meal, and Emily and John had insisted on providing it.

"How kind you are!" Sarah said, loving every moment of this, and not minding in the least that the moments before she and Robbie would be alone had not yet come. She was too sure in the knowledge that she and Robbie had the rest of their lives to make love, to make their dynasty.

So the night lingered on into the early hours, ending in merriment and laughter and too much champagne. Robbie and Sarah finally fell asleep in each other's arms, too tired for anything but the wonderful knowledge of being cherished and loved. It wasn't until the morning came, that Robert Argyll took his wife in his arms and asked her cautiously if she thought it would harm the bairn if he did what his every male instinct was urging him to do.

"I fear it will hurt me more if you do not!" his wife said pertly, her new-found status as Mistress Argyll making her bold. "I may be about to be a mother, but the time's a long while distant yet, and I've a yearning to be a bride before that, my dearest!"

He grinned, a teasing, lustful grin. "I've never made love to a married woman before. I think it may be a very pleasurable novelty."

His teasing aroused her completely, and the discomfort of the bunk was forgotten in the joy of being together in the eyes of God. Sarah had never doubted that fact, but now it was made legal, and there was an added piquancy in the thought, as well as knowing that they shared a new and precious secret.

And no, he would not hurt the bairn. If before the child was born they would need to find more innovative ways of expressing their love, it would be all the more exciting, for love like theirs would not be denied. She exulted in the maleness of her man, her eyes closing in ecstasy as the familiar sensual movements began, taking her with him to the heights and as always bringing her exquisitely down to earth with him again, always together, always perfect partners.

When their passion was finally spent and they were still in each other's arms in the afterglow, she turned her face into his shoulder, weeping a little with the sheer joy of him.

"Don't cry, my little one," Robbie said huskily.

"I think that tears of happiness are allowed, aren't they?"
She smiled at him mistily, and he gathered her close, feeling
her heartbeat as if it were his, and his were hers. He would let
nothing hurt her ever again, he thought fiercely, making his
own silent vow to that effect.

By the time the *Sea Sprite* put in at Liverpool to take on
more cargo and supplies, Sarah and Robbie said goodbye
to their new friends with real regret, but with no future plans
to rejoin. It was unlikely they would meet again by chance,
and wisely, perhaps, it was best to let the friendship go with
happy memories. Emily hugged Sarah fast for a moment.

"Good luck to you both, and the new baby. I hope it will
be what you want."

They had never discussed it, but right from the beginning,
Sarah had felt a fervent hope that it would be a boy. A new
young Argyll to carry on the family name.

The Morgans left the ship and gave one last wave before
they were swallowed up by the crowds on the dockside.
When they learned they would be an hour or so in port,
Sarah and Robbie decided to leave the ship and mingle with
the crowds and the market stalls ranging along the quayside,
which sold all kinds of wares to people looking for trinkets
or souvenirs or private provisions to take on board.

They bought nothing, just glad to stretch their legs, until
they both became aware of the odd sensation of land fever
and were glad to go back on board to await sailing time.
Once the ship set sail again, they knew they had resumed the
final part of their voyage to Scotland.

They had been fortunate. The late spring weather had
been fair and continued to be so. Very late on the following
evening the ship's siren blared out, in a little ceremony
always faithfully observed by the crew, announcing that they
were now moving into Scottish waters. Robbie clasped
Sarah's hands tightly.

They stood at the rail in the warm night air, watching the scudding waves that were silvered by moonlight. Ahead of them still were miles of sea, but already Sarah felt a great surge of optimism. They were in Scottish waters, and soon she would set foot on this new land for the first time.

"I have a very faint idea of how a pioneer must feel, stepping onto new territory for the first time," she murmured, her head on Robbie's shoulder as she stood in the crook of his arm.

"We shall certainly be new settlers on the shriveled earth of Glen Argyll," Robbie agreed. "Though thankfully the grass will be grown again these long years since the burning. It will be sweet and green, and probably grown over the ruins of the house. We shall need to build again, Sarah, but I know that the foundations will be strong and weathered."

She spoke gently, knowing how his emotions must be tugging at him. The nearer he got to his roots, the more he would be reliving all the old memories of that terrible day when he was a twelve-year-old boy and witnessed the horror.

"That's what I want. To renew what was old and good with something totally unique to us. The past will still be with us in the stones, but we'll put our own mark on it."

His arm tightened around her, and he bent his head to kiss her as the ship drifted smoothly northward on a steady course.

"How did I deserve such luck as to find you out of all the world, my lovely girl?" he asked huskily.

She didn't answer, for her thoughts echoed his so perfectly. They were in constant unison now, and Sarah was almost too afraid to speak of their good fortune, for fear that even now something might go wrong. They still had hurdles to cross, but tonight was not the time to worry about what lay ahead. Tonight was another night for celebration, because they had crossed the boundary between England and Scotland, and they were truly homeward bound.

Celebration took the form that had come to be so familiar

365

to Sarah now, and yet was always new and different. In the narrow bunk in their cabin, she felt Robbie toss aside the Spanish shawl she had worn on deck, and felt the trail of his fingers up and down her bare arms. She shivered, not from cold, but from a wave of yearning, of shuddering excitement and anticipation, knowing that the sweet seductive invasion of her body was about to begin.

Robbie was as ardent as ever to show her how pleasurable love could be. She had worn the same creamy silk gown she had been married in, seeing it as symbolic for this greeting of her new homeland, and she felt a shivering delight as Robbie unfastened it and let it slide down her body to cascade in a shimmering heap of silk at her feet. She stepped out of it and into his waiting arms.

Love could take many forms, Sarah thought mistily a long while later. Sometimes vigorous, at other times gentle, langorous, more sensual in its slow rhythmic pleasure, and always taking her to the stars. Their limbs entwined, mouths and hearts touching, each a part of the other, and she felt as though she could go on like this forever. . . .

But Robbie seemingly could not. He gave a small groan, and gathered her up more tightly, and at once a flame of matching hunger raced through her as she met her man's needs. At once, she longed for the fulfillment only he could bring her. She clung to his powerful shoulders as the piercing sweetness of his thrusting made her cry out again and again, always with a pleasure that was acutely sensual.

Each time he made love to her, Sarah thought blindly that she had never known this need to belong to another so intensely. Her blood surged with love for him. He dominated her mind and her body, and he was all that she wanted and craved.

"God, but I love you, Sarah," he finally gasped out as his seed spilled into her, and she rocked him close as if he were the child she already carried. Her man and her child were as one at that moment.

"The feel of you in my arms is the most exciting thing that ever happened to me," he said in a ragged voice against her cheek. "The feel of you and the scent of you, and the way you fit against my skin as if God fashioned you for me alone, my dearest one. There's a fever in me that only you can cure, Sarah, and I think—I *know*—that if I had to choose between my heritage and you, then I would choose you."

She was very still, the breath coming shallowly in her throat. She had never expected to hear this, and tears started to her eyes, because it underlined the depth of his feelings for her more than anything else ever could. She moved slightly beneath him, her fingers tracing the planes of his face.

"You do me the greatest honor, my darling," she whispered. "But there's no choice to be made. We've come this far and we'll see it through, and whatever the outcome we'll always have each other. But in my heart I know that we'll win. We have to win—for *him*. It's his heritage too."

She took Robbie's hand and put it on the softly rounded swell of her stomach. It was far too soon for there to be any movement or more than a hint of enlargement, but she knew instinctively that the baby lived and breathed, and it was their promise for the future.

And one day soon, God willing, there would be no more need for lies and subterfuge. They could be as they were, and wanted to be. Robert Argyll and his wife, come home at last to Scotland.

Chapter 25

Robbie acknowledged the expert way the *Sea Sprite*'s captain negotiated the narrow passages between the more densely linked Scottish islands. The panorama of the mainland remained tantalizingly close all the way now, and Sarah became aware of a new and breathtakingly beautiful land. The mornings were clouded in mist before the sun rose and magically dispersed it, and then everywhere became a verdant summer green.

Islands and mainland, it seemed to Sarah, were clothed in heather as richly colored as a king's velvet, or as pale as a drift of shadow. The mainland was a spectacle of mountain after mountain, each peak more majestic than the last. They stretched away as far as the eye could see, chased by the shifting light and shade as clouds drifted away in the path of the sun.

Sarah's eyes were dazzled by the sheer awesomeness of it all. When they reached the Kyle of Lochalsh and climbed carefully down onto the narrow quay, she had the strangest feeling that this was a moment for kneeling and kissing the earth.

"Wait here, love, while I see about a conveyance for us," Robbie said abruptly. He left her surrounded by baggage, and to her amazement she knew instantly that his thoughts were not the same as hers. They were in discord, just when she had expected them to be most closely attuned.

She watched him stride off to a place where horses and carriages were stabled. Robbie was as tense as a spring, and understandably so, she reminded herself, but she couldn't help feeling disappointment, yes, hurt, that this stepping on to Scottish soil hadn't been more momentous. She recalled her history lessons, and gave a wry smile. Even Charles Stuart's arrival on Scottish soil had been unremarkable, so who was she to complain!

Robbie returned a few minutes later.

"I've hired a carriage to take us to Inbertoon. 'Tis the only town of any size in the area, and where the Argyll lawyer has his chambers. It will take us most of the day to get there, and I pray God that Eian Fraser still practices law there. We'll take a hotel room in Inbertoon while the necessary investigations are conducted, Sarah. Naturally, we cannot expect to get things settled in minutes."

She listened to him speaking in that short rapid voice, and it was as if she listened to a stranger. It was worse than she had feared. He was remote from her, locked up in memories of the past where she had no place, and where she couldn't reach him. She could only acquiesce, and pray that time and this homecoming would work its magic for him. It was painful for her to realize that what he wanted so much now seemed to be tearing him apart. She knew it without the telling.

The carriage trundled toward them, and the driver and a ragged lad eager to earn a copper or two helped to haul the heavy baggage aboard. And then they left the landing stage at the Kyle of Lochalsh and the sturdy horses began to pull their burden on the journey toward the town of Inbertoon.

"I swear I shall have no bones left in my body if this continues much longer!"

369

Sarah hung on to the side grip several hours later. The carriage lurched over clusters of small boulders on the rugged track that traversed a wildly beautiful glen. She hardly noticed it, nor the still loch alongside which they traveled, the mountains reflected like mirror-images in its silent depths. It was all fast losing its charm for her. She longed for the civility of a decent hotel, a hot bath and a soft bed.

Robbie put his head outside the carriage and spoke angrily to the driver.

"Can you ease up there, man? My wife's feeling somewhat ill. Take things more slowly. If the journey takes twice as long, you'll be paid for your trouble."

Sarah grimaced as he sat back beside her. If the journey took twice as long as it should she would probably expire before they arrived. The careering pace, with little thought for passengers, was upsetting her. She was anxious for the baby, though she seemed to remember some matronly friend of her Aunt Lily's once commenting archly that an unborn baby was cushioned far more safely than most people suspected. She hoped grimly that it was true.

"Do you really feel unwell, Sarah? If so, I'll get the fellow to stop awhile and we can take a gentle stroll while you recover. Or we can just have a breather outside, a welcome rest from this infernal jolting."

She shook her head. "I'd rather we went on. It will only prolong it if we ask him to stop."

She tried not to complain any more. If she did, he might start to think she was regretting coming here. Her life hadn't been exactly a bed of roses every minute she had been part of his life, but the good far outweighed the bad. She wanted to let him know that, but the words wouldn't come. Not while he sat with that tight, almost frozen look on his face. She knew that he too would be reliving the past, good as well as bad. And for Robbie, the bad must outweigh the good.

370

They had to take a twisting path higher around a mountain before the track plunged quite steeply toward the small town, a seemingly hazardous path that had Sarah dry-mouthed and clinging to Robbie. Were the perils they encountered on *The Adventuress* even comparable to this? she thought sickly.

At long last the outlines of the town could be seen far below them, and as if even the caustic old carriage driver had a feeling for the aesthetics of such a scene, he paused his sweating horses for a few minutes, and shouted back that most folk got out for a minute or two to admire the view. Sarah would have declined, but Robbie was already opening the door and jumping down, holding out his hand to her to do likewise.

They walked a little way away from the carriage, and all around them the silence was total and magnificent. It was nature on a grand scale, the mountains, the glens, glimpses of small pockets of ice-blue water and wide, beautiful lochs, reflecting land and sky in equal measure. And in the distance, too far away for its rush of crystal water to reach their ears, was a tumbling waterfall, but its movement caught and captured light from the sun and transformed it into a cascade of shimmering diamonds. And now she knew exactly what the highlands were all about.

"It's time we were moving on," Robbie said, before she could begin to try and put it all into words. But how could anyone ever do that? Only poets, perhaps, who were able to put heart and soul into something as inanimate as a vision . . . she swallowed the emotion in her throat and caught at Robbie's hand.

"Does it not stun you with its beauty?" she whispered.

"Aye, it does," he answered. "But for now, I'll not let myself be stunned. My mind needs to be too canny, Sarah. Later will be the time for dreaming."

And for making dreams come true, she added silently,

knowing she would not move this strong man from his purpose, not fully realizing until now just how important this mission was to him. She could see it in the set of his head, proud and upright and defying anyone to deny him his birthright. She knew it by the imperceptible twitching of nerves beside the mouth she longed to kiss and calm and bring to a gentle passion. But now was not the time, and she knew he would not welcome her woman's wiles.

He was enveloped in a man's world that he had left in terror as a vulnerable boy, and there were still the hurdles of the lawyer and any other claims to his land that might have been registered in the past eighteen years. Sarah shivered. If all was lost, she had no idea what the effect might be on Robbie. He was here as Robert Argyll, his true identity, and he had done with subterfuge and disguise.

How cruel it would be if everything was to be denied him. She was certain they would remain in Scotland now, but the bitterness in his heart would cloud their happiness for the rest of their days, and she couldn't bear that.

They continued the journey in silence, each caught up in their own thoughts. Sarah couldn't guess at Robbie's. One minute he looked morose, the next animated with a fever that made his eyes glow like yellow fire, and then again the pain of remembering the reason for his fleeing this land would apparently overcome him, and the forced rigidity of his body told her more than words how firmly he kept himself under control.

Why could a man not weep as women wept? Sarah thought fiercely. Where was the shame in it, when a man's feelings ran just as deep as a woman's?

It was early evening when the carriage arrived at the modest Inbertoon Hotel, and it was still as light as day. Sarah remembered Robbie telling her that the summer nights remained light in these northern parts of Britain, with only a brief time of semi-darkness they called the gloaming. It was a name that had enchanted her.

Now they were here, and the travelers alighted stiffly. Sarah was never so thankful to see the inside of a building that was clean and comfortable, and when Robbie asked for the best room available, they were shown into a large bedroom with a small bathing and dressing area. He asked for bathing water to be sent up straight away, and within half an hour Sarah was blissfully sinking her aching body into a bath of steaming water and resting her head back against the high headrest, her eyes closed in the welcome caress of the hot water. Such an occasion had so often been the prelude to an hour of sheer pleasure.

"I would find it more than enjoyable to assist you, dearest, but I feel the need for some exercise. Will you be all right if I'm gone for half an hour?"

She turned her blue gaze on him, knowing that he was too restless to do anything but scout about the town for the lawyer's chambers. It was unlikely anyone would be working at such an hour, but Robbie wouldn't rest until he knew that this Eian Fraser he had mentioned was still practicing—still alive, even!

"I shall be perfectly all right, my love," she said evenly. "Don't worry. I shall lie on the bed for a while when I've bathed, and probably fall asleep if my bones will let me after that awful journey."

She almost wished she hadn't said it as she saw the look on Robbie's face. Did he think she meant she resented having been brought here to the back of nowhere? But he nodded in agreement, a smile touching his mouth.

"It wasn't the best. I have a key, Sarah, and I shall ask that you don't be disturbed before I return, so rest easy."

He bent to kiss her, and she resisted the temptation to throw her arms about him and hold him there. Like a protective mother with a child, she was almost afraid to see him go out alone on this particular day because of what he might have to face.

Robbie hardly remembered Inbertoon. The glen where he had lived with his parents was some distance from here, and in those days, people rarely traveled far from their homes unless it was absolutely necessary. His father's legal affairs were handled at Inbertoon, and old Eian Fraser was his main objective. Before he left the hotel, he had made inquiries after the doctor who had assisted the distraught young boy before he had fled to England.

The owner had frowned, and then shook his head slowly, recalling that old Dr. Blair had died some years ago. It was as Robbie had feared. Everything now depended on the lawyer. The streets were a hodgepodge of lanes with square-built, homey cottages, the more business-like establishments announcing themselves by plaques in the windows. Robbie knew he would waste valuable time searching out Eian Fraser's chambers on his own. He spoke directly to a prosperous-looking gentleman in the street and asked if he knew where he could find the lawyer.

The man looked doubtful. "Fraser, you say? There's no lawyer here by that name that I recall. There's the partnership of Dewey and Menzies in Ninnion Lane, and they may be able to help you."

Robbie's voice was harsh. "Thank you. Tell me, sir—do you know of a man called Callum Argyll?"

He held his breath. The first disappointment was acute, and he dared not contemplate it further for the moment. If this man knew of his cousin, then the battle would be on. The gentleman looked at him oddly.

"I deduce that you do not belong to these parts, laddie, or you would know of the tragedy of the Argylls."

"If you mean those who lived in Glen Argyll, I am very

well aware of it."

"No, no, not those poor folk, but some of their kin. The son Callum was a feckless lad who went to India without a thought to his elderly father. The old man took a stroke and begged young Callum to come home. 'Tis said the lad only agreed when some financial bait was dangled in front of him, and then he died in some Indian skirmish or other before he could start for home. It finished the old man. When he heard the news, he merely stopped eating and starved himself to death for the loss of his son."

Robbie kept his features under control as the tale unfolded, thanking the man and walking quickly in the direction of Ninnion Lane before he paused to sort out his spinning thoughts. His uncle was dead, and he mourned him briefly . . . but so too was his cousin Callum, who was the only legitimate contender for Argyll land in these highlands. Everything still had to be fought and won, and if he lost, the land would finally go to the Crown. But a renewed feeling of hope was beginning to stir in Robbie's veins.

"Young sir—just a moment—" He heard the voice of his recent companion calling after him, and turned until the man caught up with him. Puffing a little, the man imparted some news that was to lighten Robbie's heart even more.

"A thought has just occurred to me. I've only lived here for five years, and all else about the district I've learned through hearsay. But about the old lawyer you seek—I seem to recall hearing that the legal partners in this town allow an elderly but astute lawyer to use a corner of their chambers to mull over old documents and trivial matters. It could be that he's the one you seek."

"Thank you!" Robbie said. "Thank you very much!"

It was unlikely that such an old man would be burning the midnight oil, but he had to find out just where Ninnion Lane was, and he intended being there first thing in the morning. He found it eventually, and as he suspected, it was closed for the night. But his feeling that the old lawyer who mulled over documents in a corner would be Eian Fraser was very strong. Indeed, who else could it be?

Sarah was already in bed and asleep when he returned to the hotel, and he undressed quickly and slid in beside her, not waking her. Robbie realized that he too was exhausted after the day's travel, and he eased his aching limbs into a comfortable position as Sarah nestled against him, murmuring words in a half-sleep.

"Everything will be all right, Robbie . . . we couldn't have come all this way without luck on our side . . . have faith, my love. . . ."

Robbie became very still. Somewhere in the back of his mind a memory teased him. *Have faith . . . in the earth and our kin . . .* the words went round and round in his mind, as he filled in the missing pieces. They were the words that might be the key to their destiny. He held Sarah close in the circle of his arms, his hands soft against her stomach, where his son slept serenely. These moments were his alone, and in her sleep she stirred but slightly as he buried his lips in her hair, loving her.

Sarah awoke to find Robbie already dressed, the sunshine streaming in the window. It filled her with a feeling of optimism, sure that this must be a good day. She prayed that Robbie's feelings were the same. The moment she looked into his face she knew that something had happened.

"What is it?" she asked. She sat up in bed a mite too quickly, feeling her senses swim for a moment, and Robbie asked quickly if the bairn was all right.

"The bairn's fine," she said, using his own quaint word for the baby. "But I will not be if you don't tell me what happened last night. Why didn't you awaken me at once if you found out anything?"

He laughed. "Because, my sweet darling, you were almost dead to the world."

And then he couldn't tease her any longer. He seized both her hands in his. She could feel the excitement in him now, and the tumble of her dark hair fell across her slender shoulders, as her eyes implored him to tell her.

"I've had it on what seems reliable authority that the old doctor is dead, but so too is my cousin and my elderly uncle."

Sarah tried not to look too delighted at hearing the last, because it was surely a sin to be pleased at such events. But in this case, it meant so much.

"And I *may* have found Eian Fraser," he said.

"Oh, Robbie!" Sarah said joyfully, her eyes suddenly filled with stars.

"Just hold on. I said I *may* have found him, though in my own mind, I'm sure." He couldn't pretend, not with her. "Get dressed, and as soon as we've had breakfast we'll go around to the chambers and announce who we are."

"I couldn't possibly eat. I'm not hungry."

"But my son is," he said sternly. "Breakfast first, and then we go to Ninnion Lane."

While they ate in the hotel dining room he related all that the gentleman had told him last night.

Sarah's initial elation was tempered slightly. It was all only hearsay, after all, and there could still be a mistake. But she didn't dare suggest it, when she knew that Robbie was pinning all his hopes on what happened at the lawyer's.

He still kept something to himself. The memory had come to him suddenly, and it was too momentous even to tell Sarah, as yet. It was to be his trump card, if all else failed. All Scottish clans had their own motto, and the fact that his own had been changed was known only to an exclusive few, himself among them. But the new motto would be legally registered in Edinburgh, and Robbie prayed that his knowledge of its wording would prove conclusively once and for all that he was truly Robert Argyll.

After they had eaten, they set off for the small establishment in Ninnion Lane with the names Dewey and

Menzies painted on the windows. A youngish man answered the door, and Robbie asked directly for Mister Eian Fraser.

"Do you have business with Mr. Fraser? He no longer sees clients, and all legal business is done by myself and my partner. My name is Dewey—"

Robbie broke in. "Please, it's vital that I speak with Mr. Fraser. Will you please tell him that Robert Argyll is here to see him?"

The man looked from Robbie to Sarah, a deepening frown on his forehead.

"You'd best come in." He stood aside for them to enter and showed them into a small waiting room. Minutes later they heard shuffling footsteps and Dewey came back, helping a bent old man to sit in a chair. His eyes were rheumy and his thoughts clearly scattered as he spoke Robbie's name in a quavering voice.

"Is it Robert Argyll of Glen Argyll that ye claim to be, laddie?"

"It is, Mister Fraser. De ye not know me? Have I not the same look of my father?"

Sarah noticed at once how Robbie's speech broke into a more pronounced accent, and knew how tense he must be. The old man shook his head.

"I can see very little. The eyes have almost gone, and if 'twere not for the kindness of this one here, I'd sit and look at mountains all day long, but 'tis little I can do for him except offer something of an old man's lifetime's advice on legal affairs."

"But you must know me!" Robbie's voice sharpened with frustration. "You recall my father—Duncan Argyll!"

"Oh aye, I recall Duncan Argyll and his poor wife, Mairi. Perished at the hands of the English bastards, they did."

Sarah was sure he would spit in contempt were it not for Dewey's restraining hand on his shoulder. But then the old man's voice suddenly became clearer, and he looked more alert, as if his wandering mind began to clear a little.

"The young Argyll lad ran away and was heard of no more, but there was a cousin, Callum, who stood to gain the land. I mind that after a good many years passed, his father even took to rebuilding some of Duncan's house in preparation for when Callum returned from India. There was no law that said the house couldn't be rebuilt, so long as 'twas not lived in nor claimed legally." He shrugged. "Anyway, 'twas never to be. Callum never came back to the highlands. He died in a brawl, and his father soon after."

So that much was true. Robbie began to breathe slightly easier. And there was a bonus. His uncle had been so sure that young Robbie would never be heard of again that he had begun to rebuild the house in readiness for his own son! That was undoubtedly the financial bait the gentleman had spoken of last night. The story was probably being handed down in legend now.

Robbie leaned forward, speaking deliberately.

"Mister Fraser, I am Robert Argyll, Duncan Argyll's son. If you do not see me clearly, can you tell me if there was anything about the family that was distinctive?"

The old man seemed to look into the past, and slowly nodded.

"There was something. The eyes. The color of cats' eyes they were. Yellowy. Both father and son had 'em, but o' course, there's probably plenty of other folk with the same peculiarity. 'Twouldn't be enough to determine a claim in a court of law, and any claim would need to be properly determined in Edinburgh, laddie, just in case you were thinking an old man's words were going to hand you the Glen Argyll and all the accumulated assets on a platter."

His voice, suddenly crisp, assured them all that his mind was not yet senile, and he knew what was what when it came to the law.

"I was not," Robbie said shortly, as the young lawyer confirmed the older one's words. "But tell me this. Do ye recall being present at my father's house one night soon after

379

the Uprising, and making a new motto?"

Eian Fraser looked at him sharply, and Sarah held her breath. All of this was completely new to her.

"Aye, mebbe I do," the old man said cagily. "But there were only two men present at that, Duncan Argyll and myself, and what transpired was to be told to no one."

He stopped abruptly, and Robbie finished for him.

"Except Duncan's son—Robert Argyll."

"Go on, please." Dewey began to show a keen interest in all this now as Eian Fraser seemed to be losing his grip on the proceedings again.

Robbie spoke rapidly. "That night my father decreed that a new family motto should be made, exclusive to our branch of the Argyll clan. As you know, all such mottoes are secret until registered legally, save for the lawyer concerned. Since I was his only heir, the motto was naturally told to me, and all other knowledge of it died with my father. The sealed document to this effect will be registered at the bank in Edinburgh, and would never have been brought to a court register until I was present."

"Do you concur with all this, Mister Fraser?" Dewey wanted to know.

"All that the lad says is true, though how he knows of it, unless—"

"Gently, Mister Fraser," Dewey said, seeing the old man's agitation. "We clearly agree that since Duncan Argyll is dead, you and the son of Duncan Argyll are the only two people in the world who know the words of that new motto. Is that correct, Mister Fraser?" He handled the old man with patient courtesy, but Robbie could see that the case was arousing all his interest.

Eian Fraser's concentration was fast slipping away now. He shook his head, his balding scalp beneath his sparse white hair beaded with perspiration.

"Aye, that would be right, but dinna ask me to recall the words of the motto. It's too long ago," he muttered.

"But I remember it," Robbie spoke quietly. He looked at the young lawyer. "If you will agree to conduct my affairs in the future, I formally charge you to note exactly what the words of the new motto are, and compare it with the sealed document in Edinburgh."

Dewey became more businesslike.

"Then please come to my chamber, and we will draw up a signed statement of the motto. We will then show it to Mister Fraser. Whether he recognizes it or not is immaterial, since we still have to go through the other procedures."

"My wife will witness this as well," Robbie said, and the lawyer acquiesced, leading them to a somber room where Dewey opened a ledger and wrote the name of Robert Argyll prominently at the top of a page. He spoke with frank curiosity.

"This would seem to be a momentous time for you, sir. May I ask why it has taken you so long to claim your inheritance?"

"You'll understand from what's been said that the circumstances of my departure made very unhappy memories. I wanted to be as far from Scotland as possible, and have been in business in the southern hemisphere for many years," Robbie repeated his tale. "My wife and I met there, and were settled enough, but lately we have both felt a longing for our children to be born in Scotland."

"Of course." Dewey accepted this explanation without question, and saw the quick clasping of hands between the couple. He looked at Robbie inquiringly, quill poised in his hand.

"The old motto was *Have faith,*" Robbie said, and heard Sarah's small gasp. "The new motto is *Have faith in the earth and our kin.*"

They were all silent as the lawyer's scratching quill wrote down the words on the document. He then sealed it with his own seal. He and Robbie signed their names across the seal, and Sarah saw the pride in her husband as he wrote his own name.

They took the document out to the old lawyer and showed it to him, but it was all for nothing. He simply couldn't recall anything.

"No matter," Dewey said. "I shall leave for Edinburgh tomorrow and be back as soon as possible, hopefully with good news. I do not know you, sir, but I sense that your words are true ones."

His handshake was warm, and although Robbie had intended to go with the man, Dewey firmly forbade it.

"Leave legal matters to the experts," he advised. He neglected to add that, should the bank's document not tally with this one, he would not care to be saddled with a hopelessly despondent client all the way back to Inbertoon.

In their hotel room, Sarah put her arms around her husband and looked wonderingly into his face.

"Robbie, those words of the motto," she whispered. "It's very odd, but I dreamed I said something of the same. Was it all a dream?"

"Not all, my lassie," he said. "You were half-asleep last night, and I cuddled you into me, and you murmured that everything would be all right. You told me to have faith, and the words triggered off a memory in my mind. Without you, I might never have remembered those words."

They looked at one another. So many times each had saved the other. The fabric of their lives was interwoven so intricately and indisputably, as if theirs was a love that had truely been destined. Sarah shivered, leaning her head against his chest and feeling the pulsebeat of his heart.

The document had to be proven conclusively. She prayed to God that it would be so. She knew in her heart that nothing could prevent it now.

"Can we go to see Glen Argyll now?" she asked huskily. "I've a need to feel the grass, where our bairn will run and

382

play, beneath my feet, and to sense the memories of happier days within those walls."

"Aye, we'll go directly, for I, too, have a need to be among my own folk. And have I told you today that I love you, Mistress Argyll?" Robbie said, his mouth warm against hers. She knew he was relaxing for the first time since setting foot on his native soil.

"If you said it a thousand times a day it would never be too many times for me," she said softly.

His kiss was sweet and tender on her mouth, and but for the mission they had set themselves, she knew these moments would only end one way. But they had a lifetime ahead for living and loving, and today was very special to them both.

Robbie hired a small one-horse trap and took up the reins himself. They wanted no other person with them on this first sight of Glen Argyll. It took them more than an hour to traverse the delightful dipping valleys between the mountains, where scattered sunlight picked out isolated crofts and an occasional shepherd with his flock.

With every new vista, Sarah fell in love with the highlands all over again. And then they rounded a jagged outcrop of rock, and spread before them was a glen of great natural beauty, a shimmering loch running down its length, where tall grasses waved like the undulating waves of the sea.

Just for a moment the imagery held Sarah, awed, and then her attention was caught by a lovely old house, no longer crumbling into disrepair, since someone had obviously started to rebuild what had once been charred ruins. She gave silent thanks to the loving hopes of Callum Argyll's father, knowing all this was now hers and Robbie's.

He was watching her face.

"Will it suit, my lovely girl?" He spoke softly, using the same phrase with which he had taunted her, all those months ago, when she had been like a child in her uncle's house, playing at life, knowing none of it.

"Just as long as you're here," she said unsteadily,

"anywhere is home to me, But this above all—oh, *this* above all, Robbie—"

They continued swiftly toward the house, and decided with delighted pleasure that it would not take too long to be completed. They went inside and explored rooms that, through Robbie's uncle's fond hopes, had been given new floors and ceilings and windows, and Sarah could have sworn that just for a moment the very walls gave a sigh of welcome to these travelers who had come so far to find their rightful place.

And then all such fanciful thoughts left her mind, because the arms that were holding her and pressing her close were very real, and the sensations that seared like a flame through her body rose instantly to match his—her husband and lover, and ever her dashing pirate prince.